SENTINEL OF TIME

THE CURSE AND THE CROWN
BOOK 3

LINDSAY BUROKER

1

*O*THERS SEE THAT WHICH WE THINK WE HIDE.
  ~ *Dionadra, Essays on the Motivations of Men*

"Some instructors will tell you to watch your opponent's eyes, but I say be aware of their chest. The eyes can lie, but you can't commit to a strike without moving the core of your body."

"Is that why so many rangers check out my boobs?" Kaylina Korbian wiped sweat from her forehead and started to lower her sword to take a breather, but she jerked it defensively up again. Her new instructor tended to whack her if she dropped her guard before they stepped out of the practice ring.

"No, that's because they're rude, horny, and assume all women want their attention because they're royal rangers, which obviously makes them sexy and irresistible." Sergeant Zhaniyan, one of only a handful of female rangers, winked. Since she was in her early twenties with lush raven hair, striking green eyes, and an athletic but feminine figure, she had to understand Kaylina's experiences with the rangers.

"Obviously."

"I hear you have mystical druid powers that attract other beings too." Zhani, who'd only recently been pressed into this training duty, didn't know Kaylina well, so it was as much a question as a statement. She raised her eyebrows as she looked across the practice arena toward the passageway that led to the main courtyard and stables.

Six blue-furred taybarri congregated there, their long powerful bodies pressed side by side as they watched Kaylina—or possibly her pockets. That morning, she'd doled out samples from her latest batch of honey drops to Levitke, Crenoch, and all their furry friends. Since the first strawberries had come into season, despite the ever-present threat of frost creeping down from the snowy mountains behind the city, she'd added a touch of the fresh fruit. The taybarri had approved. Of course, they approved of almost everything except the dehydrated protein pellets the rangers fed them for nutrition rather than pleasure.

"Supposedly, I'm an *anrokk*," Kaylina said, "which means I attract animals. It's not supposed to do anything to attract men."

Unless she counted Lord Vlerion, her *previous* trainer, who was cursed to turn into a beast if his emotions—including lust—were aroused.

After an incident during which they'd found each other's heaving and sweaty bodies irresistible, and their sword practice had turned into a lips-led embrace, Vlerion had decided that someone else should teach blade work to Kaylina. He remained at ranger headquarters though, and she kept catching his eye from across the arena, where he was sparring with a number of his men. If anyone presumed to whistle, leer, or comment on her physique, he swept over to loom while issuing a stare frostier than the snow in the mountains.

"Some men fall into that category," Zhani said.

"The category of animals?"

"Yup." Zhani's smirk was without rancor. She didn't seem to mind stray comments from the male rangers. Probably because she had blade skills that twenty-year masters would envy and could flick her wrist to slice the balls off any aggressor.

Kaylina lifted her sword, determined to learn as much as she could. Of late, everyone from irate fur sharks to armed men to horned Kar'ruk had tried to kill her, and her grandpa's sling hadn't proven a powerful enough weapon to fend them off.

"For the next combination, I'll feint high, stab midsection, then swing my blade in from the side, in what I call the oak, briar, fern combination." Zhani demonstrated a high, middle, and sweeping attack with her blade.

Kaylina tried to envision the flora referenced but didn't find the description that helpful. Zhani had an extensive knowledge of altered and unaltered plants, and she often mentioned them, as if they were the perfect mnemonic devices, but it seemed like something that worked better for her than Kaylina.

"Later, I won't warn you what I'm going to throw at you," Zhani added, "but, for now, I want you to practice parrying quickly and correctly against common combinations. The rangers and Kingdom Guard both train with this attack, so you'll see it almost as often as the jab-punch in boxing."

Kaylina, who'd only been training to become a ranger for a few weeks, and was opening a meadery and eating house with her brother on the side, nodded, but she had even less *boxing* than sword-fighting experience.

As they practiced, the male rangers did too, and Kaylina often found her gaze drifting toward Vlerion. It was hard *not* to look since he, currently shirtless and battling three foes, was mesmerizing. Sweat gleamed on his torso, drawing the eye to his powerful muscles. They relaxed and flexed in the most intriguing manner as he moved effortlessly about, striking with amazing speed and power that kept all three opponents at bay.

After a failed attempt to gang up on him, they regrouped, discussed strategy, then attacked again. It still wasn't enough, not against someone with the swift grace of a panther.

Kaylina suspected the curse lent him that, some of its magic affecting him even in his human form, giving him an edge over all mundane foes. Watching him was captivating—and arousing.

Countless nights, she'd woken from erotic dreams of Vlerion, disappointed to find herself alone in bed. More than once, she'd lashed out at her brother for no good reason except frustration over not having an outlet for release.

A blade smacking the back of her hand made her jump, jerking her gaze back to Zhani.

"If we end up riding into battle together," the sergeant said, "I'll hope there won't be any naked men on the battlefield to distract you."

"Sorry." Kaylina blushed. She'd thought her glances were covert and that her instructor wouldn't notice. "If it makes you feel better about our future battles, not all naked men would distract me."

"Oh, I know who you're looking at. A lot of women ogle him, even though he's not *that* gorgeous."

Kaylina opened her mouth to protest, but she'd noted herself that Vlerion wasn't the most handsome ranger, not with the claw scars on the side of his face and a severely short haircut that made it possible to see more scars on his scalp. Vlerion's mother had pointed out that women were drawn to the cursed men of the Havartaft line, sensing on some level the danger and power of the beast and finding it appealing.

"He's... nice," Kaylina settled on.

"In that cold, aloof, you-are-nothing-to-me kind of way?" Zhani arched her eyebrows.

Again, Kaylina couldn't protest, not when she'd thought exactly that of Vlerion when they'd met. She'd called him *pirate* out loud and *asshole* in her mind, too busy bristling at his haughty dismissal of her to properly respect his aristocratic rank.

Then she'd learned his secret and that he carefully distanced himself from situations that could bestir his emotions. Now, she understood perfectly well why he came across as cool and aloof.

"Okay, he's kind of an ass," Kaylina said, since she couldn't share Vlerion's secret with anyone to explain him, and he didn't seem to care what others thought anyway, "but he's hot."

Zhani lowered her sword and gazed toward the passageway where the taybarri still congregated. "Like I said, you're not the only one to think so."

Kaylina followed her gaze, then stiffened, her sword far more inclined to raise than lower. A human visitor had arrived.

Though she had only seen him once in daylight, she recognized Spymaster Sabor, a man who manipulated the king—who manipulated the entire *kingdom*—and who was interested in using Kaylina because of her *anrokk* power.

As Zhani had pointed out, Sabor wasn't looking at her, not today. The plain-faced man with short graying hair gazed into the practice arena toward the male rangers—toward *Vlerion.*

Kaylina had witnessed that even men were drawn to Vlerion, quick to obey his orders, whether they were of lower rank or not. She wasn't sure if that was because they also sensed the beast on some level, and it made them wary of him, or if it was that his family had once ruled the kingdom and still had political power, even if his ancestor had abdicated the throne because of the curse.

Sabor's gaze had a speculative element as he looked Vlerion up and down, watching with a slight curve to his thin lips. Before Kaylina could decide what it meant, he turned toward her.

One thin eyebrow twitched in wry acknowledgment that he'd been caught staring. He didn't seem to care. And he also gave *her* a long and speculative look. Wondering if she'd learned how to *control* the beast yet? He'd once asked Captain Targon if she could do that.

Hardly.

"You don't want to garner the attention of that one." Zhani shifted to block Kaylina from the spymaster's view while bending her knees and lifting her sword, as if all she meant to do was restart their training.

"Too late." Kaylina parried a straightforward blow less complicated than the combinations they'd been working on earlier. "He's interested in me because of the *anrokk* thing. I guess it's rare."

She'd certainly never heard the term before coming north.

"It is. We have a couple in the sandsteader towns, and there are rumored to be more among the nomadic wild tribes, but not many people have that power."

"Is that where you're from? The desert?" Kaylina had wondered. The sergeant's skin wasn't as dark as hers, but it and her hair color were different from the pale-skinned, light-haired people common in this northern part of the kingdom.

"Yes, but I haven't been back in six years." A warning in Zhani's tone suggested she didn't want to talk about her home or why she'd left.

That was fine. Given how many people knew about where Kaylina had come from and her goals here in the north, she would have preferred more anonymity herself.

"What are all you taybarri doing over here?" came Captain Targon's voice from the passageway. He attempted to nudge one of the big creatures aside, but it didn't budge. The herd continued to observe Kaylina, even though she couldn't imagine the sword practice was that interesting. "Don't you have a stable full of protein pellets?"

Kaylina snorted. "Like those are going to lure them away."

"Blu seems to like his," Zhani said.

"That's the name of your taybarri?"

"Yes. Bludashar. He's a unique soul."

"They all are. If he'd had honey, I promise you he'd be less interested in dehydrated hearts and lungs or whatever those things are made with."

While Kaylina parried more simple attacks, she kept an eye on Targon and Sabor. They stood shoulder to shoulder, looking back and forth from the men to the women. No, from Vlerion to Kaylina. Sergeant Zhani's attempts to keep powerful people from noticing Kaylina were not, alas, working.

Sabor pointed at Vlerion and at her and asked Targon something. Targon nodded, then waved back toward the main courtyard. Suggesting they could speak in his office? About Vlerion and Kaylina?

She frowned as the men walked away together, not wanting to be the subject of their conversation. At the same time, if she *was* the subject, she wanted to know what they were talking about. Plans for how she could help the kingdom? By controlling Vlerion?

"I need to pee," Kaylina blurted.

Zhani blinked and stepped back.

"Can we take a break?" Maybe that would have been a better way to start her request.

"Sure." Zhani pointed her sword toward a latrine near the pool in the practice arena.

"I like the one by the stables." Kaylina leaned her sword against a rack and strode in the same direction the men had gone.

"The better for the taybarri to observe you?"

"I don't mind company in the latrine," she called back more loudly than she should have.

Vlerion and several of the men looked over, some with curious expressions, one with a lewd smirk. That ranger looked like he wanted to reply to the comment, but he glanced at Vlerion and kept his mouth shut. Good.

Kaylina glanced back at Zhani as she squeezed past the taybarri to follow the captain and spymaster. Though the sergeant didn't stop her, her narrowed eyes promised she knew Kaylina was up to something. Hoping it would work, Kaylina raised a finger to her lips before hurrying out of Zhani's view.

When she entered the main courtyard, the herd of taybarri padding after her, Targon and Sabor were already out of sight. From there, they could have gone into the stables, infirmary, mess hall, barracks, or offices. Assuming Sabor hadn't come to feed taybarri, get a muffin or bandage, or take a nap, Kaylina strode toward the offices.

A couple of rangers in black leather armor had recently arrived and were brushing and feeding their taybarri. They looked at Kaylina as she walked toward the office building.

She kept her head up, her back straight, and attempted to look like she had been summoned, or at least had a good reason for entering. She was most certainly not a furtive trainee on the way to eavesdrop. Assuming she could figure out *how* to eavesdrop. Last time, Targon had stuffed her through a secret doorway in his office, but it exited in the sewers, and she didn't know if there were any other entrances one could use from inside ranger head-quarters.

When she stepped through the two-story building's front door, she caught a voice from the top of the stairs. Targon. Good, she'd guessed right.

She eased up the steps, halting when one creaked under her feet. She couldn't hear Targon anymore. Because he'd heard the creak and stopped? Or because they'd stepped into his office?

A thump came from the level below. Someone else walking into the building?

She kept going up the stairs and groped for an explanation to give if she were caught. What reason for this errand might someone believe?

When she reached the top of the stairs, she heard nothing but silence. She peeked out, looking in the direction of Targon's office. The hallway lay empty, the door ajar. A shadow moved inside his office. If the men didn't close the door, she had a shot at eavesdropping. Perfect.

Stepping carefully along the wall to avoid creaky floorboards, Kaylina headed in that direction. Her instincts warned her of danger behind her, of someone slipping out of another doorway. She crouched to spring away and whirl to face the threat, but the person was too fast.

With viper-like speed, an arm snaked around her, yanking her back against a hard chest. Before she could do more than jab her attacker with her elbow, the blow hurting her more than him, a sharp, cold dagger pressed against her throat.

2

A MAN NEED NOT THREATEN YOU WITH A BLADE TO DECLARE HIMSELF AN enemy.

~ Sandsteader Proverb

With the dagger pressed into her throat just shy of drawing blood, Kaylina didn't try to ram her elbow back into her attacker's chest again. Her first strike had glanced off what had to be chain mail under his shirt, and the man's grip had only tightened.

Spymaster *Sabor's* grip.

She couldn't see him behind her and dared not turn her head, but her captor wasn't tall enough to be Captain Targon. Besides, Targon greeted her with snarky comments about her irreverence, not blades.

"Where are you going, girl?" Sabor asked softly. Dangerously.

Kaylina hadn't seen the spymaster fight, but she doubted a person rose to such a position without knowing how to vanquish enemies. And just because he wanted to use her didn't mean he wouldn't hurt her along the way.

Since she'd already passed two latrines, she couldn't use that excuse. "Captain Targon wants to see me," she tried.

His office door opened wider, and he leaned out. "I thought you were right behind me, Sabor."

"I noticed we had a follower. She says you want her."

The turn of phrase made Targon's lips quirk up. "Oh, yeah. I summon her every day after lunch. She likes my sword a lot more than Sergeant Zhaniyan's."

"Is that so."

"Yup. She's good fun too. Lots of vigor and a screamer."

Kaylina clenched her jaw, unable to feel gratitude toward Targon for covering for her, if that was what the idiotic words were meant to do.

"According to the reports I've received, she's saving her *vigor* for Vlerion," Sabor said.

"I had no idea your spies were reporting on Trainee Korbian's sex life. Important to the kingdom, is it?"

"They like to be thorough."

"But they couldn't figure out that Jana Bloomlong was the one to deliver poisoned mead to the queen, not me?" In her predicament, Kaylina should have kept her mouth shut, but she couldn't help but bristle, even if she'd since been cleared of suspicion. At the least, the queen of the taybarri had vouched for her. Kaylina didn't know if Queen Petalira truly believed her innocent.

"Haven't your trainers taught you not to question your superiors, girl?" Sabor asked softly. "And to address those with power over you as *my lord*?"

"No, they haven't mentioned it. Captain Targon finds me a delight in my natural state."

Targon snorted. "I keep telling Vlerion to flog some respect into her, but he's gone soft."

"Oh?" Sabor asked. "I'd heard *anrokks* made him hard."

"Well, not Sergeant Jastadar. This one on the other hand..." Targon smirked at Kaylina again, his gaze dipping to her chest.

A creak came from the stairs, and Targon didn't finish his sentence. That had to be the same board that Kaylina had stepped on, now announcing someone new coming up.

Sabor couldn't have known who it was, but he shifted to put his back against a wall, pulling Kaylina with him to keep her pressed against his chest and the dagger at her throat. She bared her teeth, wanting to jerk away, but such a movement would cause that blade to cut her.

On the stairs, Vlerion rounded the corner and came into view, his shirt in his hand, his bare chest still sweaty.

"Craters of the moon." Targon couldn't have seen Vlerion yet but must have guessed who it was. He stepped into the hallway, his lecherous expression shifting to concern.

As soon as Vlerion spotted Kaylina with the dagger to her throat, his blue eyes widened, and anger sparked in them. Anger and something more dangerous.

He sprang up the steps, skipping several as he landed in a crouch in the hall, like the panther she'd likened him to earlier. The growl that emanated from his chest was human but barely. It promised what he could become if he lost control, if the beast overtook him.

"It's okay," Kaylina blurted, hoping to keep that from happening. "I'm okay."

For a split second, she wondered if the kingdom would be worse or better off if he changed and killed these two men, the savage instincts of the beast keeping him from recognizing friend from foe. But he might not stop with them. There were dozens of innocent rangers in the headquarters compound, and the beast was a threat to her as well as everyone else.

Sabor remained calm, his only response to tighten his grip

slightly. The blade pressed harder against Kaylina's throat, making her wonder if she'd spoken too soon. Maybe it *wasn't* okay.

"What is going on?" Tension radiated from Vlerion, his muscles taut and coiled to spring. Usually, he hummed a song that soothed him when the beast threatened to arise, but he didn't now, only staring at Sabor with rage in his eyes. Maybe he *wanted* to turn, to ensure he could protect her.

"Trainee Korbian invited herself up to eavesdrop on our conversation," Sabor said. "I cannot allow that. Nobody spies on the spymaster." The bastard sounded like he was smiling. He either loved courting danger or didn't recognize how much he was in. "Captain Targon informs me that you've been lax in flogging her and drilling proper respect into her."

Vlerion clenched his jaw so hard that Kaylina heard his teeth grind together.

"Put the knife down, Sabor." Targon lifted a hand toward the men. "You're not going to kill a girl you want to use, and I'm not going to be able to stop him if you push him over the edge."

"As an aristocrat sworn to defend the crown and serve the king and his superiors, Lord Vlerion shouldn't be on any edges around me," Sabor said coolly, not taking his gaze from him.

"*Vlerion* isn't the him I'm talking about, and you know it," Targon said.

Vlerion's jaw clenched even harder, the tendons in his muscled neck standing out. The dangerous heat in his eyes threatened to shift into more, a fiery inferno that would bring the beast.

Would Sabor be too stubborn to back down? His body was also taut with tension, his knuckles tight around the hilt of the dagger. Maybe he *did* recognize his predicament.

Targon was tense too, not looking like he knew whether to jump in and try to separate the potential combatants or if he should back into his office and let events unfold as they would.

"Why don't we all relax and put our weapons down?" Kaylina suggested. "The grand opening of my meadery and eating house is this week, and I would prefer to serve my patrons without a bloody gash in my neck. I'd invite you all, but the cursed castle still isn't fond of rangers. I suppose it might not have a problem with a spymaster. We're offering ten percent discounts on opening night to anyone who comes and orders a flight of mead to sample."

Sabor and Vlerion were too busy with their staring battle to respond. Vlerion didn't even seem to see Kaylina—only the threat to her.

"Haven't you had that grand opening a couple of times now?" Targon asked, going along with her attempt to infuse some lightness into the situation, to calm both men.

"Just once, but someone rudely lit our castle on fire. And then the Kar'ruk invaded the city, so we had to wait a few weeks to try again. Funny how people aren't in the mood for drink and festivities when there are dead in the streets."

"Yes, funny."

Sabor growled softly, sounding almost as animalistic as Vlerion, and lowered his dagger. He released Kaylina by shoving her toward Vlerion while shifting farther away from them, keeping the blade ready in case he needed it.

"If he turns, that's not going to save you," Kaylina muttered. "I've seen him kill a horde of Kar'ruk warriors."

At the time, the beast had been dusted with a magical powder that conveyed invisibility, but it had still been an impressive feat.

Sabor eyed Kaylina with irritation as Vlerion took her arm and guided her to his side.

"The rangers are going too easy on you, girl," Sabor said. "Don't forget that you're a commoner, druid blood or not."

"You sure about that?" Targon asked. "Maybe the druid who screwed one of her hot ancestors was a prince."

"The Daygarii didn't have royalty. Teach her some respect, Vlerion. If you and Targon don't flog her for her insolence, *I* will." Sabor lowered his dagger but didn't put it away as he walked toward Targon.

He had to pass Vlerion on the way, and Vlerion reached out. Sabor whirled, turning the blade toward him, but, as fast as he was, Vlerion was even faster and caught his forearm, halting it before Sabor could bring the blade to bear.

"If you touch her," Vlerion said, his earlier fire replaced by ice, "or cause harm to befall her, I will kill you."

Kaylina had seen the beast arise numerous times now, and she recognized that the threat hadn't passed. Vlerion's emotions were still flaring. Could the spymaster not tell that?

Sabor tried to twist his arm free but failed. That didn't keep him from glaring defiantly back at Vlerion. "I'm the last man you want to threaten."

"No, I am the last man *you* want to threaten."

"Attack me, and you'll meet the same fate as your brother."

Vlerion's eyes narrowed. "If you admit to me that you somehow orchestrated that, I'll kill you right here." His muscles bunched, his grip tightening on Sabor's arm, and another growl rumbled from deep in his chest.

Though it felt like sticking her hand in a furnace, Kaylina eased closer to him and rested her hand on his back. She stroked his hard muscles, his bare skin, attempting to soothe him.

"There are others in your headquarters besides these two," she murmured, trusting he would understand what she meant.

Vlerion wouldn't forgive himself if he turned and killed Jankarr, Sergeant Zhani, and other rangers who'd done nothing to deserve the beast's ire. He also considered Targon a friend, even if Kaylina questioned that choice.

"I know," Vlerion said tersely without looking away from Sabor. More softly, he repeated, "I know."

He was trying not to turn, but it was hard. So hard. Kaylina stroked him gently, making sure there was nothing arousing about her touch. She wanted only to soothe.

The brand on the back of her hand warmed, and she imagined magic flowing through her fingers, helping relax him, calming the curse. It might have been her imagination that she had any power to do that, that any magic came from the brand, but Vlerion's muscles loosened ever so slightly. He released Sabor.

For an instant, defiance twisted the spymaster's face, and he looked like he would do something dumb, like slashing at Vlerion with his blade, but he smoothed his features and sheathed his dagger. Unfortunately, he also looked at Kaylina and squinted thoughtfully.

A question he'd once asked of Targon came to her mind: *Do you think she can control him?*

She didn't shake her head or do anything to indicate she could guess what he was thinking. Vast relief flowed into her when he left them, walking toward Targon without another word. The spymaster stepped into the captain's office and disappeared from view.

"Keep her out of trouble, Vlerion," Targon said, less an order than the suggestion of a friend who knew how disastrous that showdown could have turned. The concerned look in his eyes suggested there might yet be disastrous repercussions.

Would Sabor take out his anger at the situation on Vlerion? On her? By some less direct means than a confrontation with a dagger?

"It is... difficult." Vlerion wrapped his arm around Kaylina.

"Yeah, who knew an *anrokk* could be such a handful?" Targon managed a smirk. "Sergeant Jastadar is such a loyal ranger who never gives me any trouble."

"I knew the day I met her," Vlerion said.

"The day she hit you in the back of the head with a sling round?"

"Precisely."

"Get in here, Targon," Sabor said.

Targon lifted his gaze toward the ceiling before turning, entering, and shutting the door firmly behind him.

Vlerion shifted to face Kaylina, his attention fully on her for the first time. He slid his other arm around her, pulling her close and inhaling her scent.

Aware of his raw power wrapped around her, of the appeal of him—her protector—Kaylina had to resist the urge to press herself against Vlerion and kiss him. Or maybe slide her tongue over the swell of one of those hard muscles.

"This is just as dangerous," she whispered.

"I know." He nuzzled her ear and cupped her ass, making her ache with desire for him, before releasing her and stepping back. "To my great lament."

He looked her over, his eyes hungry, then turned away. This time, she caught him humming softly.

Her heart ached for what he had to endure—and the shared frustration for both of them.

"If you want to eavesdrop with me, I know where access to a secret passage to Targon's office is," she said quietly, though she didn't know if one could get in through the sewer exit or not.

Vlerion grunted without turning around.

Maybe she shouldn't have said anything. Vlerion might be too noble—in all senses of the word—to stoop to activities such as eavesdropping. She realized he might have suspected that was her intent when she'd left the arena, and that was why he'd come up here in the first place. To stop her.

"I do appreciate you coming to help," she said, "but you might have made an enemy of Sabor there. It would behoove both of us to listen in on that conversation."

"The sewer exit is one-way," Vlerion said. "Short of using explosives, you could not enter from there."

"Are explosives not a valid way to gain eavesdropping access?" Kaylina almost pointed out that the Virts, the rebels hoping to overthrow the monarchy, used black powder frequently, but he knew that well and didn't approve of their methods. She didn't either, not against people, but she wouldn't be above blowing a hole in that stinky sewer tunnel.

"Not if one wants the people being eavesdropped on to be unaware of one's presence." Vlerion turned, more composed, with his shoulders less tense, and regarded her thoughtfully.

"If it's not appropriately noble and honorable to listen in on conversations, you could leave me here and return to your training. I'll just..." Kaylina looked down the hallway. "See if there's a latrine up here."

"While pressing your ear to Targon's door?"

"Yes, naturally. They might be discussing the location of the facilities right now."

Vlerion shook his head, donned his shirt, and pointed at the stairs. "Come with me."

"Aren't you curious about *what* they're discussing?" She pointed to herself, then to him, to imply it was about them.

Maybe he'd been too busy defending against three opponents to notice Sabor looking back and forth between them in the practice arena.

"Come," Vlerion repeated, pausing at the top of the stairs to make sure she followed, "or I will carry you."

"You know women love it when you give them orders." Kaylina cast a longing look over her shoulder toward the closed office door, but she believed Vlerion *would* pick her up and tote her out, so she followed him.

"That was a threat, not an order."

"*Such* an improvement."

He looked back at her again.

"My lord," she added, then smiled at him.

He sighed, looking like he might hoist her over his shoulder, whether she followed or not.

Attempting to appear properly respectful, she followed and gave him no reason to do so. Meanwhile, she schemed up ways to slip away in time to catch the tail end of that conversation.

3

IF HE CARES, HE'LL PROTECT ME FROM THE WORLD; IF HE LOVES, HE'LL give me a step up into it.

~ Lady Dandrela the Fair, poetress

Kaylina expected Vlerion to lead her outside and back to the training arena, but when they reached the first floor, he strode down the long hallway and past an armory and numerous storage rooms. At the end, a plaque on the wall read *Visiting Officer Quarters.*

He opened the door and stepped into a suite with two rooms and a latrine that smelled of lye soap. The space was unoccupied and ready for visitors.

Kaylina thought he might direct her to the latrine, but he headed for an armoire in the bedroom and pushed it aside to reveal a square access panel. He removed it and set it against the wall, the space beyond too dark to see into. "Sometimes, fleet admirals and high-ranking rangers from other provinces will stay here at headquarters when they visit. It's important that they be able to escape if trouble arrives."

"Does this go to the same place as the hidden door in Targon's office?"

Already stepping through, Vlerion held a finger to his lips before ducking his head to enter fully.

Without hesitation, Kaylina followed him. Maybe he *would* help her eavesdrop.

If there were lanterns anywhere inside, Vlerion didn't pause to light them. He found her hand, placed it on his back, and walked into the darkness, a dusty passageway that couldn't see frequent use.

She trailed him until he paused. A faint rasp sounded as he pushed open a door before turning into a new passageway. Steps led upward, and Kaylina trusted they were the same ones she and Frayvar had once gone down to escape the compound.

As they reached the top, the sound of voices grew audible. Doing her best not to make a sound, she joined Vlerion on the landing.

They were outside Targon's office, and a touch confirmed that the wooden back of his sliding bookcase was the only thing between them and the speakers. She kept one hand on Vlerion's back as she leaned close, hoping to hear their words without needing to slide open the bookcase.

He didn't move close to it and probably had his arms folded over his chest, silently saying this was *her* plan and that he wouldn't stoop to eavesdropping.

That was fine. She would tell him what she learned later. As long as he didn't stop her...

"I don't want excuses, Targon. If you can't control your ranger, I'll have him taken out in his sleep."

Kaylina swallowed. Your ranger. Vlerion. Who else?

Targon snorted. "You could lose a lot of people trying to do that. Besides, he's a boon to the kingdom. He's as loyal as a hound, does what you ask of him, and has the fighting prowess of ten men. That's when he's just a normal human."

"What's his prowess when he changes?"

"You almost got a chance to find out in my hallway," Targon said grimly. "We both did."

"But she stopped him." Sabor's tone had turned speculative. "I was curious if she could. She denied it, but..."

"I think you read more into that than was there."

"Did I?"

"If you want to test him, do it somewhere dozens of rangers aren't around who could become collateral damage."

Not responding to that, Sabor said, "You should be training the girl's druid powers, not teaching her to poke people with swords."

"Do I look like I know how to train someone's *druid* powers?"

"I sent you books. I understand your education was somewhat deficient, but surely you know how to read."

"My education was fine, Spymaster. Books written by humans who thought they knew something about the druids aren't useful resources. They said nothing about dealing with druid magic— or someone who has access to it." After a pause, Targon added, "What is it you think she's going to do for you? For the kingdom?"

"Since I'm as yet unenlightened about the extent of her powers, I don't know, but you saw what the plant in that castle did to the Kar'ruk that came near it."

"I heard it shot magical beams and killed them, yes."

"Magical beams of power, Targon. I've never heard of an altered plant that could do that—I had no idea such power even existed in the world anymore. Even if all the girl can do is learn to control that plant—and to control *him*..."

Vlerion growled softly. As proud as he was, he couldn't appreciate the suggestion that a woman—that anyone—could control him. He probably hated the mere idea that someone might believe that possible.

Kaylina stepped closer and leaned into him, trying to convey through her touch that she cared for him and wouldn't use that power even if she had it.

That wasn't, however, entirely true. When he'd been trapped in the preserve by magical vines, with enemy Kar'ruk heading their way, she'd tried to make him turn into the beast. And just now, in the hallway, she'd used her power to soothe him. She could argue both instances had been for the greater good, but did that make them acceptable?

She had apologized for her actions in the ruins, but she might need to apologize for the confrontation with Sabor too. She shouldn't try to manipulate Vlerion, druid power or not, but it was hard when she feared what would happen if he changed.

He wrapped an arm around her, shifting her so that she remained close enough to the bookcase to hear but had her back to his chest. He rested his face in her hair. Though he didn't speak, the gesture seemed to mean he wasn't annoyed with her. She hoped that was the case. In the dark, she couldn't see his face, and she wouldn't have any idea if his eyes sparked dangerously.

"She saved your ranger Jankarr too," Sabor said, and Kaylina realized she'd missed whatever Targon's response had been, "by manipulating vines with her power."

"You continue to demonstrate how well-informed you are about the activities of my rangers."

"Don't sound so indignant. You have spies in the royal castle too. I know it. It's how the system works."

"If you mean the baker, she's not a spy. She just likes to chat while I help her frost her cookies."

"Yes, I've heard you're quite the kitchen helper in your off-time. You frost a lot of women's cookies, considering you're not that comely of a man."

"In your opinion. Is there something you want besides intel on my sex life?"

"I already told you," Sabor said. "The Kar'ruk may be gone for now, but the Virts are still problematic. I want you to figure out what that girl's powers are and how we can use them. Stabbing people with swords is beneath her. She's got access to magic far greater than that. Either you figure out how to draw it reliably out of her, or you let me take her to train."

Kaylina winced at the thought of being dragged off to the castle for whatever a spymaster's *training* might involve. It was bad enough the ranger training was being forced on her. At least it came with access to the taybarri. Nobody had officially said Levitke was her mount, but she hadn't seen the female with any other rangers on her back, and Levitke cheerfully greeted Kaylina each morning when she came to headquarters.

"Train or experiment on?" Targon asked.

Behind her, Vlerion tensed again, his arm tightening protectively around Kaylina.

"Whatever it takes to bring out her power," Sabor said.

"You make her hate you, and she'll get those vines to wrap around *your* neck."

"Is that what happened when you were attacked in Stillguard Castle?"

Targon hesitated. "None of your *spies* were around for that. Vlerion didn't tell you, and I'm positive *she* didn't."

"My *spies* are observant. When you return to ranger headquarters with a red welt all the way around your neck, people can guess someone—or something—was at your throat. Did she sic a vine on you?"

"She tried to help me."

"Tried? And failed? She helped Jankarr in the preserve, didn't she?"

Kaylina resented that she couldn't speak up to defend herself

—Targon's attack had been before the plant in the tower had branded her, before she had any power. She still didn't know if any of her new ability to communicate with vegetation came from within her or from the brand. The plant might simply have lent her some of its power because it found it useful to do so.

"He's a lot prettier and friendlier than I am," was all Targon said.

"That's the truth. Train her, Targon. Figure out what she can do so we can use it to our advantage." Sabor's voice grew less distinct, as if he was heading for the door. "And figure out if she can summon the beast—and control it."

"By all the moon gods, you weren't *trying* to make Vlerion change in the hall, were you? Did you know he was coming up? Is that why you put a knife to Korbian's throat when she hadn't done anything?"

"She was going to spy on us. I meant to teach her a lesson."

"And when Vlerion showed up? You aren't suicidal enough to have wanted to rouse the beast, are you?"

"I wouldn't mind a demonstration of what he can do—and what she can keep him from doing."

"You're a loon. He was about to *do* you. Even if she could stop the beast, who says she would to save *your* life?"

"Really, Targon. You said she tried to save yours in Stillguard Castle. I'm at least as appealing and affable as you are."

"You're an ass."

"Yes, but so are you."

Targon snorted. "Get out of my office."

"I'll be back soon to check on your progress with her."

"I'm giddy at the prospect of seeing you again."

A soft thump sounded, a door shutting. Kaylina leaned her back into Vlerion, letting her head fall against his shoulder.

Maybe she was a fool for staying in Port Jirador, but with her meadery and eating house so close to opening, she refused to leave. Even if she wanted to, she didn't know if she would be allowed to depart. Early on, Targon had spoken to the shipmasters in the port, ordering them not to give her passage home if she tried to escape. She had a niggling feeling that Sabor might have updated those orders, making sure any new arrivals knew about them.

"The spymaster risks alienating you instead of securing your loyalty," Vlerion murmured.

There wasn't any noise coming from Targon's office. Had he walked out with Sabor? Kaylina didn't know, but when she replied, she kept her words soft.

"Diplomacy doesn't seem to be his strong suit. Targon hasn't exactly won my loyalty either."

She thought about leading Vlerion down the stairs, in case his captain *hadn't* left his office, but it felt good to be in his arms, to have him holding her. He'd let her eavesdrop, even if he hadn't approved. He'd turned into her supporter as well as her protector. That meant a lot to her.

"I have." Vlerion stated it as a certainty, no question in his mind.

Kaylina was tempted to deny it, if only to pop his bubble of arrogance, but she didn't want him to question her loyalty. He'd said he appreciated her and how she wanted to lift his curse. She liked knowing it mattered to him.

"You have," she agreed. "Despite your aloof haughtiness."

Not that he was being aloof now, with his arm around her, his face resting against her head, his warm breath stirring her hair.

"You have mine as well." Vlerion ignored the rest of her comment in favor of moving aside her hair and kissing the back of her neck.

Desire trickled into her. Worrying about Targon overhearing them wasn't the *only* reason she needed to lead Vlerion away. She dared not remain in the dark alone with him.

"I'm glad." Though she longed to stay, to enjoy his lips brushing her skin, Kaylina shifted, intending to step away.

"I sensed you use your power on me."

She froze. A denial sprang to mind, but she'd just been thinking about that, about how it was the truth.

"To keep me from changing into the beast," Vlerion added, "from killing him."

"I'm sorry, but I thought you would regret it. I wasn't sure if I could soothe you, but I had to try. I was afraid for all the other rangers, not only Targon and Sabor."

"Yes. I did not want to turn, but when I saw him with that dagger..." Vlerion's arm tightened again, holding her against him. "I *wanted* to kill him." The words came out a growl.

Kaylina shivered. Even if she didn't like Sabor, hearing Vlerion say that was chilling.

"But I didn't want to kill Targon or hurt you," he added.

"I know. We'll figure out a way to lift your curse. Soon." Kaylina regretted that she hadn't made any progress on that in the weeks that she and her brother had been cleaning up the castle and she'd been training.

A few times, she'd spoken to the plant, delivering more honey-water fertilizer to keep it happy with her. She'd asked it the history of its curse and who'd placed it there, but it hadn't answered. Maybe because she hadn't let any of the vines touch her, not wanting any more of its visions. The one about the taybarri elders might have been helpful, but she hadn't forgotten the other one it had given her, the one asking her to kill Vlerion for her own good. She didn't need a plant bodyguard deciding who was and wasn't a threat to her.

The bookcase slid aside, and light slashed onto the landing.

Kaylina jumped. If not for Vlerion's arm around her, she would have sprinted down the stairs. But Vlerion didn't stir as Targon looked in at them. Targon's back was to the wall beside the entrance, a dagger in his hand that he'd used to push open the bookcase.

Vlerion only rested his chin against Kaylina's head while gazing impassively at the captain. Had he expected Targon to know they were there?

"I wasn't sure if I'd find you naked and furry in here." Targon eyed Vlerion's arm around Kaylina.

"So you decided to check?" Kaylina asked.

"It would have been quite a show." Targon's gaze lowered to her chest, though he didn't let it linger long. Maybe Vlerion was glaring at him over her head.

"You knew we were here all along?" Kaylina asked, wanting to change the subject. Sabor couldn't have, she hoped.

"I had a hunch." Targon met her eyes. "You're a proven eaves-dropper, and you..." He lifted his gaze to Vlerion. "I'm beginning to think Sabor is right."

"That I'm under her control?"

"Are you?"

"I can tell when she draws upon the power in that brand and channels it into me," Vlerion said. "So far, it hasn't been often."

"That might change. She might *like* controlling you."

Kaylina squirmed in Vlerion's grip, not caring to have them discussing her in front of her face. Not that she wanted them to discuss her behind her back either. She would prefer not to be so interesting to people in general.

Vlerion must not have been concerned by Targon's suggestion, because he slid his hand down to rest it on hers. "She doesn't want to control me. She wants to lift my curse."

Kaylina nodded. That was the truth.

"Sabor doesn't want your curse lifted. He'd like you under *his* control, a weapon he can direct toward the defense of the kingdom anytime he wants. I'm sure he'd rather have you obey him, but if he can control Korbian, and she can control you..."

"A dagger to her throat isn't going to win her loyalty," Vlerion said.

"That isn't going to win *anyone's* loyalty," Kaylina said.

Feeling self-conscious with Targon squinting at them, she tapped Vlerion's arm and attempted to step aside.

He seemed reluctant to let her go, as if he felt he also had to protect her from Targon. Did he? Kaylina didn't love the captain but believed he wanted to use her and wouldn't hurt her. He was more inclined to bribe her.

"The spymaster gets what he wants through threats, not by earning loyalty," Targon said. "He has access to all the funds in the kingdom, and he has a lot of people under his thumb, a lot of ways of manipulating those who don't obey."

"I'm aware." Vlerion must have realized he was now restraining Kaylina instead of romantically holding her, because he released her, but he didn't step away. "If Sabor attacks Kaylina again, I'll kill him. I don't need to turn into the beast to do that."

The look of exasperation Targon adopted was leveled at her, not Vlerion. As if his ranger's attitude was *her* fault.

Yes, she'd gone up to eavesdrop, but she hadn't told Vlerion to kill anyone. All she wanted was to know what fate those in power had in mind for her. Didn't she have a right to seek out that information?

"It must be nice to have your very own—" When Targon glanced at Vlerion's face, the word *beast* had to be on his mind, but, after a pause, he said, "—noble bodyguard. Not many ranger trainees get that."

"If Sabor attacks *you*, I'll also kill him," Vlerion told Targon.

"I'll bet not many ranger captains get noble bodyguards either," Kaylina said.

"*My lord*," Targon finished for her. "You're incorrigible."

"As you were just pointing out to Sabor," Vlerion said, "if she turns out to be part druid, she might not qualify as a commoner who has to *lord* you."

"Even the aristocratic ranger trainees know to use *sir* or *lord* with their superiors," Targon snapped. "She gets the same rules as anyone else. Since the druids were enemies to humans, I doubt she wants to call upon that heritage to define our treatment of her."

Kaylina lifted her hand, tired of being talked about instead of included. "If my training is over for the day, I'd like to go back to Stillguard Castle. We're preparing for our grand opening, so my brother needs me."

Targon glanced toward a clock. "Go, go, but you'd better watch out for that kid as much as yourself."

Again, Kaylina froze. Frayvar had already been hurt a number of times for no reason other than that he was helping her get the meadery started and some people didn't want that.

"Did Sabor say something?" she asked. "Before, we, uhm."

"Before you two sneaked up the back way to eavesdrop?" Targon asked.

"Yeah."

"Not about your brother, but I'm aware of his methodology. Watch the kid's back." Targon pointed toward the door of his office. "Get out of here, Korbian. But you don't go with her." The pointing finger shifted to Vlerion. "You'd better be heeding my orders about staying away from that ranger-hating place."

"I am." Vlerion touched the small of Kaylina's back and guided her out of the office.

She walked quickly, once again concerned for her brother. Targon's warning made her wish she hadn't sneaked up to eavesdrop after all.

"Too late now," she murmured.

4

POWER OF ALL KINDS IS DOUBLE-EDGED, AS MUCH A THREAT TO THE wielder as those nearby.
  ~ Ranger Lord Vlerion of Havartaft

"Come with me to the barracks before you go," Vlerion said as they stepped into the courtyard.

Kaylina pulled her mind from concerns about her brother's safety. "I believe you meant to say, please, delightful companion of mine, come with me to the barracks."

Vlerion stopped to look at her, his face hard to read.

She doubted she'd annoyed him—she'd often said such things in the hope that he would stop ordering her around, but he seemed too accustomed to issuing mandates to his men to stop. Still, she watched his eyes for signs of irritation. Just because he'd gone with her and even facilitated her eavesdropping didn't mean he was happy with her. He'd been nuzzling her in the dark passageway, but he'd admitted before he had no trouble being attracted to her and vexed with her at the same time.

"Because you are training as a ranger, and you should learn, as Targon said, to obediently do as your superiors ask without hesitation, I've attempted to treat you no differently than any other trainee. But..." Vlerion tilted his palm toward the sky. "This is a request and not an order. I should have phrased it differently."

It took a moment for the meaning of his words to sink in.

"Was that an apology?" Kaylina asked. "An admission you were wrong?"

"A confession that you were not incorrect to suggest a rephrasing."

"I'm going to interpret that as an apology. Excellent. I'd love to go with you to the barracks." She lifted her arm in offering.

Vlerion grunted and raised his to link with hers, but Jankarr and Zhani jogged out of the passageway between courtyards, and he paused.

"Everything all right, my lord?" Jankarr looked with concern at them, glancing at their upraised arms.

"Yes," Vlerion stated.

Jankarr arched his eyebrows toward Kaylina.

Had they heard or seen something to suggest otherwise?

"I think so," she said.

"Before they left, we heard Spymaster Sabor speaking to one of the guards who accompanied him." Zhani waved toward the stable. "The guard said something about your, ah, attractiveness, and Sabor told him to stay away from you, that he'd caught you eavesdropping and that you're trouble and you attract even more trouble."

"He technically caught me *before* there was eavesdropping," Kaylina said.

Zhani winced. "I knew you were up to something. I should have stopped you for your own sake. The spymaster is nobody to trifle with."

Kaylina touched her throat, the memory of the cold blade's kiss lingering. "I gathered."

"Sabor said Targon never should have handed your training off to someone inexperienced," Jankarr said.

Zhani winced again.

"You're to be punished, he said, for your infraction." Jankarr glanced at their arms, though they'd both lowered them. When he'd walked into the courtyard, had it appeared that Vlerion would grab her or hit her?

Kaylina had no idea what the punishment was for eavesdropping, but Targon mentioned flogging *often*.

Vlerion opened his mouth but glanced at Zhani and noticed several other rangers in the courtyard watching and within earshot. He gripped Kaylina's arm. "Yes. I will handle the punishment. Sergeant Zhaniyan was chosen to train Korbian for a reason, and it did not involve babysitting. Nonetheless, eavesdropping on royals and officials from the castle is not permitted. I *will* ensure Trainee Korbian does not make that mistake again."

"Sorry," Zhani mouthed to Kaylina as Vlerion led her away.

Doubting Vlerion had flogging in mind, Kaylina lifted a hand to try to convey to Zhani that it was all right. She was positive Vlerion had only said that because there had been witnesses. He probably wouldn't have put on a show for Jankarr alone.

Zhani's forehead was furrowed with concern and guilt as Vlerion led Kaylina into the barracks. Since she only knew cold and aloof Vlerion, she might well believe he *would* punish a woman. And maybe he had done so for wayward trainees in the past. But Kaylina trusted he didn't have that in mind for her. Maybe she could confide in Zhani later to alleviate her guilt, but she didn't know the woman that well yet and wasn't sure what she could say. Nothing about Vlerion's secret or their relationship.

"What *are* we going to do in the barracks?" Kaylina murmured as Vlerion led her toward his room.

"You're not open to being punished?"

"Not when you were eavesdropping right along with me."

"What if you'd succeeded in eavesdropping without me and I had been the one to catch you?" Vlerion asked.

"I suppose I might deserve it then."

"You do not." He stopped in front of his door, opening it for her. "I haven't forgotten that you didn't volunteer to train as a ranger."

"No, I did not."

"It does leave me conflicted about how to treat you. More in public than in private. Privately, you know how I feel."

"Irritated, vexed, and inexplicably drawn?" Kaylina stepped into his room, a nervous flutter teasing her belly when she glanced at his bed, even though she knew he hadn't brought her here for a horizontal rendezvous.

"I am rarely irritated and vexed with you these days. Occasionally exasperated."

"Only occasionally?"

That morning, he'd pointed out that a ranger was supposed to show up at dawn in training leathers, not ten minutes after with honey stuck to her fingers and treats to hand out to the taybarri. Exasperation had absolutely been involved.

"Occasionally each hour." Vlerion closed the door behind them. "As to the inexplicability of the *draw*, I believe we both understand it."

"Yes, you adore my whimsy and can't stay away."

"Whimsy, yes." He glanced at the top of her head. Was he remembering the mud and the reed antennae she'd stuck in her hair to make herself less sexy? If so, he didn't mention it, only pointing to his office. "I have a gift for you. Two gifts actually."

"Oh?"

Something long and wrapped in blue velvet lay on his desk, but he propped his hip on the edge and faced her instead of giving it to her. Maybe that particular item had nothing to do with her.

"I trust you've noticed my sword is magnificent," he said.

"I, what?" Kaylina glanced below his belt, memories of seeing him naked and aroused springing to mind.

"The sword I wield in battle," he said.

"Oh."

"Though the proper response to your interpretation of my first question should have been *yes, my lord, very magnificent.*"

"Uh-huh. Can't I call you Vlerion? When we're alone, at least?"

"Yes. I'd like you to."

"Then why do you always get pompous and add *my lord* to my sentences?"

"I worry about you. Your southern islands must be *very* lax and largely free of aristocratic influence."

"They are. I've mentioned that."

"But you seek to start a business here. Port Jirador, under the shadow of the royal castle and the unforgiving Evardor Mountains, is the opposite of lax. Your insouciant expressions and flippancy may get you into trouble with aristocrats who are even more *pompous* than I."

"Such people can't possibly exist."

Vlerion pointed at her. "That's what I'm talking about."

"Flippancy?"

"Flippancy." Vlerion flattened his hand to his chest. "*I* don't mind it."

"Except only occasionally?"

He snorted and flicked his fingers to acknowledge that maybe she did still exasperate him. Now and then. "I'm learning that it's a character trait of yours that I should, if not appreciate as much as your other assets, at least tolerate. I am aware that *I* have traits—and an ancestral curse—that you must also tolerate."

"*Yes.*" Tactfully, Kaylina didn't point out that the curse was easier to endure than the haughtiness. The former wasn't his fault. The latter was... a result of his aristocratic upbringing, she supposed. But he needed to get over that. "Just to be clear, are the assets you appreciate..." She waved vaguely toward her chest, though he didn't spend as much time ogling it as some of the other rangers did. Targon couldn't seem to resist—or didn't care to *bother* resisting.

"I admire your loyalty, courage, and selfless sacrifice for your family, per our previous discussions on the matter." His eyebrow twitched. "Your physical attributes draw the beast."

"Only the beast?"

"No."

The glint in his eyes—amusement and not something more dangerous—made her want to hug him. She enjoyed seeing his lighter side when he was willing to banter with her.

"Is it weird that I like that we don't have normal conversations?" she asked.

"I believe we've established a lack of normalcy in both of us."

"Yes." That made her want to hug him too.

But he was drawing his sword, the one sheathed at his hip, so she stayed back. Maybe he wanted to show her the *magnificence* that she'd never noticed. Probably because she was always watching *him* when he went into battle, not his blade. Besides, whenever he turned into the beast, he left the weapon behind, the same as his boots.

"I know you worry about me and my flippancy, my *irreverence*, and I won't deny that it's gotten me into a little trouble here and there." Kaylina bit her lip, thinking of the times she'd lost her temper and *really* had her tongue fly out of control. "But maybe my newfound powers will allow me to deal with anyone who's too uptight to respect the opinion of a commoner." She waved her branded hand at him.

Vlerion lay his sword on the desk next to the velvet-wrapped package. They were of similar length.

"I could convince nearby trees and plants to attack anyone who tried to chastise, flog, or arrest me," she added.

"Are you able to do that now?" One skeptical eyebrow rose, but Vlerion politely didn't mention that he'd found her tied and helpless in a valley after the Kar'ruk had kidnapped her. All she'd been able to convince the nearby plants to do had been to give her visions.

She hesitated. "I convinced a tree to help me fight a Kar'ruk warrior by dropping a branch on his head."

"Oh?"

"The Kar'ruk did sink an axe into the tree first, and I could tell it was peeved. It's possible that its help would have been scant if not for the offensive injury. Even with the dropped branch, I was lucky to have Levitke with me."

"That was an altered tree in the preserve?" Vlerion asked.

"A regular pine tree in the mountains where we found the press."

"Where *you* found the press." He held her gaze, beaming pride at her.

That warmed her to the core, and the urge to hug him rushed into her again. "Levitke found it. I showed her a newspaper article, and after she chewed it up, she tracked it to its origins."

"The taybarri are wonderful allies, but do not diminish your role. You will be an excellent ranger, should you be able to navigate working with your comrades and superiors without irking them."

"That *is* challenging. They're all so..."

This time, both of Vlerion's eyebrows went up.

"Stiff." That wasn't quite the word she wanted. It prompted her to glance at his groin again before catching herself and jerking her gaze away. Here she was resenting Targon for looking at her chest, and she couldn't keep her eyes off Vlerion.

"I'm glad you are as drawn by my beast side as I am by your *anrokk* side," he said softly. "It makes me feel less disturbed that you *are* able to control me now, at least in some small way. I believe I also have some sway over you."

"Yeah, you do." She thought of all the times they'd kissed against her better judgment. Even knowing the danger, she would have let him carry her off to do far more than kissing. He had the power to rouse her body with a mere look, to make her want him like she'd wanted no other. *That* was control, most certainly. And, of course, he was bigger and stronger than she, and could toss her over his shoulder at any time. It was hard to believe he worried about some vague druid magic in her.

"I can't really control you," she said. "You know that. All I was doing was trying to keep you from changing."

"Perhaps this time," he said, his eyes now brooding. "Your power is growing."

"Just because of the brand, I'm sure. The power the plant put in me may be growing." As soon as the words came out, she worried they were the wrong choice. Especially when his eyes darkened. "But it can't control *me*," she hurried to add.

He had to be thinking about the vision she'd told him about, the vision of the plant wanting her to use her knife to kill him. Maybe she should have kept that to herself.

"I hope that will continue to be true," Vlerion said. "You've kindled hope in me that you might be the one with the ability to lift my curse, even though none of my ancestors who studied it were able to make any headway. *They* did not have the blood of druids in their veins."

"I need to talk to my mother about that someday. It's hard to believe that I'm not... what I always assumed I was."

"It is distressing to have one's self-identity forcibly altered."

"Yes. And, uhm, your sword is very nice." Not sure what she was supposed to say, Kaylina waved at the bared blade on the desk. It had a jeweled hilt—was that a sapphire on the pommel?—though it was wrapped in leather that hid whatever designs it might have held. The blade was straight with few dents, a dark blue-silver metal that had recently been oiled. "Prettier than the ones we practice with."

And sharper.

"Yes, pretty weapons are what we all desire." A slight twitch to Vlerion's lips was the only indication that it was sarcasm.

Since his had an expensive jewel on the end, Kaylina knew *someone* had cared about aesthetics. She was about to say so when Vlerion lifted the velvet-wrapped item and held it out to her.

"It will be some time before your ranger training is complete and you're sent into battle, but you've found battle enough on your own, so you need a weapon for close-quarters fighting. Something superior to your dinner knife."

"You're giving me a sword?" The memory of the plant's vision came to mind again, of her thrusting her so-called dinner knife into Vlerion's chest. If she was wrong, and the plant's power somehow managed to take her over, she could do a lot more damage with a sword. She grimaced at the thought.

"I am. I can see from the delight on your face that you're appreciative and honored."

"I'm touched that you want to give me a quality weapon. I just…" She licked her lips, not wanting to remind him of what the plant had shared but feeling the need to explain. "That vision worries me. You know I'd never attack you of my own volition, but, as you pointed out, the plant…" She shrugged helplessly.

"I did consider that when contemplating this gift. I'm willing to take the risk that I can defend myself should you strike."

"You know you pass out at my feet when your beast-ness wears off, right?"

"That would be an opportune time for the plant's power to force you to attack, but... as I said, I'll risk it. You need a good weapon. I'll defend you whenever I'm nearby, but you insist on residing and working in a cursed castle that longs for nothing as much as my death."

More than once since her training had started, Targon had suggested she live in the barracks in ranger headquarters. He'd even said Frayvar could have a room there, an offer perhaps prompted by Doctor Penderbrock, who apparently appreciated all the organizing and cataloging of his medications that Frayvar had done. The system Frayvar had developed was even more thorough than the food categorization in the pantry. But Kaylina felt compelled to keep an eye on the castle, and she also needed a break from the wandering gazes of the perennially horny men here.

"I think the castle longs for all rangers' deaths equally," was all she said.

"The plant has given you visions of your knife thrusting into Targon's chest?"

"No," she admitted. "Which is a little disappointing."

"Indeed." Vlerion extended the gift toward her.

After accepting it, Kaylina unwrapped a beautiful sword, not only bejeweled with sapphires, like his, but having an intricate vine and flower pattern that started at the hilt and ran up either side of the fuller of the blade. She wasn't experienced enough to tell a good sword from a great sword, but when she swung it experimentally a few times, it felt light and balanced in her grip.

"It was my brother's blade," Vlerion said, "though if I were to have one made for you, I'd choose something similar. You are even more inextricably linked to plants and nature than a ranger."

"It's beautiful."

"Yes. Vlarek wasn't that much taller than you, so I think you'll be able to use it."

"It's a gracious offer, but I can't accept a family heirloom, especially when I'm such a novice."

"It's not an heirloom. He had it made when he was accepted into the rangers."

"So... it's just expensive?" Kaylina wouldn't be surprised if the weapon was worth more than the entire Spitting Gull building and business back home. The kind of money that aristocrats had to spend on such things was mind-boggling.

"Quality custom-made weapons are expensive, yes, but he no longer needs it."

"Oh. I'm sorry," she said, reminded that his brother had died years earlier, cut down by rangers who'd been his allies until he'd lost control and turned into the beast.

"He would not mind me giving it to you, another ranger in training, someone who will put it to good use. Besides, since he was cursed in the same way as I, he also would have been interested in you."

Kaylina blinked as she imagined *two* Havartaft brothers being attracted to her, their beast halves drawn to her druid blood. Would they have fought over her because of that? And would she have been drawn to them equally and forced to choose?

She rubbed her face. "The *anrokk* power is... alarming at times."

His eyebrows didn't rise. He could probably guess exactly what she was thinking about. "Power is double-edged, as much a threat to he or she who wields it as those nearby."

Since she'd never had any kind of power before, she hadn't contemplated it that much, but she nodded, trusting he knew all about such things.

"Tomorrow, we'll take it to the swordsmith, and you can pick out a comfortable wrap for the hilt." Vlerion nodded toward the blade, assuming she would take his gift.

It didn't feel right to accept something so valuable. She could hear her grandmother's advice from years earlier, saying not to take expensive gifts from men or they would expect sex. If only she and Vlerion *could* have sex. Still, it would be useful to have a weapon she didn't have to return to the practice rack at the end of the day. And it was beautiful. Maybe if she accepted it *temporarily,* that would be all right?

"Okay. Thank you." Kaylina held the sword up with both hands. "If I become famous and am too busy making mead to defend the borders as a ranger, I'll return it to you."

"You'd best make time to defend the borders, at least when Targon asks, or he might sabotage your business to *ensure* you have time."

"Asshole."

"As we've discussed." Vlerion smiled, but only briefly, then rested a hand on her shoulder. "Sabor may also insist, at some point, that you make time to do *his* bidding. I regret that you've come to his attention. I know this isn't what you wanted."

"It's not. Vlerion?" Kaylina gazed into his eyes, an earlier question returning to mind. "If my brother and I decided it was too dangerous for us here, or the business wasn't working out, would we be allowed to leave? Do the shipmasters who visit the harbor still have orders not to give us passage?"

He hesitated. Because he didn't know? Or because he didn't want to give her an answer that would displease her?

"They do have those orders," he said quietly. "They are to keep *you* from leaving. Your brother would be free to go."

Kaylina lowered her gaze, feeling grim and glum. A few months earlier, she'd been so eager to leave home and prove herself, but how many times since her world had grown so dangerous had she thought longingly of her bed back in the Spitting Gull? Of the family she'd butted heads with so often but loved?

Vlerion squeezed her shoulder, then brushed his fingers along the side of her neck. "If you were to feel compelled to go, it's late enough in the year that the snow has melted in the pass. You could travel that way and get a ship from another port city farther south."

"Would someone be sent to hunt me down and drag me back if I disappeared?"

"That is a possibility."

She looked into his eyes again. "Would they send *you*?"

Vlerion sighed and repeated, "That is a possibility."

5

THE TONGUE OF YOUR COMPETITOR FLAPS LOUDEST.
   ~ Derias Halkor, shipping magnate

A soft spring rain fell, hiding the sunset as Vlerion walked Kaylina most of the way back to Stillguard Castle. When they neared the closest stone bridge arching over the river, he gazed toward the structure, its towers visible over intervening rooftops. As usual, the magical purple glow emanated through the window where the plant resided.

A mulish expression on Vlerion's face suggested he was contemplating accompanying Kaylina *all* the way to the castle. Maybe what they'd heard eavesdropping on Spymaster Sabor had him concerned about her safety.

Kaylina stopped on the bridge and gripped his hand, hoping to deter him from such thoughts. When they'd believed the plant only capable of sprouting vines from the mortar to attack people, it had seemed an acceptable risk for rangers to walk close to the courtyard walls. Now that they'd seen it shoot deadly beams out to the street to kill enemies, she didn't want Vlerion anywhere near it.

"Has it given you any more visions regarding me?" he asked.

"No, but I've been avoiding letting it rub its tendrils all over my forehead."

"Perhaps wise." He gazed speculatively toward the castle.

"I'm looking forward to trying your *second* gift," Kaylina told him, hoping to drive thoughts that she needed protection from his mind. She patted her pocket to indicate a pouch he'd given her after their discussion in his office.

In the weeks that had passed since the Kar'ruk had been killed or driven out, the city had been quiet. Other than the Virts sabotaging factory equipment a couple of times, there hadn't been much trouble. The destroying of machines might irk the aristocratic owners of those factories, but Kaylina found that much less alarming than murders and assassination attempts.

"Since I expected that response," Vlerion said, "I won't be chagrined that there's much more enthusiasm and delight in your voice when speaking of that than the sword."

"Trying the first gift would mean eviscerating an enemy, so speaking of it with enthusiasm and delight might be weird. With *this*—" Kaylina patted the pouch again, which contained five high-quality varieties of local yeasts, "—I can make people happy. All I brought was our white-wine yeast, since it works with a lot of mead recipes, and is tolerant to different climates and temperatures, but I can't wait to try these."

"Good. Since I can't reward you in quite the way I wish..." His eyelids drooped, making her certain of the exact type of *reward* he was referencing. "I'm glad to at least give you something that you like, to let you know I appreciate all the work you did to help the city—and me. Captain Targon, if not the king and queen themselves, should have given you praise and recognition for your role in defending Port Jirador against the Kar'ruk."

"The queen has decided I'm no longer a criminal and ordered the wanted posters taken down. That's good enough for me. The calendar tells me summer is approaching, even if warmth and strong sunlight are rare here, so I might have started to look silly skulking around in a cloak with the hood pulled low."

"When it's raining, such a fashion choice is always appropriate, and it rains a lot here when it's not snowing."

"Yes, I've noticed how delightful the weather is year-round. At least there aren't hurricanes." Those came by a couple of times a year back home. "I can handle light rain."

It was little more than a mist now, and she let her hood fall back, not minding the dampness on her cheeks.

"You can handle much. As you've proven." Vlerion's voice was a rumble, and he gazed into her eyes.

His pride for her, especially when he'd been so indifferent and dismissive of her when they'd first met, pleased her. It made all the danger seem worth it. "Thank you."

"And you deserve more of a reward than you've gotten. One day I will give it to you." He bent to kiss her on the cheek, warm lips brushing her skin and sending a shiver of delight through her.

They couldn't linger and tempt the beast, but she caught herself leaning in, molding herself to him. Why was he so hard to resist?

Another rumble emanated from him, a growl without words. With only desire.

His lips lowered, tracing her jaw, then her neck as he lifted a hand to her head, threading his fingers through her hair. Amazing. His touch always felt amazing.

"I'd better go," she whispered, resting a hand on his chest to stop him, or so she intended, but her fingers curled into his shirt, feeling the hard contours of his pectoral muscles. He wasn't wearing his armor, so it would be easy to slip her hand under the fabric for an even better feel.

"Yes," he whispered, nuzzling her ear, cupping the back of her neck, holding her in place. "Though I want to keep you safe, it's good that you've insisted on sleeping elsewhere, not in the barracks, not close to my room. I could easily wake up in the middle of the night and make the unwise decision to visit you, and then..."

She swallowed and stepped back. "Yeah, and then we'd be in trouble."

At first, he resisted letting her go, and the thought of him pushing her against the railing and taking her leaped to mind, along with such an intense longing for him to do so that she almost sprang onto him.

But he released her, stepping back himself, and took a long breath. His voice husky, he said, "I always think I'm just going to kiss your cheek in a brief parting, but as soon as I get close, I want so much more." He tore his gaze from her, looking toward the water. "I want you."

She remembered their shared hallucination, a byproduct of a powder from an altered plant that the taybarri had given them. In it, she'd seen her brand trickling a green strand of magic—of *power*—toward him, drawing him inexorably toward her. Even before she'd been branded, something in her blood—whatever made her an *anrokk*—had done the same.

In the hallucination, she hadn't seen a similar trickle of magic wafting from him, some indicator that the curse of the beast had power to draw her, but she didn't doubt that it did. From the beginning, she'd been far more aware of and attracted to him than any other man.

"I want you too," she whispered, though he knew. He'd always known.

"Yes." Vlerion met her gaze again and looked like he would say more, but the clip-clop of hooves on the street leading to the bridge drew his attention.

Horses pulled a familiar carriage through the drizzle, but it wasn't until it headed up the bridge, and the occupant gazed out the window, that Kaylina remembered when she'd seen it. It belonged to the Saybrook family, those leasing the cursed castle to her and Frayvar.

When the carriage stopped, Lady Ghara, the elegant and beautiful blonde-haired woman who liked to touch Vlerion while leaning all over him, looked out the window.

Kaylina tried to smile at her. It may have looked more like a badger baring her teeth to protect her young from predators. She resisted the urge to step closer to Vlerion, wrap her arm around his waist, and possessively claim him. That wouldn't be a mature and self-assured move. She *did* hope Ghara had seen Vlerion nuzzling her and grasped that they were...

Craters of the moon, what *were* they? Not lovers. The curse ensured that. Were they friends who gave gifts and did things for each other? Yes, but would that keep Ghara from flirting with Vlerion and inviting him to her apartment in the city?

The door opened, and Ghara lifted the ermine-fur-trimmed hem of her cloak to step out.

"Why, good evening, Vee. I didn't expect to find you randomly roaming the city."

Vee. Kaylina had forgotten about that nickname. She wondered if Vlerion would let her use it, or if he would want that. He and Ghara and another Saybrook sister had made play forts together as children, Kaylina recalled. They were all of the same aristocratic rank.

When Ghara looked curiously at her, she offered another badger smile.

"I am accompanying ranger trainee, Kaylina Korbian, home," Vlerion said.

Kaylina tried not to wince at his classification of her as *ranger trainee.*

"Do you accompany all trainees home?" Ghara asked in a teasing tone, but no humor reached her eyes. Instead, wariness—or was that suspicion?—lurked there. "Or only the female ones?"

"The ones whose lives are regularly threatened." Vlerion's tone was stiffer than when he'd been alone with Kaylina, and that aloof mask he often adopted made his face seem harder.

It wasn't until that moment that she realized he softened himself for her. Or was it simply that he let his guard down? Now, he was the cool and distant ranger that Sergeant Zhani saw.

Ghara looked at Kaylina more closely, then blinked in recognition. "Kaylina Korbian, lessee of Stillguard Castle?"

"Yes."

"I didn't recognize you without—" Ghara waved to her own hair.

Kaylina winced, remembering she'd been disheveled, covered with cobwebs, and in rumpled clothes when they'd met. After spending her first night in the cursed castle, Kaylina thought her state had been understandable, but a childish part of her wished Ghara had seen her freshly washed and made up, dressed in elegant clothing that made her look ravishing.

"Well, your hair is damp today," Ghara finished, waving toward the rain clouds, then lowering her arm. She had more tact than most noblewomen that Kaylina had encountered. "What is this about you being a ranger trainee? I thought..." She trailed off as she looked toward Stillguard Castle, the purple-glowing tower more noticeable as it grew darker, twilight settling over the city.

"I got conscripted," Kaylina said. "Apparently, I'm an *anrokk*, and the rangers like that."

"A what?"

The carriage driver, a man sitting in the mist with his hood up, looked over at them—at Kaylina—for the first time. But he didn't say anything, as was doubtless appropriate for commoners working for the Saybrooks. For any aristocrats.

"We believe she has the blood of druids in her veins," Vlerion said. "She has a way with the taybarri. Captain Targon leaped at the chance to take her in."

Kaylina bristled at the words *take her in*, as if she were a wayward orphan that Targon had adopted out of the goodness of his heart, but she didn't correct Vlerion. Besides, he shifted to stand shoulder-to-shoulder with her as they faced Ghara. It wasn't a definitive statement that they were a couple, but it seemed to convey that.

"But what about the castle?" Ghara asked Kaylina. "I received your menu and was coming to check the preparations for your grand opening. To see if you need anything to help ensure it goes smoothly. That would be ideal. The captain of the Port Jirador branch of the Kingdom Guard came to see my grandfather last week about some Kar'ruk that died in front of the castle during the invasion. There are rumors that the tower was responsible, but I can't imagine that. It's preposterous, isn't it? That glow can't *kill* people." As firm as Ghara's statement was, a hint of doubt touched her eyes as she gazed toward the tower again. "Didn't that used to be more of a red glow than a purple glow? I'll admit I've not spent much time in the area, especially at night, but..."

"It was red," Vlerion said. "With her *anrokk* power, Kaylina has altered it."

"That was more the honey-water fertilizer," she murmured, not wanting to explain her druid weirdness to a near-stranger. Especially one who had, intentionally or inadvertently, stepped closer to Vlerion as she looked toward the castle.

As if absently, Ghara reached out and rested a hand on his chest. "How strange."

She glanced at Kaylina, her elegant blonde brows drawing together. Though Ghara didn't say it, the look proclaimed that *Kaylina* was strange.

The words of her former lover, Domas, rang in her mind, as they did so regularly: *"What is* wrong *with you? You look so normal."*

"Does that mean the castle *did* attack and kill people? Kar'ruk, I mean." Ghara eased closer to Vlerion, her hand still on his chest. "The guard said a human man claimed it struck him a blow to the shoulder, leaving a burn mark. He was someone who has nothing to do with the rangers. I'm aware of the rumors that it's killed people of your profession, but... this man is a cobbler. The guard came to my grandfather because he's concerned the castle has grown more dangerous and might need to be demolished."

"That's not necessary. It was targeting the Kar'ruk. The man may have been nearby." Doing her best to divert the conversation, Kaylina asked, "You said you saw our menu? My brother and I have been distributing copies, but I didn't realize they would reach you at your estate in the country. Or are you, uhm, staying locally?"

"Your brother—that's Frayvar Korbian, right?"

"Yes."

"He was the one to send the menu. He even signed it. Is it common for the chef to do that in your part of the kingdom?"

"Very common. It, uhm, wasn't doused in perfume, was it?" Well aware of her brother's infatuation with Ghara, Kaylina could imagine that. They'd even discussed such treatments for love letters.

"No." Ghara tilted her head, looking puzzled at the idea.

Good.

"It did smell of rosemary and something else. Herbs. Like one might dust on baking bread."

"Ah." Kaylina suspected that hadn't been an accident. That probably *was* the kind of perfume her brother would employ in an attempt to woo a woman. "He must have written it while working in the kitchen. But there's no need for you to come, if you don't wish. We have the castle under control. Well, not exactly under *control*, but the weather has gotten warmer, so we're going to seat everyone outdoors for the meal. I don't think the tower will attack anyone." She hoped. When she'd asked the plant why it had killed the Kar'ruk, it hadn't responded in any way, other than waving a vine in the air toward her head. Since she'd been determined not to receive any more visions from it, she'd backed quickly away from the offering.

"Weren't the Kar'ruk who died outdoors at the time?" After asking, Ghara eased even closer to Vlerion and gazed into his eyes, her chest brushing his. "They were horrible. The Kar'ruk burned the Lavertok estate next door, and my sister and I were sure they would come for us next. We were scared and could only tremble as the fires burned. That night was so awful. The staff were armed, and we have a handful of bodyguards for Grandpa, but... I wished you were there. You would have killed them easily and protected us."

"It was my duty to protect the king and queen." Vlerion looked at Kaylina but didn't add that he'd also been busy protecting *her* at the time. The beast, especially, had.

She wished he would. Oh, she knew he wouldn't share his secret or explain everything that had been going on, but her fingers curled into a fist as she longed for him to make it clear to Ghara that he wasn't available. She shouldn't lean her boobs all over him because...

Because why? Kaylina and Vlerion hadn't sworn fidelity to each other. They couldn't swear anything until she found a way to lift his curse.

Still, the urge to see if she could summon some druid magic to knock Ghara away from Vlerion flirted with her mind. She resisted it, instead looking toward the river, trying not to watch them out of the corner of her eye, but it was difficult.

"I understand you have your duties as a ranger, Vee, but it was so scary." Ghara's fingers curled into his shirt. "We all wished you'd been there. And I wish... you know what I wish." She licked her lips, not a nervous lip-licking but a sultry drawing of her tongue along them to capture Vlerion's eye, to make him want—

"I am aware," he said, then caught her hand and pushed her gently back.

"Come to my apartment tonight," Ghara whispered, determined despite his rejection. With her gaze locked on him, she seemed to have forgotten Kaylina stood nearby. Or maybe she didn't want to acknowledge that any competition might exist. "Let me show you what I've learned in the years since we were together. You'd enjoy it immensely, I'm certain." She ran her tongue over her lips again.

Vlerion grimaced, probably thinking of what might happen if he enjoyed himself immensely with *any* woman.

"I am with another now, Ghara." He stepped close to Kaylina and wrapped his arm around her waist.

Relieved and pleased by the acknowledgment, Kaylina kept herself from flashing a triumphant yes-he's-*mine* smile at Ghara. But she did slide her arm around his waist without hesitation. Not *claiming* him, she told herself. Simply reciprocating the gesture to demonstrate that their feelings were mutual.

"What?" Ghara asked, more dismay than shock twisting her face. "But she's..."

Common was the word that she didn't say, Kaylina suspected, though it might have been something more derogatory. No, probably not. Whatever Ghara thought, she seemed to maintain a civilized veneer.

"Your mother wouldn't approve," Ghara said instead. Then she blinked in surprise—or realization? "Your mother *doesn't* approve. This is the girl, isn't it? That your cousin, Beatrada, said has her hooks in you and is a danger to the estate."

"Ah." Kaylina lifted her finger. "I'm not *hooking* anyone, and I'm far from dangerous to his estate or..." She wanted to say *him* or *anyone else* but realized she couldn't, not honestly. Since their kisses could lead to Vlerion turning into the beast, she might legitimately be a danger to everyone around.

"You have the mien of a schemer," Ghara said coolly.

Cursed craters, her brother would have agreed. And Vlerion snorted.

Kaylina hit him on the chest with her free hand. "You're not helping."

"You let her touch you like that? A commoner?" Ghara sneered. So much for her civilized veneer. "Vee, it's so presumptuous."

"She is that." Vlerion sounded amused.

Kaylina lifted her hand to thump him again, but she paused, self-conscious now that she'd been called out as a schemer. Even though she had much more important things to worry about than what high-society women thought of her, she hated the idea of being accused of chasing after Vlerion for his money and status. That was the last thing she cared about. She intended to acquire all she needed by working hard and opening a business that people adored, not latching onto wealthy men.

Vlerion clasped her hand out of the air and lay it on his chest.

"Beatrada said there will be consequences," Ghara warned. "That she's dangerous. And your mother won't allow it."

"I have been a ranger for years, risking my life to defend the kingdom," Vlerion said coolly. "I respect my mother and listen to her counsel, but I am long past the age where I obediently do as she wishes."

"You should *always* listen to your mother. Do you remember when she said we'd make a handsome couple? I know she was also thinking that we'd be an *appropriate* couple. The Havartafts and Saybrooks are of similar social rank. It would make sense."

Kaylina frowned at Vlerion, wondering if that was true. Had Isla of Havartaft tried to encourage Vlerion to be with a woman?

When she was intimately aware of how such relations tempted the beast to appear? Lady Isla had tried to get Kaylina to stay away from her son.

This time, she was the one to curl her fingers into Vlerion's shirt and shift closer to him.

"I do not wish to hurt you, Ghara," Vlerion said, some of his aloofness fading, gentleness in his tone as he met her gaze. "This simply is what it is."

"What it *is* is her rubbing her chest on you and you liking it." Ghara stepped back and sent Kaylina a scathing look, as if she were an expert seductress and Vlerion a simpleton falling for her advances.

"I do like it," Vlerion stated. "And I like her. I apologize that we were not meant to be more, Ghara."

Though Kaylina appreciated Vlerion making that clear, she worried the words were turning Ghara into an enemy. Kaylina wouldn't have wished that, not from another person with the financial power to make her life difficult. What if Ghara ripped up the lease and drove them out of Stillguard Castle after they'd done so much to make it ready?

The plant and all its quirks didn't change the fact that it was a far more affordable building to rent than any other they'd find in the city. The location was also excellent. And, given that Jana Bloomlong was still targeting Kaylina, having a sentinel keeping an eye on the place wasn't that bad. With luck, the plant would keep any more would-be arsonists away.

"I see," Ghara said, her tone stiff. "Ms. Korbian, should you need assistance with your opening, I am available, but I will give you the message my grandfather sent me to deliver. If the castle harms any citizens who attend, or are simply walking by on the street, the Saybrooks will not be responsible in any way. Before *you* stepped into that building, it had not killed in generations and only rangers. Nor did it have the power to shoot beams to murder people. Now that I've spoken with you, I believe the rumors may be true, and that *you* are responsible for the changes."

Kaylina opened her mouth to protest, but could she? She hadn't been there when the plant killed most of the Kar'ruk, but it was possible that she had, with her infusions of honey, given it more power. The power to kill more easily. But it had shared that it would allow her customers to dine in peace, as long as those customers didn't have ill intent toward her.

"Be careful, Vee." Ghara stepped into the carriage but met his gaze before shutting the door. "She's a beautiful woman, and she knows it. She'll use her body to manipulate you, to get as much of your wealth and prestige for herself as she can."

The door slammed, and the indifferent carriage driver clucked to the horses to get them to continue over the bridge.

Kaylina, stung even though she barely knew Ghara and there was no truth in those words, lowered her hand, intending to step back. But Vlerion pulled her close, his arms locking her to him.

"I know the truth," he murmured, his lips brushing her ear. Warm pleasure swept through her. Amusement laced his words as he added, "And how much my family's *wealth* means to you."

"It's not what makes me wake in the middle of the night thinking of you," she whispered, glad he knew the truth even though she'd never doubted it.

"With only your own hand to satisfy the ache within you," he murmured, the amusement gone, huskiness in his voice.

"Yeah." She swallowed, aware of the danger rising, a threat that Ghara had no idea about.

"You'd better go," he rumbled even as he inhaled her scent and nibbled on her ear, muscled arms holding her tight against him.

She arched into him before she could stop herself. By the gods, why couldn't they enjoy one night together?

With a growl of frustration, Vlerion released her. He didn't push her back, the way he had Ghara. Instead, he looked to the sky, the mist dampening his cheeks as he struggled to gather himself.

"I'm sorry." Kaylina hated that she distressed him. She stepped back, lifting her hands in an apology.

"Don't be. *You* are not a beast."

"No, but I don't want to tempt you. I don't mean to. I just..."

His eyes were fiery with his passion when he lowered them to meet hers. "*You* were not trembling and afraid before the Kar'ruk."

"I..." Kaylina knew it was a compliment and that he liked her bravery, but a savage glint mingled with the passion in his eyes, the hunger and the promise that the beast lurked, ready to erupt. "Wasn't delighted by the experience either."

"I'll have you one day soon," he vowed.

She nodded and stepped farther away, for both their sakes. "As soon as I figure out a way to lift the curse, and I will. I promise."

His eyes narrowed with speculation, and she wondered if he'd meant he would have her whether they lifted the curse or not. That hunger in his eyes made her want to return to him to find out. Instead, she hurried off the bridge and down the trail toward the castle. She could feel him watching her but didn't look back.

6

Don't trust those with too great an interest in your passions.
  ~ *Grandma Korbian*

The last couple of blocks to Stillguard Castle, Kaylina walked slowly as night deepened around her and the mist turned into a fog that blanketed the river. Ghara's accusations repeated in her mind.

Kaylina hadn't intended to fall for a nobleman—certainly not a haughty ranger lord—so she hadn't considered that outsiders would think she was after Vlerion for his family's wealth. She doubted it mattered what Ghara thought, but what about his mother? Or his *cousin*? She had been the one to tattle to Lady Isla about Kaylina and Vlerion standing close and possibly being romantically involved before they'd ever shared a kiss.

Vlerion's mother, Kaylina felt certain, worried more about his interest causing him to turn into the beast and hurting people—a valid concern. Isla hadn't come across as someone who would worry about a girl's status or the family she came from, but Kaylina didn't know her that well.

Movement near the gatehouse at the back of Stillguard Castle distracted her from her thoughts, and she immediately suspected Jana Bloomlong of having sent spies. Or people worse than spies.

Lanterns burned on either side of the closed gate, illuminating four cloaked men lurking outside. Her instincts shouted *danger*, and she tensed, about to sprint toward the front gate, hoping she could dart through and lock it before they caught her.

But the men only glanced at her, then whispered and pointed at the menu Frayvar had secured to the wall under one of the lanterns. There was also a sandwich board facing the trail that listed the meads and their tasting notes. The men appeared to be absorbed in reading both.

Maybe her instincts had overreacted. That thought didn't keep Kaylina from stepping toward the side street that connected the trail to the boulevard out front. In the danger-cloaked capital, avoiding groups of people at night was wise.

One man lifted a hand toward her. "Are you the owner of this establishment?" He had a friendly voice. "We heard a southern woman was in charge."

Kaylina paused. "Yes."

"We're thinking of coming to your grand opening this week, but my friend is allergic to a few foods and has questions about the menu." The speaker pointed to another man in the group.

"Oh." Kaylina approached the group. Since her brother had multiple food allergies, she was sympathetic toward anyone with such issues, and these sounded more like potential customers than troublemakers. None of them were holding weapons, but she stopped several feet away. The cloaks could easily hide maces and daggers if not swords. "I helped my brother—he's the chef—shop for ingredients and can probably answer your questions."

"It's about the lamb dish." The speaker stepped toward her,

though he pointed at the menu as he moved. "It says it's a cherry *mint* glaze. Is that right?"

"Yeah, Frayvar says the mint—"

The man lunged, reaching for her as he swept his cloak aside to reveal a cudgel.

Cursing, Kaylina leaped back to avoid his grasping hand. She snatched her sling from her belt, but he kept coming, so there wasn't time to load it.

With longer legs, he caught up to her and raised the cudgel. Kaylina darted sideways to avoid a blow to her head, yanked her knife out, and slashed to keep him back.

"Frayvar!" she called as the other three men surged toward her.

She spun to run for the front gate—what she should have done from the beginning—but the cudgel wielder yelped in surprise.

A glance back revealed something catching his leg and tugging him off balance. He tilted sideways, crashing into one of the other men who was rushing after Kaylina. They both pitched to the ground, making an obstacle for the other two assailants.

Not questioning her luck, Kaylina put her knife in her mouth and loaded her sling, firing without hesitation. While chasing her, the group had moved far enough from the lanterns that she couldn't see their features well, but she could tell her lead round struck one solidly in the forehead as he sprang over the downed men.

He flinched but swore and kept coming. As she hurried to load another round, something detached from the courtyard wall and snapped around the man's waist.

A vine. Her cursed castle was helping her.

"Thank you," she whispered, aiming at one of the men who hadn't yet been impeded.

He also carried a cudgel, and the thought crossed her mind

that these people probably hadn't come to kill her, just pummel her. Not that the notion was that comforting.

He sprang for her, but she caught him in the bridge of the nose with her round. He yelled and dropped the weapon to clasp a hand to his face.

The iron gate creaked open. Frayvar ran outside with a cast-iron pan raised like a club.

One of the men on the ground rolled to his feet. Snarling, he sprang for Kaylina.

There hadn't been time to load another round, so she dropped her sling and took the knife from her mouth. In the heat of the moment, her thoughts scattered, and she couldn't remember the fighting moves she'd practiced with Zhani. She reacted only on instinct, putting her back to the wall as the man swept his cudgel at her.

She ducked, the weapon whistling over her head and clipping the wall, then lunged in with the blade. She stabbed it toward his abdomen, but he twisted, jerking his arm protectively down, and swept the cudgel toward her again. She sliced through clothes and clipped his arm but had to dive to escape being clubbed. She hit the ground, managing to roll and come up on her feet.

A hand snatched her ankle—one of the men on the ground, a vine keeping him from rising. She barely kept from pitching to the ground herself.

There were foes everywhere, damn it. She should have run.

Loosing an anemic battle cry, Frayvar struck someone with his pan. The thud was impressively loud in the misty night.

Relieved that she had help, Kaylina stabbed downward. Her blade sank into the man's wrist, and he screamed and released her ankle.

She leaped back, turning toward the man who'd swung at her with a cudgel, expecting him to be on her. But another vine had snaked out of the courtyard wall. Did it have him by the neck?

"The cursed castle is attacking!" someone cried.

"By all the moon gods, this isn't worth it."

A splash sounded, one of the men jumping into the river. The attacker that Frayvar had clubbed followed, staggering and grabbing his head before half-leaping and half-falling into the water.

The man on the ground, hand bleeding, cudgel lost, tried to roll away from the vine that had him. But it tightened its grip as another tendril grew from the mortar and lashed toward his face —toward his neck.

Kaylina grabbed her sling and backed away from the ensnared men. Gagging sounds came from both as they thrashed and tried to escape the vines.

The plant would choke them to death.

"Don't kill them, please," she said in the castle's direction, though she didn't know if the plant could hear her. She assumed *it* was behind the attacks and that the vines themselves weren't sentient, but who knew? "I want to question them."

Even more, she didn't want a pile of bodies that she would have to explain. Lady Ghara had *just* complained about the carnage the castle had been responsible for during the invasion. Dead humans would be even worse than dead Kar'ruk.

The gagging sounds grew feebler. Kaylina rushed toward the man trapped against the wall, intending to grab the vine and use her newfound power to convince it to release him. But when she gripped the tendril, a buzz of electricity zapped her. She stumbled back, her palms burning and her arms numb.

"Let them go," she ordered, trying to will the brand to do something.

No hint of warmth or suggestion of magic emanated from the spot on her hand. A snap came from the man on the ground, and his thrashing stopped. Had the vine broken his neck?

Kaylina gripped her knife, turning toward the remaining man against the wall. She was tempted to hack at the vine choking him, but she'd tried before to cut the rubbery tendrils and failed. Even using a sword, she wasn't strong enough. If her power wouldn't do anything to affect the vines, she was helpless against them.

Unless... What had the word been that she'd used in the preserve?

"*Sywretha!*" she called into the night.

The vine that wrapped around the dead man released, sliding back across the ground toward the wall. But the other finished its task, remaining tight around the man's neck until the fight—the *life*—drained out of him.

Kaylina shook her head grimly.

"I've only got an illusion of power," she murmured, eyeing her hand.

"Are you okay?" Giving the body on the ground a wide berth, Frayvar joined her, his frying pan at his side.

"No, but they didn't hurt me. Thanks for coming out to help." Though numb from the vine's magic—and watching the castle kill two men in front of her—Kaylina made herself nod at him. "That was timely. I didn't realize you had it in you to leap out with a weapon, like a warrior." She waved at the frying pan.

"That wasn't my intent. I heard someone asking about the cherry-mint reduction and doubted you were sufficiently familiar with the recipe to answer questions."

"You would have been deeply offended if I told them you muddle the mint instead of cutting it up?"

"*Deeply.*" Frayvar looked toward the river, but the men who'd jumped in had disappeared, swimming downstream to who knew where. "Who are—were—these guys?"

"I don't know." Kaylina thought of Targon saying Sabor might be a problem, but if he wanted to use her power, would he order her clubbed? "I've irked a few people since we got here."

"I've noticed. You should try to help people instead of irritating them."

"You think if I'd offered to organize their medicine cabinets, they wouldn't want to club me?"

"It's possible. Uhm, what should we do about...?" Frayvar pointed his pan at the dead men. Both vines had receded now, disappearing as if they'd never existed. "Not to sound callous, but we don't want them here for opening night."

"Not the kind of ambiance a restaurant should provide, huh?"

"No."

"I'll ask the rangers to come take a look in the morning." Kaylina was far more inclined to go to Vlerion for help than wander up to one of the Kingdom Guard outposts in the city. The rangers could figure out who these people were, who had sent them, and what their goal had been.

A brightening of the ambient light made Kaylina look toward the front of the castle. Though the plant's tower window faced the boulevard, the purple glow was strong enough to see from behind. As they watched, it throbbed three times before lessening again.

"I guess it's good that the plant is watching out for you." Frayvar's tone was dubious. He wasn't *sure* if it was good.

Kaylina wasn't either.

"It might just be watching out for its own interests," she murmured.

7

NOBODY LOVES YOU LIKE FAMILY; NOBODY LECTURES YOU LIKE FAMILY.
    ~ Actress Lady Verova of Islemark

"They don't have any identification." Vlerion crouched beside one of the two dead men, the morning air chill with fog that hadn't lifted. "I haven't seen them before."

"So they're not notorious assassins?" The question Kaylina truly wanted the answer to was whether more would come after her.

"Notorious assassins don't get choked to death by plants." Captain Targon stood nearby, having invited himself along when Kaylina had entered ranger headquarters at dawn to share the news with Vlerion.

She politely didn't mention that *Targon* had almost been choked to death by a vine. She doubted he'd forgotten. Even though they were outside the courtyard wall, he'd cast numerous glances toward the castle—especially the tower—since arriving.

Kaylina couldn't blame him. The curse was proving it could reach beyond the courtyard walls to deal with enemies.

Soft concerned whuffs floated through the fog. Six taybarri, including Levitke, also stood nearby, not watching the investigation but congregating. From the way they kept looking at Kaylina, she had a feeling she was the subject of a discussion.

Targon noticed the taybarri and their focus. "They're pissed at me."

"Because of the loathsome protein pellets you feed them?" Kaylina asked.

"You're full of snark today." Targon glared at her, and then Vlerion, probably still wishing his ranger would flog obedient reverence into her.

"Yes, my lord," Kaylina said agreeably.

The glare shifted back to her. "I gather they're pissed that you were attacked after I told them ranger taybarri have to live in the ranger stables. They've tried to leave the premises a few times to come here and serve your divine *anrokk*-ness."

"I would love taybarri visitors, except..." Kaylina looked toward the tower, terrified at the thought of the plant attacking them because they were associated with the rangers.

"Exactly." Targon had followed her gaze. "They're forbidden from coming close to this place. So is Vlerion. I tried to bring Doc Penderbrock instead, but someone and his huge furry mount insinuated himself."

"I'm not the one who stepped on your foot." Vlerion joined them, holding a cloth band in his hand. He lifted it toward Kaylina. "This was in that man's pocket. I believe it was meant to be your gag."

"Meaning these were kidnappers and not assassins?" When Kaylina had seen the cudgels instead of swords, she'd assumed the men hadn't meant to kill her, but why would anyone want to kidnap her?

When she'd eavesdropped on the Virts a few weeks earlier, some of them had admitted they wanted to use her supposed druid abilities. Did they think they could lock her in a room somewhere, and she could magically spew power through the walls and into the city to inconvenience aristocrats and assassinate key people? Hardly. She hadn't even been able to keep the plant from killing these men.

"You piss off someone else by not being properly respectful?" Targon asked her.

"Dozens of people. It's my hobby."

Targon squinted at her, then looked to Vlerion again. "I'm shocked someone hasn't tried to gag her sooner."

Ignoring him, Vlerion gazed gravely at Kaylina. "I should have insisted you take the sword home with you last night."

He'd brought it this morning, the hilt freshly wrapped for her, and it leaned against the wall nearby.

"I don't think that would have changed anything. I had... protection." Kaylina also didn't know if she could drive a blade into a human being's heart. Some predatory animal's, yes, and maybe that of a Kar'ruk, but she didn't want to kill people. Cracking them with lead rounds suited her more. Her sling could leave a bruise, but it didn't kill.

"Protection? From the castle?" Targon grumbled under his breath. "I wouldn't trust that place—or that *plant*—as far as I could kick one of its crumbling bricks." He waved his foot toward the courtyard wall.

"Frayvar also came out with a frying pan."

"Oh, yeah, better than a legion of bodyguards."

"You will stay at ranger headquarters until we figure out who hired these thugs," Vlerion stated. An order.

Kaylina started to reply but caught Targon watching her and refrained from pontificating on how women liked men to say *please* and make suggestions instead of issuing mandates.

"May I have a word with you, my lord? Alone?"

Vlerion snorted, probably guessing the exact thought process that had led to the polite request.

"I'll hear your words." Vlerion gestured for Kaylina to walk away from Targon with him. "It's doubtful we'll be fully alone." He looked at Crenoch and Levitke as they separated from the other taybarri to follow Kaylina to the river's edge.

"I don't mind if they hear. They're indifferent to me snarking and don't care about people saying *my lord* and *my lady*."

"They exist outside of our social mores and cultural expectations."

"Must be nice."

Before she could complain about his order, Vlerion held up a hand. "For your safety, and my peace of mind, I request that you accept a room at ranger headquarters."

"You couldn't say it that politely in front of your captain?" Kaylina couldn't object to that phrasing, even if she didn't intend to comply.

Vlerion considered Targon, who was scowling at the bodies. "No."

"Because I'm a commoner or because I'm a trainee?"

"Because I'm a noble and command rangers."

"So you can't make polite requests."

"Not to subordinates."

"Would that apply to lovers as well, should you acquire one of those?"

"To a lover training to be a ranger, yes," Vlerion said.

"Ranger life is complicated."

"More so than mead-making life, I believe so."

"Remind me why I agreed to start this training?"

Vlerion held a hand out toward Levitke, who was alternately watching the street and looking toward them. "I believe so you could ride taybarri and learn to defend yourself from all the many and varied nefarious thugs who wish to kill or use you."

"Ah, right. I knew there was a reason to put up with the crap."

"*Whuff*," Crenoch said.

"I suppose I should get them honey drops since they came all the way here to check on me."

That prompted a more exuberant *whuff*.

"Will you also get Targon honey drops?" Vlerion's eyes glinted.

"If he wants some. I might spit on them and dust them with rat droppings first."

"It's odd that he believes you irreverent."

"I think so." Kaylina lifted a hand, tempted to touch Vlerion or lean on him to let him know she appreciated his presence, but she lowered it again, reminded of the bridge—of how every touch was a temptation. For both of them.

He gazed sadly at her and clasped his own hands behind his back.

"Is it okay to join you?" Frayvar stood in the open back gate several yards away, probably not sure if they were having a romantic interlude.

Kaylina *wished* they were. Though she would prefer to do that without anyone watching.

"Yes." Kaylina waved an invitation. "We've determined that these people were trying to kidnap me."

"Oh. That's good news."

Vlerion arched his eyebrows.

"How so?" Kaylina asked.

"The odds of surviving a kidnapping attempt are much better than surviving a murder attempt," Frayvar said.

"You've calculated them?"

He tilted his head. "I calculate everything."

"When he charged out, he must have been a fearsome sight to the kidnappers," Targon said as he walked over, apparently disinterested in letting Kaylina and Vlerion continue to chat without him.

"If you insult my brother, he won't invite you to our grand opening," Kaylina said.

Targon scoffed. "No ranger is going to show up for that. Are you seriously going to invite people here to this cursed death trap of a building?"

"To the courtyard outside," Kaylina said.

"We've set up tables and fire pits," Frayvar added. "I've made a seating chart to ensure the comfort of all guests while allowing sufficient room for servers to move about."

"I'm sure the *fire pits* will entice people to come to a place inundated with sentient killer vines," Targon said. "You know the rumors about this place have gotten worse since those beams shot out, right? You must have noticed the lack of foot traffic."

"The beams struck *Kar'ruk invaders* who were killing innocent people," Kaylina said. "The citizens of Port Jirador should be praising the castle for its brave defense of the city."

"Uh-huh. Nobody's going to show up for your mead."

"They will. They'll be curious. Besides, aren't you the one who *wanted* us to open this place?" Kaylina pointed at Targon. "You sent us furniture and mead-making equipment."

"Don't remind me. I didn't know rangers and taybarri—" Targon glared at the herd, "—wouldn't be able to stay away from the place and would immediately give away that you're aligned with us."

"You didn't think that your conscripting of me to train as a ranger would have resulted in the same thing?"

"She has a point," Vlerion said.

"I was adapting to changing information. When we first questioned her, who knew she'd turn out to have druid blood and be catnip to furry animals?" Targon squinted at Vlerion. "Of all kinds."

Vlerion squinted back at him, the look a touch dangerous.

"Hello?" a woman called from the side street. "Do any of you know where the mailbox is for this, uhm, establishment?"

Targon dropped a hand to his sword and peered through the fog. "This *establishment* has been vacant for generations and has only recently gotten a renter."

The woman walked closer, though she kept throwing wary glances toward the tower. With fog lingering in the streets, she hadn't noticed the bodies yet.

"I have a letter for Frayvar Korbian." She wore the green and white uniform of a postal worker and carried a large mail satchel.

Targon dropped his hand, nodding toward Frayvar and Kaylina.

Frayvar stepped forward and raised a finger. "That's me. The castle doesn't have a mailbox that we've noticed."

"The Saybrooks weren't fans of solicitations," Targon said.

"The plant isn't either. Are you expecting mail, Fray?" After the attempted kidnapping, Kaylina was wary of anything unexpected that showed up, whether person, animal, or envelope.

"I did write to Grandma last month. Oh, maybe she sent money and honey. That's what I asked for."

Kaylina eyed the slender envelope the postal worker waved and doubted it held either.

The woman noticed the bodies with a start. To her credit, she took a deep breath, skirted them, and reached Frayvar. "Here you go, sir."

"Thank you."

With the message delivered, the postal worker hustled up the river trail and away from the castle.

One of the taybarri whuffed, and she jumped, her letter satchel almost falling from her shoulder. Kaylina wagered the woman was *glad* Stillguard Castle didn't have a mailbox.

"It's from Grandma. She got our letter." Smiling, Frayvar drew his utility knife to open the envelope.

"Your letter. *I* didn't know you sent one." Kaylina did remember that her brother had asked if it would be allowed or if the shipmasters Targon had instructed not to give them passage would also refuse to carry their mail. "I wouldn't have asked the family for coin."

She might have asked them for honey, but now that she knew about the hives in the preserve, the delicious honey inside created by bees that foraged on magical altered plants, she didn't think they needed to import more from the Vamorka Islands. They could use the local stuff. From what the taybarri queen had said, few were permitted near those hives, but the bees had allowed Kaylina to walk up and take the honey. One perk of being marked by a magical plant.

"I have no trouble asking for financial assistance." Frayvar unfolded the single page—there weren't any liviti bills inside. "Due to unlikely benefactors, we've not spent as much money on the start-up costs as I thought we would..." He nodded toward the still-scowling Targon. "But it's still been expensive, especially since a fire forced us to delay our grand opening. Unless you count the private orders I've lined up and fulfilled, we're not bringing in an income yet."

"You fulfilled private orders?" Kaylina had been so busy training that she hadn't noticed any missing mead bottles.

"Three." Frayvar lifted his chin. "All from aristocrats with country estates around the city."

"Good work." Kaylina caught Vlerion smiling slightly and wondered if he'd had anything to do with the aristocrats finding out about their endeavor.

"The *mead* is what's good. Excellent, in fact. The word is already getting out. I'm..." Frayvar had been reading while he spoke and trailed off with a, "Hm."

Targon walked up, jerking his chin toward Vlerion. "Send someone to collect the bodies. I'll talk to Captain Deetrok at the Guard and see if anyone can identify them—or if he's heard anything about kidnappers in the city. This is too sloppy to be Spymaster Sabor's work. I suspect the Virts."

"Agreed," Vlerion said.

"It could also have been Jana Bloomlong," Kaylina said.

Targon looked blankly at her. She didn't know if it was because he didn't remember the rival mead-maker or couldn't imagine her masterminding a kidnapping.

Kaylina had no trouble envisioning the scenario. The woman had sent poisoned mead to the queen and framed Kaylina for it. And when that hadn't worked, Jana had delivered a vial of her special blend in case Kaylina wanted to nobly take her own life. She was *definitely* a mastermind.

"Has she threatened you further?" Vlerion asked.

"No, but I caught her watching the castle a couple of weeks back. From across the river, we made rude gestures to each other."

"Women have interesting ways of dealing with their grievances with each other," Targon said.

Kaylina half-wished Jana would come at her with a sword. She didn't mind a confrontation. Having to worry about sneak attacks was stressful.

"She didn't like that I was going to be her competition even before I found the druid honey, which is letting me make *amazing* mead. I don't want to sound cocky, but we could be legitimate competition for her." Kaylina hoped they would put the vile woman out of business, defeating her not with a blade but with the vast superiority of their mead. "That's an idea Jana doesn't like," she added.

"I'll return tomorrow," Vlerion told Kaylina, "and we can go visit her together. Her meadery doesn't open until late afternoon, but people can come and go at all hours for the inn." He knew because he'd skulked in Nakeron Inn on Kaylina's behalf before, seeking evidence.

She nodded to him, grateful for all he'd done for her.

"The taybarri will also come," Vlerion added. "We'll stand at your back and look threatening while you ask her questions. Maybe she'll be nervous."

"I would be," Frayvar said. "The rangers and taybarri *are* threatening."

A chuffing sound came from the herd. One of the taybarri was scratching his furry rump on the corner of a building. He rolled onto his back and started rubbing it on the cobblestones with all four legs in the air, his thick lizard-like tail swishing back and forth.

"Yes," Targon said, "It's surprising more people don't wet themselves when we ride past."

"Crenoch knows when to look serious and menacing. I'm not sure about that one." Vlerion pointed at the upside-down taybarri. "Or why he's here."

"We all know why." Targon flicked a finger at Kaylina. "You talk our trainee into living in the barracks yet, Vlerion? To keep her safe from the machinations of sixty-year-old female rival mead-makers?"

Kaylina curled a lip at him. Why was he mocking her when he knew that Jana had almost been responsible for her death?

"No," Vlerion said. "She changed the subject."

"If she's going to stay here, we'll have to post a guard to keep an eye on her, and I'd rather not waste manpower on that. She's a *trainee*, not..." Targon lifted a hand, groping in the air.

"She *is* someone special and worth protecting," Vlerion said coolly to finish the sentence.

"Right now, she's a special pain in the ass."

"She was integral in helping defeat the Kar'ruk scheme and shutting down the rebel press."

"That doesn't make her less of a pain in the ass," Targon said.

"No." Vlerion smiled.

Kaylina, who'd spotted her sister's name in the letter, frowned and elbowed him. "You're not supposed to agree with that."

"Will you stay in the barracks where you'll be safe *without* the need of a bodyguard?" Vlerion asked.

"Does my ass-pain status depend on me agreeing to that?" she asked.

"It does."

Targon nodded firmly.

Kaylina sighed, feeling ganged-up on. She might be safer from kidnappers in ranger headquarters, but she and Vlerion would be sleeping in the same building, and that, as they'd discussed, would be problematic.

"I need to be here this week for the grand opening to help set everything up," she said. "I also need to be here for—"

"Our sister's arrival," Frayvar cut in, lifting the letter.

"Uhm, what?" Kaylina stared at it, horror blossoming.

Silana, their perfect older sibling, was coming to Port Jirador?

"Grandma and Grandpa got my letter and are considering our request—"

"—*Your* request," Kaylina said.

"Yes. They're sending Silana up—it sounds like she's already on her way—to see if there's true potential and if we've chosen a good location. They also want to make sure we're serving mead that's up to the family standards."

"She's coming to check on us," Kaylina interpreted. "And butt in if she doesn't think we're doing things right."

She couldn't keep from making a sour face.

"I believe I said that, yes. Help from the family is contingent upon Silana's approval."

"We don't need their help. *Or* their approval." Kaylina sounded petulant, but she didn't care.

"You woke up with bodies outside your meadery," Targon pointed out.

"My *sister* can't do anything about that. She'll probably blame *me* for it."

Frayvar lifted a finger—he wasn't going to point out that they were there because of her, was he?—but maybe he read the irritation on her face, because he lowered it again without speaking.

"When does she arrive?" Kaylina thought of all the things they would have to do to ensure Silana didn't find the place a disaster. Removing the bodies was only the start. How would Kaylina explain the cursed plant? The cursed... *everything*?

"This said her ship should arrive... looks like two days from now."

"That *soon*?" Kaylina drew back, stress tightening every muscle in her body. "Is it wrong to hope someone kidnaps *her*?"

"Yes," Frayvar said. "She has children."

"Damn."

8

IN MEAD, THERE IS TRUTH.

   ~ Grandma Korbian

Kaylina washed dishes and mead-making equipment in the kitchen while her brother made his signature spice blends. She'd started all the batches she could until she could visit the druid preserve for more honey—or until Grandma sent some up from the south.

Numerous varieties were ready for the grand opening, including a delicious strawberry mead that Frayvar kept sampling. He promised he was contemplating a dessert that would complement it, but the way his eyes rolled back in his head and his lips smacked made her doubt anything other than pleasure was involved in the tasting.

A clang came from the rear courtyard. Something ringing off the gate?

When Kaylina looked out the kitchen window, she spotted a

blond man in overalls and a homespun shirt. When their eyes met, he smiled and waved.

She grimaced. He wasn't wearing a hood and cloak, with a gag dangling from his fingers, but the other thugs hadn't looked like kidnappers either.

The smiling man pantomimed drinking from a mug.

"We're not open yet," she called out the window.

He made the drinking gesture again, then dug in his pocket and fished out a wrinkled liviti bill. Was that a five? That was enough for a couple of goblets of mead.

The part of her that was all businesswoman—and that craved recognition and to prove herself, independent of her family—wanted to take his money and give him a drink. Maybe he had lots of friends and would tell them how fabulous it was. The wiser part of her was wary after the previous night's experience.

"Can you scrub my stock pot while you're washing the carboys?" Frayvar hadn't noticed their visitor yet.

"No. I only scrub containers and equipment slathered with honey."

"I could put a few drops in the pot."

"No. Come over here, please. Does this look like a potential customer? Or a kidnapper?"

Frayvar joined her at the window. When the man saw a second person, his brows rose and he lifted the bill again.

"The other guys pretended to be interested in our food too," she added.

"I remember. They used my signature cherry-mint reduction against you."

"In a most dastardly way."

The man clasped his hands over his chest and bowed his head in a popular prayer gesture for several of the gods.

"I'll offer him a goblet through the gate," Kaylina decided. "If that's all he wants, he won't mind drinking it out there. After all, there's a nice view of the river."

"A view that's now free of dead people, thanks to the rangers sending a wagon over to collect the kidnappers."

"Be sure to mention the lack of corpses in our marketing material."

"Yes, such selling points must be highlighted." Frayvar waved toward the visitor again. "Do you want me to go out and ask him which mead he wants?"

"Nope. I'm picking for him. See those freckles? He looks like a fruit lover. I'll give him the red currant-raspberry melomel."

"I was afraid you'd say the strawberry."

"Because you want all of that for yourself?"

"Not *all* of it, but if I decide to pair it with a dessert, I'll need plenty on hand."

"You're more likely to pair it with your tongue."

"Not *more* likely," Frayvar protested.

"Equally likely?"

"That might be true."

Kaylina took a bottle from the root cellar and grabbed one of the dented metal goblets that had come with the castle—one she wouldn't be disappointed to lose if the man ran off with it. She also strapped the belt and scabbard holding Vlerion's brother's sword to her waist. *Her* sword, he'd called it, but she considered it a loaner.

The man smiled when she walked into the courtyard—if the presence of the sword fazed him, he didn't show it—and waved his bill again. His cheekbones stood out, and Kaylina thought him on the verge of being gaunt, but he was still handsome.

"Five liviti is enough for two goblets." Kaylina stopped outside of his reach and showed him the bottle. "Do you have any thirsty friends with you?" Thirsty kidnapping colleagues, her mind silently added.

"No, but *I'm* parched, and that looks fantastic. The weather is really heating up."

Southern-bred Kaylina couldn't help but scoff at the words. She'd yet to be tempted to wear fewer than two layers of clothing, all long-sleeved. Even when the wan sun was out here, it rarely provoked a sweat.

"If you think this is warm, you might collapse in the Vamorka Islands." Kaylina eased close enough to take the bill, then stepped back to pour.

"That's where you're from? I wondered. There's speculation, you know."

"Yes, I've somehow aroused a lot of interest, considering how short a time I've been in Port Jirador."

"Well, you *did* move into a cursed castle that's recently started shooting streams of purple fire at enemies." His eyebrows rose.

"Enemies, arsonists, kidnappers, and patrons who don't tip well." Done pouring, she watched his face as she spoke to see if he would react to the mention of kidnappers.

"Oh." It was the last bit that made his eyebrows rise further in concern. "Here." He dug into his pocket and offered a two-liviti bill. Then, after glancing toward the tower and at her sword, pulled out another bill. "Is that enough?"

"Yeah." Feeling guilty for prompting the tip—she'd only meant it as a joke—Kaylina added more mead to the goblet, filling it to the brim, before handing it to him. "Plenty. The plant that's responsible for the curse is in a good mood this morning."

"Because of the heat." He smiled and took a long drink before tilting his head. "Wait, did you just say a *plant* is responsible for the curse? I'd heard about vines killing people..."

"One that the Daygarii left to guard the castle."

"Huh. I guess it makes sense that druids would use plants to oversee their interests." He drank again and smiled. "This is really good. I heard you're the mead-maker. Is that right?"

"Yes."

"I guess that's another reason to hope we can get you on our side." His easygoing smile reminded her of Jankarr.

"You're with the Virts, I assume?"

"I work at the brick factory, the same as my brother. Our father used to work there too, but we lost him in an accident that could have been prevented if the lord in charge cared about the safety of his workers."

"That was a *yes*, right?"

Kaylina wasn't unsympathetic, not in the least, but she couldn't help but feel wary. Not only had the Virts set fire to Stillguard Castle, apparently to test her and see if she was associated with the rangers, but, as she'd been thinking about before, some of them wanted her for her supposed druid powers. Still others had discussed killing her before she could use her powers on behalf of the aristocracy. The Virts were far too interested in her.

"It's a yes. I don't agree with everything our leaders do though." Maybe he was watching her face for reactions. Negative reactions. "We need change, and I'm not above..." Before continuing, he lowered his voice and glanced left and right. "I'm not above a little sabotage, *especially* sawing the spokes in the wheels of Lord Yarrowfall's carriage, but I'm no murderer, and I don't condone the assassination attempts. I want a *peaceful* solution. If we had a little more power, we could force the king and the nobles to negotiate with us. All we want is better wages, shorter working hours, more safety in the factories, and a day off here and there so people aren't so tired on shift all the time." He grimaced, the memory of his father's death perhaps haunting him. "I wouldn't be *opposed* to a new system of government in which we aren't absolute nobodies, but... I think that's unrealistic. It seems like the other stuff is more achievable." He held the empty goblet out for a refill.

"One would hope." Kaylina took it and poured more mead in, waiting for him to implore her to help him. "There are more commoners than aristocrats, and you're working in the factories where you're capable of sabotage, as you just said, so it seems like you do have power. What'd you say your name was?" She planned to report this guy's visit to Vlerion.

He hesitated. "Grittor."

Kaylina would apparently have to give Vlerion a fake name. She handed the man the refilled goblet anyway. After all, he had paid and tipped.

"Thanks. The problem with *that* kind of power is that the owners know who's responsible and there are repercussions." Grittor shuddered. "Serious repercussions. You're aware of the hangings?"

Kaylina shook her head. "Sorry, I haven't kept up on the local news."

"It's hard to keep up on news that pertains to commoners, now that the indie press has been destroyed." Grittor looked at her as he drank.

That look was probably to inform her that he knew she'd been involved in that.

"I hear presses get destroyed pretty often when you let horned national enemies man the letters." She refused to feel guilty about her role in halting the Virt newspaper.

Grittor sighed and pushed his hair out of his eyes. "I suppose so. That wasn't a wise plan. I had nothing to do with it."

"Naturally. Take your time finishing that. I've got to get back to work."

"Wait," he blurted, lifting a hand. "I have a request."

"If it's for the blueberry mead, that's a small-batch specialty, and five liviti will only get you half a goblet." Kaylina had no interest in hearing his request.

"That sounds fabulous. If I order it, will you stay and talk longer?" Grittor smiled flirtatiously.

"Only long enough to pour it for you." Maybe she would send Frayvar out to handle that.

Grittor fished in his pocket again but was slower to produce money this time. "As I was saying before, the authorities *used* to throw suspected saboteurs in jail, but the king is extra grumpy right now. The, uhm, Kar'ruk alliance was a bad, bad idea. We all knew it, but some of the leaders... Look, I think the best thing we could do is find someone with a little power to help us. Maybe the kind of power that could convince an ancient druid plant to shoot up the city. Or just *threaten* to do it." Grittor handed her another bill. "The royals and nobles would listen and come to the negotiations table if we had druid magic on our side."

"No, they would send assassins to kill the plant wrangler." Kaylina took the bill and turned to leave.

"I have intel that may be helpful to you," Grittor called. "It's about the other mead maker in town. Jana Bloomlong."

Though Kaylina's instincts told her to walk inside and send her brother to deliver the next drink, she couldn't help but turn around. Since Jana was her other suspect when it came to orchestrating that kidnapping, she had to accept any information offered about her.

"If it's that my mead is far superior, I'm already aware of that."

"I'd say you're cocky, but after drinking two goblets, I can't disagree with your assessment."

"Good." Since this guy was flattering her because he wanted her help, Kaylina shouldn't have felt any pride at the comment, but she did lift her chin, positive her mead *was* superior.

"She's looking to hire people—commoners—who are struggling to get by and will take her coin without asking a lot of questions. She wants them to show up at your opening night and spread rumors to all those about to walk in, reminding everyone that you tried to poison the queen and might serve *them* poisoned mead."

Kaylina clenched her jaw in irritation, but she'd expected Jana to continue to be a pain.

"If it helps," Grittor said, "I haven't heard of many taking her up on the offer. As much as commoners like me could use money, the recent and lethal demonstration of what this castle can do hasn't left people eager to come close to it. Just those fools who love trying new drinks and can't resist the chance to speak with a beautiful woman." He backed up from the gate so that he could bow to her.

Ignoring that comment, Kaylina lifted the liviti bills he'd given her. "You don't seem to have a shortage of money."

Had he perhaps accepted what Jana was offering and come over to scout the place? To see if it would be safe for his people to show up at the grand opening and do exactly what he'd told her about?

"Oh, don't be fooled. My purse is never overflowing, but sometimes it's worth giving up a few meals to lay a foundation for future prosperity." Grittor set the empty goblet on the crossbar of the gate. Those pronounced cheekbones *did* suggest he missed meals often. "Do consider my words, please, Ms. Korbian, and let me know if there's anything I can do to make amends for past transgressions my colleagues have inflicted upon you. If it's any consolation, some of them are hanging even now in Banker Square."

"I wouldn't wish death on anyone, transgressions or not." She didn't comment on him knowing her name when she hadn't shared it. By now, this entire city knew far more about her than she cared for. Why couldn't she become known for her mead, not whatever funky blood flowed through her veins?

"I'm glad to hear it. Before I go, is there any other information I might offer you that would make you think kindly of me and mine? I do have large ears that I turn often toward gossiping coworkers." Grittor tapped one of them.

They weren't that large, but they did protrude a touch.

"I'll give you another goblet for free if you can tell me who sent the kidnappers who attacked me last night."

Grittor blinked in surprise. "I... don't know. I'd heard the rangers wanted you—and may already have you, much to my consternation. And some of the Virt leaders have contemplated that your *forceful* acquisition could be useful, but I believe I talked them out of that. People who are kidnapped tend not to want to work faithfully with their captors."

"Imagine that." Kaylina wondered if he had enough sway in the Virt organization to talk anyone out of anything. He wasn't much older than she, and his smiles made him seem boyish and naive. She reminded herself that Mitzy, who was about Frayvar's age, had some pull.

"I'm not aware of anyone else who might be interested in kidnapping you." Grittor spread his arms, his expression apologetic. "I will keep an ear turned into the wind and let you know if I hear anything. Another serving of your excellent mead would be most appealing." Grittor bowed again and departed.

Kaylina collected the empty goblet and headed inside, relieved he hadn't asked her to open the gate or tried harder to inveigle a promise from her. Even if he seemed more reasonable than the other Virts she'd dealt with thus far, she didn't want to pick a side —or be caught in the middle.

"Did he like the mead?" Frayvar asked from the sink, his sleeves rolled up as he scrubbed the stock pot he'd tried to foist on her.

"That's your most burning question?"

"I heard the rest through the window, but I couldn't see his facial expressions from here."

"He seemed to like it, but he was here to recruit me and would have pretended to enjoy it even if it was loathsome."

"We don't serve anything *loathsome*." Frayvar gave her an

affronted look. "We don't even have anything loathsome in the kitchen."

"One of the traps caught a rat this morning." She pointed toward the pantry where it had been laid.

"We're not *serving* that."

"Not contemplating my earlier suggestion of a rat tartare, huh?"

"Your sense of humor is dreadful. Maybe we *are* less related than I always assumed." Frayvar squinted thoughtfully at her.

"At the least, we have the same mother. And sister." Kaylina winced at the reminder that Silana would show up before long. "I'd better clean more than the mead equipment today."

"I would."

"You don't think she'll try to convince us to go back home with her if she doesn't believe this is a good business venture, do you?" Kaylina reminded herself that she was an adult and her sister couldn't force her to do anything.

"She might try to convince you to go home if she finds out people are trying to kidnap you."

"We won't mention that to her."

"What happens if the next kidnapping attempt occurs while she's here?" Frayvar asked.

"It won't."

"You're being optimistic."

"Isn't that something you usually encourage me to be?"

"I just tell you to quit having funks where you lie in bed, read, and don't do anything else."

Kaylina wished she still had the luxury of those funks, but with her sister coming, the grand opening in the works, and kidnappers after her, there wasn't time. She had to keep pushing forward, whether her brain went on strike or not.

9

To inspire youth to grow up and do great deeds is to create a future you want to live in.

~ Queen Henova

Kaylina walked side by side with Vlerion along the river trail, clasping his hand as they headed for a park they'd visited once before. The last time, they'd kissed on the bank, leafy trees giving them privacy from others in the area. It had been dangerous, tempting the beast, but she'd more than once dreamed of being with him there, of him pushing her against a tree and satisfying the unquenched desire that had tormented her since she'd met him.

"We will resume what the arrival of the Kar'ruk interrupted last time," Vlerion squeezed her hand, giving her a sultry look.

"I wish we could, but we both know we can't." She squeezed his hand back, then tried to let go and step away. They couldn't tempt fate —couldn't tempt the beast.

But he didn't let her go, instead stepping closer and wrapping his arm around her. "I can't be without you any longer."

"Vlerion, I want you too, but—"

His mouth came down upon hers, hungry and demanding as it stole her words. And her breath.

She wrapped her arms around his shoulders, unable to keep her body from responding to him with fiery desire. She kissed him back, pressing herself into his hard length, tempted to wrap her legs around him. He growled as he gripped her, pushing her against a tree, and a frisson of fear shot through her. That growl was as much animal as human, a promise that he was on the edge of turning.

Breaking the kiss, she pulled her head back enough to see his eyes.

The savageness of the beast rose in their blue depths, lust driving out the man. Even as she opened her mouth to say they had to stop, fangs erupted, and the change began.

Before he gained his supernatural power, Kaylina slipped her knife from its belt sheath and stabbed it into Vlerion's chest. Again and again, she struck him, killing him before he could kill her.

His eyes locked onto hers, stricken with pain and betrayal. Immense betrayal. As he crumpled, dying at her feet, he never took his gaze from her.

Kaylina woke with a scream, her sweaty nightclothes plastered to her body, sheets tangled around her waist, and something hard clasped in her hand.

Her knife.

She stared at it in shock and looked around the second-floor bedroom that she'd cleaned and claimed for herself weeks earlier. As she struggled to push aside the dream—the nightmare—and remember reality, a terrified part of her thought she might find Vlerion in the room with her, dead on the floor, knife wounds perforating his chest.

But she was alone, enough morning light creeping through the shutters to confirm that. Kaylina reminded herself that Vlerion wouldn't come into the castle. Further, she never could have killed him that easily, even if he *had* been in the middle of changing. Both as the ranger and as the beast, he was far too powerful a fighter for her to overcome.

But waking with her knife in her hand chilled her, and she set it on the bedside table. When she'd gone to bed, she'd left it in her belt, the same as she always did, and hung it and her sling by her clothes near the door. She must have sleep-walked to grab it, but she'd never been told she did such things before. An alternative was that the plant had used its power to float the knife into her grip to make a point, that it wanted Vlerion dead. It still believed he was a threat to her, one that had to be dealt with.

Shaking, Kaylina pushed damp hair away from her eyes. "I'm going to lift his curse, not *attack* him."

She looked in the direction of the tower, though she couldn't see its glow from the window of the room she'd chosen. She had deliberately picked one on the far side of the castle from the plant.

A knock sounded at the door, and she almost lunged for the knife again. What if the nightmare had been a warning that a threat was coming?

Frayvar called through the door. "Kay, are you all right?"

"Fine," she said, though she wasn't.

"The curse didn't attack you, did it? Should I send Lord Vlerion to get Doc Penderbrock?"

"No and no. Don't bring any rangers here under any circumstances." She climbed out of bed, afraid he wouldn't go away until she showed him that she was all right.

The vestiges of the nightmare clung to her, and she kept seeing Vlerion fall to the ground, half-changed into the beast, her knife in his chest. On the way to the door, she pushed open the shutters, hoping more light would drive away the memory of the dream.

Had it been a dream? Conjured by her own mind? Or had the plant sent it? Like the visions it had shared with her?

Kaylina didn't know. Since moving into Stillguard Castle, she and Frayvar had both received visions in the form of nightmares, but she didn't know how much to blame on the plant and how much was their subconscious fear finding a way to arise.

When she opened the door, she found her brother dressed, a broom and damp, dusty rag in his hand.

"How late is it?" she asked.

How long had she been captured by that dream? When she should have been helping him prepare for their sister's arrival?

"A couple hours past dawn. It's raining, so it's not surprising that you slept in."

"Slept in, right." She snorted at the idea that her sweaty night-mare-plagued thrashing had anything to do with something as restful as *sleeping in*.

"You're sure you're okay?"

"Yeah." No. She rubbed the back of her neck. "I will be."

Frayvar studied her face with concern. "Yesterday, I checked out some other commercial buildings with space for lease."

"Oh?" she asked with wariness, though maybe she should have made it an enthusiastic inquiry. After all she'd endured in Still-guard Castle, she shouldn't *want* to stay here.

But she'd put in so much work. Not only in cleaning the place up—twice, thanks to the fire—but forging a relationship with the plant. She glanced at the brand on the back of her hand, all too aware that she was now tied to this place. Even if she left, that wouldn't change.

"Yeah. Just in case. I thought rates might be down due to all the trouble in the city of late."

She snorted again. "No kidding. Were they?"

"No. I guess the hardy northerners are used to constant trou-ble. Invading Kar'ruk killing residents and lighting fire to the city and the countryside aren't viewed any differently than pirate attacks and hurricanes back home. People endure."

"Yes," Kaylina murmured, glancing at the brand again.

"The going rates are well out of our price range, unfortunately. I think we have to stick it out here and find a modicum of success before we can afford to move. Further, if we broke the lease, we would be responsible for the ten months of rent we would still owe to the Saybrooks. As shrewd businesspeople, they wouldn't let us out without demanding those payments, I suppose."

"No." After her last encounter with Lady Ghara, Kaylina couldn't imagine her showing leniency. It wasn't as if she and Frayvar hadn't known the castle was cursed when they'd signed that paperwork.

"I assumed not. I don't suppose... now that you're... friends with Lord Vlerion... do you think he might wish to back your fledgling business venture? If he would give us a loan..." Frayvar raised hopeful eyebrows.

"I don't want to ask him for money." Kaylina shied away from the idea, especially after Ghara had accused her of wanting exactly that from Vlerion.

"Ah. I thought when you said he'd given you that fancy sword that he might be plying you with gifts to win your love. Like in those romance novels you like."

"They're romantic adventures with swashbuckling, and Vlerion isn't *plying* me. He lent me the sword so I can better protect myself. What's with this interest in leaving all of the sudden?" Kaylina couldn't blame him, but he hadn't spoken of this before.

"I've had some nightmares too."

"About me killing Vlerion and him dying at my feet?" She doubted the plant was sending her brother nightmares of that, but who knew? It had given them shared visions before.

"No. Of Silana showing up and everything going wrong. In one of them, vines came out of a bowl of stew that I was serving a customer and tried to strangle him. At the time, Silana was standing behind me with a clipboard and a checklist. She shook her head and crossed something off. It felt like a teacher grading a test—a very substandard test." He winced.

"I'm not sure whether to be relieved or saddened that you're also stressed about our sister's visit." Kaylina wagered the letter was what had prompted Frayvar to look at other buildings for lease. "I'd offer you a hug, but I know how you feel about touching."

"Yes." He stepped back as if she might forget and spring upon him. "*Silana* will hug me when she arrives. And then tease me for being tense and weird."

"Normal people don't understand un-normal people."

"I *know*. I think we're stuck here though. Maybe you and Lord Vlerion can figure out who hired the kidnappers today and convince them to stop."

"That would be ideal. Wait, did you say earlier that you wanted to send him for the doctor? He's not *here*, is he?" She pointed toward the courtyard.

"I think he's waiting on the bridge or up the trail a ways."

"How do you know?" Kaylina imagined Vlerion stopping a safe distance from the castle while chucking rocks over the courtyard wall to get their attention. But he would have thrown such projectiles at her window instead of Frayvar's.

"Uh, a hunch." He walked to her window, pushed the shutters open wider, leaned out and pointed.

They had a view of the back of the courtyard, including the gatehouse, and she could make out two blue-furred snouts pressed against the bars.

"Ah. Give them some honey drops, will you? I need to dress."

Frayvar left, muttering about abundances of taybarri saliva, and Kaylina hurried to wash and put on clothing that wasn't rumpled. She would have to clean and press everything before

Silana arrived. Their sister would doubtless be fastidiously put together, even after a long voyage at sea.

Reminded that she and Vlerion were going to see her nemesis, Jana, today, Kaylina belted on the sword. Despite Vlerion saying that his brother hadn't been much taller than she, having the long blade dangling in a scabbard from her hip made her feel awkward as she walked. Some of the rangers wore their swords on their backs, and she would look into that if she didn't grow accustomed to this.

As she'd guessed, Crenoch and Levitke were the taybarri at the gate. When she arrived, they were lapping at the cobblestones with their large tongues.

"Frayvar didn't *throw* your honey drops to you, did he? Like you're stray beasts and not intelligent beings who prefer being hand-fed?" Kaylina had no idea if the taybarri cared how they ate their food—when traveling, the rangers put their piles of protein pellets on the ground—but thought they might be offended by having their treats chucked through the gate to the ground.

Crenoch and Levitke *whuffed* with no indication that they minded, but when she offered a few more in her palm, they butted shoulders in their hurry to get to them first. A few birds chittering from a nearby tree branch flew down to investigate. One landed on her shoulder and dared swoop down to pluck up a honey drop that had somehow evaded the tongues. A cat meowed and padded past, then darted away when a couple of stray dogs ambled down the street with their noses in the air.

Since Kaylina didn't want to end up feeding all the animals in the area, she wiped her palms and pointed toward the bridge. "Is Vlerion here?"

After whuffing again, Crenoch ambled in that direction. Levitke waited for Kaylina to mount, not rolling her eyes—or the taybarri equivalent—when Kaylina got the scabbard tangled in her legs.

"Being a ranger takes a lot of practice, doesn't it?"

Levitke whuffed agreeably and padded off after Crenoch.

When they'd battled the Kar'ruk they'd stumbled upon at the Virt press, Kaylina had somehow drawn upon the brand's power to communicate with the taybarri, even hearing Levitke's telepathic words in her mind, but she hadn't tried to do so since. The elder taybarri could project their thoughts to those without any druidic power, but the young taybarri didn't seem to be able to.

Vlerion was indeed waiting at the bridge, and the memory of the nightmare flooded her mind. She took a deep breath and pushed it away. He was fine, not a single knife hole in his chest.

Unaware of her anxiety, he smiled, his brows drifting up as he took in not only the two taybarri, but the dogs trailing after them. No, after *Kaylina*. She hadn't seen them before and suspected the scent of honey drops had drawn them.

"If I had any doubts about you being an *anrokk*, I suppose seeing you lead packs of strays would squelch them."

"Two dogs isn't a *pack*, and I didn't think you had any doubts."

"Oh, I don't. Levitke isn't the only taybarri who tried to leave headquarters this morning when I grabbed Crenoch. I didn't say where I was going, mind you, but they knew."

"It might have been a guess," she said, though the elder taybarri could read minds, and the young were quite perspicacious too. "We do spend a lot of time together."

"To my mother's consternation, yes."

Kaylina hadn't seen Lady Isla of Havartaft since their first meeting when she'd warned Kaylina of the beast curse. She'd also warned Kaylina to stay away from Vlerion and under no circumstances flirt with him. It hadn't been bad advice, especially in retrospect, but Kaylina had not succeeded in heeding it.

"Have you seen her recently?" she asked as Vlerion mounted Crenoch and led the way into the city.

"She came to ranger headquarters yesterday to let me know

about repairs that are ongoing at the estate—as I feared, it was targeted the night of the Kar'ruk invasion. Fortunately, no one was hurt. They only lobbed incendiary devices at the stable and a couple of storage buildings. Other estates weren't so lucky." Vlerion gazed toward the top of a building they were passing.

When Kaylina looked, she didn't see anything up there except a chimney and a weathervane. "I'm glad your family wasn't hurt."

"Thank you. She also wanted to make sure we weren't seeing each other." Vlerion's attention shifted from the roof to her, his expression hard to read. "For our own good."

"I hope you didn't tell her you've ordered me to move into the barracks. Also for my own good."

He sighed. "I didn't, but I didn't lie to her. Even if I had been inclined, I know she talks to Targon occasionally and would find out the truth."

"Do you think she'd be less distraught about us if I sent her more mead?" Kaylina smiled, but it saddened her that they were causing Vlerion's mom to worry. Since she'd lost her husband *and* her older son when their beasts had been out, Kaylina understood perfectly why Isla was worried about Vlerion. Of all people, Isla knew that Kaylina was a threat to his safety. To *both* of their safeties.

"I don't think she would be less distraught, no."

"But she'd drink it, right?"

"Likely so. She has mentioned on numerous occasions that it's a delight."

"Good. She needs some delight in her life."

"Yes." Sadness lurked in Vlerion's blue eyes, but he waved toward the street, and the taybarri turned to take them deeper into the city. "We'll go see Bloomlong and get to the bottom of the kidnappers."

"Thank you for coming to help me with this."

"Of course."

As they rode, Kaylina told him about Grittor and the information he'd shared.

"That's interesting," Vlerion said when she finished.

"That the Virts are still trying to recruit me?"

"No, I knew about that. But would Jana Bloomlong be trying to discredit you and ruin your opening night if she had a plan to make you disappear?"

"Since the kidnappers failed and two died in the process, she's probably assuming her plan didn't work and is now trying something else."

"That's possible. I had assumed she would try again."

"I hope not. Even if my brother says the odds of surviving kidnapping attempts are better than surviving murder attempts, I don't want to experience either again."

"Understandable. You said the Virt's name was Grittor?"

"I don't think that was his real name."

"I don't recognize it."

Kaylina hesitated before asking, "*Are* there hangings taking place in that square?"

Face grim, Vlerion nodded. "Yes. In the aftermath of the invasion, the king is adamant that punishments be severe for any who made deals with the Kar'ruk and invited them into our city." He lowered his voice and guided Crenoch closer to Levitke. "Unfortunately, I believe many who are being hanged *aren't* guilty of that. Of lesser crimes, yes—there's been an uptick of sabotage in factories—but the Kingdom Guard, under orders from the royal castle, is being ruthless."

"You don't approve." Kaylina didn't either, but she was a nobody.

"No. I've said as much, but the Havartafts don't have the sway with the throne that they once had."

"Because the king won't listen? Or because he's not the one making the decisions?"

"Some of both. My grandfather was close to Gavatorin Senior, King Gavatorin's father, but the older men are both long gone. The current king has kept my family's secret, so it's difficult for me to openly oppose him." Vlerion lifted a hand. "The reprisal has even benefited me, as the Virts are so busy trying to avoid hangings that I haven't heard any new accusations about the beast. But I cannot wish their deaths. Such harsh measures will have repercussions."

Everyone's measures were harsh here in the north. Kaylina could have argued that the Virts had brought the hangings on themselves—those who'd been in charge—but she had little doubt that a lot of innocent people were being punished.

Kaylina caught Vlerion looking toward another rooftop, this one three stories up and flat. She didn't see anything, and he soon turned his attention back toward the street. But was it her imagination or was his hand sitting closer to his sword hilt?

They'd entered a market area, and the dogs who'd been trailing the taybarri wandered off, their noses in the air as they investigated cooking tents serving everything from skewers of roasted meat and early-season vegetables to raw octopus and caviar. The latter were kept chilled, lying atop blocks of crudely chiseled ice, and Kaylina remembered Jana mentioning that ice houses in the city preserved pieces carved from glaciers. There was nothing like that in the Vamorka Islands, where glaciers—and snow, for that matter—existed only in story. Since the northerners apparently sweltered when the sun grew vaguely warm, she would have to investigate the cost to purchase ice for the eating house. She trusted the root cellar would keep the mead pleasantly cool without need for it, but Frayvar might use it in some dishes.

Giggles from the side drew Kaylina's eye. A couple of girls working in a market stall selling skeins of yarn pointed at Vlerion while whispering.

They were younger than Frayvar but old enough to appreciate men. When he glanced over, they turned away, cheeks reddening as they straightened already-straight skeins. Blushes, Kaylina noted, were easy to see on the pale-skinned northerners.

Surprisingly, a girl selling fish in the next stall focused on Kaylina instead of Vlerion, her eyes shining.

"Mom," she whispered to a middle-aged woman recording sales in a logbook, "another girl ranger. I thought Sergeant Zhaniyan was the only one."

This time, *Kaylina* blushed, the attention surprising her. She also felt like a fraud since she was only a trainee. She didn't wear a ranger's black leather armor, but the taybarri were so associated with the rangers that Kaylina wasn't surprised someone might make the mistake, especially since she now carried the sword.

The mother glanced at Kaylina but only flicked an I'm-busy hand.

"Maybe I really *can* be a ranger," the girl continued unfazed. "They sometimes allow commoners in now, you know. There are a *bunch* of male rangers who aren't nobles. *She* doesn't look noble."

Since the taybarri didn't slow down for the conversation, Kaylina missed whatever came next.

Vlerion ignored the girls who'd gone back to giggling, and he smiled at Kaylina. Because he agreed that she didn't look noble?

"She can tell because the tilt of my chin isn't haughty," Kaylina said.

"Are you sure that's it? Your chin can assume a haughty tilt when you're discussing the superiority of your mead."

She squinted at him. "I don't believe that's true."

Had Queen Seerathi, the taybarri elder who'd read her mind when she'd been thinking about how good her mead was, spoken to Vlerion about her thoughts?

"When you're *thinking* about its superiority then," he said, eyes glinting with humor.

Damn, Kaylina wagered Seerathi *had* ratted her out. "Is Sergeant Zhani a commoner?"

The subject hadn't come up during their training.

"Far from it," Vlerion said.

"What does that mean? She's more than an aristocrat?" Kaylina thought of Zhani's accent. "I thought she came from the desert. She once mentioned growing up with the sandsteaders."

"Yes. You'll have to ask her if you want more details. Only Targon and a couple of other rangers know her background. She may still technically be in hiding, though I suspect her family knows where she is."

Curiosity about her instructor made Kaylina want to probe him for more details, but Vlerion said, "We're here," and pointed toward a two-story brick building with a corner on the market square.

Signs labeled the intersecting streets as Fountain and Second, and the inn stood across from a nursery painted in cheerful yellow with blue trim. Something about that struck Kaylina as familiar, but it took her a moment to remember why. Vlerion had once mentioned it as a place with catacombs access in the basement.

But his focus was on the brick building, not the nursery. A wooden sign over the door held a tankard with the words Nakeron Inn.

Kaylina sniffed. "That's an unimaginative and generic sign. No *wonder* she's worried about competition."

"Not everyone sets up shop in an establishment with such a reputation that a sign isn't needed," Vlerion said mildly.

"I'd be willing to give her the plant if she wants a building with a reputation of its own."

Vlerion swung down from Crenoch's back to knock on the door. Above it, a second-story curtain stirred, but nobody came down. Vlerion tried the door, but it was locked.

Kaylina pointed to a sign made from paper in the window. It said the eating house and meadery wouldn't open until dusk because the owners had "gone to the hanging."

"That's awful," Kaylina said. "People go to *watch*?"

"Always." Vlerion pointed at another sign that said an inn access door was around back. "This time, the crown is encouraging it."

"As entertainment?" Kaylina couldn't imagine wanting to watch people die.

"As a lesson. The crown wants to deter further uprisings." Vlerion kept saying *the crown* instead of *the king*. If he believed someone else was making the decisions, maybe that made sense.

Kaylina dismounted and followed Vlerion toward an alley that presumably led to the back entrance. Even though Jana was her nemesis now, Kaylina hadn't had time to check out the establishment before. Maybe she would come later to buy a goblet of mead —to sample the competing beverages.

The alley was wide, free of garbage, and offered few hiding spots, but Vlerion paused in the entrance, his hand finding the hilt of his sword.

"Trouble?" After seeing him glance toward rooftops numerous times, Kaylina wondered if he believed they were being followed. She touched Levitke's shoulder, making the question for her as well. With their keen senses, the taybarri might detect enemies sooner than humans.

"Maybe." Vlerion's gaze probed the rooftops again.

There weren't any windows on the first level, but a row of them looked down onto the alley from the second floor, the inn rooms perhaps. All were closed, and Kaylina didn't see any faces pressed to the panes. The building on the other side of the alley lacked visible windows.

Crenoch cocked his head, a floppy ear twitching. Levitke lifted her snout in the air, nostrils flexing.

"My instincts are telling me," Vlerion started, but he didn't get to finish.

A crack came from behind them, a ceramic jar striking the side of a building next to the nursery. It exploded with a deafening boom that made Kaylina cover her ears.

The explosion caused both taybarri to roar in alarm. Broken ceramic shards flew everywhere. One struck Crenoch in the head, and he sprang away.

"Put your back to the wall," Vlerion ordered Kaylina, his sword already in hand.

Smoke flooded the street and square as the noise of the explosion dwindled, replaced by alarmed shouts from the market area.

The threat, however, came not from that direction but from the alley. Several men in loose white and tan garb dropped down from the rooftop of Nakeron Inn with swords in their hands. Without a word, they charged at Vlerion and Kaylina.

10

ENEMIES ARE GATHERED MORE EASILY THAN SEASHELLS.
  ~ *Dainbridge III, the playwright*

Near the mouth of the alley, Vlerion pressed Kaylina against the brick wall of Nakeron Inn, ensuring she obeyed his order to protect her back. Then he charged to meet the approaching swordsmen. Three of them. She caught him humming as he went.

She reached for her sword but, after so few lessons, didn't trust that she had learned enough to hold her own in a fight. Instead, she pulled out her sling and loaded a round.

Metal clashed as Vlerion met the swordsman in the lead. Instead of putting *his* back to the wall, he kept it to Kaylina and the street, positioning himself in the middle of the alley so the attackers couldn't get by—couldn't get to *her*.

She fired at a man far enough to the side of Vlerion that she wouldn't risk hitting him. All three attackers were focused on him, no doubt deeming him the greater threat, so her target didn't see the blow coming. The lead round struck him in the temple, and he reeled back, almost dropping his sword.

The man snarled, clutching the wound, then shouted something in a foreign language and pointed at her.

Watch the girl, Kaylina wagered was the translation.

The other two fighters engaged with Vlerion, angling themselves to try to flank him. His feet blurred as he darted about, keeping them from their goal as he returned the attack.

But his opponents were surprisingly fast. Even with her limited sword-fighting experience, Kaylina could tell they were good. Not only did their blades whip about with rapid and precise combinations that Vlerion was hard-pressed to defend against, but they must have practiced together often. They simultaneously launched attacks and never got in each other's way.

Shifting to the defensive, Vlerion drew a dagger and used it to help parry the blows raining down on him.

Afraid Vlerion would be outmatched if the third attacker joined the fight—he already would have if not for the width of the alley limiting space—Kaylina fired the sling again.

This time, her target had an eye toward her and saw it coming. The man ducked, and the round clacked off a brick wall.

"Stay out of this, girl," he snarled in accented Zaldorian as blades continued to clash, the noise echoing in the alley.

More than once, Vlerion glanced back at Kaylina as he fought. Worried a kidnapper would sneak up and get her from the other direction?

She hoped not. If he believed she was in trouble, he could change into the beast. That might help him against the capable swordsmen, but with dozens, if not hundreds of people nearby, their skirmish could turn into a massacre of innocent citizens.

"Where are the taybarri?" Vlerion called.

Another boom came from the street, another explosive

smashing into a wall. Kaylina was glad there didn't seem to be any children at the nursery that afternoon.

Crenoch roared. Someone ran into view at the mouth of the ally, and Kaylina spun in that direction. But the person—another swordsman in white and tan—kept running. Levitke was chasing him.

"They're busy," Kaylina replied.

A cry of pain followed by a curse made her turn back to Vlerion's battle. One of his attackers staggered back, blood weeping from a long gash in his arm.

Vlerion had done the first damage. Unfortunately, the third man had recovered from her attack and was ready to take the other's place.

Kaylina loosed another round at him. Once more, her blow struck him on the side of the head. He'd been slashing toward Vlerion, but he flinched, fumbling his sword, and Vlerion knocked it out of his grip.

A victory, but the movement left Vlerion open to his other foe. The man's blade whipped in, clipping Vlerion's jaw.

Cursed craters, that one was fast. Unnaturally so. Usually, *Vlerion* was the one with the superior speed, but they were an even match.

The man she'd struck pointed at Kaylina and ordered something in his tongue. Probably a command for someone to take her sling—or kill her.

The injured attacker glanced at his comrade, then focused on Kaylina. The blood dripping from his arm didn't keep him from charging at her with his sword raised.

After seeing him fight, Kaylina knew she wasn't his match, and fear almost made her run. But she couldn't abandon Vlerion—even if he might have preferred her to get out of trouble.

She jammed her sling into her pocket and drew the sword.

Barely in time. Her attacker stabbed his blade straight for her heart.

She leaped sideways, scarcely parrying the blow. Had he launched a second attack, she might not have managed to deflect it, but he seemed surprised when she avoided the first. He must not have expected to need much finesse to defeat her—to *kill* her.

"You're more than his pretty lay, huh?" the man asked in a clipped accent.

"Who are you?" Kaylina didn't long for a conversation with the guy, but if she kept him busy, it might give Vlerion time to finish off the other two. Assuming he could.

Her attacker didn't answer, instead advancing on her with testing probes, quick strikes that she struggled to read. Were they feints or real attacks? Neither his eyes nor his chest—per Sergeant Zhani's advice—seemed to hold the answer, and she hastened to parry each one, just in case. More than once, she swung at empty air.

When another boom shook the street, her assailant swept in with deadly intent, launching a stab at her chest. She parried it, but he followed up with a swift sweep toward her head. She ducked and tried to back up again, but her shoulder bumped against the wall. She stumbled, and he shifted his grip, raising his sword to brain her.

Help me! she called silently to her blood—to whatever druid power ran through it.

Warmth surged from the brand on her hand, and the man gasped, his head whipping back as if a beam had smashed into his face. What would have been a deadly blow clipped Kaylina's ear instead of killing her. Pain burst from the wound, and warm blood flowed down the side of her face and neck. She hurried to return to a defensive stance, her blade up. But the man was stumbling back, his sword wavering, his face contorted in pain.

"What did you *do*?" he demanded.

A roar from behind Kaylina startled her. Levitke surged past, brushing her shoulder, and barreled into the attacker.

"In the alley!" someone shouted from the smoky street. "Lord Vlerion is in there!"

More taybarri rushed past Kaylina, these with ranger riders, and she backed to the wall, as worried about being trampled by allies as slain by foes. She kept her sword up, not trusting that her attacker had given up. But he turned and sprinted away.

One of Vlerion's opponents lay dead in the alley, but the better fighter remained. He saw the odds shifting and threw something at the ground. A crack echoed from the walls, and a cloud of black smoke filled the alley. In it, Kaylina lost sight of the men until she glimpsed Vlerion's attacker climbing the brick wall like one of the monkeys back home.

"Up there," one of the rangers called, then loosed an arrow.

But the man was too fast, catching the lip of the roof and pulling himself over and out of sight. The arrow struck the gutter and was deflected away.

The taybarri managed to catch up to the injured man who'd attacked Kaylina. He whirled, fighting instead of letting himself be captured.

"Subdue him without killing him," Vlerion ordered.

He didn't turn away from the skirmish, but he did back toward Kaylina, glancing at her as the rangers surrounded the remaining attacker.

Blood dripped from Vlerion's jaw, and a rip in his sleeve promised at least one other wound, but his humming had kept him from turning into the beast. Kaylina nodded to him, assuming the danger of that was past, but his glance turned into a stare when he saw the blood running down the side of her neck.

Fury leaped into his eyes, her wound charging him with more dangerous emotion than threats to himself ever did.

Afraid he might yet turn, Kaylina rushed to him. "I'm fine."

She rested her hand on Vlerion's hip and gazed into his eyes so he would see the sincerity in hers. The wildness of the beast in their blue depths made her feel like she was sticking her fingers into the maw of a rabid wolverine.

"It barely hurts," she added. "It's just my ear." Just the tip of it, she hoped, but it was bleeding a lot so she wasn't sure. "Don't worry. If it falls off, I've got another ear, so I'll still be able to eavesdrop." She winked and shifted her hand to his chest. "Are you okay? That guy looked good." She patted him, hoping her inane chatter—or at least her calmness—would allow him to more easily wrangle his emotions.

Her palm tingled, and magic seemed to flow from her hand, as it had in ranger headquarters when he'd confronted Spymaster Sabor. Soothing warmth trickled into Vlerion.

He took a deep breath and closed his eyes.

"Everything is fine," Kaylina said softly, aware of the sounds of fighting dwindling and another taybarri approaching them. "Thank you for your concern and for protecting me."

"Always." His voice was gruff, but he slid a gentle arm around her waist. When he opened his eyes again, his full humanity was there. He'd tamped down the beast.

Or *she* had.

Vlerion looked at her hand, straight at the leaf-shaped brand, and she knew he'd felt the magic, its influence over him.

She swallowed. Before, he'd said it was all right, but was it? He was so used to being fully in charge, as a ranger and an aristocrat —having power over others. Now, she, whether she wanted to or not, had power over him. Would he come to resent that?

"I'll take you to headquarters and have Doc Penderbrock treat that." Vlerion pointed his chin toward her ear.

"And maybe your wounds too?" Kaylina lifted a hand toward his face but refrained from touching his bleeding jaw.

"Maybe." He managed a quick smile. "That man *was* good.

Even without his allies, I would have struggled to best him. I have no idea who these people were. Their fighting techniques weren't based on any of the styles typically taught in the kingdom, and it took me time to get used to it—to them." Vlerion looked toward the end of the alley where the rangers had dismounted.

Their opponent, the one Kaylina had tangled with, was on his knees, several swords pointed at his throat. Instead of looking at the rangers, he glared down the alley toward Kaylina with loathing burning in his dark brown eyes. Fortunately, the rangers removed his weapons, so glaring was all he could do.

"That man wanted to kill me," she murmured, realizing that this attack probably hadn't had anything to do with the kidnapping attempt.

Vlerion followed her gaze to him and growled.

Since he might not have seen all of her fight—and how close she'd been to dying—she wished she hadn't said that. Especially when his eyes hardened again, and fresh tension tightened his muscles.

"It's all right," Kaylina said, patting him again. "I'm just pointing out that I don't think they wanted to kidnap me. I was an afterthought for them. They were after you."

"It is not *all right*," he said. "They attacked you as well as me."

"Yeah, but only because I hurled lead rounds at them. Men get inordinately crabby about that."

"True. You should have stayed out of it."

"Of course. I should have picked up a snack from the market, taken a seat, and watched while they killed you."

Vlerion squinted at her. Fortunately, the dangerous glint had faded again.

"Am I not being properly reverent with my tone, my lord?" She smiled, relieved the moment had passed.

"You are not."

"I'll try to do better."

"Good." Vlerion noticed a couple of the rangers looking toward them and released her, stepping back. "It would be unfortunate if I had to flog you after you assisted me in a battle."

"Or at any time ever."

"Indeed." Vlerion opened his mouth to say more, but a blue-furred snout leaned between them.

Crenoch had arrived. He carried something in his fanged mouth and seemed to be offering it.

"What is that?" Vlerion held out his hand.

Crenoch carefully released one of the ceramic jars that held explosive material, this one not yet detonated, and Vlerion caught it. Crenoch also released—less carefully—a hand that had been gorily removed from the rest of its body by taybarri fangs. It flopped to the ground at Vlerion's feet.

Kaylina cursed and leaped back, as distressed by that as anything else that had happened.

"Good work, Crenoch," Vlerion said, unfazed.

The taybarri lifted his head and swished his tail.

"Extra protein pellets for you tonight," Vlerion promised him.

One of Crenoch's ears twitched, and he looked to Kaylina.

"Uhm, yes." She pulled her gaze from the hand. "And honey drops."

That prompted more vigorous tail swishing, from Levitke as well as Crenoch.

"Lord Vlerion?" A scarred ranger about ten years older than Vlerion stepped up, speaking deferentially though he wore more rank on his sleeve. "We've bound that one, and we've got the wagon coming for the bodies. Do you have any orders?"

"Let me know what you learn by questioning him." Vlerion pointed at the man who'd been tied and tossed over the back of a taybarri, face down in fur. "Use kafdari root. Find out who sent them and from where. These weren't random thugs." He looked toward the rooftop where the other combatant had disappeared. "I believe they're trained assassins."

"Yes, my lord. They were. That one has the sagebrush tattoo on his forearm."

"Ah." Vlerion's eyes sharpened. "Interesting."

"Sagebrush?" Kaylina only vaguely knew the plant from books.

"You've heard of the sandsteaders who have settlements in the drylands east of the mountains?" Vlerion asked her.

"Yes."

"There are also nomadic wild tribes over there who aren't interested in obeying the rules of civilization and settling in one place. They roam the deserts, surviving in hostile land with little water, and they have some of the best fighters in the world. It's said they eat a certain altered plant that gives them greater speed and strength than a normal human being. I always thought that a myth, but..." Vlerion touched his wounded jaw. "Perhaps there's something to it."

"Because one managed to cut you?" Kaylina asked. "You *were* outnumbered."

"I was," he agreed, lowering his hand.

"Hardly anyone ever touches Lord Vlerion with a blade," the ranger told her. "Even when he *is* outnumbered."

True. Kaylina had seen that for herself. As the beast, he was almost unstoppable, but some of that power conveyed to him as a man too, making Vlerion faster and stronger than his opponents.

"Find out if they were all sage assassins and who hired them. Also, find out if I was the target or..." Vlerion extended a hand toward Kaylina.

"Oh, they wanted you," she said, certain of her assessment.

"If that's true, we've both earned new enemies of late."

"At least my enemies only want to kidnap me." Kaylina looked toward Nakeron Inn, though nobody had come out, as far as she'd seen, to observe the fight. Since explosions had been taking place in the street, that was understandable. A few of the curtains in second-story windows were stirring.

"They could have been kidnapping you to deliver to someone who wants to kill you," Vlerion said.

"A cheery thought."

"Yes." As the rangers took the prisoner and the bodies away, Vlerion gazed thoughtfully at Kaylina. "I wonder if your plant is capable of influencing people who don't have druid blood."

"Can we not call it *my* plant, please? Just because we're house-mates now doesn't mean I claim any ownership over it." She glanced at her hand. If anything, the plant had an ownership claim on *her*. "As to the rest, it's given Frayvar bad dreams and visions, the same as it has me."

"Hm."

It took Kaylina a moment to realize what he was suggesting. "I don't think it hired the assassins."

"I said influence, not hire. Though, at this point, I wouldn't be that shocked to see it using its vines to wave bags of coins at people through its window."

She shook her head. "It still wants you dead—I'm positive—but I doubt it had anything to do with this. You have a new enemy."

"Not surprising. The Virts may be behind it, but their schemes thus far haven't suggested that they have a lot of money to spend. Hiring sage assassins isn't cheap. *They* wouldn't have been lured here by promises of access to their holy catacombs." Vlerion pointed at the cobblestones under their feet.

"Maybe the Virts have gotten some monied backers." Kaylina looked at the inn again.

"We'll talk to her, but let's get your ear fixed up first."

"How gory does it look?"

Vlerion pointed at the dismembered hand full of taybarri teeth marks.

"It *can't* be that bad. My sister is coming to visit."

Not visit. *Judge.* And report back to the family.

Grimacing, Kaylina probed her ear carefully, relieved to find only a cut, not the entire top half missing.

Warmth came from the back of her hand, and she jerked it down. The brand—the druid power—had saved her. She couldn't deny that, but that didn't make her comfortable with it.

"I was joking," Vlerion said. "It's not that bad. Ears always bleed a lot. Come." He pointed to their mounts.

The rest of the rangers and their taybarri had left with their prisoner, but Crenoch and Levitke waited. Vlerion winced as he mounted. Maybe her ear wasn't the only reason he wanted to see the doctor.

As they rode away, he leveled a long look back toward the rooftop of the inn, but the assassin was long gone. That didn't mean that he and however many of his allies had survived wouldn't try again. And next time, they wouldn't assume Kaylina was a frill only with Vlerion for a *lay*. The assassins would be better prepared.

11

HOPE MAKES US EASILY LED.

~ *Talivaria, Daygarii wise woman*

"You've dusted that table four times," Frayvar observed.

"I'm nervous about our grand opening tomorrow." Kaylina shifted her hair to make sure it covered the stitches in her ear, though she'd already told her brother about the adventure—the *mis*adventure—with Vlerion. Doc Penderbrock had sewn them both up the evening before.

"Are you nervous about that or about Silana coming?"

"*Both.*"

Between her concern that kidnappers would try to snatch her again, possibly in front of their sister, and that Vlerion's assassin would go after *him* again, Kaylina had a lot to be nervous about.

"I'm anxious too," Frayvar admitted.

He was also wiping tables when he wasn't tending a flatbread dish crisping in the oven. The scents of butter and garlic filled the castle, making Kaylina's mouth water.

"I hired a couple of servers to help us tomorrow," he added, "but if we don't get enough customers, paying for staff will put us in the hole. *More* in the hole. We've invested a lot in buying ingredients—twice now. I tried to find servers who would work for only tips, but the reputation of the castle made it hard to entice anyone, regardless." Frayvar sighed wistfully. "It's too bad the curse hates rangers."

"Why? Do you think you could press them into helping serve? For tips?" Kaylina snorted at the idea of her haughty Vlerion looming beside a table to take orders, then holding his hand out for liviti coins afterward.

"I thought their *taybarri* might help. They would do anything for you, and can you imagine how delighted people would be to see them carrying trays on their backs?"

"They'd eat the food instead of delivering it. And don't forget how drawn they are by mead—and the consequences."

"I suppose that's true. I—"

"Hello?" came a familiar voice from the vestibule.

Silana.

Nerves assaulted Kaylina's stomach. She willed a silent message to the plant in the tower: *That's our sister. Please don't attack her, give her horrible visions, or do anything weird.*

Since she'd rarely attempted to communicate mentally with the plant before, especially from a distance, she didn't expect anything to come of it. But a vague sense of indignation or maybe affront wafted down from the tower.

"We're back here," Frayvar called when Kaylina didn't respond. He poked her in the arm and waved for her to go first. "She's going to hug me," he muttered under his breath. "I know it."

Though Kaylina had reservations about Silana's arrival, her smile was genuine when she met their older sister's dark brown eyes. Almost as tall as Frayvar, with more maternal plumpness,

Silana wore an airy white dress and seashell bracelets that evoked memories of their island home.

"Kaylina, there you are." Silana crushed her in a hug. "Hiding in this humongous stone— Does this qualify as a castle? I've always wanted to tour one. They're all over the place up here. I kept seeing them along the coast from the ship. Oh, and the big castle perched on the plateau up there is where the king and queen live, isn't it? Frayvar! Are you eating? You're more gaunt than ever. Ah, but I smell something delicious cooking."

Their brother hung back, but that didn't keep Silana from releasing Kaylina and advancing on him with her arms spread.

He opened his mouth, either to say he *had* been eating or, more likely, to remind her of his hugging preferences, but he wasn't quick enough to utter either. Silana enveloped him—*smothered* him—and he gritted his teeth as he briefly returned the embrace.

"I *told* you," he mouthed to Kaylina.

She nodded. She hadn't doubted his prophesying. "It *is* a castle, Silana, and it's got an interesting history. According to the locals, there's a curse."

Kaylina felt disingenuous downplaying it—she knew all about that curse by now—but such things existed only in stories back home. She expected scoffing and dismissal from their sister.

"Yes, the driver mentioned that as he rudely hurled my trunk and bags to the ground outside the gate and urged his horses to leave as soon as my feet touched the ground." Silana released Frayvar and stepped back to look them up and down. "I thought it a rather extreme reaction, but the gossip on the ship was that there have been assassination attempts up here lately, and Port Jirador is on edge."

"It is." Kaylina didn't know where to start or how much to share.

"A shocking amount of information was not making it into the newspapers that are distributed to the southern province." Fray-var's voice dripped disapproval.

A meow came from the open front door, and a couple of cats sashayed in. Kaylina held up a finger, saying she would be back, and hurried outside. She intended to grab her sister's belongings and close the door before any more strays could wander in. The word seemed to have gotten out among the furred that she was a softy and often shared food.

Kaylina halted in the courtyard, spotting more than cats. A familiar black, silver-trimmed carriage was parked in front of the castle, with magnificent stallions nickering softly as they looked toward her.

At the gate stood the same tidy gray-haired chauffeur who'd once picked up Kaylina to take her into the country to see Vleri-on's mom. When the man spotted her, relief flashed across his face. Maybe gossip about the recent deaths caused by the cursed castle had made it out to the estate.

The chauffeur bowed toward her and, without stepping through the gateway, called, "Lady Isla requests your presence at Havartaft Estate today, Ms. Korbian."

"She requests it?" Kaylina walked through the courtyard so they wouldn't have to yell. "It's not an order?"

"It is not, but she urges you to accept her invitation."

"I've just had a family member arrive, and our grand opening is tomorrow. It's not a good time."

The chauffeur blinked slowly, and she knew he couldn't believe a commoner would turn down a request from his aristo-cratic employer. He looked back to the driver on the bench, but the man didn't comment.

"Perhaps you will reconsider, Ms. Korbian. She has not given me the full details of that which she proposes, but I believe she is considering an investment in your business endeavor."

That surprised Kaylina. Isla had enjoyed her mead and

proclaimed it of good quality, but, with everything else going on, it was hard to believe Isla had business investments on her mind. Hadn't Vlerion said his family's estate had been set on fire during the Kar'ruk invasion?

"Oh, that's quite promising," came Silana's voice from the courtyard.

She and Frayvar had come outside to listen in. Eavesdropping tendencies ran in the family.

"If there's a chance to receive funds from a friendly backer," Silana said, "you shouldn't pass it up."

Frayvar nodded but didn't add verbal support, maybe because he also found the timing odd. Even unlikely. Was this a pretext? Did Isla want something from Kaylina? Maybe to again request that she stay away from Vlerion?

"Don't you want me to stay and give you a tour? It is a castle, after all." Kaylina refrained from glancing toward the tower. With the sun out today, the purple glow wasn't that noticeable, but her sister would see it sooner or later. Kaylina hadn't yet figured out how she would explain the plant.

"I'm certain Frayvar can give me a tour." Silana gripped his shoulder.

He nodded and made himself smile, though it looked like more of a grimace.

"We'll catch up when you get back, and you can tell me all about your plans," Silana added. "Grandma is curious to know if you're adequately making the family recipes."

"The mead is very adequate, thank you," Kaylina said.

"We'll see." Silana smiled, but it was the I'll-be-judging-you smile of an older sister watching younger siblings for faults. "Help me with my luggage, won't you, Frayvar? There's honey and a few supplies to help make your eating house a success. Grandma didn't want to send anything until she heard a report, but I was positive she would want you to succeed, so I slipped a few key ingredients out of the pantry." She winked while she nudged him in the direction of the trunks.

Frayvar shot Kaylina a you'd-better-hurry-back-and-save-me look as he hefted one.

"I even brought you both personal gifts." Silana walked to one of the bags and unbuttoned a flap. "Here, Kaylina. You'll appreciate this on your ride. The latest Pirate Plunderer novel, a romantic adventure and most certainly not, as Grandma would say, trashy fluff."

Silana usually called the books trashy fluff too, but Kaylina was so delighted to have the latest installment from the southern publisher that she didn't mind. She managed a genuine *thank you* and another hug for her sister before pirouetting, her mood much improved.

"This way, Ms. Korbian." The chauffeur smiled pleasantly at Silana.

Kaylina held up a finger and hurried into the castle to pluck a bottle of her favorite semi-sweet mead from the root cellar. Whether Isla was a potential investor or not, Kaylina would bring her something to enjoy.

On the way to the carriage, she crossed back through the courtyard, receiving an approving nod from Silana, who was delving into her bag again.

"Here you are, Frayvar. I brought you an article recently published by Professor Zymollar on prehistorical accounting methods. There are also a couple of blank ledgers for the business or whatever other use you might have for them."

"Oh." Genuine delight infused Frayvar's voice. He might also have pirouetted.

Silana was annoyingly perfect, and Mom's and Grandma's favorite, but she did pay attention to what everyone in the family liked so that she could give good gifts.

"Oh, charts with data and footnotes with further references,"

Frayvar murmured, managing to read the front page of the article while tugging a trunk inside. "I wonder if I can find them in the university library here."

Feeling less guilty about abandoning Frayvar now that he had fresh reading material, Kaylina let the chauffeur give her an arm up into the carriage. With her book clutched to her chest, she sat back for the ride while hoping that Lady Isla genuinely wanted to back the business.

As the carriage pulled away, she glimpsed the tower and again willed the plant to be good for whatever tour Frayvar gave their sister. She trusted he wouldn't take her to see it, but the *sentinel*, as it had called itself during one of their communications, could make its presence known whether one visited it or not.

12

WHEN YOUR FORCES ARE INSUFFICIENT FOR A FORWARD ASSAULT, YOU must tempt the enemy into a trap.
  ~ Lord General Menok

The carriage pulled off the highway and onto the drive for Havartaft Estate, and Kaylina put down her book. The sign and manor house were as she remembered them, but, as Vlerion had mentioned, a silo and the stable had been damaged by fire. Work crews were replacing the charred wood, the bangs from hammers drifting across the countryside.

Since her last visit, the snow had melted, and greens thrust up from garden beds, while fruit was starting on vines and trees. On a grassy hillside, lambs cavorted about between grazing sheep.

With the mountains rising beyond the estate, peaks still blanketed in snow, it was a beautiful area, the kind that made a visitor feel at peace and long to stay. Now that the weather was warmer, Kaylina could imagine reading her book underneath one of the trees, with a gentle breeze rustling through the grasses.

If not for the family curse, Havartaft Estate would have been a wonderful place to grow up. But that had to loom over everything. Kaylina well remembered Isla speaking of eventually losing Vlerion, the same as she had her husband and her firstborn son. She'd spoken of *when* it would happen, not if.

Since she had warned Kaylina to stay away from Vlerion, to keep the beast from rising unnecessarily, Isla couldn't have given up on him completely. But she was probably the pessimistic sort. With her background, how not? Maybe she always expected the worst even as she fought for something better.

The same butler answered the door, passing the mead bottle to the kitchen staff and leading Kaylina into the castle. Isla sat in a room of tufted couches and chairs, a low table waiting with a pitcher of tea, cups, and a plate of biscuits and butter.

The last time Kaylina had visited, there had been sweets as well, and Isla had liked her honey drops. Maybe Kaylina should have brought those instead of the mead. Or in addition to the mead.

Isla, her dress plain and her face without makeup, the same as it had been before, nodded when the butler led Kaylina in.

"I'm pleased you could come, Ms. Korbian, and do I understand that you brought another bottle of your wonderful mead?" Isla smiled, and, unlike with so many others Kaylina had encountered recently, it seemed genuine, if sad. There was a graveness in her blue eyes that probably never left.

"I did. Word travels fast in your home." Kaylina couldn't help but glance at the scars—the *claw marks*—on Isla's neck.

During her first visit, she hadn't known where they came from, not until Isla told the tale of being wed to Vlerion's father before she'd learned about the curse. Her husband might not have killed her when he'd turned into a beast, but he'd hurt her when they mated. Now that Kaylina had seen Vlerion change a number of times—and knew his beast wanted to claim her as *his female*—seeing the scars was much more chilling.

"The house is quiet with Vlerion moved out and only me here most of the time," Isla said. "The staff lacks for gossip or much to talk about, so they overexert themselves in that area when visitors arrive. I do wish it were possible for my son... Well, I've told you why there should never be a wife and children for Vlerion."

"Yes," Kaylina said, her mouth dry. She was nervous, expecting the worst. What had Isla *really* invited her here to talk about?

"You've seen it—*him*—now." Isla held her gaze, the words a statement of certainty, not a question. "You understand fully."

"I... yes."

"You've not been able to stay away from him." It also sounded like a statement of certainty. Surprisingly, it didn't come across as an accusation. Isla almost sounded sympathetic, as if she understood fully. Of course she did. She'd spoken of the allure of the beast, of how women were drawn to the Havartaft men, even when they knew better.

"Well, I'm training to be a ranger." Kaylina felt she needed to give an excuse. It wasn't that she'd *wanted* to defy Isla, who had given her good advice and who doubtless wanted the best for her son. "And with everything going on... the gods keep throwing us together."

"So he said when I spoke to him." Isla sighed and leaned forward to pat a chair adjacent to the couch. "I do not blame you. And, as you might guess, I was unsuccessful in convincing Captain Targon to put aside his notion of training you to be a ranger. He's convinced you have some... power." Isla's forehead creased as she looked Kaylina up and down as if she couldn't believe it.

Since Kaylina struggled to believe it herself, she wasn't offended. She doubted she had much in the way of inherent power, maybe nothing more than the ability to attract animals. It hadn't been until the plant branded her that she'd started being able to do odd things. Most likely, she was a conduit for *its* power.

"More than that of an *anrokk*," Isla added.

"It's hard to explain." Kaylina perched on the edge of the seat. "I do seem to have a link to Stillguard Castle and its curse. Do you know about the druid plant that resides there?"

"Vlerion mentioned it, but he's terse whenever he speaks about you—and things revolving around you. He knows I feel you two should stay apart, and he doesn't want to upset me, but I can tell... Well, I understand he's not been successful in staying away from you either." Her mouth twisted, the sadness in her eyes deeper.

"The gods keep throwing us together," Kaylina said again.

"The gods are capricious."

"Yes."

A soft knock sounded, and a female server brought in another tray. It held the opened bottle of mead, more than a few sips missing, and two crystal goblets.

"Did it pass the taste test?" Kaylina recalled that even a horse had gotten a lick last time.

The server smiled, dimples appearing. "Yes, ma'am. If the kitchen staff—and the butler and the gardener and the stable master—didn't know my lady enjoys your mead, the entire bottle might have disappeared."

"Really," Isla murmured.

The server bowed her head, poured drinks, then departed.

Last time, Isla had only seemed moderately interested in the mead, surprising Kaylina when she'd spoken of its excellence toward the end. This time, she didn't hesitate to pick up the goblet and take a sip, swishing it thoughtfully in her mouth before swallowing.

"A different recipe, for certain, but was it also made using different honey?" she asked. "The first varieties you brought were wonderful, but this has something extra to it."

"You have a sensitive palate, my lady." Kaylina found it easier to throw the honorific on her sentence for Vlerion's mom than for him. Maybe because she wasn't pompous. "That's one of my first batches made from honey crafted by bees gathering pollen from altered plants in the local preserve." Kaylina waved in the general direction, though the dense forest didn't border Havartaft land like it did some of the other estates outside of the capital. "I stumbled upon ancient druid hives while I was, uhm…"

She wondered how much Isla had heard about the poisoning charges and Kaylina being chased around the countryside by the authorities. Her cheeks warmed. It shouldn't have mattered what Isla thought of her, but, for some reason, she didn't like the idea of Vlerion's mom believing she was a troublemaker. Even if she'd eventually been cleared of that crime, she couldn't help but feel she'd been shortsighted along the way and gotten herself into that mess.

"While I was temporarily unable to stay in my home," Kaylina finished.

Isla's graying eyebrows twitched faintly at that interpretation of events. Kaylina had a feeling she'd heard the story from Vlerion or someone else. After all, her wanted posters had been all over the city for a while.

"When that was resolved, I went back and collected enough honey to turn into mead," Kaylina added.

"There are Daygarii traps on this land, vestiges of their previous settlement, that are quite dangerous to those who don't know to avoid them. We've used it to our benefit when it comes to pirates and other marauders from the strait and the mountains, but one is left with the impression that their kind loathed humans —or anyone who presumed to touch what they claimed." Isla tilted her head. "Are there not traps on the hives? One would think such a precious commodity wouldn't be given up lightly—by the bees or those who placed the hives centuries ago."

"The taybarri and probably the local animals aren't able to raid them. There's some magic that guards them." Kaylina thought of the star-shaped leaf mark on the hives, the one that matched her brand, and glanced at the back of her hand. "I was able to take honey without being attacked."

"Interesting." Isla also glanced at the brand. She didn't appear surprised by its presence, so maybe she'd heard about that too. "Not long ago, when I was visiting the capital to arrange some business matters, Spymaster Sabor's minions showed up and invited me to a meeting at the royal castle. I would say *commanded* me to attend a meeting, but Sabor phrased it politely. He plays by the rules and lets us nobles pretend we outrank all those but the king and queen themselves." She smiled tightly.

"I met Sabor. He's an ass."

"Yes." Isla chuckled and sipped from her goblet. "You've a blunt tongue for one lacking the protection of a noble title."

"I know. Captain Targon keeps suggesting Vlerion flog me."

Isla's eyebrows twitched again. She wasn't the most expressive woman and even reminded Kaylina of her grandmother, but Grandma was much more acerbic.

"I was about to say I'm surprised Targon wouldn't handle discipline of ranger trainees himself," Isla said, "but I realized Vlerion wouldn't allow such actions when it comes to you, and Targon won't cross him."

"Targon says Vlerion has sworn an oath to him and the crown, and that Vlerion is honor-bound to do whatever he commands." Kaylina made a face, not liking the idea of Targon making Vlerion do something unpleasant, whether Vlerion had sworn an oath or not.

"When it comes to normal ranger duties, yes, Vlerion would follow Targon's orders, but I assume that you... He will protect you." Her eyes sharpened, and she lowered her voice. "Am I wrong?"

"No."

"Targon wouldn't risk arousing the beast by harming one of Vlerion's... friends." A twist to Isla's lips promised she knew they were more than that.

Since she'd ordered them *not* to become more than that, Kaylina didn't know what to say. She sipped from her own goblet to give herself time to think.

"Sabor, on the other hand," Isla continued, "must believe his position would somehow insulate him because he's more interested in rousing the beast. He asked me if you can control him in that state."

"I can't." Kaylina lowered her eyes and took another sip, guilt creeping into her because it wasn't a complete truth. She felt compelled to amend it. "I mean, I've been able to kind of soothe him when I can tell he's getting irked and might change, but I definitely can't control him once he's changed. He listens to me as the beast, but he's not willing to, ah, put aside what he wants."

"You." Isla gazed steadily at her.

"Yeah."

"Has he...?" Isla glanced at her neck, as if expecting to find scars there.

"No. So far, I've gotten lucky, and he's only come to me after a battle. He's been tired and collapsed before he... did anything." Did *much*, she thought, remembering the tear to her dress. But that had been a minor thing. He hadn't hurt her.

"But he wanted to," Isla said softly.

"Yes."

"I'm sorry." Isla shook her head and set down the goblet.

"It's not your fault. And it's fine anyway. Nothing happened." *Yet*, the back of her mind whispered.

"It *is* my fault. He is my son. I bore him even after I knew all about the curse. After Vlarek, my husband and I decided not to have more children, but he came to me again as the beast, and I had no choice." Isla held her gaze. "Kaylina, it is not a path you should continue down. It's dangerous—and could be deadly—for you. Vlerion is at *least* as strong as his father was—as dangerous. And you... You have a gift." Isla waved at the mead. "And you're so young. To die because of this curse... It would be tragic."

"I agree. I'm not planning on dying. I'm doing some research and figuring out how to lift Vlerion's curse." Kaylina didn't know if pouring honey-water on a plant counted as research, but she continued to believe that lifting the curse in the castle would give her a clue about how to remove Vlerion's curse.

"It's noble that you wish to help him, and I believe you've a good heart for wanting to do so, but it's not possible. As I told you before, numerous cursed Havartafts have dedicated their lives to trying to figure out how to remove the curse."

"They didn't have the blood of the druids in their veins."

"And you do?" Isla sounded skeptical.

Vlerion must not have explained his belief that such ancestry was what gave her the *anrokk* power.

"So I've been told by numerous people, er, entities. The taybarri queen said so, and the cursed plant in Stillguard Castle implied the same. It gave me this, which is conveying... I'm not sure exactly but some kind of power." Kaylina showed Isla the back of her hand. "I intend to use it to help Vlerion."

"I wish that were possible, but everything has already been tried." Isla shook her head sadly.

Vlerion didn't think Kaylina would be able to lift the curse either. She didn't know if she was naive to believe otherwise, or if a fatalistic streak ran in their family.

"Also, for your sake and his, I wouldn't speak of what that does or doesn't convey." Isla reached over, clasped Kaylina's hand, and pressed it down onto the chair, as if that could hide it. "Sabor is already too interested in you. And in Vlerion. He wants to control the beast, supposedly for the good of the kingdom, but I think for his *own* interests. He's heard about the power Vlerion has in that form and wants it for himself. I know Sabor isn't aligned with the Virts, but... I'm also not positive he's interested in maintaining the current order. He seems content to have a hand in ruling now while Gavatorin is going senile, but when the king passes, I suspect he might not throw his weight behind Prince Enrikon as the successor."

"I just want to help Vlerion, my lady." Kaylina wouldn't say she didn't care about politics or whether the existing regime retained control, since politics had decided to care about *her*, but her interests were in much more personal matters.

"I appreciate that, and you're a good girl, one I would approve of for my son if circumstances were different."

Longing crept into Kaylina, a wish that circumstances *could* be different. She would love to have the approval of Vlerion's mother, for Isla to believe Kaylina good enough for her son, even though he was a noble.

"Thank you," she murmured.

"Unfortunately, I can't encourage you two to spend any more time together. I don't want the beast to ravage the city and end up killed, the way Vlarek was. I also don't want *you* to be mauled or murdered."

"That won't happen."

But hadn't it almost happened? More than once?

Kaylina bit her lip and looked away.

Eyes all too knowing, Isla gazed at her for a long moment before rising and walking to a table with drawers. She slid one out and extracted a thick envelope, the edges filigreed in lacy gold. She returned, sat, and placed it in front of Kaylina.

"Dedrik, my chauffeur, told you I'm interested in investing in your business?"

"Yes." Kaylina didn't know what to make of the abrupt topic change and flattened her hands to her thighs instead of picking up the envelope.

"Stillguard Castle sounds like an unwise place to launch such an enterprise."

Something Kaylina could not deny, not when Frayvar had been out hunting for affordable leases that very week.

"It presents a few challenges," she murmured.

"That envelope contains twenty thousand liviti. It's yours to invest in your business, no equity required to be shared with me, *if* you return to your homeland to open it."

Kaylina blinked. "Pardon?"

"Go back south, dear," Isla urged. "To your Vamorka Islands or elsewhere in that province. You'll be closer to your family. It'll be for the best. Don't let yourself fall into the clutches of the Virts or Spymaster Sabor, and don't..." She closed her eyes. "Please don't see Vlerion again."

"Oh," Kaylina whispered with understanding.

This wasn't an investment. It was a bribe.

"I'll leave you to consider my offer." Isla rose. "I urge you to take it."

Goblet in hand, she walked out of the room, leaving Kaylina alone with the envelope, with more money than she'd ever seen before.

With twenty thousand liviti, Kaylina and Frayvar could do exactly what Isla asked, start over somewhere else, somewhere far less dangerous. She could pursue the dream she'd left home to follow without all the caltrops that had been thrown in her path. She could prove herself to her family. Once, that had been all she wanted to do, everything that mattered.

Now...

Now, other things were as important to her. To leave without helping Vlerion... Kaylina couldn't do it.

Without looking in the envelope, she rose and walked out of the room. Maybe she was supposed to wait for Isla to return, but she didn't want to discuss the matter further with her.

The hallway was empty, with no sign of Isla or any of the staff. Since the back door was closer, Kaylina left the manor that way, though she would need a ride back to the city, so it wasn't as if she could simply walk away without speaking to anyone else.

"Too bad I can't summon Levitke," she murmured, glancing at her hand. She'd succeeded at telepathically communicating with the taybarri before but not from miles away.

Assuming the chauffeur would take her back, Kaylina followed a path past flowering gardens and manicured hedges that led around the side of the manor to the front drive. The carriage wasn't there, so she headed for the stable.

A few horses hung their heads over half doors, waiting for their pasture time. Their nostrils twitched as she approached, and she again regretted not bringing honey drops.

The front door was open, and Kaylina heard voices inside, so she slowed to listen.

A horse nickered at her. She held up a finger to her lips. It whuffed, not dissimilarly to the taybarri. It might have been one of the horses that she'd fed honey drops to the last time she'd been here.

"This is a lot of coin to deliver to a random thug in a rough part of town," a man inside the stable said. "Maybe I should take an escort."

"You're afraid you'll be mugged along the highway on the way to the city?" a woman asked.

Kaylina debated between listening—*eavesdropping*, as Vlerion or Captain Targon would be quick to call it—and walking in to ask about a ride.

"More likely *in* the city," the man said. "Though after the fire—the whole Kar'ruk invasion—I don't feel that secure riding through the countryside either. I wish my lord Vlerion were on patrol on the border, not bogged down in that quagmire with the rebels in the city."

"Deliver that coin then. If my lady is correct, he'll be less endangered once the girl is gone."

Kaylina lifted her eyebrows.

The girl? *Her*?

"She is pretty, and I can see how a young lord would be distracted by her, but I don't understand why some fling matters so much that Lady Isla is willing to pay to get her out of her son's life."

Kaylina frowned at the paint on the side of the stable. This had to be about the bribe. But that didn't make sense. Nothing about the bribe should have required a staff member delivering coin to someone in the city. The money for it was presumably all in that envelope.

"She's a commoner," the woman said. "And Lady Beatrada and Lady Ghara think she's after his money."

"Cheaper to pay *her* to stay out of his life then, don't you think?" A bag of coin jangled. "This is a lot of gold, not to mention that Lady Isla already paid for one attempt. If this one succeeds, what's to say the girl will stay in the south after she's ousted?"

"She will if she knows what's best for her. My lady could as easily pay to have her killed, but she's got a good heart. She only wants to protect her son."

Kaylina leaned back as the realization slowly dawned. Jana Bloomlong wasn't the person paying to have her kidnapped. Vlerion's *mom* was.

A horse harness jangled, and hooves clopped on the flagstone floor of the stable.

Kaylina scurried away from the building. She managed to back up about ten steps before a horse and rider appeared in the doorway. A middle-aged man with a goatee, he gaped when he spotted her.

"Hi," she blurted with a wave to pretend she'd just arrived. "I'm looking for the carriage. My meeting with Lady Isla is over, and she said her driver would take me back to the city."

Even as she spoke, hooves rang out on the cobblestone driveway. The carriage and the chauffeur came into view, exiting from a structure on the other side of the manor.

The horseback rider gave a long look over his shoulder into the stable—toward the woman he'd been speaking with?—but he only pointed Kaylina toward the approaching carriage. He had to suspect she'd heard them speak, but she hoped he wasn't certain. She also hoped he wouldn't tell Lady Isla. She might adjust her plans if she realized Kaylina had learned about them.

Not that Kaylina could do anything even with this knowledge. All she could do was brace herself for another kidnapping attempt.

No, she decided. She had to put a stop to this. With her sister in town and the grand opening a day away, Kaylina couldn't risk having hired thugs come after her again.

Once she returned to town, she would tell Vlerion and hope he could talk his mother out of this. She would tell him about the bribe too—the supposed investment. She didn't want to drive a wedge between Vlerion and his mother, but this was a problem that only he could solve.

13

PATHS ARE RARELY AS DIRECT AS WE WOULD LIKE.
  ~ Lord General Avingatar

Evening approached as the carriage rolled into Port Jirador. Kaylina asked the chauffeur to drop her off in a park along the river between Stillguard Castle and ranger headquarters. She said she needed to walk a bit after the two long rides. The arched eyebrow he slanted back at her suggested he knew she was up to something, but he didn't object.

Though she felt guilty for not going to the castle first to check on Frayvar and Silana, Kaylina worried she didn't have a lot of time until the next kidnapping attempt. On the way back, Isla's rider had passed them on the highway, and she'd imagined she could hear the bag of coins jangling as the stallion galloped by.

After stepping out of the carriage, she waved to the chauffeur and headed toward Stillguard Castle. As soon as he was out of sight, she turned and veered across the grass toward a path headed to ranger headquarters. The sooner she let Vlerion know what his mother was up to, the sooner he could convince her to put a stop to it.

Clouds had wafted in, and rain drizzled from the gray sky. With the deteriorating weather, the park was empty of visitors. Or so Kaylina thought. She was almost to the street when a shadow detached from a tree and lunged for her.

She sprang away, reaching for her knife—why hadn't she thought to bring the sword?—but the man was too fast. Before she could draw the blade, he grabbed her and spun her to grip her from behind, his arm wrapping around her. She tried to stomp on his instep, hoping his grip would loosen, but he evaded her foot and pressed a cold blade to her throat.

She snarled. This was happening to her *way* too often.

"I wish only to speak," the man said in a soft accented voice.

"We couldn't *speak* without you manhandling me? And *knife-handling* me?" Kaylina didn't know what in all the moon craters that meant, but she was flustered and afraid.

"I suspect you'd be less motivated to tell the truth in such a situation," he said mildly.

That accent. She'd heard it before recently. Where?

The sleeves of his brown shirt were loose, and the one on the arm holding the knife to her throat had fallen back enough for her to glimpse a long tattoo pointing toward his wrist. In the fading light, it was hard to tell, but it might have been a sagebrush branch. Yes, that's why the accent was familiar. This was one of Vlerion's would-be assassins.

"What truths do you want?" Silently, Kaylina attempted to marshal whatever power flowed through her veins to call out telepathically in the direction of ranger headquarters. *Levitke, if you can hear me, I need help!*

Did the brand on the back of her hand warm slightly? Or was it her imagination?

"Tell me what power Lord Vlerion of Havartaft commands," the assassin whispered.

"What power? He's just a man. What power do *you* command? You guys are fast and deadly, and you skimmed up a brick wall like a caffeinated banana spider."

The knife dug in, and a drop of blood dribbled down Kaylina's throat. She closed her eyes, fear rather than power surging through her veins.

"When you are in the position you are in, with me in the position I am in, it would be wise for you to answer *my* questions."

"Nobody's accused me of being wise before."

"It was chance that brought you to the encampment we've chosen, yes? We have been watching the ranger compound to study our prey, but since fortune has favored me, I will now know what you know."

"What do you want to know? I don't understand what you mean by power." Kaylina eyed the nearby trees, wondering if she could convince any of them to help her. In the mountains, a pine had kindly dropped a branch on a Kar'ruk attacking her, but it had also been pissed because he'd sunken his axe into its trunk.

She stared at a willow alongside the path, its branches dangling overhead. *Will you help me?* Kaylina attempted to ask it. *I'll bring you a special fertilizer if I can get away from this guy. It uses delicious honey made by bees that forage on altered plants.*

"Lord Vlerion moves faster and has greater strength than a man should," the assassin said.

"You were speedy yourself." Kaylina kept herself from mentioning that Vlerion *usually* beheaded his opponents without receiving any wounds, at least when he was in his human form and battling fellow humans, but that would only support the assassin's beliefs about him.

"You are his female, yes?" His tone was more thoughtful now, and the knife dug less deeply into her skin. "If you were used as bait in a trap, he would come for you."

She'd liked it more when the guy had simply been threatening her. She didn't want to be used against Vlerion. "He's a good man. He would come for any woman being brutalized, threatened, and held against her will."

Again, she tried to stomp on the assassin's foot. This time, she clipped the inside of his boot, but he didn't flinch.

When her foot touched the ground again, a faint vibration came up through her sole. From the dirt? Or maybe caused by the tree's roots?

Help me, please, she urged again. *The honey water is great. You'll love it. I'll gently and lovingly bathe your roots in it.*

The vibration came up through the ground again. She squirmed as much as she dared and gripped the assassin's wrist to distract him. She was surprised he hadn't yet reacted to the vibration—unless it was some magical message directed only at her?

"A mouthy warrior woman is what attracts him?" he asked calmly, his grip remaining implacable. "Like the chieftain Delzari? Strange. It is our way that women raise children and cook, not make battle. The men protect them and value them."

"Thanks for the culture lesson."

"What marks your hand? I saw it earlier but not well."

"A leaf."

"It is magical. When I use my gods sense, I can feel it."

What in all the altered orchards was a *gods sense*?

"No, you're mistaken," Kaylina said. "It's just a brand. They're trendy in Port Jirador this season. You should get one too."

"Have you any other marks on your body?"

"No, I do not."

The dagger lowered from her throat, but she couldn't feel any relief because the assassin used the sharp blade to cut open her shirt. Bastard.

She jammed her elbow backward and tried to twist away, but his grip around her waist was of steel. Even though she struck him hard in the abdomen, he again didn't flinch. He didn't even seem to feel pain.

"Careful," he said softly, the tip of the dagger touching her breast. "It is not our way to harm a female, but accidents happen in situations such as this."

"You maiming me with a knife wouldn't be an *accident,* asshole."

His dagger moved, lifting her shirt.

"I sense..." He'd closed his eyes, and he inhaled slowly. Maybe his gods sense came in through his nostrils. "Only your hand is marked by magic, but all of you... Yes, your blood has power. From a plant? Or from an ancestor?"

She drove her elbow into his gut again.

The bastard smiled, opening his eyes and regarding her again, first her face and then his gaze shifted lower, to the flesh he'd exposed. "You are most appealing."

"Thanks. I love it when strangers with daggers think so."

"I see why he has claimed you as his female, and I believe he *will* come for you."

Yeah, he would. That was the problem.

"Look, why don't you let me go, and I'll tell Vlerion you're looking for him. You say you're staying here in the park? I'll send him to visit." With a squadron of guards and rangers at his side...

The assassin snorted softly. "Tell me what altered plants he eats to gain his power. He is not part druid. I am certain. Tell me what I wish to know, and I will release you. To use a female as bait in a trap would not be honorable, even if pragmatism prompts me to contemplate it. Though my tutors taught me this language and the ways of Zaldor, I am at a disadvantage as a newcomer to this land."

Another vibration, a greater one, emanated from the ground.

"You didn't seem disadvantaged in that fight." Kaylina hoped the tree was doing something. "What altered plants do *you* eat?"

Before Vlerion had mentioned the possibility, she hadn't heard of plants that could convey greater fighting ability to a man, but she wouldn't be surprised if they existed. The fact that the assassin was asking about it seemed a confirmation that he used such things himself.

A crack came from above them, and branches rattled, foliage rustling. The assassin tensed as he glanced up.

A thick willow branch swept toward his back. He released Kaylina and dove to the side, rolling away so quickly that it left her off-balance. The branch caught *her*, sending her tumbling forward. She flailed but kept her feet, then ran toward the river.

The assassin had already risen, crouching with his knife in hand as he glanced from the tree to her, his eyes narrowed. Only after the branch returned to its original position did he run after Kaylina.

A roar came from the far side of the park. A *taybarri* roar.

Though she hoped that signaled help for her, Kaylina didn't slow down. Even with an ally, she didn't want to fight the assassin and risk losing, being caught again and used in a trap against Vlerion. Whether it was *honorable* or not.

She sprinted for the river, the sliced open halves of her shirt flapping.

The assassin stopped, turning to face the long-bodied blue-furred taybarri that ran toward him. Levitke.

Thank you for coming, Kaylina thought, willing the brand to convey the words to her, to let them communicate telepathically as they had before. *But don't get in a fight with that guy. He's dangerous. Just keep him distracted for a moment, will you?*

These ones attacked us before, came Levitke's reply, along with an image of the battle in the alley, of an assassin almost cleaving Kaylina's skull in two with his sword.

Oh, I remember.

She reached the river and turned to follow the trail that ran along it, but she spotted a cloaked figure at the apex of a bridge ahead. A hood and twilight hid his face. Another of the sage assassins?

Cursing, Kaylina followed her original instinct and veered toward the water, hoping she could swim away from the area and that the assassins would lose her in the darkness. As she leaped off the bank, more taybarri roars came from the far side of the park, and she glanced back. Several rangers rode off the street and onto the grass. Her assailant had disappeared.

As Kaylina hit the water, its glacier-fed iciness shocking her body, she realized she might not have needed to douse herself. She swam out into the current anyway. The person on the bridge was far enough from the approaching taybarri that he might not worry about them.

Unfortunately, the flow of the current took her in that direction. She thought about swimming against it, but if the man had a bow or other ranged weapon, her movements would draw his eye, and, unlike his colleague, he might shoot at her without having a chat first.

Kaylina stayed still as she floated under the bridge, hoping the darkness would hide her.

"Where'd she go?" a familiar voice called from the park. Was that Jankarr?

I'm heading out to the harbor, she thought but didn't yell, not when she was passing under the bridge. The cloaked figure didn't miss seeing her. He switched sides so he could watch her as she continued downriver. If he held a weapon, she couldn't tell, but she kept her mouth shut. He continued to watch her, unconcerned by the rangers in the park.

She was far downriver before he disappeared from her sight.

14

CONTROL IS NEITHER A TRUTH NOR AN ILLUSION BUT CREATED IN THE
minds of others.
~ *Planting Moon Priestess Zarestha*

Sodden and cold, Kaylina hurried toward ranger headquarters. Thanks to the powerful current of the river, she hadn't managed to pull herself out of the water until she'd washed out into the harbor.

If Stillguard Castle had been on the way, she might have stopped to dry off and change clothes, though she might not have. Explaining her soggy state and cut shirt to her sister wouldn't have been appealing.

Besides, Levitke and the rangers who'd charged into the park didn't know what had happened to her. When word got back to Vlerion, he would be worried. And furious. She didn't want to risk the beast erupting.

When the stone wall around ranger headquarters came into view, she pulled her shirt closed, folding her arms over her chest to keep her skin from showing. Maybe she *should* start spending the nights in the barracks, if only so she would have a room and a change of clothing. And so creepy assassins who could gods-sense her magic wouldn't be able to reach her.

Had it been coincidence that had brought Kaylina within his reach? Or had his power somehow let him sense her coming? She believed he'd been watching ranger headquarters but not that chance had taken her into his grip.

"Hello, Corporal Opank," she greeted the gate guard, having learned more of the rangers' names by now.

Lanterns that burned in the courtyard provided enough illumination to show numerous taybarri lined up and ready to go somewhere. Rangers were mounting them, weapons clinking and clanking as the men swung up.

"Trainee Korbian," the corporal blurted, "a squadron is looking for you."

"A lot of people are looking for me lately."

"Kaylina?" Vlerion called from the courtyard, concern lacing his usually calm voice.

"Yes." She waved, picking him out of the group of riders as Opank pushed the gate open for her.

Vlerion sprang from Crenoch's back and ran to Kaylina, enveloping her in a hug before she'd made it two steps into the courtyard. She returned the embrace, glad she'd reached him before he'd ridden out and all over the city looking for her.

"Jankarr said a man attacked you in the park. Between the dark and the trees, he couldn't see much, and then you both disappeared, and he didn't know if you'd been hurt or where you'd gone." Vlerion released her from the hug but gripped her arms, standing back so he could look at her. "He thought there might have been more of them and one might have gotten you. He—"

His gaze snagged on the bare skin visible through the shirt the assassin had cut open, and his eyes bulged. Fury surged into them.

Fury and more, that dangerous wild glint that promised the beast wasn't far away.

"I'm fine," she blurted, gripping his shoulders and trying to get him to look into her eyes. "It was the sage assassin, one of them. He threatened me and wanted information about you, but he didn't hurt me. He was thinking about using me to bait a trap for you but not anything else."

Was that a lie? The assassin's words repeated in her mind: *You are most appealing.*

"He cut open your shirt," Vlerion growled. "He wanted to do more than use you for bait." His angry gaze lifted to hers, his eyes still savage. "I will kill him. Where did he go? Do you know?"

"He said he was camping in the park, but I'm sure he'll move his tent. He didn't offer a forwarding address." Kaylina rested her palm on his chest, trying to make her tone light and to soothe him, to keep the beast from rising, especially with all his ranger comrades scant feet behind him. Sensing the danger, the taybarri shifted their weight uneasily, some moving back. "He was quite presumptuous and rude," she added.

Vlerion bared his teeth and looked toward the gate, his muscles taut, deadly power radiating from him. Speaking so the others wouldn't hear, he hoarsely whispered, "As the beast, I could smell his scent and track him."

He inhaled deeply, muscles bulging against the sleeves of his shirt. Damn it, did he *want* to change?

"Stop, Vlerion," Kaylina ordered, keeping her voice soft, knowing he wouldn't want his men to hear her giving him an order. But she willed her power into the words, needing him to hear them, to *obey* them. "It's too dangerous to change here, and you know it. The beast might kill other people on his way to track down the assassin. A *lot* of other people. Calm yourself. Stay with me. I need you here with me."

His fiery gaze swung from the gate to her, so intense, so close to the edge, that she almost withdrew her hand and stepped back. But she rooted her feet to the ground and met that scary gaze.

"I need you here with me as Vlerion, the man," she said.

Cool power flowed from her hand and into his chest. Soothing him, keeping the beast at bay.

"I'll help you find him." Kaylina hoped he wouldn't resent her for again presuming to use the plant's power on him. She also hoped he wouldn't come to resent her for anything else, such as that he'd been able to control the beast without help before she'd come into his life. All his recent changes, and his almost-changes, had been because of her. That, she knew without a doubt, was why his mother wanted her out of his life.

"I will find him," Vlerion said, his body still tense, but his voice less hoarse—less of an animalistic growl. "I don't know yet who sent him, but he shouldn't be after you. *Nobody* should be."

"I agree, and I'd love it if you found him." She patted his chest.

As she lowered her hand, a familiar voice spoke from the doorway to the office building.

"That's twice now," Spymaster Sabor said, looking to Captain Targon, who stood at his side, as if they'd stepped out of a meeting. "I think she *can* control him."

Dread swept into Kaylina, and she pulled the fabric of her shirt close to cover her exposed skin.

Targon glanced at the rangers; they'd also been watching the exchange. With Vlerion's back to them, they shouldn't have seen or heard much, but Sabor and Targon were to the side. Kaylina didn't think she'd been speaking loudly enough for them to hear, even if they'd been there the whole time, but her touch and Vlerion's body language might have said enough.

Vlerion gave Sabor a dark look as he turned toward the men, standing so that he blocked the view of Kaylina's cut shirt from them. "Numerous sage assassins are in the city. I am their target.

Go out, and ask around to see if anyone knows where they're staying. Remain in pairs or threes. They're dangerous."

"We'll find them and handle them, Lord Vlerion," an eager young ranger said, nudging his taybarri to lead the way out.

"Simply find them, and tell me where they are." Vlerion lifted his chin. "It is my problem, and *I* will handle them."

The ranger hesitated and glanced at his comrades before saying, "Yes, my lord."

A determined set to the young man's jaw made Kaylina certain that he—maybe all of them—wanted to personally end the threat to Vlerion. Sergeant Zhani was among them, and she nodded, the same determination on her face.

Fear joined the dread curdling in Kaylina's stomach.

"Maybe she should skip this assignment," she whispered.

Sergeant Zhani was as capable as the men—Kaylina had no doubt about that—but the assassin's creepy assessment of her as *appealing* as he'd touched her skin with his knife... She didn't want him to catch Zhani and do the same—or worse—to her.

Vlerion regarded Kaylina, his gaze assessing, and something told her he was following her line of thinking as perfectly as a telepathic elder taybarri. Maybe she shouldn't have said anything, but she also couldn't remain quiet and let Zhani ride into danger.

"Sergeant Zhani." Vlerion lifted a hand. "You will remain at headquarters. Kaylina requires more training after she changes into dry clothes."

As Zhani looked over, frowning as if it were a punishment to be removed from the assassin-hunting duty, Kaylina couldn't help but prop an indignant fist on her hip. *Training* was the last thing she wanted to do more of tonight. She also didn't want Zhani to resent her.

The movement exposed her bare stomach and the curve of her breasts again, and Zhani noticed, perhaps for the first time. Her gaze was sympathetic instead of resentful.

"Yes, I see," she said, stopping her taybarri.

A couple of the other rangers riding past glanced at Kaylina's skin, and she crossed her arms again.

"Get our trainee some clothes, Vlerion," Targon said, walking up behind them. For once, he managed to avoid ogling Kaylina. Was that even a hint of concern in his eyes when he looked at her?

Unfortunately, Sabor had walked up with him, and there was nothing but calculation in his eyes as he gazed speculatively at her.

"Yes, Captain." Vlerion wrapped an arm around Kaylina's shoulders, as if he could shield her from the attention of the men —and the spymaster—and guided her toward the barracks.

As they walked away, Kaylina could feel Sabor's gaze upon her, and she couldn't help but shiver from more than her wet clothing.

15

FEARS NEVER ADMITTED IN A CROWD MIGHT BE SHARED IN PRIVATE WITH another.

~ Writings of the Divine Servants

As soon as they stepped into Vlerion's barracks room, he removed his weapons belt, closed the door, and caught Kaylina's hands and gazed into her eyes.

"Are you truly all right?" he asked softly. "Did the bastard try to... or *did* he..."

"No," Kaylina said firmly, not needing the sentence finished. "He was a weirdo—I'm not going to lie—and maybe he was starting to think... Oh, I don't know what he was thinking, but he saw the mark on my hand and wanted to know if I had any marks elsewhere."

Vlerion's brow furrowed.

"He said he could sense its magic—gods sense, he called it. Have you heard of that?" She asked the question out of genuine curiosity and because she wanted to distract Vlerion from his dark thoughts.

Even if the wildness had left his eyes, he remained tense. It wouldn't take much to rile him up again, to rouse the beast. She didn't want him dwelling on the possibility that the assassin might have been contemplating rape.

Vlerion took a deep breath, visibly trying to release his tension, and walked to a cabinet to withdraw a towel. "It's mentioned in the religious songs of the nomadic tribes. They don't have texts, as far as we know, and hand down their knowledge vocally. They believe that some of their people have the ability to sense the magic of altered plants from miles away. Since some of the plants only grow near water, those with the gods sense are highly valued foragers because they can lead their people to desert oases. I suppose if there were other kinds of power, they might be able to sense them too."

Returning with the towel, he glanced at her hand.

"Like very slight amounts of druid blood that might possibly flow in a person's veins?"

"Yes." Vlerion wrapped the towel around her shoulders, covering her bare skin. "I'll get you some ranger blacks to wear."

"Thank you."

Kaylina shivered again, and she wasn't sure if it was from the chill or fear that lingered. Fear of the assassin, fear for Vlerion's life, and fear of Sabor and whatever machinations he was planning.

Vlerion must have noticed because, instead of leaving to retrieve clothes, he wrapped his arms around her and pulled her gently against his chest.

"I regret that you were endangered because someone has hired assassins to kill me." He rested his face against her head.

"It's not your fault." Comforted and always pleased to be in his arms, Kaylina leaned into him. She felt safe and was glad Vlerion cared, glad he wanted to protect her, especially since her life had grown so dangerous of late. She worried about him getting into trouble because of her, but being with him felt so good. So right. She closed her eyes and rested her face against his shoulder. "Maybe I should let your mother's hired thugs kidnap me and send me south after all."

She said it as a joke before remembering that she hadn't yet shared that information with him.

His body tensed again. "What?"

She hesitated, but she'd already said too much to retract the words or promise to tell him another time. Besides, she didn't want to be evasive with him. She explained her visit to Havartaft Estate, hurrying through it because she could feel the danger in the tautness of his body around hers and worried the beast might yet arise.

She rested her palm against his chest again, in case she needed to try to stop it. He clasped his hand over hers, and she realized he might be remembering the courtyard and the other times she'd used her power to soothe him. He might also be remembering Sabor's words about her controlling him. She didn't want to do that—never that. She just didn't want to be the reason the beast killed innocent people.

"It is unacceptable," he stated, his voice hard.

"I'm sorry," Kaylina whispered, afraid she'd overstepped her bounds.

"It is not your fault."

"I'm afraid it is. It's been a conscious choice. I just..."

He spoke over her, as if he hadn't heard her. "She is my mother, and I understand that she wishes to protect me, but she should not presume to interfere in *your* life. Further, you could have been hurt or *killed* by those brutes."

"Oh." She realized he hadn't been following her thoughts and wasn't talking about her power over him.

"I will speak with her and tell her to *un*-hire whoever Tavos was taking coins to. And I will talk to him and the rest of the staff. No one will deliver her coin to kidnappers. None will take actions that could lead to your harm." His hand still covering hers, Vlerion leaned back enough to look into her eyes.

"Thank you. I know she's trying to help you, but I'd prefer not to be kidnapped."

"You will not be. And you will not be harmed by that assassin. Or any other." His jaw clenched for a moment before he added, "You will stay here tonight. Train, rest, and remain within the walls. I will go out and hunt down the remaining assassins."

"Alone?" Alarm flashed through her. "Or in pairs or threes as you *wisely* ordered your men?"

"I will go alone so that I can give the assassin the answer he sought to scare out of you," Vlerion said, the corners of his eyes tight. "I will track him down and kill him after finding out who hired him."

Kaylina shook her head, grasping what he meant, *how* he would track the assassin down. "Not in the city, Vlerion. You can't change. It's too dangerous. If you hurt or kill anyone else, you won't forgive yourself." Her voice lowered to a whisper as she held his gaze. "You won't forgive *me*."

Her hand was still on his chest. Dare she try to soothe him again? Would it even work?

She could tell he wasn't on the verge of changing. But he had to believe he could bring it about later, when he was alone in the park and wanted the beast's superior senses to track the assassin. Maybe he would imagine her in danger, imagine what the assassin could have done to her, and that would be enough to prompt the change.

He looked down at her palm splayed on his chest, his hand still clasped over hers. This time, she knew he was thinking about the power she'd used on him, the power he could *sense* when she used it on him.

"A part of me is affronted that you have control over me." Vlerion lifted his gaze as he raised his hand to the side of her face, brushing his fingers over her damp hair to grip the back of her head and rub her scalp. "What, I wonder, could you prompt me to do if you tested your power further?"

"I doubt it goes any further, but I wouldn't try to prompt you to do anything even if I could." Kaylina licked her lips, nervous even as her body responded to his touch, to the delicious sensations his rubbing fingers raised. She caught herself tilting her head back and arching toward him. "I'm not that horrible spymaster who keeps popping up like a cockroach."

"No. You are most certainly not he." Fingers kneading her scalp and the back of her neck, Vlerion's gaze lowered to her lips and then further to her chest.

Had the towel slipped? She needed to tighten it and ask for dry clothing. She needed to resist the desire to step closer to him, to press her bare skin against his chest. Having the beast arise in the barracks wouldn't be any better than in the streets.

"The other part of me," Vlerion murmured, "the beast drawn to your *anrokk*, perhaps, wants to let you do whatever you wish, to bask in your power, to serve it."

His eyebrow twitch promised that he, the aristocratic always-in-charge lord, did *not* wish to serve her. His other hand came to her hip, under the towel and her shirt to graze his fingernails over the bare flesh of her abdomen.

She quivered, her skin alive under his touch, her body heating with pleasure and intense longing. She lost her grip on the towel, and it slid to the floor.

"I think you have more power to control me than I do you," she whispered, her body throbbing as his fingers trailed higher, cupping her. She turned into his touch, pushing into his hand, even as she failed at ordering herself to step away. She needed to soothe and calm him, not arouse him, but his touch made her crave him like nothing else.

"Good," Vlerion whispered, a pleased gleam in his eyes. His gaze roved over her, as if he couldn't get enough of drinking her in. "Good."

She shook her head, catching the dangerous glint creeping into his aroused eyes. This was a bad idea. They needed to—

He surprised her by releasing her with both hands and stepping away. It was what she wanted—no, not what she wanted but what they needed to do—but such disappointment flooded her that she almost sprang onto him and kissed him, wanting everything his touch had promised. Wanting him.

Vlerion bent to pick up the towel and wrap it around her again. "Stay here tonight. Stay safe."

With a final look at her, he grabbed his sword belt and walked out the door.

16

"I WANTED TO RIDE A TAYBARRI."
  ~ *Princess Sergeant Zhaniyan*

Despite the numerous suggestions that Kaylina take up residence in ranger headquarters, nobody had shown her to a room. After Vlerion departed, she found a lavatory on the floor that wasn't being used by any of the men—many had gone out to look for the assassins.

Inside, she risked removing her clothes to scrub off the salty harbor water—and the taint of the creepy guy scraping his dagger all over her. She didn't linger, not wanting anyone to walk in and ogle her, and wrapped the towel around herself to hurry back down the hall to Vlerion's room.

She'd assumed he had forgotten saying he would get her some dry ranger blacks, but Sergeant Zhani stood in front of the door to his room with clean clothing folded in her arms. She looked like she'd just knocked. At Kaylina's approach, she turned, her eyebrows lifting.

"Ah, that makes sense." Zhani pointed her chin in the direction of the lavatory. "Lord Vlerion said I'd find you in his room, but I didn't want to presume and walk in to leave these."

"Thank you for bringing them." Kaylina accepted the clothes. "I'm sorry you got pressed into errand duty though. I'm sure sergeants aren't supposed to tote clothes around for people. And I'm also sorry you didn't get to ride out with the others."

"Oh, you get assigned menial chores often in the rangers, no matter what your rank. It's more frequent in the beginning, as you'll see. Expect lots of extra duties if you don't care for your taybarri properly or keep your room clean. Oh, and if you can't quote long passages from *The Ranger's Guide to Honor, Duty, and Tenets.*"

"That book makes for dry reading."

"Indeed it does. Later on, you also get extra chores when younger rangers serving under you fail at things since you didn't properly school them in the ways. I don't mind chores. It's better than the life I would have had if I'd stayed at home." She shuddered.

"Do you have a perfect older sister and family members with impossible standards?" Kaylina asked lightly, though she doubted anyone else would have left home for reasons similar to hers, reasons that seemed silly in retrospect.

"No, I have... *had*... an arranged marriage to someone loathsome."

"Oh. I can see where that would be rough. It's been canceled?"

Zhani hesitated, then lifted her chin. "*I* canceled it."

Had she? Or had she run away from it? Maybe *that* was what had brought her to Zaldor.

Either way, Kaylina couldn't blame her. She thought of Lady Isla and how she'd had an arranged marriage to Vlerion's father and hadn't learned about the family curse until *after*ward. Women should not be forced into such things.

Zhani waved at Kaylina's towel-covered torso. "You might want to put on clothes."

"So we can resume training?" Kaylina couldn't keep from twisting her lips into a grimace, and she groped for a way to get out of that, at least until after the grand opening. She needed to return to Stillguard Castle. By now, her siblings would be worried about her. Of course, as long as the assassins remained out there, it would be dangerous for her to go anywhere alone.

"We can if you like. If you're... feeling all right. I couldn't tell in the courtyard but, ah, saw your clothes."

"I'm all right, but I'd like to return to Stillguard Castle. Would you walk there with me?" Kaylina always hated to impose, so she added, "I'll give you some mead." She made a mental note to also take some of her honey-water fertilizer to the park the next day. She owed that willow tree for its distraction.

"You don't have to give me anything, though I have heard your mead is good."

Taking that as acceptance, Kaylina said, "I'll dress," and turned back toward the lavatory.

But a naked man wandered out of his room and ambled toward the door while scratching his balls. He noticed them, jerked his hand away from himself, and bellowed, "Female on the floor!" That warning voiced, he sprang through the door and into the lavatory as if fleeing from an overseer with a whip.

"Men are an interesting species," Kaylina said.

"I believe we're all the same species." Zhani smirked.

"I wonder about that sometimes."

Since the lavatory was occupied, Kaylina stepped into Vlerion's room, trusting he wouldn't mind if she changed in there. He wouldn't even know. He was out... She glanced toward the window, full darkness having long since fallen outside. If he went through with what he'd seemed to be planning, he might even now be in the park and tracking his enemy. In his furry form.

Would it be safe for Kaylina and Zhani to ride through the streets with the beast, assassins, and kidnappers about?

Maybe she should send someone with a message to let her sister and brother know where she was and that she was fine. But who would she send? The rangers couldn't get close to Stillguard Castle. If Zhani rode back with her, Kaylina would have to make sure she stopped a couple of blocks away. It would be hard to reward her with mead then.

Her shoulders slumped as she second- and third-guessed herself. But what if the assassin did enough research to learn that Frayvar and Silana were Kaylina's siblings? Would he think to kidnap one of them to draw her in as bait, thus to be able to use *her* as bait for Vlerion?

Kaylina groaned and dropped her forehead into her hand, a headache forming behind her eyes.

"Are you sure you're all right?" Zhani stood in the doorway and hadn't departed. She probably worried Kaylina was hiding an injury. "I trained for years—my entire childhood—as an herbalist and a healer under my grandmother's instruction. I help Doc Penderbrock in his infirmary sometimes, especially when it comes to our handful of female rangers."

"Sorry, I am all right. I'm just thinking of... my complicated life." Kaylina moved farther into the room and shucked the towel so she could dress. "If you had all that training as a healer, why did you become a ranger when you came to Zaldor?"

"I wanted to ride a taybarri."

Kaylina laughed. "Me too."

"They're amazing."

"Absolutely."

Zhani hesitated, then glanced down the hall as someone walked through singing—someone else naked, though this man had a towel wrapped around his waist. Zhani stepped into the room and closed the door.

"There's something I should tell you, Kaylina. Actually, I *shouldn't* tell you, not if I value my life and my career, but..."

"I trust this isn't about your love of taybarri?"

"Sorry, no." Zhani lowered her voice. "Earlier, Spymaster Sabor approached me. He wants me to watch you carefully during our training sessions and report anything unusual to him."

"That's... not surprising."

"No? I felt affronted and appalled that he wanted me to spy on a fellow ranger. We all serve the crown, and we—I thought—were above reproach, above suspicion."

"I doubt anyone is above suspicion these days. Not here." Finished dressing, Kaylina waved toward the window to indicate the capital city. "Since I can't seem to say *my lord* without sarcasm when I'm talking to my superiors, I'm especially not above suspicion."

"Is that really it?" Zhani cocked her head. "Sabor can't care about that."

"No, this is what interests him." Kaylina held up the brand, then grabbed her boots to put them back on. The leather was still wet, and she had to extract seaweed from the laces.

"Is there anything you want me to tell him when he asks for a report? I resisted his attempt to recruit me, but he reminded me that I'm... something of a refugee here and could be kicked out of Zaldor any time he wishes. It was irritating, since I've served the rangers and your king for six years, and I was tempted to openly defy him, but... I decided it might be best to..."

"Closedly defy him?"

"Is that a word?"

"We can ask my brother. He reads dictionaries as a hobby."

"He may not find that word in one, but, essentially, yes." Zhani shrugged.

"You can tell him I'm a dim-witted slow learner who can't tell the difference between a longsword and a rapier and whose only hope of winning battles is to thrust my boobs at men."

"I... feel it would be less of a betrayal to report on your actual activities."

"I'd like him to underestimate me." Kaylina was glad the sage assassins had. If the women in their culture predominantly raised children and tended their homes, it made sense that they hadn't expected a fighter—however novice she was. She doubted the assassins would underestimate her a second time.

"I see. Perhaps I'll consider other words to convey that."

"You're a polite refugee."

"Yes. I also don't want to discuss boobs with Spymaster Sabor."

"Wise." Kaylina led the way to the courtyard but halted a couple of steps after walking out the door.

Not only was Levitke standing on the cobblestones, ready to head out, but numerous other taybarri waited, their eyes all swinging toward Kaylina. Drizzle fell from the night clouds, but they all appeared ready to go on an adventure.

"You might not need me to escort you home." Zhani pointed at one of the male taybarri with a torn ear. "But Bludashar is there too, the one I ride, so I guess we're going."

"He's handsome."

A ripped ear couldn't detract from the appeal of a furry taybarri face, and Kaylina touched her own recently maligned ear in sympathy.

Bludashar swished his tail, raised his jaw, and padded over to stand beside Levitke.

The gate guard, someone new on duty since Kaylina had entered, frowned as he watched Kaylina and Zhani mount. With eight other taybarri padding along beside them, they approached the gate.

"Captain Targon said you're to stay in ranger headquarters

tonight, Trainee Korbian. He said you and Sergeant Zhani would be busy with weapons practice."

"We're going to practice how to ride across the city flanked by a herd of taybarri," Kaylina said.

"Step aside, please, Corporal," Zhani said, emphasizing his rank. To remind him that she was his superior? Bludashar and Levitke continued toward the gate as she talked. "I'll keep an eye on Trainee Korbian."

The corporal shook his head. "Captain Targon distinctly said—"

The taybarri hadn't slowed, and he had to jump to the side to avoid being trampled. Levitke also roared, drowning out any further protests he might have made.

Kaylina remembered the taybarri ripping the portcullis open at the royal castle and feared they would do the same here— Captain Targon would have snippy words if she was responsible for that. But Levitke sashayed up to the gatehouse, leaned her head inside, and used her snout to push a lever. The gate swung open, and the herd ambled out.

"This is highly unorthodox, Sergeant," the corporal called after them.

Zhani waved at him but didn't otherwise respond.

"Thanks for the help," Kaylina said.

"Are you thanking me or the taybarri?" Zhani touched her chest, perhaps pointing out that she hadn't done much.

"Everyone who supports me in my endeavors."

"Ah. I'll accept that gratitude. And the mead you promised." Zhani winked. "I'll even trade you this." She delved into a pouch at her belt. "I wasn't sure when I went up to see you if you'd need them."

"Uhm?"

Kaylina accepted a small packet that reminded her of some of the wrapped pills in Penderbrock's office. Since her brother had shown off the infirmary cabinets he'd organized when he'd stayed there, she had seen all manner of medicines.

"I hope you won't need them, but should you involuntarily have intercourse with a man, those will keep you from getting pregnant."

"I— Oh." Kaylina's first instinct was to hand the packet back.

"Also if you *voluntarily* do," Zhani added. "Given your business aspirations, I assume you might not be ready for motherhood."

Kaylina's cheeks warmed. Zhani had to be thinking about the comments Kaylina had made about Vlerion—and the looks of longing she'd directed across the practice arena toward him.

"Thanks," Kaylina said and tucked the medicine into her pocket.

"You can take them continuously if you're having sex, or one for three mornings after if it was a chance event." Zhani's worried frown suggested she was imagining *chance* events with the assassin who'd cut up Kaylina's shirt.

Kaylina hoped not. "Thanks," she said again. "Do you know of any herbs that can keep assassins away?"

"A traipse through the sewers might be your best bet for that."

"I've taken that traipse before. It was unpleasant."

"Any herbs potent enough to keep assassins away would have to be similarly aromatic. Unless... did you mean poisons?"

"No. It was a joke. I couldn't convince that guy to let me go, so I'm positive I couldn't have convinced him to ingest something."

"In my homeland, there are historical tales of female assassins who took an antidote or built up a tolerance to a certain poison, and then mixed it into their lip paint and killed their victims by kissing them."

"Your homeland sounds interesting."

"The sandsteaders have been at war with the nomadic tribes for centuries if not millennia. The tribesmen are particularly cruel and ruthless, but both sides have learned to kill."

"Odd that you were so eager to leave home."

"Yes. Odd." Zhani smiled, but emotions other than humor lurked in her eyes. Regret? Homesickness? In the dim lighting, it was hard to tell.

Kaylina decided to cross the eastern side of the Evardor Mountains off her list of potential places to visit and sell mead. Northern Zaldor was a forbidding enough environment in which to do business.

When they passed the park where the assassin had accosted her earlier, Kaylina peered into it, probing the shadows for signs that the man lingered. She also worried that the *beast* might be lingering, seeking his trail.

That turned into more of a concern when several taybarri sniffed the air and started swishing their tails in agitation rather than their easy contented sway. Had they caught the scent of a predator? Of the beast?

Despite the twitching nostrils, the taybarri hurried through the park without pausing. Kaylina didn't object. After her encounter, the city parks felt more menacing to her, especially at night.

Soon, the castle came into view, the purple glow of the tower not diminished by the drizzle. What were the odds that Silana had stayed inside all day, hadn't noticed it, and also hadn't heard more about the curse?

"I'd better stop here." Zhani brought her taybarri to a halt. "Targon forbade the rangers from coming within two blocks of that castle."

"I know."

"Normally, I might risk extra duties to bend the rules for a good cause, but..." Her gaze was locked on the glowing tower.

"Oh, I understand completely."

"And yet you're going to spend the night there." Zhani nodded toward the castle. "Even though it hates rangers, and you're training to be one."

"It's protecting me."

"Because of your druid ancestry?" Zhani glanced at the brand.

"I guess so. I don't know for sure about any of that. Not really. I..." Kaylina trailed off, realizing she might, for the first time, have a resource she could consult. Someone old enough to remember the events around her birth—no, her *conception*.

Maybe. Silana was a little over five years older than Kaylina. Little more than a toddler back then, she wouldn't have been Mom's confidante. Still, maybe she recalled something. Such as if someone besides the father Kaylina had always assumed she shared with Frayvar and Silana had been around back then?

"I need to go. Thanks for the escort." Kaylina waved to indicate the taybarri as well as Zhani. She assumed the sergeant would take the herd back with her. After all, Targon's forbidding had included the furry ranger mounts.

"You're welcome."

As Zhani departed, Kaylina slid off Levitke's back and patted her side. "You may want to go home too."

The taybarri gave her a solemn look. Though Kaylina hadn't attempted to call upon her power to communicate, Levitke's soft voice sounded in her mind. *No leave I.*

"You're going to stay here? In the rain?" Kaylina wished she had a stable in the courtyard that she could offer, but it wouldn't be safe for the taybarri anyway.

Levitke whuffed and walked toward the castle. Surprisingly, the rest of the taybarri, all save the mount Zhani was riding, also padded off into the rain around the castle. They didn't attempt to enter the courtyard but spread out and took positions around the outer wall, each within view of at least one other. Once arranged, they lay down, heads resting on their furry forelimbs, and watched Kaylina.

"You're staying to stand guard?" She touched her chest. "For me?"

Only Levitke, the closest taybarri, answered, giving an affirmative whuff.

Emotion tightened Kaylina's throat. She didn't know what she'd done to deserve their faithfulness, their willingness to sleep out in the rain to keep an eye on her.

A part of her wanted to argue that they should go home to the safety of their stable, but the taybarri could take care of themselves if trouble came. The memory of Crenoch dropping a dismembered human hand on the ground at Vlerion's feet came to mind.

"Thank you," she whispered, patting Levitke again before she headed for the gate.

With her jaw set and her back straight, she braced herself to ask her sister about her heritage.

17

THE HERD NEVER FORGETS.

~ *Elder Taybarri Seerathi*

The kitchen smelled of rosemary, thyme, sourdough bread, and roasted pork, and Kaylina veered straight toward a number of pots and pans sitting on the counter. At first, she thought Frayvar and Silana had gone to bed, but as she cut a piece of bread and slathered butter onto it, her sister stepped out of the pantry with one of Frayvar's logbooks in hand.

"It would have been warm if you'd been here two hours ago." Silana pointed her chin toward the pans.

Ignoring the censure in her sister's voice, Kaylina said, "Frayvar's food is fabulous even when it's cold."

She checked the oven and found the pork inside in the pan, kept warm by the lingering heat, and she skipped to the cupboard for a plate. When had she last eaten? The snacks at Havartaft Estate had been ages ago.

"It is excellent, even if he's handicapped by a lack of key spices."

"If you're referring to nutmeg and the other ones he's allergic to, he does fine without them. You can hardly blame him for not wanting to risk touching and ingesting them."

"I don't. Did you know your tower is glowing purple?"

So much for hoping Silana hadn't noticed that.

"Is it? Huh."

Silana set the logbook on a counter and raised frank eyebrows. "The rumors about this castle being cursed are more than rumors, aren't they?"

"What did Frayvar tell you?"

"Nothing. I've heard about the curse from passersby, delivery drivers, and a ten-year-old boy who ran into the courtyard on a dare. *Frayvar* only told me about his recipes, your mead, and his budget and the income you've made thus far from bulk orders."

"Those are the things Grandma sent you to investigate, aren't they?"

"*Some* of the things. She also wants to know how you two are doing emotionally. Everyone wants to know that. You left without talking to anyone." Silana's eyebrows climbed again. They conveyed censure as effectively as her tone. "If not for Frayvar's letter, we wouldn't have even known where you were."

"I wanted to prove that I could start a business without..." Without everyone telling me what to do all the time, Kaylina thought. What she said was, "Independent of the family's influence."

Silana's snort suggested she heard the unspoken words. "And you thought setting up in a cursed castle would be the way to do that?"

"It's a magnificent cursed castle, and the rent is cheap. *Very* cheap."

"They say people have died here. Or... been *murdered* here?"

"There was a Kar'ruk invasion a few weeks ago. People died all over the city. The north is harsher than the newspapers led us to believe. There's a faction of rebels that call themselves the Virts—short for virtuous and righteous—that have tried to assassinate the king and were in league with the invading Kar'ruk. They want to overthrow the monarchy and set up some other system of government." Kaylina didn't know how much her sister would care about all that and mostly gave the information in the hope of distracting Silana from the curse.

Judging by how many times her lips pursed with disapproval, it didn't work. "Five hundred liviti a month is too much for a building in the middle of all that."

"Frayvar told you about our lease, I see. And that's not too much. Lord Vlerion said you'd be hard-pressed to rent a stable stall for that in the city."

"Lord Vlerion," Silana mouthed.

"The son of the woman—Lady Isla of Havartaft—who I went to see today about backing the business. She made a robust offer, but it had some stipulations that wouldn't have been good for us, so I had to refuse. Her interest is encouraging, though. She loves our mead. Others who've tried it have too. Maybe a couple of other wealthy benefactors will be interested in investing."

Doubtful. Unless someone else wanted to bribe Kaylina to leave the area. Still, she smiled for her sister, longing for her blessing on the endeavor. Oh, she didn't care that much about *Silana's* approval, but since she was acting as the eyes and ears of Grandma and Grandpa...

"The mead *is* good." Silana sounded grudging.

"Yes." After setting her plate on the counter, Kaylina cut off a piece of pork and ladled drippings over it that she could sop up with the bread.

"Especially the varieties from what Frayvar said is a new batch from local honey. I wouldn't have thought you'd find anything as good as what we get from Grandpa's hives."

"We got lucky." Kaylina decided not to explain that a taybarri had led her to the valley of hives because he'd wanted honey for himself. "Apparently, the bees in the druid preserve outside of the city also forage on altered plants, plants left long ago by the Daygarii. Do you know anything about them, by chance?"

"About the ancient druids? Nothing more than we were taught in school. You know I'm not the history student that Frayvar is. I'm too busy doing Mom's chores as well as my own while caring for the children. Hagenth is watching them while I'm gone. We thought about coming as a family for this visit, but inklings of the chaos up here have trickled south. That was another reason Grandma wanted someone to check on you. You picked a strange time and destination for your endeavor." Silana's lips pursed again. They were good at that.

Refusing to be diverted from the topic of the Daygarii, Kaylina said, "I suppose that means you've never seen a druid. Or possibly someone who might have been descended from their people?"

"Of course I've never seen a druid. They left our world centuries ago, right? Or maybe millennia ago? There aren't even ruins or anything in our province, so it's not like they hung out down there."

"I know, but I thought you might have seen someone around the Gull when we were kids. No, when *you* were a kid. Before I was born."

Silana's brow creased. "The druids lived in our world centuries ago. I'm not *that* much older than you."

"I know that." Kaylina couldn't keep from rolling her eyes. Her belief that Silana might be a useful resource was dwindling fast. She would have to go home and talk to Mom if she wanted to know if there'd been another man.

"I don't know what a Daygarii descendent would look like,"

Silana added. "The history books don't even say much about what *they* looked like, do they?"

"Exotic and magical, I think."

"That's vague. Why are you asking about this?"

"Because..." Should Kaylina explain further? A part of her wanted to share everything, but she doubted her sister would believe much of it. She'd had a hard time believing the part about her having a hint of druid blood herself, and she'd been living through all the strange things that had happened in the weeks since she'd arrived in Port Jirador.

Her hand warmed slightly, and an image wafted into her mind.

Framed between two ancient trees stood a handsome man with reddish-bronze skin that reminded her of the bark of the cedars that grew in the foothills of the mountains here. He had deep brown eyes and windswept green hair that fell to his shoulders. After a moment, the image faded.

Who is that? Kaylina asked silently, directing the words toward the plant in the tower.

The image returned, this time with the green-haired man standing in the bow of a ship that was sailing past familiar rocky cliffs with seagull nests perched in the crags. That was the mainland behind the small island where Grandpa hunted birds with his hounds and gathered honey from his hives.

Is that a druid? Or someone with partial druid blood?

The image disappeared, and she didn't receive another response.

"Kaylina." Her sister prodded her in the shoulder.

"Sorry." Kaylina blinked and focused on her. "Did anyone with green hair ever come around the Gull when you were little?"

Silana opened her mouth, as if to issue a swift rejection, but she paused and looked thoughtfully toward the fire that burned low in the hearth. "Yes. I do remember that. He liked the mead and always ordered Grandma's seafood vegetable stew. He stayed in one of the rooms upstairs for a while, but he left eventually and didn't come back." Silana squinted at her. "That was before you were born. I was only four or five. How do you know? Did Mom say something about him?"

Not wanting to explain the plant and that it communicated with her, however vaguely, Kaylina shook her head. "No. Is there a reason she would have said something about him?"

"Just... I think they spent time together. Maybe..." Silana shrugged.

"Romantically?" By the moon gods, was it possible Kaylina *did* have a different father? Some weirdo with green hair? It was hard for her to see any of herself in the man in the image, other than maybe in the eyes, but her siblings had dark brown eyes too. And their brown skin was a similar hue to hers with no barky reddish tint.

"I don't know. I was too young to know about things like that. But it was between... Well, you know how Dad came and went and never would settle down and help out at the Gull when he was there."

"He was a deadbeat."

Kaylina expected her sister to object to the derogatory term, but Silana shrugged and said, "Yes. I didn't understand what Mom saw in him except that he thought *she* was hot and loved that she gave him mead and food for free. Grandma hated that—and him. But he kept trying to win her over by bringing gifts for her and Mom every time he came back."

"He brought us gifts too."

"Yeah, that was how he bought love and forgiveness for his absences. And for the fact that he never did anything to help out." At least Silana's lips were pursed disapprovingly for someone else, this time. "I'm pretty sure they were stolen gifts half the time. He was a thug and a pirate, even if he always said he was a buccaneer and worked on behalf of the kingdom."

"I know." Kaylina waved in the air, wanting to bring the conversation back to the other man, the possibly druidic man. She already knew the man they'd called Dad when he'd visited over the years.

"The green-haired guy *made* us gifts," Silana said. "I remember that now."

That surprised Kaylina, and she dropped her hand.

"Me and our cousins," Silana clarified. "Since that was before your time."

"He was nice?"

Since the druids had supposedly hated humans, Kaylina had assumed anyone with their blood who'd visited would have been aloof, if not an outright enemy.

"Well, he was quiet, from what I remember, but he made things out of driftwood and gave them to us. He might have been trading them for lodgings. I think Mom still has the stuff he made her. You could ask her if you give up this crazy business here and come back with me."

Kaylina frowned. "Is that what the family wants? Did they send you to drag us back?"

"Not necessarily but to check on you, yes, and see if you're all right. But now that I've heard about this curse and all the trouble going on in the city, *I* think you should come back with me."

At least she wasn't talking about all the trouble going on with *Kaylina*. With luck, Silana hadn't heard about the kidnappers and assassins yet.

"Try this again somewhere closer to home," Silana urged. "I've got enough money that we can transport the bottles you've already made. Why did you pick the capital? It's so far from our islands."

Kaylina decided not to mention the Queen's Corner in the newspapers and her dream of having the royal family try and adore her mead. Now that she'd met the queen and king, she was less enamored by the thought of them visiting her business. She would prefer that Queen Petalira forget she existed altogether. The king probably already *had* forgotten about her.

"I wanted a place with a large population of people who would enjoy the mead. There are also good distribution lines from here. Oh, you have to go by sea, since the roads over the passes close for a large portion of the year, but ships come and go all the time from the harbor and head directly to all the major ports. I envisioned the mead becoming so popular, maybe helped by complimentary write-ups in the newspapers based out of the capital, that orders would flow in."

Silana touched her chin. "That's actually a good point. We've struggled with distribution since so few freight ships come to the Vamorka Islands."

"Yes." Kaylina was pleased her sister thought she'd had a good idea. Admittedly, Frayvar had helped her realize that and only after they'd arrived in the capital, but... whatever made the family believe this expansion was a good idea was fine by her.

"Let's see how the grand opening goes," Silana said.

"Yes." Kaylina smiled, encouraged.

Silana's lips twisted. "Frayvar wants me to help out by serving and washing dishes."

"Aren't you glad you arrived in time for the event?"

"Oh, terribly." Silana yawned and headed for the door. "I'm going to bed. There are a lot of rooms up there if you ever want to expand this place into an inn."

"We did consider that."

Especially after they'd cleaned the skeletons out of the rooms...

Silana paused with her hand on the doorframe and looked thoughtfully back at Kaylina. "Mom talked about him sometimes after he left."

"The green-haired guy?"

"Yeah. His name was..." Her eyes drifted toward the ceiling as she dredged in her memory. "Arsonli? Arsonti? Something like that. I never thought about it before, but it was after he left that Mom started taking the tarmav weed. She used to lose her temper and be moody when I was little—I always thought I'd done something wrong and it was my fault—but she seemed happier when he was there. Then he was gone, and she... wasn't. I'm not sure I'm remembering it all correctly or if it means anything. You'd have to ask Grandma."

Kaylina couldn't imagine asking their aloof and completely rational grandmother about Mom's love life, but she nodded, as if it was a reasonable idea. "Goodnight."

Kaylina hoped that the castle wouldn't moan or drop any chandeliers in the night—nothing to make her sister believe this place truly was cursed. It had seemed more content since she'd been feeding it the honey water, but who knew how long that would last?

After putting the leftovers away, Kaylina headed upstairs toward her room. She sensed a presence in the back of her mind. The plant.

Was the green-haired man my father? she asked silently. *Is he still alive?*

She didn't know how even a sentient magical plant in Port Jirador could know what had happened in the bedroom between two people more than a thousand miles to the south, but... maybe it could somehow see things in her blood.

The plant didn't answer except to again share the original image of the green-haired man between the trees.

18

By the moon's silvery glow, shadows stark and long, the hunt begins.

    ~ Dainbridge III, the playwright

Kaylina awoke before dawn with her heart hammering and her mind whirling with fear. She lurched upright in her bed and peered around the dark room, her hand diving under the pillow for the knife she'd started sleeping with.

It was still night, with the city quiet, and she didn't hear anything. Nor could she pick out any alarming shadows in her room—no assassins crouching to spring at her. She liked to think the castle—the plant—would protect her if someone skulked toward her room with the intent to kill, but she didn't know for certain that she was safe within these walls.

With the knife in hand, Kaylina slid out of bed and unshuttered the window, revealing fog that had crept in during the night. From the second floor, she could see rooftops over the courtyard walls and streetlamps burning at intersections in the distance, but everything was indistinct from the haze. She almost missed spotting one of the taybarri sleeping on the river trail, still guarding her.

She wiped her damp palm on her pajama bottoms. If Levitke and the other taybarri were snoozing, maybe nothing was wrong. Maybe some dream—or nightmare—had plagued her sleep, and she couldn't remember it.

Lingering at the window, she listened for long seconds but heard nothing except the jangle of a horse harness as a wagon making an early-morning delivery passed. She stepped back, about to close the shutters and attempt to reclaim sleep, but a distant roar sounded, one that she instantly recognized as belonging to the beast.

"Vlerion." Kaylina leaned out the window and looked in the direction the roar had come from.

The park where the assassin had accosted her earlier. Had he returned to camp there again? And had Vlerion—the beast—been waiting?

She bit her lip, worried because that roar had sounded more like one of pain and fury than a battle cry. What if the sage assassin had set a trap and was getting the best of the beast?

The roar came again. Her fingers curled around the stone lip of the window. The beast *was* in pain.

Going out there at night would be foolish, especially when he was a threat to her as well as others, but if he was wounded, she couldn't leave him to fend for himself. What if he collapsed in an alley with blood streaming from his injuries, and he fell unconscious, as he always did when he turned back into a man? For long minutes, he would be unable to defend himself, completely vulnerable to an assassin's blade.

Terrified for Vlerion, Kaylina hurried to dress. She belted on the sword as well as her sling and knife. Only after she ran out the back gate did she wonder if she should have told Frayvar where she was going. If she got herself killed... Well, there wouldn't be anything he could do. He would find out when the authorities came to report her death to him.

Grimacing, Kaylina jogged up the river trail in the direction of the park. She'd only taken a few steps when Levitke loped out of the shadows and caught up with her, matching her pace and looking over. Was that a *reproving* look?

"I don't think you and the other taybarri want to come with me on this errand." As much as Kaylina would love their help if she had to face the assassin, they were understandably afraid of the beast. He was as much a threat to them as their enemies.

Her hand warmed, and she heard Levitke speak into her mind. *Ride.*

More taybarri caught up to them, the bodyguards who'd been sleeping around the castle.

"All right." Kaylina stopped to swing onto Levitke's back. "But don't feel you have to stick with me if we run into the beast."

One of the taybarri issued an uncertain whine, and several others exchanged concerned looks. She believed they knew exactly what—*who*—she was talking about. Maybe they'd also woken when they'd heard the roars?

As Levitke carried her faithfully up the trail, across a bridge, and toward the park, Kaylina patted her on the shoulder.

"You're a good friend."

Levitke's head came up proudly, and she increased her pace. The other taybarri let her lead, and they kept exchanging looks with each other, what-have-we-signed-ourselves-up-for looks.

Maybe foolishly so, Kaylina was more worried about the assassin, and whatever allies he'd brought along, than Vlerion in his furry form. She believed the beast would focus on her if she arrived with taybarri, and he didn't want to kill her but to make her his mate. Hopefully, if he was injured, that wouldn't be on his mind.

The taybarri galloped into the park.

"Slow down," Kaylina warned. "This is where he is. Where *they* may be."

She gripped the hilt of her sword, glad she was armed but dreading coming face-to-face with the sage assassin again. With whatever power he possessed, he'd easily immobilized her.

"I didn't have taybarri with me last time," she tried to reassure herself, looking across the fields and into the trees as she did.

Streetlamps burned along the periphery of the park, but it was dark within. Without a command, the taybarri spread out to search the area.

Levitke padded along a trail leading to the path where Kaylina had been attacked earlier. Even though she doubted the assassin was waiting for her behind the same tree, she tensed, her hand almost hurting as she gripped the sword hilt.

As they passed the spot, Levitke sniffed a few times but continued on. She glanced back at Kaylina, as if asking what they were looking for.

"We need to find Vlerion. I think he's injured. And he may still be the beast." Since the taybarri all knew his secret, Kaylina didn't need to worry about telling them, but she kept her voice low in case the assassin was around. "That guy who attacked us yesterday might be here too," she added.

Levitke's whuff sounded like one of acknowledgment.

She passed one of the other taybarri, his snout in the air, nostrils flexing as they sampled the foggy night air. His nose led him across the park, and he gazed toward the flat rooftop of a building across the street. Kaylina recalled how well the sage assassin could climb.

Still on the park trail, Levitke halted abruptly, as if she'd caught a scent. After sniffing a few times, she lowered her snout to the ground. She veered off the trail and through the grass, eventually trotting between trees and coming out on a sidewalk along the street. Still following her snout, she headed for a lamp, then stopped and looked up at Kaylina.

"You found something?" Kaylina slid off the taybarri and crouched. Dread socked her in the stomach. Blood spattered the sidewalk, and it was still damp. "Is it... Vlerion's? Or the assassin's?"

The latter, she hoped, but the grave look Levitke gave her suggested otherwise.

"Can you follow his trail? We need to find him." Again, Kaylina imagined Vlerion unconscious in an alley, the assassin poised to strike.

Levitke whuffed, and Kaylina climbed onto her back again.

Leaving the park, they headed down a street that paralleled the river. Had Vlerion run toward ranger headquarters? This was the right direction for that, but she didn't think he would take trouble to his colleagues—or show up there in beast form.

Of course, as she told herself, he didn't possess his faculties, his rational thoughts, as the beast. As he'd often reminded her, he couldn't tell friend from foe in that state and was motivated by different things than he was as a man. It was surprising he'd believed he could convince his beast half to track down the assassin. Or... maybe not. In both forms, he wanted to protect her. Maybe he'd known the beast would seek to eliminate someone who'd threatened her.

A few of the taybarri followed Levitke down the foggy street, where more riders and wagons were out now on early-morning errands, but others remained in the park.

"Are they tracking the assassin?" Kaylina hoped that meant he'd gone in a different direction, that he wasn't right on Vlerion's trail.

The answering whuff didn't sound that certain. Maybe Levitke didn't know what the others were tracking.

She passed the turn that would have led them to the gate of ranger headquarters. She paused, again near a streetlamp, and pointed her snout to a light-hued cobblestone. The color made it easy to spot the drops of blood.

Moving quickly, with her nose to the ground again, Levitke continued down a side street, passing wide marble steps leading into a building Kaylina recognized. The Gentleman's Steam and Strigil. She and Frayvar had once come out of a catacombs entrance in the basement of the establishment.

At first, she thought Levitke was passing it, but she turned into the adjacent alley. She stopped at a side entrance to the building, the metal door not only ajar but half ripped off the hinges.

"I'm guessing he went in there."

Levitke whuffed.

"At least we know he's still got his strength." Kaylina swung down.

The next whuff was uncertain, Levitke pointing her nose at the door.

"You're too big to go in, huh?" Kaylina paused, debating the wisdom of going in by herself, but, just because the beast had been strong enough to rip open a locked door didn't mean that her fear couldn't come true. If the magic left him unconscious, and if the assassin was nearby... "I have to go in."

Levitke made a mournful sound.

Kaylina bit her lip, wanting to send her for backup, but Vlerion might still be in beast form, and she didn't want to endanger anyone else. Nor did she want to expose his secret. The beast might not have Vlerion's thoughts or be as rational, but he wasn't dumb. He might have deliberately come here because he knew the bathhouse wasn't yet open for the day and people wouldn't be inside.

"Will you get Captain Targon?" Kaylina finally decided on. "But not anyone else, please. He'll help me, and he... already knows everything there is to know."

The answering whuff didn't sound like one of agreement, but Kaylina couldn't stay to discuss the situation further. Vlerion needed her help.

19

FOR THE LOVE OF A WOMAN, WARS BEGIN.
  ~ Lord General Avingatar

Kaylina squeezed in past the broken door, entering a short hall with a wine cellar and food preparation area on one side and giant linen closets on the other. The beast wasn't in sight, but she spotted a lantern burning low and grabbed it.

"Nobody's ever served me wine while I bathed," she muttered, walking by rows of casks stacked against one wall in the hallway.

Kaylina held the lantern ahead of her, looking for drops of blood on the tumbled-travertine floor tiles. The hallway ended, offering options that led to laundry facilities, the reception area up front, and stairs heading down.

Since she'd briefly been in the building before, she knew the layout, but that didn't mean she knew which route Vlerion—or the beast—might have chosen. Why had he come here? To hide? To nurse his wounds?

She cocked her head, listening for sounds of someone in pain. Or anything at all.

Faint hisses came from below, but that was it. Though the Strigil wasn't yet open for the day, warm steam wafted up the stairs, dampening her cheeks. Maybe the fires were kept going and the water heated around the clock.

Thinking Vlerion might have needed a towel to staunch the blood flow, she started for the laundry room, but she halted, realizing he might have gone into the catacombs. He knew them well, and an assassin from a distant land wouldn't. Maybe he'd thought to set a trap or lead his stalker past some of those Kar'ruk statues that spat poison vapors—one of the ones with its reservoir still full.

Lantern in hand, Kaylina descended the stairs. On the second step from the bottom, a spatter of blood promised she was going the right way.

"Vlerion?" she risked calling softly, though if he'd gone into the catacombs, he could be long gone.

No, not *that* long gone. The blood she kept finding was still damp. She was close behind him.

He didn't answer her, however. Only a hiss of steam sounded, making her jump.

At the bottom of the steps, the walls were tiled, droplets of moisture on them glistening in the lantern light. She stepped into the first of several bathing rooms. Towels and brushes were stacked on trays on benches around large pools wafting steam into the air. Walkways between them allowed one to easily move from one to another.

By day, with numerous bathers about, the atmosphere might have been appealing, but with only the lantern to brighten the shadows, and all the hisses of steam releasing, Kaylina found it eerie.

"Vlerion?" she called again. "Are you here? I'm pining for you."

Another hiss was her only answer. A hiss and... was that water rippling?

She set the lantern on a bench, drew her sword, and turned toward the noise.

A shadow stirred in the steam, and the sage assassin stepped into view, again wearing loose tan and white clothing. He gripped a sword, the tip pointed toward her, but his other hand held a bloody towel to his side. Sweat bathed his face, his jaw stubbled, his eyes lined with fatigue and pain.

If he was here, what scent trail had the taybarri in the park been following? Had Levitke led Kaylina after the assassin instead of Vlerion?

"Where is he, girl? And *what* is he?" His hard gaze held hers as he lifted the towel to reveal shredded clothing and three deep gashes in his side. Claw marks.

"Someone you shouldn't trifle with."

The assassin snorted. "*That* I figured out. We should have demanded much more coin." His voice lowered to a grumble as he added, "Or avoided this assignment altogether."

"Who's paying you to hunt him?"

"An honorable assassin does not reveal his employer's name."

Like this guy was *honorable.*

"Does he spring on an innocent girl in the park and cut open her shirt?" Kaylina pointed her sword toward the man as she risked glancing around. If her taybarri had been following the assassin's trail of blood here, where was Vlerion? Had he led this guy here, as she'd been thinking, or had the assassin come of his own volition, looking for a towel?

No, he'd asked her where Vlerion was. He had to believe he was in the area. And Levitke would have known who she was tracking. Maybe they were *both* wounded.

"He does not," the assassin said. "That was inappropriate, but I was curious about what you are."

"Just a girl with a sword."

"You are not." He glanced toward her branded hand.

Kaylina looked toward the back of the room, beyond two pools and a couple of statues of gold miners with picks. The steam made it hard to see the wall, but she'd come out of the catacombs back there. She would be hard-pressed to pick out the door since it blended seamlessly with the tile. It had been easier to see from the other side.

"You are not," the assassin repeated, looking toward her face again. "After what I've endured, I am more certain than ever that you might be used as bait to lure him close."

He took a step toward her.

"Maybe so, but are you sure you want that?" Kaylina pointed the tip of her sword toward his wounds. "It looks like you lost in your last confrontation with him."

"I am not the only one wounded. I was chasing him." His brows rose. "*It.*"

"Oh, he's male in both incarnations."

"In one, he's stronger, but that did not keep me from wounding him. He fled here to hide."

Kaylina didn't object aloud, but she had never seen the beast flee anything and thought her earlier guess might be right, that he'd been leading the assassin into a trap.

"What magic possesses him, girl? I know you know."

"Why don't you set down your sword, turn yourself over to the authorities, and we can discuss it?"

That was a lie. She wouldn't discuss anything about Vlerion with this guy. But she wasn't sure what to do. Fight him? Even wounded, he could best her.

"I think not. I simply want him dead." The assassin glanced toward the corners of the room and clucked his tongue.

Even before Kaylina saw or heard anything, her stomach sank

as she realized they weren't alone. The steam had hidden people from her.

"These pools are shallow," the assassin said softly. "You'll not escape into the water this time, girl. And, unless I'm mistaken, your furry allies are too large to come to your rescue."

"You *are* mistaken. I can summon them anytime I wish." Kaylina shifted to put her back to one of the pools. Shadows in the corners of the room stirred as a second assassin stepped out of the steam, his sleeves rolled up to reveal a sagebrush tattoo. Another assassin stepped out of the hallway, blocking her escape route. Also armed with swords, they strode toward her.

Levitke, Kaylina called silently, willing the brand to give her the power to reach the taybarri. *Please tell me you're on your way back with Targon. I need help.*

As if sensing her calling upon magic, the lead assassin glanced at her hand. "I believe you *can* summon them, girl, but not that they will fit down here." He nodded to his men and spoke words that sounded similar to, "Get her," followed by, "We bait our trap."

A muffled roar came from somewhere outside the building. A taybarri roar.

The lead assassin frowned, but the two men arrowing toward Kaylina didn't pause. She cursed and flung her sword at one to slow him down, then turned and jumped into the pool.

He dodged the blade, and it clattered onto the tile floor. At least it stopped him from leaping in after her. She couldn't let one of them catch her again, couldn't let herself be used to ensnare Vlerion.

If she could reach the taybarri, they would be more than a match for three humans, even humans enhanced by whatever altered plant they consumed.

Half swimming and half wading, Kaylina attempted to make it to the far side of the pool before the assassins, but one ran around the corner to head her off. She backed into the middle of the pool.

Glowering, he crouched to spring in after her, but a roar sounded, and he froze.

That roar didn't belong to the taybarri, and it didn't come from outside the building.

The lead assassin cursed as the hidden tile door ground open. The beast charged out of the catacombs entrance and straight for him. Another roar echoed through the bath chamber, far more fury than pain in it.

His short auburn fur damp and sleek, the beast ran, sure-footed on the slick tiles, his muscles rippling. His blue eyes were savage and locked on his target. The lead assassin.

Instead of leaping in after Kaylina, the frozen man remained on the edge, glancing from her to the beast racing toward his leader. She took advantage of his indecision and paddled toward the far side of the pool.

Sword in hand, the assassin leader dropped his towel and delved into a pouch at his belt.

"Look out," Kaylina yelled, certain he had a trick to pull out.

As the beast sprang for him, the assassin threw down a smaller version of the ceramic containers his allies had used near Nakeron Inn. When it exploded, the boom thundered in the confined space. Tiles rattled and water sloshed while a cloud of smoke spread, mingling with the steam.

In the haze, Kaylina lost sight of the beast and the lead assassin, but she heard a loud splash. The man diving into one of the pools? Or the beast knocked in by the power of the explosion?

Kaylina drew her knife and climbed out of her pool. Her sodden sling would be useless, but she had to help if she could. These guys were more than human, and they'd thus far survived their encounters with the beast.

Unfortunately, the smoke and steam made it hard to see what was going on or even where everyone was.

A scream rang from the walls. A scream of pain. It halted

abruptly, and another smaller splash sounded from the pool Kaylina had exited. She crouched and looked toward something starting to sink. A head.

"Shit," she swore and backed up, almost pitching into another pool.

The head belonged to one of the assassin's assistants, but that didn't make it less disturbing.

A moist thud came from the walkway to her side. The rest of the man's body hitting the floor?

Splashes, the sound of someone swimming, came from one of the pools. A heavier splash followed. The beast jumping in after his prey?

Something shattered against one of the walls not far from the catacombs exit, and another boom followed. The floor quaked under Kaylina's feet, and smoke again flooded the chamber. She couldn't see more than a few feet but had a feeling the lead assassin was trying to get away while his men distracted the beast. Or *died* to the beast.

Kaylina backed to the chamber's main exit, thinking to head off the lead assassin if he was running. She didn't want to fight him, but if she could delay him, maybe the beast would finish off the others and have time to take care of him too.

But the only sounds came from the back of the chamber. More splashes and were those footsteps? She realized the leader had to be heading for the catacombs. He'd heard the taybarri roars and had to guess they would attack if he ran outside.

Dashing sweat and water from her eyes, Kaylina followed the wall around the pools. She wanted to avoid the beast but catch the assassin before he slipped out.

Another scream of pain rang out, this time from one of the pools. Splashing—*thrashing*—sounds announced a man dying.

Kaylina reached the back wall but caught a grinding noise over the splashes. The catacombs door closing.

She hurried, her foot slipping more than once on wet tiles, but was too late. The door had closed, and it was so well hidden from this side that she couldn't find it again. She patted around but feared it was too late. The leader had gotten away.

In the pool behind her, water rippled. A grunt sounded, and she spun in time to see the beast pull himself out, landing in a crouch on the walkway.

Blood mingled with the water dripping from him, but he didn't appear as injured as the assassin had suggested. He certainly hadn't been too injured to fight. The smoke had cleared enough to see a body floating in the water behind him, the assassin she'd thrown her sword at.

The beast placed his paws on the wall. Seeking the hidden door? Since he'd just come out of it, maybe he knew how to get through it from this side.

Before he'd done more than push and grunt a couple of times, the beast spotted her through the steam and smoke. His head swung around, his gaze locking onto hers.

"You're right. The lead assassin went through there if you want to catch up with him." Kaylina smiled at him and pointed at the wall, though she had no idea if he was in the right spot.

Fur sleek and wet over his powerful muscles, the beast fixated on her. He'd either given up on finding a way through the door from this side, or... he'd forgotten about his foe. She was the reason he'd come forth tonight, after all. Maybe he felt his duty was done?

"Through there." Kaylina pointed again. "He's getting away."

The beast looked her up and down, all interest in the assassin gone. They were alone now, he with the woman he'd once called his mate.

Kaylina licked lips that had gone dry in the steamy air. She felt vulnerable with her sodden clothes clinging to her body, making her curves easy to see. She knew well from past encounters that the beast was drawn to those curves, drawn to her.

The back of her hand tingled.

What did that mean? If he came at her, there weren't any vines or trees down here that she could call upon for help.

"My female," the beast rasped, stepping closer. His gaze was hungry as it roved over her, but he also sounded weary. How long had he been in that form, hunting the men?

"Your *mate*, right?" Kaylina smiled again, but nerves knotted in her gut. Every time she faced him, she worried it wouldn't end well, that he would catch her and mate with her, leaving her scarred from those claws—or worse. This time, there were no rocks to hide under.

"My mate," he agreed, his maw parting, his sharp fangs far from human. Lust mingled with the savagery in his eyes, and he strode toward her on powerful legs, ready to claim her.

Fear tempted Kaylina to flee, to race around the pools and try to reach the stairs and the exit where the taybarri could help her. But what if Targon was up there with other rangers? Or what if *only* rangers were there, and not Targon? They would think the beast an enemy and attack him. She dared not run.

But he was almost upon her, crouching, as if he would spring at her like a panther, not a man. The hazy air couldn't hide how sharp and deadly those claws were as he raised them.

Her hand tingled again.

She willed it to send soothing power at the beast, to make the raw wildness fade and return Vlerion to her. "Easy, my friend."

His lips rippled with a snarl of objection.

"My mate," she corrected, though she didn't know if he objected to the term or her using her power on him. Before, he'd definitely objected to her attempt to command him to stand down. "I want you but later, all right?"

When you're human, she thought but didn't add.

The beast didn't spring, but he stalked closer. Though she wanted to stand fearless before him, he was so tall and powerful, so deadly, that she couldn't keep from creeping backward until her shoulder blades hit the tile wall.

"My mate," he whispered in that rough animal voice. "Protect you."

"You did. I appreciate that. You're a good mate."

Her hand tingled again. What, did she have to touch him for her power to work? Last time, she'd kissed him, but he'd been half unconscious, so it hadn't seemed that daring.

Mouth parted and fangs visible, the beast looked at her chest. He reached for her, claws leading.

Though she was tempted again to run, she couldn't. Instead, she swallowed and stepped closer, letting him touch her as she reached toward him. He growled with approval, cupping her and shifting closer as she stroked the side of his furred face and tried to hide the tremble in her hand.

"You've worked hard tonight." Kaylina tried to make her voice soothing, to let the power of the brand flow through her fingers and into him. "Why don't you rest for now? The battle isn't yet over."

"Mate first," he said in a hungry snarl and pushed her against the wall, his hard body trapping her.

Fresh fear blasted into her, the tremble not only in her hand but throughout her entire body. She pulled her fingers from his face to plant her palm on his chest.

"Mate *later*." She managed to say it without a shake in her voice, but defiance sparked in his eyes. He wanted her now, not later.

Since it had worked before, she leaned in and kissed him, lips brushing fangs—terrifying fangs. At the same time, she again attempted to call upon her power to soothe him, to make him change back. He returned the kiss, hungry and eager, his muscled body crushing her against the wall.

Soothing him wasn't working. He was too roused. Too *aroused*.

Later, she thought, willing him to back off, to obey her wishes. She was the one with druid blood, damn it. Her ancestors had made him with their curse. He ought to do as she wished.

His weight shifted away from her, his mouth parting from hers, and he gazed into her eyes, confusion there.

"Later," she repeated. "You didn't get the lead assassin yet, and he'll be after you again. He's still a threat."

The beast looked toward the hidden door.

"After you deal with him, we'll mate." And after she lifted the curse. "I'll help you get him, but you need to rest first."

"Rest," he whispered, some of the savagery finally fading from his eyes.

"Yes." Kaylina gripped his shoulder. "Rest."

He lowered to one knee, though his hand—his paw—ran down her body as he dropped, reluctant to release her. His head rested against her abdomen, his claws curled around her waist. From there, he slumped against her.

Sensing the tension—the magic—flowing out of him, she placed her hand on the back of his head and repeated, "Rest."

As he dropped to the floor, gradually shifting from furry beast back into Vlerion, she realized they weren't alone in the chamber.

Clad in black and with his sword out, Captain Targon walked around the pool toward them. The steam stirred in the doorway, revealing another man in dark clothes. Spymaster Sabor.

"So, you *can* control him," he said. "I thought so. Excellent."

The steamy air didn't keep Kaylina from seeing the calculating gleam in the spymaster's dark eyes.

20

Feed and care for your mount before you care for yourself; your
survival will one day depend on the loyalty of the taybarri.
  ~ The Ranger's Guide to Honor, Duty, and Tenets

Kaylina sat astride Levitke's back with Vlerion draped in front of
her, unconscious with his clothes shredded. She'd retrieved her
own sword but had no idea where his boots or sword were and
hoped he remembered when he woke up. Assuming Spymaster
Sabor would *allow* Vlerion his weapons. Sabor rode a brown stallion and was leading Kaylina and the rangers, not to their headquarters but toward the royal castle.

Targon, who rode his taybarri at her side, had protested, saying
Vlerion needed a doctor to stitch up his wounds. All Sabor had
said was that the royal castle had a surgeon, doctor, and pharma-
cist and that he would be adequately tended.

Though the rest of the taybarri who'd been accompanying
Kaylina that night ambled along with them, it was clear Sabor was
in charge. Targon, irritation tightening his eyes, glared at his back,

but it seemed a kingdom's spymaster outranked a kingdom's captain of the rangers.

As they rode through the streets, dawn creeping over the city, Sabor kept glancing back at Kaylina and Vlerion. Waiting for him to wake up? Or wondering if she would veer away and use her sway over the taybarri to convince them to help her escape the city?

That *had* crossed her mind. But she'd already endured being a fugitive on the lam. She didn't want to do anything to incriminate herself. Or Vlerion. Besides, as she kept reminding herself, they hadn't done anything wrong. Sabor wanted to use them.

That wasn't much more appealing than being a fugitive. Kaylina rested her hand on Vlerion's back.

"We caught the end of the battle," Targon said quietly.

She winced. She hadn't been sure how long the two men had been standing in the doorway to the bath chamber, watching across the pools as the beast advanced on her. If they'd seen the end of the fight, that meant they'd seen them together, him touching her, her kissing him. Her cheeks flared with the heat of embarrassment. It wasn't as if she could have done anything else, since touching had been required to assert her power, but she could imagine what they thought of a woman who would kiss a furry, fanged beast.

"Despite knowing about the curse for years," Targon continued, "that was the first time I'd seen him fighting as the beast. He *is* powerful. As evinced by the torn-off head at the bottom of one pool and the body floating in the other." The captain's grimace suggested that even he, surely inured to death, had found that gory.

"Yes. It would be unwise to irritate him." Kaylina spoke firmly, the words more for Sabor than Targon.

The spymaster had to know that, because he looked back, his smug smile unconcerned.

"I don't recommend people irritate him when he's a man either," Targon said. "I seem to remember giving *you* that warning once."

"You did." Kaylina lowered her voice. "What's he planning to do with us?" She nodded toward Sabor.

Though she didn't like Targon, he was closer to an ally for her than Sabor. He at least considered Vlerion a friend as well as a loyal subordinate, and cared what happened to him. Sabor, she had no doubt, didn't care if Vlerion lived or died. All he saw was a potential tool.

"I don't know. Study him maybe. Study you two together. Figure how he can use the beast to help protect the kingdom." Targon eyed Sabor's back and spoke the next sentence so softly she almost missed it. "And further his own ambitions."

"Will he—*we*—be safe?"

Targon turned his palm toward the sky. He didn't know. Great.

The thought of being *studied* didn't appeal in the least to Kaylina. Would the spymaster lock them up so he could have scientists poke and prod at the beast? And order her to soothe him so he could be controlled?

She shuddered at the thought of being used against Vlerion. All she wanted was to help him and be with him.

She closed her eyes and stroked Levitke's fur, again tempted to urge the taybarri to flee, to take her and Vlerion out of the city. But her siblings would be in danger if she acted against the crown's wishes. And Vlerion's mother lived nearby too, his cousins and friends. People that someone like the spymaster could use against him.

Sabor led the taybarri herd away from the last buildings and toward the cliff on which the royal castle perched, overlooking the harbor and the city. Before the road began its ascent, Kaylina noticed someone peeking out of an alcove. The person wore a hood, but she glimpsed a familiar face under it. Mitzy, the Virt girl who'd come to the castle numerous times and who'd tried to recruit Kaylina for the movement.

Targon followed her gaze, and Mitzy ducked back into the alcove.

"The Virts are watching." Kaylina hoped the captain wouldn't feel compelled to chase Mitzy down.

Mitzy mostly seemed like a messenger, and she had argued against getting rid of Kaylina, as one of her allies had wanted to do. One whom the plant had later killed before he could leave Stillguard Castle. Kaylina doubted Mitzy would dare act against her now.

"Yes, that's the third one I've noticed." Targon looked forward, giving no indication that he would pursue Mitzy. "Your taybarri herd was making quite the commotion at the Strigil. Most of the city knows something happened there."

As the taybarri climbed toward the castle, the road growing steep, gravity shifted Vlerion back toward Kaylina. She leaned forward to compensate, imagining being trampled if they both fell off with more taybarri coming behind them, and gripped the thick fur of Levitke's neck to anchor herself.

"I'm expecting an invoice for destruction to the bathhouse," Targon added dryly.

"The lead assassin is still alive. He got away into the catacombs." Maybe Kaylina should have reported that earlier, but by the time the men had walked in, she'd assumed the assassin long gone.

Targon grunted, not sounding surprised. "I'd hoped he'd gotten them all. They blab to you who hired them?"

"I asked, but the assassin wouldn't say. He was fixated on wanting to use me as bait for Vlerion." Kaylina shifted her hand to rest on his back again, worried that he hadn't yet woken. Were his injuries graver than she'd realized?

But he stirred under her touch, as if he'd only been waiting for it to waken. Since he was draped belly-down over Levitke's back, his first view was of fur and the ground.

He issued a disoriented grunt.

"I'm here," Kaylina told him, lest he think some kidnapper had gotten him—though the blue taybarri fur should have told him he was with her or another ranger. "We're being escorted to the royal castle for..." She looked at Targon.

Sabor was the one to answer, though she'd been speaking softly and hadn't expected him to hear. "A chat." He waved an airy hand.

"More likely scientific study," Kaylina muttered as Vlerion shifted around.

"There's not much that's more unmanly than being carried helpless in a woman's lap." Vlerion managed to get a leg over Levitke's back so he could sit up.

"Levitke is doing the carrying," Kaylina pointed out. "And you were more in front of my lap than in it. You'd be heavy for that."

"I see." His back straightened and shoulders tensed as he took in their surroundings—and their company.

The taybarri were cresting the plateau, and the royal castle loomed ahead of them. At Sabor's approach, guards opened the gate without hesitation. Of course they did. He was halfway in charge here, after all. Kaylina remembered the way the aged king had looked to the spymaster for cues when he'd addressed the Kar'ruk and taybarri elders in the courtyard.

"About time you woke up," Targon told Vlerion. "You look rougher than an archery target at the end of the summer."

"I wasn't perforated *that* many times. I don't think." Vlerion touched his side, a wound visible through one of many gashes in his shirt. Most of the rips in his clothing were from the beast changing, prompting muscles to bulge out, but that one had to have been a gift from one of the assassins.

"Not as badly as they were. The lead assassin got away, but

even he has garish claw marks deep in his side. The ones who didn't get away..." Kaylina glanced at Targon again.

"*More* garish claw marks," he said.

"Do you remember much of the night?" Kaylina touched Vlerion's shoulder as they rode through the open gate.

"As usual, it was a blur. I remember seeking the assassin's trail, as I'd planned, and then fighting and..." Vlerion looked toward the cloudy gray sky as he tried to recall the events. "More men showed up. Some were his, but there were guards too. They heard our battle and came. The beast *almost* attacked them, but he—I—had instincts enough to realize we didn't want to be seen, that the guards would turn on us." He waved at the plural pronouns, as if to acknowledge they weren't correct, but he didn't amend them. *We* was probably right. He truly was two different beings when he was Vlerion versus the beast. "We wanted to lead the assassins to the catacombs and take care of them down there. I remember that. We tried to let them think we were more injured than we were, that the assassins had us."

"It was working. I... I guess I screwed up the beast's plans. I'm sorry. I woke up and heard a roar of pain and worried the assassins would catch you after you changed back, and they'd take advantage."

"That would have been a possibility, but the beast was dead set on ending the threat to you. He wouldn't change back until you were safe."

The taybarri came to a stop in the courtyard, Sabor having dismounted and handed the reins of his horse to a stableboy.

Vlerion shifted his gaze to Targon. "Are we being detained for some reason, Captain?"

"*Chatting,*" Targon said sourly.

"Your presence is requested for a brief discussion, Lord Vlerion." Sabor bowed politely to him. "And that of Ms. Korbian as well. It's not a detainment. There may even be snacks. Croissants? Jam? I trust you haven't had breakfast yet?"

"He chewed the head off one of the assassins," Targon grumbled.

Vlerion didn't wince, but he did clench his jaw, and Kaylina was positive he didn't want to be reminded of the details—or for them to be a joke.

"One would think croissants a more palatable meal," Sabor murmured.

"Will they be served in the dungeon?" Kaylina asked.

"Certainly not. The dungeon is reserved for criminals." The way he twitched his eyebrows and looked at her made Kaylina think he still believed her such. Or, if not that, he could envision her becoming one.

This time, *she* clenched her jaw.

"You may leave, Captain," Sabor said. "This won't concern you or the other rangers."

"It involves one of my men."

"Lord Vlerion, I am certain, is capable of handling a chat without you holding his hand. Especially when he has someone far more appealing to do that." Sabor inclined his head toward Kaylina.

Maybe it was meant to be a compliment, but she doubted it. She barely resisted the urge to bare her teeth at him.

"As his commanding officer," Targon said coolly, "I have the right to know what the crown needs that would involve him. What *you* need." His narrowed eyes suggested he knew fully well that the crown and the spymaster might have different desires in this instance.

"He is welcome to report the minutes of our meeting to you if he wishes." Sabor waved toward Targon before pointing Kaylina and Vlerion toward a door that she hadn't been through before. "And do take your furry herd with you when you go, Captain."

Levitke issued a defiant grunt. Several of the taybarri did, and a number of them sat or lay down.

"The furry herd looks like they're sticking with their *anrokk*," Targon said dryly. "I might be able to convince Terkarik to come along for a promise of breakfast." He patted his own mount. "Croissants with jam, perhaps."

A floppy blue-furred ear lifted with interest.

"If that's what you feed them," Sabor said, "they're spoiled."

"They are intelligent beings and eat and do what they wish. Don't forget that if you have more than chatting in mind. You may recall that they've been in the castle before. They helped protect the king and queen from the invaders."

"What I remember is picking up droppings in the great hall," Sabor grumbled.

"I'll wager a thousand liviti that you didn't personally pick up anything."

Sabor smiled thinly. "Privileges of rank."

He shooed the captain toward the gate.

Before budging, Targon looked to Vlerion. Vlerion sighed and nodded to him.

"I'll take that report when you're done," Targon told him and directed his men and the taybarri toward the gate, though many looked back at Kaylina. Even his loyal mount did.

Levitke swished her tail on the cobblestones, not leaving.

Vlerion sighed again and dismounted, noting his bare feet for the first time.

"We weren't sure where you left your boots and sword," Kaylina said, "or I would have grabbed them."

"It's all right. I trust I won't need them for this meeting." Vlerion directed a sour look toward Sabor, but the spymaster was already heading for the door. "Assuming the *droppings* have been cleaned up."

Kaylina also dismounted. She started to give Levitke a

customary pat but felt the urge to turn it into a hug, wrapping her arms around the taybarri's thick neck and pressing her face into the fur for a moment.

When she stepped back, Levitke gazed at her with concerned eyes.

"We'll be fine," Kaylina promised and hoped it wasn't a lie.

21

HE WHO STANDS TO GAIN MOST CAN BE TRUSTED LEAST.
  ~ Grandma Korbian

Kaylina and Vlerion followed Sabor into the castle, the taybarri remaining in the courtyard. As Targon had predicted, they didn't leave.

Too bad they wouldn't be able to do anything if Sabor dragged Kaylina down to the dungeon again. When several uniformed members of the Castle Guard came out of a side hallway and walked beside and behind them, Kaylina felt certain that would be their fate. She and Vlerion would have to negotiate for their freedom from behind bars.

Did Sabor know Vlerion wouldn't likely be able to change into the beast again so soon after his last shifting? She'd once given that information to Captain Targon to defend why she and Vlerion had risked kissing in the preserve. Targon and Sabor didn't seem to like each other, but she wouldn't be surprised if they shared information. Of course, Sabor had proven capable of gathering information whether anyone shared it or not.

Despite her concerns, the spymaster didn't detour toward the door that descended deep into the plateau under the castle. Instead, he took them to a third-floor sitting room with views over the castle wall to the Strait of Torn Towers. With day progressing, the fog was finally clearing.

Nobody waited in the sitting room, but as soon as they arrived, staff bustled in with the promised croissants, coffee, and tea. They laid plates, cups and saucers, and silverware on a low table between two sofas.

"Shall we stay in the room, Spymaster?" One of the guards pointed to a spot beside the door.

Sabor glanced at Vlerion. "No. I trust a ranger and loyal member of the aristocracy won't spring upon me with his blade." He took in Vlerion's bare feet and absent sword belt. "Or fists."

"Yes, Spymaster." The man nodded toward Vlerion, as if to say he hadn't wanted to stand watch anyway, and Kaylina remembered other times when it had been clear the guards didn't want to restrain or fight him. Even though they didn't know about the curse and that he could become the beast, they'd all heard or seen how deadly Vlerion was as a man.

"Besides," Sabor said, as if continuing the conversation, though the guards had shut the door after stepping out, "I intend to make what I believe is an appealing offer to you, Lord Vlerion. And perhaps to you as well, Ms. Korbian. I don't think you'll be tempted to extend your claws toward me." He glanced at her, a tight smile quirking his lips. It did nothing to make him look friendly. "Nor should you."

"I'm clawless." Kaylina looked toward the window and thought of the taybarri—*they* had claws—but the courtyard wasn't visible from this side of the castle.

Had Sabor chosen the room so her furred guardians wouldn't

be able to help if she yelled? Vlerion positioned himself, not quite to block Sabor's view of her but to shield her from him. And protect her if he attacked?

"True," Sabor said, "but you might be able to get that potted rubber tree near the window to do dastardly things to me."

Kaylina probably shouldn't have looked wistfully at the tree's large leaves and imagined them smothering the spymaster.

Sabor's lips twitched. He could surely guess her thoughts.

"What is your offer?" Vlerion asked in a flat tone. "I don't suppose you know who's sending the sage assassins?"

"I am researching that." Sabor sat on one of the sofas and waved to invite them to the one opposite him, then poured himself a cup of coffee. "They rarely come to the kingdom and should know they aren't welcome here. Since our nation is vastly more powerful than their nomadic tribes, even if you include the modest might and standing military of some of the sandsteader settlements—" his disdainful sneer promised he didn't, "—they shouldn't risk the ire of Zaldor. It's brazen of them to hurl explosives about and attack an aristocrat here in our capital." He used a spoon to scoop sugar from a bowl, tapping it on the lip to level it, tipping out a few grains, then tapping it again until the amount suited him precisely, then stirred it into his coffee. "I have alerted the Kingdom Guard to their presence, and they're seeking however many remain."

Vlerion's grunt suggested he didn't think the Guard would be up to the task. After watching the assassins stand toe-to-toe with him, Kaylina didn't either.

"Interesting that you let their leader get away." Sabor watched Vlerion over the top of his cup as he sipped.

Vlerion didn't respond right away and kept his face neutral. Kaylina wondered if he remembered that moment.

"The beast chose that," he finally said.

He didn't look at Kaylina, perhaps not wanting to draw Sabor's attention to her, but he shifted slightly closer to her. The man was as protective of Kaylina as the beast was. It touched her that he cared, and she longed to place a supportive hand on his arm or back, but it worried her that Sabor knew that Vlerion cared. And might use that against him.

"You've no control over what the beast does?" the spymaster asked.

"Once I shift forms, no."

"No? You didn't direct the beast to go after the assassins tonight? Unless I've the order of events incorrect, they didn't start the night attacking you. You sought them out and convinced your furry half to hunt them down." Sabor looked at Kaylina, as if for confirmation.

Not wanting to give him anything, she attempted to keep her face as masked as Vlerion's. How did Sabor know as much as he did? She knew he had a spy—at least one—among the rangers, but she and Vlerion had spoken of his plans in private.

"I sought them out as a man because they attacked Kaylina in a park yesterday."

"And did you find them? As a man?" Sabor waved toward the sofa and drinks again. "Please, you must be hungry after a night of such vigorous activities."

Kaylina looked wistfully at the croissants and jam, her stomach rumbling. It *had* been a long night. She longed to eat and also to return to help her siblings with the grand opening.

"What is the point of these questions?" Vlerion didn't take a step toward the food. "As a ranger, it's my duty to assist the crown against enemies, but you've no reason to interrogate me about my private life."

"Your private life creeps into the realm of kingdom security. Do you deny that the beast usually has no control over his targets and is as much a threat to innocent subjects as enemies?"

"I do not deny that, but the beast killed no innocents last night. Of that I am certain. He was focused only on the assassins."

"Because they threatened his mate." Sabor smiled before sipping again, as if he'd made his point.

What *was* his point? Something about the link between Kaylina and Vlerion?

"They're also trying to kill *me*." Vlerion touched his chest, though Kaylina knew that he wouldn't have risked calling forth the beast only to defend himself. Like her, he found it easier to fight for others than for himself.

"Of course," Sabor murmured, his smile lingering as he sipped. "But since, on Ms. Korbian's behalf, you seem able to focus the beast in the way that it could not be focused before, I am most interested in discussing this matter. Should she order it, would you —or the beast—go after a certain enemy? One who might not necessarily threaten her specifically but one who is a threat to the kingdom?"

"She's not my commanding officer."

"No, and I think the beast could not be directed by Captain Targon either. Perhaps I should have said *if she requests it*, as a favor, would the beast do it?" Sabor's tone shifted to a higher pitch to emulate a woman. "Dear mate of mine, those Kar'ruk invaders are vexing me. Please slay them mercilessly, won't you?"

"That's a horrible impression of me," Kaylina muttered. "I don't use the word *dear*. Or *vex*."

Vlerion smiled slightly at her, probably thinking how she might not use the word vex but she could inspire the emotion in others, but he didn't make the joke. He probably didn't want to banter in front of Sabor or do anything to emphasize his feelings for her. Though he did that whether he spoke or not, in the way he stood so close to her.

"For the good of the kingdom," Sabor said, "which you've

admitted you're sworn to, I would like to do some experimentation."

Kaylina scowled, remembering her concern about scientists studying her. *Them.*

"I invite the two of you to enjoy a special room in the castle, one with sturdy walls and a metal door which I have had further reinforced."

"That sounds like a dungeon cell," Kaylina said.

"It is not. It's in a tower with a window and a view. I have had bars placed over the window but only for the safety of those in the castle. Should you turn into the beast, I have to ensure you can't escape and harm the king and queen or anyone here. After all, this is my idea, and I'd be responsible for anything that happened."

"Why would I turn into the beast in a room in the castle?"

"It's a furnished room with a bed." Sabor extended a hand toward Kaylina.

Instead of looking at her, Vlerion squinted suspiciously at Sabor.

Kaylina might have worn a similar look.

"I understand lust is as likely to arouse the beast as anger or other strong emotions," Sabor said dispassionately, like someone who'd never experienced lust himself. "And with such a voluptuous female nearby, you've had to work hard to sublimate it."

Vlerion crossed his arms over his chest again, his jaw tight, and didn't respond. His wide stance and cold gaze said he didn't want to continue this conversation.

"I'm offering you two a safe place where you can do as you wish without worrying about hurting others. That tower isn't soundproof, but it's well insulated and removed from the main part of the castle. You wouldn't need to worry about being interrupted. You—or the beast—could be with your mate." Sabor extended his hand toward Kaylina again.

Her mouth had gone dry with anxiety or terror or... she didn't quite know. What if Vlerion said *yes* to the offer?

As much as she longed to be with him, she feared the beast—and what he would do to her if he mated with her in that state. Even if a part of her found that more intriguing than she should, she thought often of Lady Isla's words that not all women survived mating with one of the beasts. And the scars on her neck spoke of her own experiences with Vlerion's father. For all Kaylina knew, she had scars all over her body from his claws. Who knew how harrowing those sexual encounters had been?

"I'm not going to let the beast touch Kaylina. Touch *any* woman." Vlerion's voice was firm, but he did glance at her, a hint of emotion in his blue eyes. Angst? Regret? Anxiety? Because he knew the beast had touched her before? He might not remember it, but he'd seen the claw rip in her shirt.

She hadn't blamed him for that, not then and not now.

Sabor cocked his head, as if surprised that Vlerion hadn't jumped on his offer.

"I'm also not interested in mating with the beast," Kaylina told Sabor, though he hadn't given any indication that he cared what she thought, that any part of this decision was up to her. His focus was solely on Vlerion, other than to point at her, offering her as a prize.

She loathed the man.

"No?" Sabor asked with the lip-quirk smile. "Some women fantasize about such things."

"I don't fantasize about having sex with furry beings, thank you very much." Kaylina couldn't believe she was discussing such a topic with a near stranger. A near stranger who didn't have her best interests in mind. She had no doubt of that. "Besides, Lady Isla promises that being with one of the beasts is not a good idea."

"Oh, I'm aware. She's quite determined to make sure you two can't consummate a physical relationship, isn't she?"

Vlerion scowled, and Kaylina wished she hadn't brought up his mother.

"I understand she's hired kidnappers and is trying to oust your woman from this part of the kingdom, Lord Vlerion." Sabor shook his head, as if he were deeply sympathetic, but the calculation remained in his eyes, as it had throughout this conversation. "I could talk to her on your behalf, let her know how safe the tower would be for—"

"Stay away from my mother," Vlerion snapped.

"She's trying to get your woman out of your life. I wouldn't do that. If Korbian can control you once you've turned beast, we can use you. It's time to drive fear into the Virts once and for all. They're not afraid enough of the hangings— they use it as ammunition to win sympathizers... Even some of the nobles are speaking up for them. But they'll fear the beast. We *know* from those desperate newspaper articles they printed that they do. If the beast starts killing them..."

"I'm not a murderer," Vlerion said. "I won't allow myself to be used dishonorably."

"Even if Korbian kisses you?" Sabor arched his eyebrows. "Wouldn't you then?"

"*She* would not use me dishonorably."

"Even if I could talk your mother into leaving her alone so you two could be together? You could be together every night as long as you changed now and then to deal with the enemies of the crown. In the room I've had made." He issued an oily smile.

Bastard.

"You should be with the woman you love, with nothing standing between you," Sabor continued.

Kaylina and Vlerion hadn't used that word with each other before, and she didn't like hearing it come out of Sabor's mouth. His tone wasn't mocking, but it was... smug. Knowing. He felt certain Vlerion would come around to his way of thinking.

But Vlerion was angry. Oh, he kept his aloof mask, as he'd practiced so often, but Kaylina could sense the tension emanating from him.

"I have to believe you would appreciate it if I ameliorated the situation for you," Sabor added.

"I would not." Vlerion stepped around the couch so that he loomed close to the spymaster.

With his muscles bulging under his sleeves and the tendons standing out in his neck, Vlerion would have intimidated most people. Sabor sipped again from his mug, appearing confident that Vlerion wouldn't move against him.

"You will stay away from her," Vlerion said.

"If that is your wish, certainly." Maybe the looming *did* unsettle Sabor, because he set the mug down and stood, his hands at his sides and whatever weapons he might have secreted under his tunic. "But you *do* want to be with Ms. Korbian, do you not? I thought this generous offer would appeal to you. After all, we don't invite other rangers to spend the night in the castle. This is an honor and an opportunity for you to be with a beautiful young woman without worrying about repercussions."

Sabor shifted to stand almost side-by-side with Vlerion to look toward Kaylina, inviting *him* to look too. "Even I, so rarely moved by such things, can appreciate her beauty. There's a certain exoticness to her, is there not? Originally, I thought it was her southern roots, but perhaps it is the druid blood within her that lends her that intriguing and tantalizing appeal. She must excite you." Though he faced Kaylina, he watched Vlerion sidelong. "You must wake nights, hard with desire, devastated that she isn't within your arms. Look at her voluptuous—"

"Would you mind *not* speaking about me like I'm a statue instead of a person standing in the room with you?" Kaylina asked.

Irritation flickered in Sabor's eyes, but all he said was, "I'll admit her tongue is sharp. *It's* certainly not responsible for her appeal, but some men might enjoy taming the likes of her. Surely, the *beast* would."

Kaylina reached for her sling. By all the craters in the moon, she wanted to brain him with a lead round.

"Cease." Vlerion gripped Sabor's arm, fingers tight, and something sparked in his eyes. The wild glint that heralded the beast's emergence.

It hadn't been that long since his change, but maybe it had been long enough. Or maybe Vlerion had been wrong about his hypothesis. Maybe the beast *could* come again within hours of changing.

Alarm flashed across the spymaster's face. Maybe he knew he'd gone too far. How much trouble would Vlerion get in for attacking him?

Kaylina bit her lip and didn't lift her sling. As a commoner with a knack for irritating aristocrats, she would get in a lot *more* trouble for attacking the spymaster.

"Just ask me what you want, Sabor," Vlerion said softly. Dangerously. "If it's for the good of the kingdom, I'll do my best to help. You don't have to play games and try to manipulate me. The kingdom has my oath." His voice was taut with irritation, and it sounded hard for him to make himself add, "You have my sword."

"The kingdom wants the *beast's* sword. Fangs."

"The kingdom does or you do?"

"I *am* the kingdom. I serve the crown, the same as you."

"I wonder," Vlerion murmured.

Sabor jerked his arm as he stepped away. Vlerion released him, and he almost overcompensated—maybe he'd expected resistance—but he recovered easily enough. "You don't have to accept my offer. I'm not here to manipulate you."

Vlerion scoffed.

Sabor lifted a hand—an apology. "All right, it's my nature and what I do. Manipulation is how I serve the crown and learn everything I do to keep its interests safe. But can you blame me for wanting the beast to also serve? You're an excellent warrior, Vlerion, and a boon to the rangers, but when you change into that form, you're nearly indestructible. Even those with magical weapons, like the Kar'ruk, and magically enchanted bodies, like the sage assassins, aren't a match for the beast. I'll work with you to get what I want, and I'll make sure you—or the beast—are rewarded with what *you* want." He pointed his chin at Kaylina. "If it's not a secured room in the tower, then tell me where. I'll set it up."

Vlerion stepped away from Sabor. "It's too dangerous. Too dangerous for Kaylina and for all around when the beast changes. If you think you can control things when that curse unfurls... you're foolish. The druids were too powerful." He waved for Kaylina to come with him and faced the door. "Find another way for me to serve, Sabor," Vlerion said over his shoulder as he walked out.

Kaylina followed him, but she couldn't keep from looking back to gauge Sabor's reaction—to see if he would *let* them walk out.

He did, but he had parting words for her, his first that were for her alone instead of for Vlerion's benefit. "Watch out for kidnappers, Ms. Korbian."

The urge to fire her sling at him returned. Instead, she made the same rude gesture she'd once given Jana Bloomlong.

Sabor snorted and returned to his coffee.

22

THE LIES THAT TARGET OUR INSECURITIES ARE MOST LIKELY TO BE believed.

~ Lord Professor Varhesson, Port Jirador University

"I hate him," Kaylina announced as the guards accompanied her and Vlerion out of the royal castle and into the courtyard where the taybarri waited.

Some were in the stable, noshing from buckets alongside the horses. Maybe they found oats more appealing than protein pellets. The stable boy, who might have tried to shoo the taybarri away or presume to put them in stalls, was rubbing his arm. Because one of them had bitten him? Levitke *was* swishing her tail in irritation, standing outside the stable—she might have refused to be lured in. Fortunately, there weren't any tears in the boy's clothing, so she must have only used her lips to nip him. Kaylina wished someone would nip Spymaster Sabor.

"I am displeased with his new interest in me—in us," Vlerion said, staying vague with witnesses within hearing distance.

"You hate him too."

He managed a faint smile, though the tension hadn't left his body. "I almost hoped you would use your sling on him. I saw you draw it."

The guards that had been escorting them eyed the taybarri herd and stopped at the door of the stable.

"I was tempted." Kaylina walked between Levitke and Crenoch —Vlerion's taybarri hadn't been there earlier, but Targon might have sent him, or the rest of the herd might have called him some- how. Now, the two taybarri stood in the shadow of the stable while the others finished their snacks. "I didn't want to be a fugitive again though. Or get you in trouble. I could tell you would have protected me from him."

"From anything." Vlerion rested a hand on her shoulder, drawing her under the overhanging roof of the stable. "I'm trou- bled that he's not only aware of you now but wants to use you."

"So he can effectively use *you.*"

No, not him. The beast. As Vlerion had pointed out, the king and his spymaster, whether it was ideal or not, already had his vow. The beast... was another matter.

"Yes." Vlerion stepped closer and leaned his forehead against the top of her head. "I regret that you've been wrapped up in my life."

With the taybarri to either side of them, and the stable roof overhanging above, they had a semblance of privacy, though Kaylina supposed the guards walking on the castle walls might have glimpses of them. That didn't keep her from leaning into him, relishing being close, as she always did, whether it was wise or not. The part of her that wished she'd used her sling on Sabor also wished Vlerion had sprung upon him, beating him until he realized he'd made a mistake in trying to manipulate them.

"When I left home, I dreamed of proving myself and becoming somebody," Kaylina murmured. "Now, I wish I was nobody."

"Not even a famous mead maker?"

"Well... I wish I was nobody that the government cared about."

"So, you haven't given up your dream."

"I guess not."

"There have been times that I've wished... you would commit fully to becoming a ranger, so that you'd always be near, doing the same work as I."

"And then you came to your senses and realized how much better I am at making mead than chasing down bad guys?" Kaylina spoke the words lightly, but her voice might have been firmer when she added, "And how much more I want to do that."

"You could learn to very effectively chase down bad guys, if you wished, but I do understand that your dream is different from mine."

"And that's okay, right?"

"It is."

She let out a breath she hadn't realized she'd been holding. Somewhere along the way, Vlerion had started caring about more than protecting her, something she'd often wondered if his beast side compelled him to do. But Vlerion, the man, understood her dream and wanted to support her in pursuing it. That meant a lot to her.

"I know this is your big night." Vlerion rubbed the back of her neck. "When the taybarri have finished eating, you can head to Stillguard Castle. I'll tell Targon you can't train today."

"Thank you." Kaylina slumped against him, appreciating his support—and the way his touch ignited fire in her nerves, making her want more than they could have.

"I must also consider..." Vlerion sighed softly, his fingers stilling.

"Sabor's offer?"

"No. You know I want you to be with *me*, not the beast. And not in such a way that we would owe Sabor a favor. I do not trust him at all. He may wish to use the beast to end the Virt threat, but that is not where his ambitions end."

"I agree."

"What I am considering is if I should, after your grand opening, let my mother's ham-fisted kidnappers succeed in taking you away from the capital. At least until things settle here."

Kaylina leaned back so she could effectively scowl up at him. "No, you should not. Even if *you* would let them, *I* wouldn't. Nor would the castle."

"You're ensconced in that castle less often than you should be," he said, more amused than deterred by her scowl.

"Only because I heard *someone* roar in pain and was afraid he needed help." Which, she reluctantly admitted, she hadn't given him. Not for lack of *wanting* to assist, but she was the reason his enemy had gotten away. When she'd bumbled down into the bathhouse, the beast had been effectively luring the sage assassins into the catacombs for whatever trap he'd laid.

"It's not wise to run out into the night when you hear roars of any kind." Vlerion gazed at her through his lashes, not appearing irked or frustrated that she'd joined him.

"We've discussed before that wisdom isn't a trait I possess in great amounts." Kaylina leaned her head back, wishing he would resume the neck rub.

"That is true. And I understand the need to protect those you care about." His half-lidded gaze drooped to her chest, making her realize she was leaning in a way that thrust it toward him.

"And those you lust after?" She straightened, glad the taybarri were indifferent to embracing humans next to them.

Crenoch yawned.

"They can be the same." Vlerion stepped closer, pulling her into an embrace. "I wish I could come tonight to support you in your mead endeavor."

"And spend the night afterward?" That was what *she* wished.

"The plant would never allow that, but yes. You know what I want."

"Me."

"Yes," he said, his voice husky.

She needed to step back, mount Levitke, and leave before any dumb ideas came to mind, like scooting into the stable with him so they could get intimate in one of the stalls. If they did, Sabor might come out to offer them that room again. She didn't want that, but she wished...

"How have you... or how did you... you've had relationships with women before, right?" Kaylina caught herself asking.

"Not relationships, no." Vlerion looked toward the courtyard wall. Glaring at someone presuming to peer in their direction?

"But sex, right?"

"Yes."

"And it didn't rouse... you know."

"Once, when I was younger, it did. That taught me to be careful."

"Was that, uhm, Lady Ghara?" Maybe Kaylina shouldn't have pried, but curiosity loosened her tongue. Curiosity and wondering if there was any way they could be together without the beast showing up.

"No. With her and some others, I've been able to find... release, if not total satisfaction, without changing."

"Because you weren't so into it that you were..." She lifted a hand from his shoulder, waving at the air.

He had no trouble interpreting it. "Correct."

She shouldn't have been smug that Ghara hadn't excited him so much that the beast had erupted, but after the insulting things Ghara had said, Kaylina couldn't help but feel pleased that she stirred Vlerion more. She shouldn't have because if she hadn't, they could have been together. But she wanted him to want her like nobody else. She *wanted* to excite and arouse him.

Her fingers curled around his shoulders as she imagined what being with him would be like. Based on how she'd felt with their brief kisses and touches so far, she believed it would be amazing.

"I've thought a few times," he murmured, watching her face, her lips, and perhaps following her thoughts, "about the rewards I've promised you."

"Yeah, I think about those too."

"I've thought that if I took a drug to calm my libido, I might satisfy *you* without endangering you, but I doubt even a dulling medicine could tame what I feel when I'm close to you. Even when I'm not close to you, you're in my thoughts and can evoke... Well, in the park, it wasn't thoughts of protection that brought forth the beast to hunt the assassin. I was indignant and *did* want to end the threat to you, but it was remembering you in the druid ruins, your lips trailing over my flesh, your hand stroking me, arousing me."

She flushed, turned on by his admission but also ashamed by the memory. "I shouldn't have done that. It was presumptuous."

"It was exquisite."

"It wasn't what you wanted."

"It was what I wanted more than anything else," he admitted ruefully. "*You're* what I want more than anything else. If I could ensure I wouldn't hurt you..."

"You'd accept Sabor's offer?"

"Of the room, maybe. To do his bidding, no."

Her heart pounded at the thought of a private tower room with Vlerion. But it wouldn't be *only* with Vlerion. At first, it might be, but they both knew the beast would come, and the beast... She wasn't yet sure if she could truly control the beast. Keep him from hurting her. Even if she could, she wanted Vlerion, the man who'd sung to her, who protected her from enemies, and who'd given her the perfect gifts of a sword and yeast for her mead.

"I would make sacrifices if it meant I could have you," he whispered, bending to kiss her neck.

"I know. I want you too. I want—"

Crenoch stirred, shifting his rump so he could swat Vlerion in the back with his tail.

Vlerion scowled but noticed someone approaching and released Kaylina.

As always, she struggled to lower her arms and let him go, but a guard was walking up with something in his hand. An envelope.

Assuming it was for Vlerion, she straightened her clothing—how had her shirt gotten rucked halfway up her back?—and took another step away.

The guard glanced warily at Vlerion, then extended the envelope to her.

"Spymaster Sabor said to ride after you and give this to you." A bemused expression crossed the guard's face as he glanced from Kaylina to the castle gate.

Yeah, he hadn't had to ride far to find her.

Not commenting on that, Kaylina opened the envelope and stepped closer to Vlerion so she could share whatever message it contained. After Sabor had mostly ignored her, using her only as a prize, she was surprised he'd sent something to her.

"Uhm, you're to read that alone," the guard told her, glancing at Vlerion. "The spymaster said it's a matter of kingdom security."

"Uh-huh." Kaylina was inclined to lean against Vlerion so he could read with her, but he was far more loyal to the crown—and the notion of kingdom security—than she, and he stepped away, nodding for her to read it in private.

Speak to him, and bring him around to my way of thinking.

Kaylina almost snorted, but the next line caught her attention.

I can do more than ensure no kidnappers trouble you and provide a way for the beast to satisfy your sexual needs. I have means and many, many capable researchers at my disposal. I may soon have knowledge that you would find useful in lifting his curse, which I will allow to happen once the threat of the rebels is past. I already know something you should be aware of. The Symbol of the Sentinel, as the brand you've received is called, binds you irrevocably to that plant until it releases you. It conveys power, but there's a downside. Your life force is linked with its, and if it dies, you die. You'd better not forget to water it.

Kaylina stared at the words in horror. Were they true? Or was Sabor trying to manipulate her, the same as he'd tried to manipulate Vlerion?

"Oh, there's no doubt he's doing that," she muttered. The question was if the words were lies or truth.

23

RELIABLE ALLIES FORTIFY BETTER THAN STONE WALLS.
  ~ Ranger Sergeant Myorkdar the Grim

"You don't have to escort me all the way back." Kaylina rode side-by-side with Vlerion, following the river trail toward Stillguard Castle. She didn't mind the company, but she always worried when he came anywhere near the plant. He also hadn't yet seen Doc Penderbrock about his injuries.

"I'll see you to the door to make sure kidnappers don't spring out." Grim-faced after their interactions with Spymaster Sabor, Vlerion looked toward the north. In the direction of Havartaft Estate and his mother?

"I do hate springing kidnappers, especially ones who pretend they're interested in our food and our mead, only to use that against me."

"Feigned mead interest is the primary reason they irked you?" His gaze shifted to her, and he managed a smile.

"The mead *and* the food. My brother was put out that they inquired about his mint-cherry glaze to bait me into a trap."

"I might have thought their intent to grab and gag you would have been more egregious. With cloth stuffed in your mouth, you wouldn't have been able to call them pirates."

"That *would* have been horrible. I would have had to find other ways to demonstrate my irreverence."

"Perhaps by pelting them in the skulls with lead rounds."

"Perhaps."

Kaylina beamed a smile at him, in a better mood than she should have been, given the day she'd had. But now that they knew the source of the kidnappers, Vlerion ought to be able to talk to his mother and put an end to them, and she was on her way back to Stillguard Castle in time to help with the grand opening. Further, the plant had implied it would allow people to sit and enjoy the mead and food without attacking them, as long as they didn't represent a threat to her.

Her smile faltered when she remembered Sabor's note and parting words about the plant. The *sentinel.* She glanced at her brand. *Was* her life now tied to its?

Given how many people had tried to maim and remove the plant from the castle over the years, that might not matter. The thing could take care of itself. It had not only shocked her but used its vines to *kill* people with ill intent. And it had lived for centuries, maintaining its curse on the castle. And keeping an eye on the city and humanity in general? Probably.

"I should take these taybarri back to ranger headquarters after dropping you off." Vlerion waved to the herd following them. Kaylina's self-appointed bodyguards. "They are bonded to rangers who are doubtless wondering where their mounts have gone. I don't know if I would succeed, however, in convincing them to leave."

"They're also determined to help with springing kidnappers."

"I think that's Sergeant Zhani's Blu," Vlerion mused. "And is that Jankarr's Zavron?"

Kaylina spread her arms, feeling guilty about collecting taybarri who had other duties.

"Why don't you guys go home with Vlerion and get some rest?" she suggested to them. As much as she appreciated the body-guards, they might intimidate diners coming for the grand open-ing. Besides, the castle—the *sentinel*—ought to keep an eye out for her. "I'll bring you some leftovers tomorrow—and honey drops too."

At the mention of treats, the taybarri whuffed with interest.

"Will you also bring *me* leftovers?" Vlerion asked.

"Yes. Do you want honey drops too?"

"The strawberry ones."

"I can arrange that."

He smiled wistfully. "I wish I could come tonight to enjoy the event."

"I wish that too."

Stillguard Castle came into view, the glow of the tower not visible by day or from the back approach, but Kaylina trusted it remained. Even so, she would go up and feed the plant later. She had more reason than ever to ensure it stayed healthy and happy.

"Do you think Sabor will be able to figure out who hired the assassins?" Kaylina asked. "Do you think he *cares* enough to do so?"

"I believe he cares little about me, but having sage assassins traipsing through the capital is a matter of kingdom security. They might pick up other contracts while they're here. He's aware that the Virts still want the king gone. Sabor *should* be looking into the assassins and who brought them into Zaldorian territory."

"Hm." Kaylina had little faith that Sabor would do anything helpful and wondered if *she* could somehow ferret out the infor-mation. Of course, she hadn't yet figured out how to lift Vlerion's curse, so she couldn't proclaim herself an expert researcher. As soon as the grand opening passed, she vowed to drag Frayvar to a library to delve into books on druid magic. Specifically, druid *curses*.

"I'll look into it myself after I visit my mother and tell her to call off her hounds," Vlerion said.

"Good." Kaylina touched Levitke's shoulder to guide her toward the front entrance. She wanted to see if Frayvar had set out the mead list she'd made as well as his dinner menu.

A sandy-haired boy stood out front, peering through the open gate. That was closer than most people got to the cursed castle. Maybe he could smell the scents of Frayvar's cooking wafting out and hoped for a taste.

When the boy noticed the herd of taybarri approaching, he spun toward them.

"Oh, a ranger!" he blurted, looking at Vlerion. "Will you help, my lord? Some thugs attacked my family's cart at the market." He glanced at Kaylina and pointed down the street behind them. "They're shaking down my dad for money. It would be moon blessed if a ranger and all his taybarri showed up."

"These are not all *my* taybarri," Vlerion said mildly. He glanced at Kaylina, but maybe he didn't want to explain what an *anrokk* was to a boy with troubles on his mind.

"I'll be fine." Kaylina dismounted and waved for Vlerion to deal with the problem.

The boy nodded eagerly, glancing at her again and also into the courtyard for some reason.

She thought of the kidnappers who'd feigned interest in the menu to catch her off guard and looked at Vlerion, almost saying something, but the boy ran around the herd and headed down the street, waving urgently for Vlerion to follow.

Vlerion noticed Kaylina's gaze and lifted a single finger. Promising he would return soon?

"Don't worry about me. Protect those without fangs and claws to call upon." Kaylina pointed to indicate the taybarri, though the description also applied to the beast.

"Hurry, my lord," the boy urged. "They'll get away with all our coin!"

Vlerion's eyelids drooped slightly. Because the boy presumed to order an aristocrat? Or because he thought the kid was up to something? Either way, he *did* follow.

"You'd better wait out here," Kaylina told the taybarri—only Crenoch went off with Vlerion.

She looked toward the tower. From the front of the castle, the purple glow was visible. Every time she returned and saw it hadn't turned back to red, she was relieved, but the plant could be in a good mood and still attack rangers—and their mounts.

Levitke followed her gaze and whuffed, though her nostrils also twitched in the direction of the kitchen.

"I'll bring some honey out in a bit," Kaylina said. "And you all can have whatever leftovers there are tonight after the diners leave."

That prompted several agreeable whuffs.

Kaylina gripped the hilt of her sword and walked warily through the gate. She peered left and right into the courtyard, half-expecting a trap.

A man with a pad of paper and a pencil stood between the gate and the front door. He was alternately looking toward the tables and chairs set up in the courtyard and a menu posted on a stand. He *hmmed* to himself and scribbled on his paper, like an auditor coming to check the numbers. Or maybe some building-code enforcer, determining if the castle was structurally stable enough for guests to visit.

"May I help you?" Kaylina didn't see Frayvar or Silana and assumed they were prepping in the kitchen.

"Ah, yes." The man turned, holding up the pad of paper and

pointing the pencil to the front page. Was that actual writing? It looked like nonsensical scribbles. "Ms. Korbian?"

"Yes?" she asked warily, looking around the courtyard again as he approached.

"You're wanted back in your home of the Vamorka Islands." He put away the pencil and withdrew a piece of cloth. Was that another *gag*? "If you can see here—"

Movement from the walls by the gate drew Kaylina's eye, and she jumped, not hearing the rest. Damn it, four men with truncheons had been pressed into the shadows, two on either side of the gatehouse. If not for the pencil-wielder, she would have noticed them right away.

One man leaped to close the gate before the taybarri could surge through.

Drawing her sword, Kaylina scurried away from the intruders. The pencil man tossed the pad to the ground and pushed aside his jacket to withdraw a truncheon of his own.

"Put down the sword, girl," he said as Kaylina backed until a table blocked her way. "We can make this rough if you want, but it doesn't have to be that way."

"I'm not going anywhere." She raised the blade and crouched to defend herself. "It's my grand opening."

She thought about calling for her siblings, but they weren't warriors. They would only be hurt if they rushed out.

A clang from the gate made two of the men jump. Levitke and two other taybarri had bashed their shoulders against it. Rusty and bent after centuries of neglect, it rattled alarmingly. They might break it. Kaylina knew from experience that it didn't lock. If she could manage to get past the two men blocking it, she could open it for her allies.

"Even if you catch me," she said, "the taybarri won't let you out of here. They're my friends."

The pencil man scoffed. "They serve the rangers."

Levitke snarled, and he flinched, doubt creeping into his eyes.

"You sure we're getting paid enough for this?" one of the thugs muttered, glancing from the taybarri ramming against the gate and up to the tower.

Was that a vine slithering through the window and down the outer wall?

"Tadzt said we were," another replied.

"He's full of—"

Levitke snarled again.

"Tadzt?" one asked the pencil man uncertainly.

"Get her, you idiots." Tadzt pointed his truncheon at Kaylina, though he didn't advance on her himself. "We'll go out the back to the boat. Those animals won't catch us."

The vine reached the ground and slithered toward him. He didn't see it approaching.

"Go out the back gate by yourselves, and never come back. If you want to live." Maybe Kaylina shouldn't have pointed out the vine, but she did. As much as she appreciated the plant's protection, she didn't want to watch it strangle more people, especially not in the courtyard. This was the heart of her grand opening, damn it.

At first, Tadzt didn't look, probably suspecting her of a trick. But one of his men swore and pointed at the vine creeping toward him.

Tadzt spotted it, eyes bulging, and skittered back. "What the—"

Someone who must have come in through the back gate ran out from behind the corner of the keep and sprang upon him. Vlerion.

He ripped the truncheon out of Tadzt's grasp as he grabbed him from behind and held a dagger to his throat.

Kaylina lifted a hand, afraid she would spot the glint in his eyes that meant the beast was close to the surface. But Vlerion's blue eyes were cool and calm, and she suspected he'd known all along the boy was part of a ruse.

"Drop your weapons," he told the other kidnappers.

They'd halted their advance, looking in horror from Vlerion to the vine and back. It was still creeping toward Tadzt. At least it seemed to consider him more of a threat than Vlerion.

Kaylina jogged toward the vine and stood to block it. Not that it couldn't easily get around her.

"We've got this handled," she told it and willed the words to travel to the plant in the tower as well.

Only then did she notice more vines had sprouted from the wall near the gate, waving in the air, threatening the other kidnappers.

"Drop your weapons, and leave if you wish to escape with your lives," Vlerion said. "The cursed castle protects Kaylina Korbian, she who is possessed of druid blood."

From the wide-eyed looks the men shared with each other, Kaylina doubted anyone had mentioned that information to them. One spotted the vines stretching from the courtyard wall behind them. He dropped his truncheon and ran toward Vlerion before jerking to a stop, probably as intimidated by his cold eyes as by the magical plant.

"You can tell the person who hired you that Ms. Korbian is not *going* anywhere," Vlerion said. "She belongs here now." *With me*, his eyes said, his gaze shifting to her, intense and protective.

One of the vines flicked its tip. Maybe it felt the same way.

Several of the taybarri growled. In agreement?

Maybe Kaylina shouldn't have wanted so many people—and beings—deciding that she should be here when she hadn't yet decided for herself that she wanted to stay in Port Jirador forever. As fraught as her existence in the north had been so far, she'd longed for home and her bed above the Spitting Gull more than once. But, at the same time, she *was* starting to feel tied to this place, to the strange plant, to the taybarri, and, of course, to Vlerion.

The brand on her hand tingled. Not threateningly or alarmingly but to draw notice.

"I'd feel better about you if I hadn't read Sabor's letter," she muttered to it.

More rattles came from the front gate. A taybarri was nosing the bars—trying to figure out how to open it without ripping it off the hinges? Not long ago, they'd done that to the portcullis at the royal castle. Maybe, because Kaylina was leasing this place, the taybarri were being more polite about forcing their way in. Or because they saw that Vlerion had the situation in hand. Vlerion and the *plant*.

One of the vines flicked again, this time stretching toward the closest man's neck. He'd already dropped his truncheon, but at this movement, he yelled and ran through the courtyard. He weaved between tables and knocked over a chair in his haste to escape through the back gate, to whatever boat was waiting for them in the river.

Vlerion, his dagger still to Tadzt's throat, gazed coolly at the others. The remaining three also ran toward the back gate.

Levitke whuffed. It sounded like a question.

"Let them go," Vlerion said, though he tightened his grip on Tadzt. "You will return the coin to the person who hired you. He serves Lady Isla, who *mistakenly* thought that it would be wise to kidnap my..."

Kaylina raised her eyebrows, recalling another time when Vlerion hadn't known what to call her. Unlike the beast, who knew exactly what she was to him, Vlerion hadn't quite figured it out yet.

"My *mate*," Vlerion said, his eyes meeting hers, charged with feeling.

At the words, a tingle of warmth flowed through Kaylina, pleasure at the admission that he felt linked with her. Maybe he *had* figured it out.

Tadzt licked his lips, eyeing the hand holding the blade to his neck. "We did gather forces and make an attempt to fulfill the deal. I can only return ninety percent. My men must be paid."

"Your men *lived* today when they could have all died." Vlerion removed the dagger, but he didn't release Tadzt as he pointed it at the vines. They'd stopped advancing, but they remained, like guard dogs on the alert, watching to see if they were needed. And watching Vlerion, Kaylina feared.

"Ninety percent." Tadzt licked his lips again, glancing over his shoulder to check Vlerion's response. "I can return ninety percent of the fee."

Vlerion snorted and released him. "Fine. My mother deserves to lose something for this scheme."

"Thank you, my lord." Tadzt bobbed his head toward Vlerion and sprinted off in the direction the others had gone.

The taybarri who'd been fiddling with the latch succeeded in releasing it, and the gate creaked open. He stood shoulder to shoulder with Levitke, the others crowded behind, and gazed in, but they looked toward the vines and didn't enter the courtyard.

Vlerion shouldn't have been in there either, but as soon as the last of the kidnappers disappeared, he strode forward, dagger now sheathed, and engulfed Kaylina in a hug.

Though she worried the plant wouldn't like that and, with the other threat gone, would send its vines after him, she returned the embrace. She might have survived the encounter without his help, but he'd known what to say to the man to make a deal. And it had been worth enduring the situation to hear him call her his mate.

Kaylina smiled against his shoulder, feeling more drawn to him than ever. Feeling more that she *belonged* with him.

"Thank you," she whispered.

"As I said, I will ride out to the estate and speak with my

mother. She will *not* hire anyone else to kidnap you." His tone was harsh, almost savage, and she knew he was tired of people going after her—and relieved nothing had happened this time. As if to verify that, he kissed her neck and slid his hand down her back to cup her butt, drawing her into him. "You *will* stay in Port Jirador with me."

It was an order rather than a request, so maybe she should have bristled, but her body molded to his, eager to obey the command. She *wanted* to stay here with him.

He kissed her, not on the neck but on the mouth, claiming her, ordering her to stay with his body as well as with words.

His touch roused desire within her, making her forget the danger as she instinctively tightened her grip on his shoulders and arched into him, pressing her mouth to his. Passion infused the kiss. Passion and *feeling*. Maybe Vlerion had been more worried than he'd let on. Maybe he'd envisioned her being taken from him, parted from him forever.

His passion fueled hers as his hungry touches built urgency within her. She couldn't keep from writhing against him, her grip shifting so her fingers could explore, so she could feel his hard body through his clothes, clothes she longed to push aside. Oh, how she wanted to reward him for helping her time and again, for supporting her even when he disagreed with her goals. And she wanted to reward herself, damn it, to sate her need, to experience the exquisite pleasure that only he could give her.

A faint rustling announced one of the vines snaking closer. Vlerion broke their kiss and gripped his dagger as he turned toward it. Panting, Kaylina struggled to focus, to remember the threat.

The tip raised up like a cobra's head, pointing at Vlerion. Kaylina swore she heard the vine hiss.

"*No*," she commanded firmly, as if it were a dog trained to obey.

It paused, considering. The vines that had sprouted from the wall had lengthened, stretching toward Vlerion. They wavered in the air, contemplating the situation.

As much as Kaylina wanted to return to kissing Vlerion, wanted him to be welcome in her new home—and in her bed— she made herself release him and step back.

Perhaps it was for the best. His deep breaths and the fire in his eyes promised he hadn't been far from losing himself to his emotions—to the beast.

"You'd better go," Kaylina whispered, not delusional enough to believe she could command the plant. If anything, it had the power to command *her.*

As if to remind her of that, the skin of her hand warmed, the brand tingling again.

"I will go talk to my mother," Vlerion said, though his gaze raked her up and down, making it clear he would rather stay with her. Perhaps upstairs in her room...

His interest never failed to arouse her, even when he touched her only with his eyes, not his hands, not his hungry lips.

She made herself look away and say, "Good. Thank you. If I get a chance, I'll find out who hired the sage assassins."

Vlerion's eyes narrowed. "You will stay within these walls where you are safe, and you will *not* seek out the sage assassins or those who hired them."

It wasn't *bad* advice, but... "You know how much I like it when you give me orders."

"You may not like it," he said softly, glancing at the vines but also stepping close to her again, leaning in to whisper in the ear that hadn't been injured, "but it makes you hot."

"*You* make me hot."

"Good," he breathed, then nibbled softly on her lobe as he stroked her waist through her shirt. His touch teased her deliciously and seemed to promise they would be together later, when the plant wasn't watching.

Kaylina knew that couldn't be but couldn't help moaning and shifting toward him, her body loving his attention, craving more.

"Good," he repeated, and kissed her on the neck again before walking toward the gate.

The tips of the vines remained elevated, flicking as he strode past them, but he didn't hurry his pace. Unlike the kidnappers, he wouldn't be scared away by them. Maybe it would have been better if he had been, but he was a predator, not prey, and he wouldn't run.

Kaylina watched him depart, disappointment replacing the heat in her body, and she lamented that she couldn't run after him.

She looked up at the tower window. "We need to have a chat."

24

FERTILIZE THE PRESENT, AND THE FUTURE WILL BEAR FRUIT.
   ~ *Master Gardener Lady Fomalia*

Before heading up to speak with the plant, Kaylina stopped in the kitchen to make a fresh batch of honey-water fertilizer and check on her siblings. Both hard at work on the evening's menu, they hadn't heard the confrontation out front, though Frayvar had been confused when he'd spotted some men running out the back gate.

"They won't return," Kaylina said. "Don't worry about it."

She didn't know if Vlerion would succeed in talking his mother out of additional attempts to have Kaylina kidnapped—Lady Isla seemed stubborn and quite determined to protect her son—but she doubted that particular group of men would return.

"Kaylina," Silana said primly, "you're in the service business. You *want* people to return. Often."

"Not those people," Kaylina said.

"Why not?"

Frayvar raised his eyebrows, doubtless curious how she would answer.

Since Kaylina hadn't mentioned the kidnapping attempts to her sister, and didn't want to worry her, she decided on, "They don't have any money. They're not getting paid for their most recent work."

Silana's brow furrowed.

Maybe sensing he should distract her, Frayvar grabbed a stack of flyers from a counter. "I had these made for tonight. Do you want to distribute them around the area, Kay?"

"I just got here, and you want to send me away?" Kaylina glanced at the flyers, reading the promise of free mead samples with the full-price purchase of a meal at Stillguard Eating House. Promoting the business was a good idea, but Vlerion wouldn't be happy if Kaylina ventured into the streets, and she'd sent the taybarri back with him.

"We've got the cooking in hand and everything ready to go. Silana has been helping." Frayvar smiled at their sister, then leaned close to Kaylina to whisper, "She hasn't hugged me today."

"Well, you're not that huggable of a guy. I shouldn't think you'd have to endure that except after long absences and near-death experiences."

Frayvar wrinkled his nose to suggest even those weren't acceptable reasons for touching.

Kaylina pointed at the flyers. "Let me fertilize the plant—" and discuss whether my life is linked with its, she didn't say aloud, "—and then I'll hand some of those out."

"All right."

"Plant?" Silana asked.

"It's tied in with the curse you heard about. If we keep it happy, it won't act up when diners are here." Kaylina didn't explain that *acting up* involved killing people with vines.

Though Silana had heard about the curse and hadn't

dismissed the notion outright, her brow did furrow again at the statement. If she hadn't yet seen how the castle could act out, that relieved Kaylina. Better that their sister not be traumatized—and report to the family how inadequate a facility this was for a meadery and eating house.

Silana watched as Kaylina made the fertilizer and carried the heavy pot out of the kitchen, but Frayvar said a few things about his recipes to distract her, and she didn't follow Kaylina or ask any more questions. Good. This needed to be a private chat.

Kaylina dragged a chair under the hole in the tower floor, stacking a crate on top of the cushion so she could climb high enough to lift the pot up. With a grunt and much sloshing, she hoisted it onto the floorboards.

By the time she pulled herself through, fallen leaves crinkling under her knees, the plant had draped its odd combination of branches and vines into the water, hungrily drawing it up. Before she could pull away, a star-shaped leaf much larger than the one on her hand caressed her cheek.

"Stuff like that is creepy," she said.

At least the plant hadn't thrust a vision onto her. She'd been avoiding letting it touch her out of the fear of receiving more of them—especially the kind that showed her killing Vlerion.

She looked out the window into the courtyard, but the vines that had sprouted from the wall earlier had disappeared.

"I do appreciate you helping to intimidate those kidnappers," she added.

As her brother had pointed out, it wouldn't hurt to show gratitude toward the plant. *He'd* thought she should call it *my lord* or some such. That, she refused.

"And not killing them. I know you're not human, and the druids weren't either, but we have laws against such things. Even if you're protecting someone."

One of the vine tips flicked. Dismissively, she thought. That didn't keep the rest of the plant from absorbing honey water. She ladled more over the soil in the pot.

"Let me know if you want me to bring in any fresh dirt for you. Or maybe some compost? If your soil has been here as long as you have, it has to need some amendments." Kaylina glanced at her brand, debating how to bring up the question that Sabor had raised. No, the *threat* he'd raised.

Better to make the plant extra happy first. She ladled more honey water onto the soil.

"I could bring you mead to try too," she offered. "I don't know if it has nutrients, the way the fertilizer does, but you might like it. I'm making a batch using some of the yeast that Vlerion gave me. He's a good guy, you know. The beast curse isn't his fault."

One of the vines rose toward her face, the tip wavering in the air.

Kaylina flinched and drew back, afraid it would punish her for speaking well of a ranger it considered a threat. The vine hung there in the air. Waiting.

She longed to have a discussion with the plant far more than she wanted it to give her visions, but that was how it had communicated with her in the past. She still didn't know if it had spoken into her mind during one of the visions or if that had been a taybarri elder, somehow talking to her across countless miles. When she and Vlerion had visited their kind in the mountains, Queen Seerathi had been the only one to speak with her, and she'd had a different telepathic voice.

As it had once before, the vine hovered near her temple, not yet touching her. It was asking for permission.

"No visions of me killing Vlerion," she told the plant. "Of *anyone* killing him."

It didn't move. Vines didn't nod.

Kaylina sighed. "Go ahead. And, if you could, let me know if my life is bound to yours and if I'll die if you die. I didn't sign up for that."

She hadn't signed up for *anything*. The plant had branded her without asking, and it had hurt. A lot. The presumptuous thing.

The tip stretched toward her temple, and she cleared such thoughts from her mind.

She already knelt but she rested her hands on the floor, bracing herself. Last time, she'd passed out, and Frayvar had run to Doc Penderbrock for help. What would Silana think if she ventured to the tower and found Kaylina unconscious on her back?

The rubbery flesh of the vine was cool against her skin. At first, nothing happened. Had the sentinel not decided yet what vision to share? Then she sensed a presence in her mind, the *plant's* presence.

Instead of pushing a vision onto her, it stirred up her memories, rousing thoughts of the previous night when she'd woken to the pained roar of the beast. Kaylina winced, certain it would see her encounter with Vlerion in the bathhouse and see that he'd torn the head off an enemy. That might, in its mind, prove that he was a threat. It wouldn't help that he'd also leaped onto the walkway and stalked toward her with the intent to have her.

Yes, she'd kept him from hurting her, as she had in their other encounters, but, on each occasion, the beast had been weary from battle and on the verge of collapsing. As he had this time, dropping to one knee and leaning against her, the fight fading from him. One day, she might rouse the beast when he was fresh and there weren't enemies for him to battle, and then... then what would happen? She could guess, and the plant, she had no doubt, could too.

She swallowed as the memories shifted. The viewpoint did as well. Now, she was looking down into the courtyard from the tower as Vlerion sprang into view and grabbed the lead kidnapper from behind.

The plant had been prepared to strike—she sensed that through the vision, and she'd known it at the time as well. But it had paused to watch and see what happened. It had seen that Vlerion had defended her. Only when he'd kissed her had it grown concerned again, tempted to lash out. The plant's duty was to keep those with the blood of the ancients safe. Kaylina's Daygarii forefathers would have wished that. Her Daygarii *father* would have wished it.

Surprised jolted Kaylina. Her Daygarii... father? The green-haired man?

She'd assumed any druid blood she claimed had been diluted through generations, that the man who'd visited her mother at the Spitting Gull had been only partially one of their kind. Druid enough to have some strange hair and exotic facial features, but...

Perhaps the sentinel made an incorrect assumption, a dry male voice spoke into her mind. It was the same one that had communicated with her before. *Perhaps enough of the Daygarii is within you that you can control the cursed one and keep him from harming you.*

I don't want to control Vlerion. I want to lift his curse.

That is the punishment for his line.

It's not the fault of his line *that starving people hunted in the preserve hundreds of years ago. He's committed no crime. He shouldn't be punished.*

Someone had to be for that crime. Those lands, and all that thrives there, must be preserved for when the time of man passes and the Daygarii return. Without the curse, men would not remember and would again threaten those lands. The memories of their kind are short, their minds feeble.

Really. Kaylina couldn't help but feel affronted on behalf of humanity.

If you can control the cursed one, perhaps he does not need to die.

Though she wanted to argue again that she wished to lift Vlerion's curse, not *control* him, Kaylina couldn't help but lean forward with hope. *Does that mean you would let him come to the castle without threatening him? You would let him come see me to talk and...*

And what? Even if vines stopped trying to strangle Vlerion when he visited, he would still turn into the beast if she roused his lust. They couldn't be together.

The plant finished her thought with another look at them in the courtyard, again from the tower window viewpoint. It shared something between wryness and mockery as she writhed in Vlerion's arms, gripping and groping far more than she'd realized she had, and she flushed with embarrassment. She hadn't been aware of being *that* into the moment, into his kisses and his caresses. No wonder she—and her enthusiasm—roused the beast.

He desires you carnally.

Yeah, I know. Kaylina desired him carnally too. Something she did *not* want to discuss with a plant.

That is not how you control him, however. He is drawn to you carnally but also magically, and it is because of the power in your blood that he is compelled to listen to you—to obey *you—and doesn't spring upon you and force you to mate.*

Cheeks still warm at the uncomfortable conversation, Kaylina shook her head and didn't point out that Vlerion wouldn't be forcing anything if he took her, that even as the beast, he stirred her libido. Even if it was beyond dangerous, and she was afraid of the beast, she was also... She would be his if he wished it.

That was something else she didn't want to discuss with the plant. *All I need to know is if you'll let him in, if it's safe for him to enter the courtyard, the castle.*

A long moment passed as the plant seemed to consider that. *In his human form, he is not a threat to you. He may approach.*

All right. Thank you.

That was something. Kaylina smiled, feeling she'd won a victory. If Vlerion hadn't been on the way to his family estate, she would have run off to tell him he could come to the grand opening. He didn't drink alcohol, but he could enjoy the food. Or she could put him to work clearing dishes, as Frayvar had suggested. She smirked at the idea of her haughty aristocrat employed at such a task.

Reminded that *Vlerion* wasn't the reason she'd come up to speak with the plant, Kaylina said, *Spymaster Sabor wrote that he's done research on the druids and on you. Is it true that we're linked now? Because you branded me?* She tried to keep reproach out of her mental voice but didn't know if she succeeded. Though the power of the brand had proven useful, she couldn't help but resent it.

The human knows nothing.

She doubted that was true—Sabor knew far too much when it came to her and Vlerion—but allowed herself a modicum of hope. *Then our lives aren't linked together? If you die, I won't die?*

You will continue to feed me the superior honey fertilizer, the plant stated firmly.

Yes, I'm planning on it. I wouldn't stop. Even though the plant had gained in power, alarmingly so, since she'd started fertilizing it. She shivered at the memory of a purple beam shooting out to kill a Kar'ruk invader. *But is my life tied to yours? Did you brand me to make sure I would stay here and keep feeding you?*

I did not. It was necessary to waken your somnolent blood.

My what?

The brand helps you access your power, your birthright.

Kaylina digested that for a moment. *So... the times I've seemed to draw upon magic, it's come from me? Not the brand? Not you?*

The power of the Daygarii is within you. It is why the cursed one is drawn to you and will protect you. It is why the sentinel is drawn to you and will protect you. It will not allow you to be manipulated by some feeble human.

At first, she thought the plant meant Vlerion was a *feeble human*, but through another vision, it took her up through the roof of the tower where a vine she'd never noticed thrust between the slate tiles. Like a tall stovepipe, it rose high enough to have a view in all directions, above the rooftops of the city and to the harbor, and even over the wall and toward the highway heading along the river toward the preserve and the mountains.

In the vision, it was dawn, and two dark horses with hooded riders were visible on the highway. When they turned to point back at the city, Kaylina could see their faces. One was the lead sage assassin, the man who kept getting away. The other figure was Spymaster Sabor.

They chatted easily, like allies. Or... like one man hiring the other?

If so, Sabor had lied about knowing the assassins. He'd lied about everything. Could Kaylina be surprised?

Sabor delved under his cloak and pulled out a small bag of coins and deposited it in the assassin's hand. He pointed at it, then gestured to indicate a much larger coin bag. The reward should the assassin succeed at killing Vlerion?

What in all the altered orchards? Kaylina asked.

Why would Sabor hire assassins to slay the very man he kept saying he wanted to use? One of his own people. A loyal kingdom subject.

Kaylina roared in fury on Vlerion's behalf.

"Kaylina?" an alarmed voice spoke, startling her.

The vision grew wispy, Sabor's face fading.

"Kaylina?"

The voice sounded close but also far away. She struggled to focus on it and remember where she was. Her vision had turned inward, toward memories and the plant's conversation, and she had to blink several times before the vine-draped stone walls of the tower room came into view.

"What is that hideous plant *doing* to you?"

"Silana?" Kaylina croaked, recognizing the voice now.

Her sister stood on the crate on the chair, the top of her head poking through the hole in the floor. "Yes, of course. Why are there vines all over you? And why..." Her gaze lowered to Kaylina's hand. To the brand. Had she not noticed it before?

Kaylina shifted. There *were* vines all over her.

Alarm flooded into her veins before she realized they weren't restraining her in any way. It was as if they'd simply grown over her.

A leaf brushed her ear, and the plant's earlier words repeated in her mind: *It is why the sentinel is drawn to you and will protect you.*

Better than being attacked by it, but she gently plucked the vines off so she could slip away. Silana was in the way, though, frozen as she stared through the hole, her gaze focused on the brand.

Kaylina lifted her hand, about to joke that the mark was the trendiest thing in the capital. Then she saw what was alarming her sister. It was glowing green.

It had happened before but only in a dream. No, that had been a hallucinogenic vision induced by consuming those altered berries for the taybarri test. According to Queen Seerathi, they'd allowed her to see a broader spectrum of light. There was nothing altered about her vision now, and her sister could also see the glow.

Oh, well. By now, Kaylina was used to the plant—and her brand—doing odd things. That last vision had left more pressing matters on her mind.

"I need to talk to Spymaster Sabor. No, I need to catch him talking to the sage assassins he's hired while Vlerion is observing, and then we need to tell..."

Who? Queen Petalira? The king couldn't be trusted to act, even

if he believed that his spymaster was having members of the aristocracy hunted down. He might not even comprehend the problem. If he did, Sabor might convince him that Vlerion was a traitor,
someone who couldn't be trusted. But would the queen even care?

"Spymaster Who?" Silana asked.

"The guy manipulating the king. And probably the entire
kingdom."

Silana shook her head slowly, staring back and forth from the
glowing brand to the vines and leaves all around Kaylina. "I don't
know what you're involved in up here, but—"

"I need to go." Kaylina scooted to the hole, waving for Silana to
climb off the chair so she could drop down. "It's important."

She didn't yet know what she would do, but she couldn't stay at
Stillguard Castle and serve mead while one of the most powerful
people in the kingdom tried to get rid of Vlerion, the man who
cared about and supported her like no one else ever had. The man
she was falling in love with.

"What's important," Silana said tartly as she held up a hand,
"is for you to explain what you've gotten involved in. I'm worried
about you. Frayvar is being evasive whenever I ask him for information. I know he's protecting you, but, Kaylina, the family cares.
We need to know what's going on. Grandma and Grandpa can
help."

"Not from the far end of the kingdom."

Even if they'd been close, they couldn't have done anything
about Spymaster Sabor.

"Nonetheless, I insist on an explanation."

Kaylina shook her head. "This isn't the time."

Though Silana didn't move, Kaylina squirmed past, swinging
down without using the chair. She started down the hall, but her
sister spoke again.

"If you want my endorsement of this business—and of you

staying up here in the capital—you'll take the time to give it to me."

Temper roused, Kaylina turned with a scowl, about to tell her sister to drop it, that she didn't care about the business. But that wasn't true. And Silana was still glancing at her hand, her face twisted with worry.

Kaylina rubbed the back of her neck, reminding herself that she didn't know what to do next. She couldn't talk to Sabor alone —she doubted she would even be permitted in to see him, not by herself. She needed to wait for Vlerion to return. That meant she had time to talk to her sister.

"All right. I'll try to explain everything."

"Kaylina?" Frayvar called from the stairway. "Silana? The first guests are here."

"I guess I'll explain later," Kaylina said.

"No." Silana hopped down from the chair and strode toward her. "You'll explain while we're pouring glasses of water and telling patrons about the tasting notes for the mead. If you learned nothing else at the Spitting Gull, it should have been how to multitask."

"That's the truth." Kaylina managed a smile for her sister as they headed toward the stairs. "I'll do my best."

25

THE MOTHER OF THY MATE CAN DETERMINE YOUR FATE.

  ~ Kar'ruk proverb

Kaylina and Silana didn't speak *while* they were explaining tasting notes and taking orders from the guests, but every time they ended up in the kitchen together, Kaylina told her sister about her experiences with the plant and druid magic. She also explained that she now believed the green-haired man who'd visited Mom years ago had not only been her father but a full-blooded Daygarii. She emphasized what she'd done and seen firsthand rather than mentioning that the plant gave her visions. Her sister wouldn't believe in those, however accurate and prophetic they'd thus far been.

Now and then, Frayvar chimed in when he wasn't too busy carefully cutting and placing his food on plates, then wiping the rims to ensure that not a stray speck of sauce marred what he called the *frames* for his *masterpieces*. Every time they carried plates out for him, he rushed to the door and held it so they could make it to the courtyard tables without jostling his precisely crafted meals.

Kaylina expected her sister to be more skeptical of everything and to balk at the idea of magical blood and Kaylina having a Daygarii ancestor. The way Silana remained quiet through most of the explaining, except to glance often at her with pursed lips, did nothing to ameliorate that expectation.

But in the end, while they poured flights of mead in the kitchen for guests who'd laid down hundred liviti bills, asking to try every variety in the cellar, Silana said, "You were always different. Our whole family is a little quirky, with Grandma the Head Quirk, even though she'd glower in exasperation at you if you said anything like that, so I never thought much about it, but Grandpa's hounds did always love you and show off for you. And then there were those stray cats that would show up at your window and follow you every time you did chores outside. Oh, and remember the summer the jaguar was sleeping on the roof over your room?"

"I'd actually forgotten about that."

"Mom thought it was going to eat you. Grandpa said it would be fine. Grandma hired an artist to draw it and said it would have to become a mascot if it stayed. She's always the business-minded opportunist."

"Yeah."

"And the green-haired guy being a druid... I never would have guessed that, but he really didn't seem fully human. And Mom was *so* into him. After he left—" Silana set down the bottle she'd been pouring from. "Like I said before, that's when Mom got depressed and started taking the tarmav weed. I'm pretty sure. We could ask Grandma, but she was more of a normal mother before that. She took me to the beach to play and taught me to read and write before school started. After he left, she seemed lost, and she forgot how to be happy. Or even *normal*."

"Normal is overrated," Kaylina murmured.

"I'm not surprised you would say that."

"I'd say that too," Frayvar added from the hearth.

Silana gave them both exasperated looks, then called in one of the servers they'd hired to help for the night, and they carried the mead flights out together.

"This all reminds me..." Frayvar set his stew pot on a back hook and walked to a drawer. "We've been so busy that I forget to tell you I got a chance to research that rubbing you gave me."

It took Kaylina a few seconds to remember what he was talking about.

At her blank expression, he said, "The rubbing made with a horrific *pollen* that made me sneeze up and down every aisle of the library when I was looking up druid runes."

"Don't you sneeze up and down every aisle every time you go to the library?" Kaylina joined him at the drawer as he pulled out the rubbing and a page of notes. "You're allergic to dust mites, after all."

"Usually, I only sneeze in every *other* aisle." Frayvar handed her the notes and went to the oven to pull out fresh loaves of bread, scents of herbs mingling in the air with the black-currant glazed baked salmon and roasted lamb. "Anyway, that's the translation of those runes. A rough one. Even though the university library has more information on the Daygarii than I'd ever seen before, they were a reclusive and secretive people, and they had more than one written language. Much of the work we have was done by archaeologists piecing things together from old ruins and cave paintings rather than anything the druids provided to our people when they visited."

"I've gathered they didn't like humans much."

"No. One wonders why your father was drawn to Mom."

"She's beautiful. Even now, she still is."

Frayvar grunted, as if he couldn't imagine someone being

drawn by such a thing. Kaylina did not mention his instant adoration of Lady Ghara.

"Maybe he was lonely," she added. "If most of the druids left and he remained behind for some reason, he might have missed his people and sought out what company he could find. Silana said he liked the mead. Since the honey has always been made by bees foraging on altered plants—altered by the druids—it might have been comforting for him."

"I guess. Anyway, read that. It's interesting." Frayvar pointed a spatula at his pages of chicken scratches. "You said you found the runes on a plaque in the middle of some flowers?"

"What had probably once been a cultivated flower garden, yes."

"Huh. Did your weird hand lead you to it?"

"My *hand* isn't weird. The brand may be." Kaylina glanced at it. Fortunately, the green glow had faded before she'd had to serve guests. It must have been stirred up by her interaction with the plant—and it draping vines all over her.

"Whatever."

Silana returned to the kitchen to take out more goblets of mead, and Frayvar didn't say more. Kaylina read his translation.

These lands are protected by the magic of the Daygarii, the first race to walk on Keyvilar, the only race sworn to protect this world and others. Step with care. Enemies of the Daygarii and the world will be slain. One species may not subsume another. When imbalances occur, and one species dominates, fear not, for all will return to equilibrium eventually. The universe watches over all and appoints protectors to ensure that in balance the world thrives.

"That's... less helpful than I'd hoped," Kaylina said.

"It says something about what the druids believe their role in the world is. In the *worlds.* Do you think there are others in the cosmos?" Frayvar gazed wistfully toward the ceiling. "I found it fascinating."

"I was hoping for instructions on how to lift curses, so Vlerion and I can..." Have sex, she thought, before deciding that sounded selfish. Besides, she hadn't told Frayvar about the beast curse. "Just to lift curses," she said.

"I doubt instructions on that are found on garden plaques, but maybe there's a clue there for you. If the Daygarii believe in balance, maybe they placed the curse to bring this area back into what they would consider alignment."

"By putting a killer plant in a castle?" Kaylina was tempted to bring up the beast—how could *he* offer alignment?—but she was still sworn not to share that secret with her brother.

"Nobody has hunted in the preserve since then, at least from what I've heard. The curse is probably a reminder that the druids still protect that area and will punish those who do."

"So, what? To lift the curse, I have to make sure people won't hunt in the preserve even without a reminder? Fray, I don't think most people know the castle has anything to do with the druids and that forest out there."

The words made her pause to wonder if the beast might have been intended to prowl the lands around the preserve and keep people out. But Vlerion had never mentioned urges to do that. And the beast came forth when he lost control of his emotions, not when people wandered into the forest with bows. She shook her head.

"Oh, I don't think that's true. The people who live here know the castle's curse was a result of the rangers poaching in the preserve. That's part of the story." Frayvar used the handle of his spatula to scratch his cheek as he looked thoughtfully toward the tower again. "But the plant is content now that you're here feeding it, isn't it? The castle has stopped moaning creepily, I haven't woken to unexplained noises at night, and a chandelier hasn't fallen in weeks."

"A sure sign of contentment."

"We haven't had nightmares either. Those horrible visions about the castle killing people. At least I haven't." He peered at her.

Before she could respond and tartly say she *had* experienced nightmares, the kitchen door opened with a bang.

"Kaylina, Frayvar," Sevarli, one of their young helpers, blurted. A blonde freckled girl a year younger than Frayvar, she had experience in the eating-house business and had taken right to the work. "A fancy carriage with two drivers just rolled up. It's an aristocrat, I think. Maybe more than one! And did you see that Professora Vesimoor is here? She's a retired enologist who started a column in her hometown of Potato Patch, and she's making vintners famous. She's got a flight of mead right now and is penning notes in a binder. If she does a favorable write-up, you could get visitors from all up and down the coast."

"That's good news." Frayvar twirled like an eight-year-old girl. "It took years for the Spitting Gull to receive its first critic. How did the professora find out about us? Was it the pamphlets I sent out?"

"I overheard some discussions and know that a number of people are here because of Lord Vlerion," Sevarli said. "He's been telling other nobles about the grand opening, and you know everyone listens to the Havartafts. They used to rule the kingdom, and there are even rumors that Lord Vlerion is going to storm the castle one day and take back the crown." Her young eyes gleamed at this notion.

Since Kaylina hadn't heard any of *those* rumors, she was surprised by the words, but she was also touched that Vlerion had made an effort to tell people about her endeavor. When had he found the time?

"Oh, Lord Vlerion." Frayvar beamed at Kaylina. "He's turned into a wonderful benefactor. Are you having sex with him? You should *definitely* have sex with him."

Kaylina's jaw dropped, not because she wouldn't enjoy doing

exactly that, but her brother wasn't someone who usually brought up such topics. After the words came out, Frayvar looked at Sevarli, as if wondering if he'd made the right suggestion, if *sex* was the appropriate reward for someone getting the word out about one's grand opening.

The server nodded encouragingly, her eyes still gleaming.

Kaylina cleared her throat. "For now, let's just focus on making sure the guests enjoy the food and drink."

"Yes. Especially Professora Vesimoor," Frayvar said. "I do hope she likes the mead. Did she order a meal? Maybe I should bring her something special to complement the different varieties." He sprang for the cupboard to grab plates to prepare a fresh masterpiece.

"An excellent idea." Sevarli smiled as she watched Frayvar's enthusiasm—or maybe just as she watched *him*. "I've heard she likes lamb."

"I have lamb. *Delicious* lamb. I'll put extra glaze on hers. Oh, and the bread." He darted to the oven.

Kaylina put the translation away and vowed to follow her own advice, focusing on guest satisfaction, at least for the evening. The meadery was her dream, after all. Even though a few million things had happened to derail it, or at least distract her from it, she wanted to savor that things were finally going well. A write-up by Professor Vesimoor would be amazing. Kaylina had heard of the wine reviewer and read some of her articles. Some were scathing, but Kaylina knew her mead was good. The woman wouldn't write anything bad about it. She *couldn't*.

"What color is the carriage that you mentioned?" Kaylina asked, following Sevarli out with a couple of orders. She didn't know the emblems and colors of the various noble families well, but after a couple of months in the capital, she'd come to recognize some.

"Black with silver trim."

Kaylina stutter-stepped, almost sloshing gravy onto the side of the plate. There were a lot of family crests that used black, but she had a feeling...

"Are you okay?" Sevarli had noticed her misstep.

"Yes, but will you deliver these to the right tables? I want to check on our visitor." Kaylina nodded toward the open front gate as she handed the plates to Sevarli.

"Of course. Don't get too excited and fawn over an aristocrat though. You're a dignified master mead maker, even if you've common blood." Sevarli winked with encouragement.

Kaylina almost pointed out that she'd never fawned over anyone in her life—Captain Targon would have preferred it if she *had*—but she glimpsed a familiar chauffeur through the gate and only waved an absent acknowledgment.

The chauffeur caught her eye and pointed toward the carriage door. He couldn't have come to retrieve her for another meeting with Lady Isla, could he? This late in the day? Twilight was descending.

The chauffeur nodded and pointed again at the carriage. Two lamps burned to either side of the door, and a shadow moved behind the window. It already had an occupant? Was it possible Lady Isla had come to the grand opening? Maybe Vlerion had talked her out of the kidnapping quest. Maybe he was even in the carriage with his mother, and they'd come to eat.

Uncertainty and hope mingled in Kaylina's gut as she walked through the courtyard and past the occupied tables, guests chewing, drinking, and chatting amiably. Focused on the meals, they hardly glanced at the glowing tower.

Wistfulness filled her as she envisioned Lady Isla sitting at a table, having come to enjoy the mead and support Kaylina, not check to see if she'd been successfully kidnapped yet.

As she walked through the gate, passing a couple with linked arms perusing the menu, the chauffeur opened the carriage door.

Kaylina glanced at the man and woman, wondering what it would be like for her and Vlerion to be able to visit an eating house together without having to worry about kidnappers, assassins, or beasts being roused.

One day, she promised herself. One day.

Inside the carriage, a woman sat alone. It was, indeed, Lady Isla, her graying auburn hair drawn back with ivory combs, her skin pale in contrast to the navy-blue dress and shawl she wore. As usual, her attire was far more somber than festive, a sign that she still mourned her deceased husband and son—and that she hadn't likely come to enjoy a night of fine dining and mead tasting.

"Will you join me, Ms. Korbian?" Isla patted the empty portion of the upholstered bench beside her.

"If it's about your interest in investing in the business..." Kaylina barely kept herself from using the word *bribe*, "...my brother and I have decided not to take money from anyone outside the family at this time." She lifted her chin, letting her eyes add the rest: *I'm not leaving Port Jirador* or *abandoning Vlerion.*

"So I gathered when you left the envelope unopened on the table." Isla smiled gently.

Kaylina hoped the woman respected her for that, even if Isla still wanted to get rid of her.

"I spoke with Vlerion today," Isla added. "He was quite stern."

Kaylina was glad. "Where is he now? I have good news and alarming news for him." She waved toward the tower at the mention of the former and pointed in the direction of the royal castle at the latter.

A troubled expression lined Isla's face. "Vlerion said he would hunt down the assassins that are after him, that he would finish them off."

"I have some information for him about that, about who hired them."

"Oh? Then you must join me." Isla patted the seat again. "I received an invitation to a meeting with Spymaster Sabor."

"Uh." Kaylina debated whether to blurt out that *Sabor* was the one who'd hired the assassins. But Vlerion was the only one who would believe her if she admitted she'd learned that from a plant-induced vision.

"He wishes to see us together," Isla added. "That's why I came here first to collect you."

"Uh," Kaylina repeated. How was she supposed to rat out Spymaster Sabor *in front* of him? "It's our grand opening."

"Yes, I heard. It looks like it's going well. I'm pleased for you, but..." Isla looked wistfully toward the courtyard.

But she still wanted Kaylina gone?

"My lady, did Vlerion talk you out of... Look, I know you hired the thugs who've been trying to kidnap me."

Isla winced.

"I understand that you want to protect your son—I want him to be safe too—but I'm not leaving Port Jirador. And I'm not leaving him. We're not doing anything that's going to cause him to be hunted down like his brother." Kaylina tried to make herself add *I promise*, but could she? Hadn't she and Vlerion come close, more than once, to letting their desire for each other rouse the beast?

Yes.

"I wish I could believe that, Ms. Korbian. Kaylina. But just this morning, Lady Ghara came to see me and—"

"I'm not spending time with Vlerion because I care about his money. Or because he's an aristocrat." The heat of indignation seared Kaylina's cheeks as she imagined Ghara repeating her loathsome accusations to Isla—and Isla believing them.

"Oh, I know that." Isla waved in the air to dismiss the idea. "But she spoke of the way you stood together, how possessive and devoted to you he was, and it reinforced what I have known since the beginning." She lowered her voice to finish. "That the beast part of him is drawn to the *anrokk* part of you. That he's obsessed."

"He's not obsessed. Neither am I. We just enjoy each other's company."

"Even though you met when he arrested you, and you struck him in the head with a rock?"

"It was a lead round, and yes. We're the kind of people who enjoy overcoming adversity."

Isla laughed softly. "That may be true. Vlerion has certainly never walked away from it. To answer your question, my son *did* talk me out of... I refuse to call it misguided maternal interference, as he did. It was a plan that I sought due to desperation, because I didn't want to lose another son. I do apologize that you were necessarily the recipient of it. I'm relieved that it doesn't look like you've been hurt. If it mollifies you at all, I did start out by requesting that Captain Targon station Vlerion far away from here."

"Far away from me?"

Isla tilted an apologetic hand toward the night sky. "I would have missed him, of course, but it would have been a more reasonable choice than kidnapping you."

A less *criminal* choice.

"I also believe that he would have, despite his obsession, obeyed his captain and left," Isla said.

Kaylina hated the word *obsession*. It sounded so negative, when what she felt for Vlerion was... As she'd been thinking earlier, she was falling in love with him. It was a *positive* emotion that spoke of their bond, the bond forming from more than magic and being *drawn*. She was sure of it.

And yet... the plant's memory of her embrace with Vlerion in the courtyard came to mind. Her sentinel would probably agree that they were obsessed with each other.

"Targon refused to send his best fighter away," Isla said. "He was adamant that Vlerion is needed in the capital."

"I don't want to make life difficult for him or you, my lady. I care about him."

"I believe you. Come, let us face Spymaster Sabor together."

Kaylina hesitated, but she *did* want to talk to Sabor. She didn't know what she would say, but with an aristocratic lady there, he ought to be on better behavior than if Kaylina went alone.

"Did he say why he wanted to see me?" She couldn't help but feel suspicious.

"He said he wants to give you another chance to consider his proposal." Isla arched her eyebrows. "I received a message from him. We haven't yet spoken. So I couldn't ask for clarification."

"He ran that proposal by Vlerion and me earlier." Kaylina bared her teeth.

"It was that appealing?"

"Nothing about that man is appealing."

"Agreed. Visiting him in numbers is generally wise."

"All right. I'll tell my brother I'm leaving." Kaylina stepped into the courtyard and asked Sevarli to let her siblings know.

The serving girl looked frazzled, with numerous patrons asking for more bread, water, mead. One also wanted to know if it was safe to go into the lavatory, despite the vines flickering around the doorway. What were they doing? Keeping an eye on all the visitors?

"I'll be back as soon as possible," Kaylina added, feeling guilty about abandoning her family.

She was halfway out the gate when she remembered the sword. It would be best to visit Sabor armed with more than lead rounds. Just in case. She ran up to her room and grabbed it.

"Thank you for being reasonable, Kaylina," Isla said as she slid into the carriage. "I do apologize for my choice earlier. I—" She spotted the sword as Kaylina rested it between her knees. "Is that... That looks like Vlarek's scabbard. His sword."

"Yes, my lady." Kaylina licked her lips, assuming from the words and stunned expression that Vlerion hadn't told his mother. "Vlerion gave it to me. I'm learning sword fighting as part of my ranger training."

"*Gave it*," Isla mouthed, still looking stunned.

"It's too nice a gift to accept," Kaylina hurried to say. "I'm thinking of it as a loaner. That's all. I'm sorry if he didn't tell you."

"I..." Isla pressed her lips together and shook her head.

"The royal castle, my lady?" the chauffeur asked.

Isla looked away from the sword—and Kaylina—and nodded curtly at him. "As we discussed."

"Yes, my lady." He closed the door.

As the carriage rolled into motion, Kaylina hoped she wasn't making a mistake.

"Has Vlerion told you anything about how powerful and intelligent the plant in Stillguard Castle is, my lady?" she asked, both to take Isla's mind off the sword and because she had to figure out how to warn her about Sabor in such a way that she would believe it. Especially since they were going to *see* him. For all Kaylina knew, Sabor was inviting them up there to get rid of them since he hadn't succeeded in having Vlerion killed. Or maybe he intended to set a trap for Vlerion.

"He's spoken of it and that you seem to be linked to it."

"It's linked itself to *me*."

"Hm." Isla's face suggested she found the whole notion unappealing.

Kaylina did too. She looked out the window as the carriage rolled through intersections, streetlamps burning in what would soon be full darkness. A misty haze wreathed the flames, fog rolling in from the harbor.

"It won't take long for us to get to the royal castle, so I'll spit this out," Kaylina said. "The plant uses its power—power given to it long ago by the druids—to see what's going on around the city. It shared a vision with me of something it saw recently."

Isla mouthed, "*A vision*," but didn't interrupt.

"Sabor is after Vlerion." Kaylina explained what she'd seen.

"That doesn't make sense. Sabor wants to *use* my son. I'm not pleased about that either, but you—ah, your plant—must be mistaken."

"I don't understand it either, but the plant's visions have thus far..." Kaylina paused before saying *always been right*. That wasn't quite true. They were in the right vein, but the beast hadn't ripped her to shreds after defeating the Kar'ruk in that mountain valley. "The ones it shares of past events have always been accurate," she said instead.

That was the truth. It was the prognostications that needed work.

"It's given you... many visions?"

"Quite a few now. Other plants have too." Maybe Kaylina shouldn't have added that because Isla's expression only grew more dubious. "Altered plants. Regular ones don't give me visions."

The nose wrinkle and forehead crease promised the addition didn't help alleviate Isla's dubiousness.

Kaylina spread her arms. She didn't know what else to say, and the carriage was rolling to a stop.

Wait, why were they stopping? They hadn't yet gone up the steep switchbacks that led up the royal castle's plateau. Kaylina would have felt that.

A horse neighed. She looked out the window, but the fog had grown denser. Because they were closer to the water?

"Where are we? The harbor?" Through the fog, Kaylina could make out the muted light from lampposts and the masts of ships.

"Yes. This is where Spymaster Sabor asked to meet us."

"And you agreed? This isn't where normal people have meetings. And, wait, you told your chauffeur to take us to the castle."

The carriage door opened. It wasn't the chauffeur but two burly men in Havartaft uniforms with swords drawn.

Isla smiled sadly. "You're sharp, aren't you?"

"Sharp, maybe. Wise, no." Kaylina slumped against the seat as the obvious sank in. Lady Isla was still trying to have her kidnapped. And there wasn't a sentient plant here to defend her.

26

IF YOU WISH TO KNOW SOMEONE, SHARE ADVERSITY WITH THEM.
  ~ Grandma Korbian

"Out," Isla's strongman said, flicking his sword tip at Kaylina.

Still sitting on the bench, she wrapped her hand around the hilt of her own sword, but should she attack when these were Isla's people? Essentially *Vlerion's* people?

"Put that away, Kolaff," Isla said. "She's just a girl, and you're not to hurt her."

"She is not *just a girl*, my lady." Because of the shadowy interior of the carriage, the strongman hadn't noticed the sword yet, but he eyed Kaylina's marked hand. He'd heard all about that, had he?

She willed a branch to fall on him, but she didn't think there were any trees near the waterfront. Other than a patch or two of grass, there wasn't any foliage at all. No plants here could help her.

"Nonetheless, you'll subdue her without violence and carry her to the *Blowing Whale*. The crew has been paid to take her south." Isla looked toward Kaylina without meeting her eyes. At least that suggested she felt some shame about lying, about these tactics. "They'll give you a cabin as soon as the ship is underway. It shouldn't be an unpleasant voyage as long as you don't try to escape. And there'd be no point in attempting that once you're at sea. Once you've reached your Vamorka Islands, I beg you to stay. Don't make this more difficult than it needs to be."

The strongman sheathed his weapon, but his tone was no less gruff when he repeated, "Out," and crooked his finger toward Kaylina. "We're going to the ship."

Kaylina scooted to the door with the sword in her hand.

"Actually, *both* women will be going to the ship," a new voice spoke from the fog behind the men. An accented voice that Kaylina had heard before. "The ship *we've* hired."

Isla's strongmen whirled, raising their weapons. Kaylina slumped back on the seat and groaned.

Blades clashed, the noise muted by the fog but still alarming. She jumped out, abruptly afraid for her life—and for Isla's life too. Isla had been responsible for this, but Kaylina wouldn't be able to look Vlerion in the eyes if his mother died at her feet.

Cloaked sage assassins had come out of the night, two Kaylina hadn't seen before and one who stood back to supervise. It was the leader who'd attacked Kaylina in the park. He looked past the battle and straight at her, his face cool.

Isla swore as she crouched in the carriage doorway, gaping at the battle. She glanced at Kaylina, saw she had the sword, and surprised Kaylina by taking it from her.

For a bewildered second, Kaylina thought Isla was a secret sword master and would leap out to slay their enemies, but she tossed the weapon back into the carriage.

"They'll kill you if you dare swing at them with that," she whispered.

"We can't let them kidnap us." Or *kill* us, Kaylina added

silently and drew her sling. "Stay in the carriage," she ordered before thinking to add a proper, "My lady."

"I was planning to!"

Trusting the assassins would get the upper hand soon, Kaylina planned to shoot them. But they were shorter and faster than Isla's muscled men, and she struggled to find a decent target.

Only when one of the strongmen cried out and dropped to one knee, raising his sword over his head in a last-ditch effort to defend himself, did she get a clear view of his attacker. As the sage assassin lunged in, knocking the blade aside to deliver a killing blow, Kaylina loosed a round.

Her lead ball slammed into his forehead, startling him for a second. Isla's man rolled away and tried to scramble to his feet, but the assassin recovered and sprang after him. Kaylina fired another round but wasn't fast enough. Her target's blade plunged into the strongman's back, piercing his heart. Too late to help, her round struck the assassin in the jaw.

With fury burning in his eyes, he pulled his sword from the other man's back and whirled toward her.

Fear made her hands shake, and Kaylina barely managed to get another round into her sling. Again, she was too late. Moving faster than any normal human being could, the assassin sprang and caught her, fingers wrapping around her wrist, stilling the sling.

She tried to punch him with her free hand, but her fist caught only air. The assassin kicked her legs out from under her as he spun her about, pressing her back to his chest and restraining her with his arm.

Another cloaked assassin leaped into the carriage. Isla screamed, a cry for help rather than pain, but she had to be terrified.

The scream cut off abruptly. Because she'd been gagged? Or— Kaylina winced—knocked unconscious?

Isla's captor leaped out with her hefted over his shoulder like a rolled-up rug instead of a noblewoman. She groaned weakly. The bastard must have struck her.

In an equally bad position, Kaylina could do nothing to help. Worse, her captor twisted her wrist until pain made her release her sling. He pulled her knife from its sheath as well.

The lead sage assassin watched dispassionately. He hadn't moved, instead letting his men handle Isla's people. It had been enough. The chauffeur wasn't in sight and might have run away, but the two strongmen were down—dead. They'd been no match for the assassins.

Kaylina made herself meet the leader's eyes and glare defiantly at him. Any second, he would make some demand, wanting to know where Vlerion was or talking about how she would be good bait for a trap.

But maybe he'd spoken to her enough. He pointed his chin toward one of the docks stretching into the fog, then looked toward the city, in the direction of the royal castle and ranger headquarters. Was he waiting for Spymaster Sabor to show up with the larger bag of gold? But that was for Vlerion's death, wasn't it? Not for capturing his mother and girlfriend.

The assassin didn't explain, merely waiting as his men carried Isla and Kaylina down the dock. Kaylina found herself hoisted over a shoulder, the same as Isla.

She wasn't bound and might have kneed her captor, but she didn't see any point. After watching the sage assassins fight—her ear throbbed at the memory of her own experience against one—she doubted she would get the best of any of them. At least she and Isla were being kidnapped, not killed. Frayvar's words about the odds of surviving that being better than living through murder attempts came to mind. She decided to bide her time for a better chance to escape.

Though it wasn't late at night, the harbor lay quiet, and they didn't pass anyone on the dock. Now and then, voices floated off the decks of moored ships, but if anyone had heard the struggle on shore, they didn't come to investigate it. Maybe Lady Isla, not wanting anything to interfere with Kaylina's kidnapping, had arranged for people to look the other way.

Their captors took them past several docked ships, some fully dark and others with lamps burning on the decks, to one partially lit at the far end.

Kaylina twisted as they approached a gangplank and looked back toward the waterfront. The fog was dense enough that she could no longer see the assassin and could barely make out the buildings across the street from the docks. She couldn't see the royal castle or the plateau it perched upon at all. She did manage to read the name of the ship her captors were boarding.

It wasn't the *Blowing Whale*, the one Isla had arranged to take Kaylina south. This was the *Hunting Osprey*, and a pale-skinned man waited on deck near the gangplank. He wore a horned helmet, had a greasy and scraggly beard, and gold chains dangled around his neck. He reminded Kaylina of the pirates she'd encountered back home. They tended to wear whatever bounty they fancied that they'd stolen from innocents, and they bathed infrequently.

"I thought we were only holding one girl for you boys, a young pretty one." The pirate looked at Kaylina, then raised his eyebrows when he took in Lady Isla.

"Fortune has delivered two," Kaylina's captor said. "You're to keep them locked belowdecks, nothing more. You'll be paid after Venegarth completes his assignment."

Venegarth? Was that the leader? He'd failed to introduce himself to Kaylina during any of their encounters, but assassins were known to be rude.

"Nothing more?" The pirate eyed Kaylina's rump, which was,

unfortunately, thrusting upward since she was slung over her captor's shoulder.

"Nothing more," the assassin said in an icy tone. "These are bait for a trap. They're not to be molested. Our people are honorable, and if you're taking our coin, you'll be honorable too."

The pirate's grunt didn't convey agreement that Kaylina could detect. Isla moaned softly again and lifted her head.

"Belowdecks," the assassin said. "Lock them up, and be prepared to stand guard. We'll be waiting nearby, but the one who will come for them is dangerous."

"Vlerion," Isla whispered softly. "This is a trap for my son."

"Don't be alarmed if you hear growls or roars," the assassin said.

"The guy you're waiting for might bring a taybarri?" the pirate guessed. "Is it a ranger?"

"Something like that."

The assassins handed Kaylina and Isla to the crew, then waited with weapons drawn as the pirates searched their captives. They didn't bother with bindings, but numerous men pushed Isla and Kaylina down steps leading belowdecks, and Kaylina didn't like their odds of escape.

In a narrow corridor, the pirates tossed her weapons into a storage cabin before locking her and Isla in another. Inside, there were no furnishings, only a bucket to pee in and a ceramic jug of water.

Kaylina was tempted to call it a cell, not a cabin. The only opening was a circular window in the metal door, cross-shaped bars ensuring nobody could squeeze out through it.

"You ladies are lucky." The door clanged shut, and one of the men turned a key in a lock. "We don't take on a lot of prisoners, so we don't have a proper brig. These are the accommodations that usually get reserved for the cabin boys."

"The cabin boys don't warrant bunks?" Kaylina asked.

"Nah, you gotta keep 'em lean and tough so they learn how to be properly respectful to their superiors." The man winked before ambling away.

"Everyone in the north is obsessed with instilling respect into people."

Isla, who'd flopped onto her side as soon as her captor released her, groaned softly.

"Are you okay?" Kaylina looked around, as if she might find a first-aid kit or something else useful that she'd missed in her initial perusal of the tiny cabin. "I didn't see what happened. Did one of them club you?"

"That big oaf struck me, yes." Isla pressed a hand to the side of her head. "Which I did not appreciate, but I'm mostly bemoaning the situation I've gotten myself into." After a pause, she added, "With actual moaning."

"It was more of a groan."

Kaylina removed Isla's shawl, impressed that it hadn't fallen off, and moistened it with water. She knelt and pressed it to her head, though she doubted it would do much. The cool water might at least make the knot that had to be swelling there feel better.

"I thought I was being clever by engineering this, clever if deceitful." From her side on the deck, Isla turned her face toward Kaylina. "Maybe I deserve this fate."

Kaylina almost said, *I don't deserve this fate*, but decided not to be snarky with Vlerion's mom. "Let me think for a minute. I've read dozens of romantic adventures, some with heroines who've been kidnapped by pirates. Maybe I can remember something one of them did to escape."

"I don't think fictional tales are meant to offer practical advice."

"I'm not sure that's true. Anyway, my brother has read countless encyclopedias and says they don't teach you how to escape from cells either."

"Perhaps there's a deficiency in the kingdom reading materials."

"In one of my favorite books, the heroine seduces the captain of the pirate ship and manages to pickpocket the keys while they're, uhm, engaged."

"A method I'd have to rely on you to pursue since I'm past the age of effectively seducing anyone. Even when I was younger, I wasn't the most voluptuous maiden."

"If that guy with the horned helmet and greasy beard is the captain, I might pass on seducing him. He's not nearly as appealing as..." Kaylina stopped herself from saying Vlerion, since her interest in Isla's son was what had prompted this whole kidnapping scheme. The *first* kidnapping scheme anyway. Isla couldn't have anticipated the sage assassins butting into her plot.

"Vlerion?" Isla managed a chuckle. "He was never the most handsome boy, but we've discussed the allure of the beast."

"He is handsome." *Hot,* was the word Kaylina almost said, his rugged face forming in her mind.

"Polite of you to say that."

"Especially with his shirt off."

"The rangers do train hard and have admirable physiques," Isla said. "More than once, I've caught myself noticing... Well, it wouldn't be proper for an older widow to notice the physiques of younger men."

"You're not that old, and, since your husband has passed, I think you get to admire anyone you wish."

"The young men might be horrified to be lusted after by a woman more than twenty years their elder."

"Nah, they'd be pleased and smug about it. Which one stirs your fancy?"

While they spoke, Kaylina eyed her hand, wondering if her

magic could help them escape. If the sentinel had spoken the truth, she had power of her own; it wasn't lent to her by the brand or the plant, as she'd previously believed.

Isla sounded shy when she answered. "Vlerion's friend, Jankarr, is quite appealing."

"Oh, yeah. He's hot. Especially when he smiles." Something Kaylina hadn't seen him do since she'd commanded the vines to release him in the preserve—and it had worked. Now, he looked at her warily every time their paths crossed.

"Yes. It would have been helpful if you'd developed an interest in him instead of Vlerion."

"Then we never would have met. Wouldn't you feel bereft without my presence in your life?"

"Not if it meant we weren't now sharing a cell. And those men —those *assassins*—weren't using us to lure Vlerion into a trap. They know what he is, don't they? They'll be prepared to face him." Her voice turned grimmer. "He might die tonight."

"He won't. We're going to escape and warn him to stay away from the harbor." Kaylina patted Isla's shoulder, handed the shawl to her, and rose to her feet to peer out the window in the door.

"Are you seeking a pirate to seduce? With your beauty, it might be feasible."

"We'll put that on our list of escape ideas under the heading *last resort*."

The corridor outside was empty. Quiet voices floated down the ship's ladder from the deck above, but Kaylina couldn't make out the words.

A squeaky chitter came from the opposite end of the corridor where crates were tied down. Some animal? Shadows hid it from view.

"Hello?" Kaylina called encouragingly to whatever it was. She'd been mourning the lack of trees and bushes near the docks, but if an animal was drawn to her, maybe she could get it to help. "What are you?"

It didn't sound like a cat or a rat, and she didn't know what else might be stowing away on a pirate ship. The odd squeaks sounded again, and an animal scurried into view.

"A beaver?"

No, it was too small for that. More familiar with southern animals than northern, Kaylina dredged through her memory, trying to recall some of the critters she'd read about in the ranger handbook.

"A muskrat?"

It squeaked again. It probably would have responded no matter what she said.

"Are you a stowaway or a mascot?" Kaylina patted her pockets, hoping to find a pouch of honey drops, but she didn't have anything. With the way her life had gone lately, she might have been wiser to bring sweets instead of the sword.

"Who or what are you speaking with?" Isla pushed herself into a sitting position against the wall.

"I think it's a muskrat."

The brown furry creature looked curiously up at Kaylina.

"Can you climb?" she asked it. "Like a ferret? Maybe you could fetch the key and bring it to us." She patted the rim of the window, as if she were speaking to an animal as intelligent as the taybarri and it would understand and hurry to obey.

The muskrat wandered past, sniffing the deck, probably hoping for food.

"The seduction plan might have more merit," Isla said dryly.

"I know, but there aren't any horny pirates in the corridor at the moment."

"Alas."

Though the muskrat had its back to her now, Kaylina willed her power to allow her to communicate with it in a way it could understand. She tried to thrust a vision into its mind, showing it retrieving the key, climbing to the window, and delivering it to Kaylina.

The animal squeaked and slapped its long tail on the deck a few times, then paused, snout in the air. Again, Kaylina tried to share her vision with it. Her brand warmed faintly but not with the intensity that it had at other times. Maybe her power was telling her this wouldn't work and it was foolish to bother.

When the muskrat moved on, it left droppings behind. It bounded up the steps without looking back.

"It's possible my great druid magic wasn't successful in convincing it to help," Kaylina said.

"Is that the druid magic you intend to use to lift Vlerion's curse?" Isla's tone wasn't exactly mocking, but it was dry.

"No, I'd hoped to find instructions on how to do that in some druid ruins." She thought about mentioning the plaque that Frayvar had translated, but since nothing curse-related had come out of that, there was little point.

"There are some ruins on the estate that have never enlightened anyone. Traps too that their people left behind. Or at least deterrents."

"It would be hard for me to check them out from the Vamorka Islands," Kaylina said.

"Many of the cursed Havartaft men have studied them over the years. And other Daygarii relics as well. As well as all the books in the university library. None of them ever found a way to lift the curse."

"None of *them* had druid blood."

Isla grunted noncommittally. Maybe skeptically.

Kaylina sighed, wishing she could do something to prove to Isla that she *did* have power that could be useful in lifting the curse. She gripped the bars in the window and willed magic to flow into them and break them, or at least loosen them so that she might twist them free. This time, her hand didn't warm in the slightest. Metal, it seemed, wasn't anything a druid could manipulate.

A faint roar drifted to her ears, muted by the distance and the fog. Even so, she recognized it.

"Uh-oh."

"What is it?" Isla must not have heard it.

"Vlerion is about to walk into their trap."

27

Do not underestimate the lone tree. It provides shade from the merciless desert sun.

~ Abayar, Founder Sandsteader Press

Though Kaylina still gripped the bars, she accepted that her power wouldn't do anything to them. Desperate now that Vlerion —the *beast*—was in the area, she tried to reach out with her mind to find some plant or animal near the docks that she could bestir to help. Whether druids had the power to do that, she didn't know, and she lamented that her green-haired father hadn't stuck around to teach her.

A presence beneath the ship made her pause. Some fish or sea animal swimming under the hull? No, it felt like an altered plant, something with magic inherent in it, something the druids had long ago used their power to create.

Confused, Kaylina envisioned a tree or bush growing under-water and tried to understand how that could have come about. Then she felt foolish as she realized it must be kelp or seaweed or some other aquatic plant that grew in the harbor. She hadn't heard of such fauna being altered, but some certainly could be.

But was whatever was down there capable of helping her on the ship? Kelp wouldn't be able to ooze up the hull, across the deck, and deliver a key to her.

Another roar came from land. The beast sounded irritated. Because the assassins had presumed to capture Kaylina again? And his mother too? Or because he knew it was a trap, and he had to be careful?

Kaylina hoped it was the latter. In the past, the beast had proven himself clever. She crossed her fingers that he would be too smart to walk into whatever the assassin planned.

"I heard him that time," Isla whispered, joining Kaylina at the door. "I haven't seen Vlerion change in years, not since his brother's death, but the beasts have a distinctive roar."

"Yeah."

Eyes closed, Kaylina focused on that plant she sensed, willing it to reach up to them and— And what? It was seaweed, not a kraken. It couldn't fling tentacles onto the deck, ensnare pirates, and hurl them into the harbor. Sadly.

Isla, unaware of her attempt to use her magic, rested a hand on her shoulder. "Kaylina, no matter what happens, I apologize. I don't think I was wrong to try to protect Vlerion—by the moon gods, I hope he can outsmart those assassins tonight—but I'm sorry for hiring people to kidnap you. It wasn't... You don't deserve..."

The faintest of noises sounded, not in Kaylina's ears but in her mind. At least, that was how it seemed to her. Short bleeps repeated.

They reminded her of the flowers that had shrieked in the druid ruins, though those had made noise that she'd heard with her ears. Sharply. This was different, but it also seemed like an alarm. Could the plant she'd touched with her mind be sending out a warning to other aquatic vegetation in the harbor?

Something rocked the ship, and Isla's grip on Kaylina's shoulder tightened.

Had that been her seaweed? Bumping against the hull? Maybe the altered aquatic plant was more substantial than seaweed. Though she could sense its magic, Kaylina had no idea what it looked like.

"Was that a wave?" Isla asked. "The harbor waters are usually quiet, even in storms, and it's not stormy."

No, it was foggy. Kaylina hoped the beast could use that to his advantage.

Thank you for your help, she thought to the plant—or, more likely, mass of plants—below. *If you could do more like that, it might assist us.* At the least, it might help Vlerion if the ship was rocking about as the assassins fired at him, or whatever they planned.

She almost asked if the plant could break through the hull and reach up to their cabin. Visions of swimming out through a hole came to mind, but Kaylina doubted even a substantial aquatic plant could do that.

The ship rocked again. A few raised voices sounded on the deck above.

"What in all the altered orchards is going on?" someone demanded.

Altered *sea* orchards maybe, Kaylina thought, feeling a little smug. Though maybe she shouldn't have since she was still trapped.

A few bangs and thumps floated down from the deck. She imagined men running around, trying to figure out what kept nudging the ship. It rocked again, as if another wave had swept in from the Strait.

A squeak came from the ship's ladder, and the muskrat bounded into view. It had something in its mouth. Kaylina sucked in a breath, hoping for a key, but the creature might have caught a mouse.

Her reaction must have made Isla curious, because she leaned her shoulder against Kaylina's so she could look out.

Whatever the muskrat gripped in its mouth clinked as it ran, hitting the floor.

"Maybe it *does* have a key," Kaylina mused, trying not to get her hopes up, but when the animal bounded up crates tied to the wall near the door, she couldn't help but believe it was working with them.

Even with that thought in mind, the muskrat startled her when it jumped toward the window.

Isla shrieked and scurried back. Kaylina managed not to cry out, but she did leap out of the way. Only as the muskrat sailed through, clipping one of the bars and dropping what it held, did she realize it might hurt itself if it landed hard. It wasn't a *cat*.

She lunged out and caught the animal. Its long tail slapped her arm, and its startled squeak was almost as loud as Isla's shriek.

Kaylina hurried to set it down when its claws scratched her through her shirt. Once down, the muskrat ran around the cabin. It didn't help that the ship rocked again, hard enough to tilt the deck.

"Check on the prisoners," someone near the ship's ladder barked. "They're making a lot of noise."

"They're scared by the ship rocking. There aren't any waves. What's hitting us? Whales?"

"There aren't any whales in the harbor. Water's too shallow, you idiot."

"*Something* is down there."

Kaylina willed the muskrat to calm down, trying to use the same magic that she'd drawn upon to soothe the beast, but she didn't reach out to touch the animal. Its claws had been bad enough. She didn't want to experience its bite.

Footsteps sounded in the corridor. The muskrat stopped squeaking and ran behind the bucket.

A shadow preceded one of the pirates stepping up to the door to peer in. Isla, who'd recovered from her surprise, lunged to step on something.

"What's going on in there?" one of the pirates who'd escorted them to the cell asked. "You girls are getting a mite feisty."

"We're afraid, you criminal ass," Isla snapped, angry for the first time Kaylina could remember. "What's happening to the ship?"

"We'll let you know when we figure it out, but the *Osprey's* sturdy. Don't you worry. Some *waves* aren't anything you need to worry about."

"What about whales?" Kaylina asked, adding concern to her voice. Whatever kept the pirates from thinking they were up to something. Thankfully, the muskrat remained out of sight behind the bucket. "Or *sharks*?"

The man snorted. "Neither can bother the ship."

As if to deny his words, something bumped against the hull, and the vessel rocked again.

"There's something swimming out here," came a call from above decks.

"It *is* a whale!"

"You can't see that in the fog, you idiot. There's nothing—"

The ship rocked again.

"One of the mooring lines snapped!"

"Look, there's another whale."

Kaylina spread her legs for balance. She had no idea what was happening. All she could think was that the altered plant had raised an alarm that other plants—and sea life—in the area could sense. And they were responding. Protecting the plant? Protecting *her*?

The pirate squinted at her, and she attempted to mask her face.

"The assassin said to especially watch you," he growled. "He said you've got some *power*. I scoffed, but I wonder."

Kaylina spread her arms and attempted to look innocent. "Humans don't have power. I'm just a girl, and I'm as worried about whatever is happening as you are. *More* worried. It's not like we can run if there's a hole in the ship, and it starts sinking."

"Ship's not going to sink while docked." He eyed her chest.

Realizing she'd invited that with her spread arms, Kaylina crossed them over her chest.

"But if you're scared, I can come in there and comfort you."

"That's not necessary," Kaylina said, though she caught Isla raising her eyebrows. Thinking about the seduction plan they'd discussed?

If Isla had under her foot what Kaylina *thought* she had, she had no interest in kissing a pirate.

A roar sounded, closer this time. The beast had to still be on land, but he might be perched on a roof near the docks, looking in this direction.

"All hands on deck," came an order from above.

Their unwelcome visitor pulled his gaze from Kaylina's chest. "I'll be back to comfort your fears later." He winked before leaving.

"Won't that be a joyful time," she muttered.

Isla moved her foot and stared down at a bronze key on the deck. Her mouth parted, and she gazed at Kaylina. In wonder? Or like she was strange? Kaylina couldn't tell, but it reminded her of the looks Jankarr gave her these days.

The muskrat sniffed its way out from behind the pot and wove between Kaylina's legs, much like Isla's cat had done when Kaylina had first visited. She refused to pick it up and pet it, especially after it had clawed her arms.

"I understood and believed from the beginning that Captain

Targon was right," Isla said softly, "that you are an *anrokk* and that animals are drawn to you. But I didn't..." Her gaze shifted to the brand. "Everything you said is true, isn't it?"

Uncomfortable under the scrutiny, Kaylina stepped past the muskrat and picked up the key. "Everything I told you is true as I experienced it. People—and plants—could have been lying to me about some things or might not have known for sure themselves, but, by now, I do believe that some ancestor of mine was a druid. Maybe my father."

Isla watched her take the key to the door and reach her arm through the window. Now, her gaze was almost reverent.

As Kaylina groped for the lock hole, her shoulder twisted awkwardly, she hoped she wouldn't prove herself a klutz by dropping the key. She didn't know if the muskrat would be willing to fling itself through the window a second time.

As she found the lock, the ship rocked again, pitching her against the door. She barely kept hold of her prize, and it took another moment to slide the key in. Finally, it turned, and she pushed the door open.

"Freedom," she whispered to Isla, then glanced left and right, making sure the corridor was empty.

The muskrat scurried out first, brushing past her leg and whacking her with its tail. Yes, she truly had the adoration of wildlife.

"I underestimated you," Isla said.

"It's all right."

"Maybe... maybe you *can* lift Vlerion's curse." For the first time, hope entered Isla's eyes.

Even though she didn't yet know how she would do it, Kaylina nodded firmly. "I will."

"Steady!" someone above ordered. "Wait until you're sure it's near."

It. The beast?

"He's a he," Kaylina whispered, stepping into the corridor and holding the door for Isla as the ship continued to rock. "We'll have to see if we can dive over the edge while they're distracted." Kaylina suspected the gangplank had been retracted, and if mooring lines were snapping, they might not be close to the dock anymore. "Can you swim?"

"Yes." Isla crept after her. "Will your power protect us from the whales?"

"I think the fact that humans don't taste good to whales will protect us." Kaylina ducked into the cabin with her weapons. Her sling and knife had fallen to the deck, but they were there.

"Hold your fire," a voice called from farther away than the others. Someone on the dock? It wasn't Vlerion, but it sounded familiar. "I'm coming aboard to speak with Venegarth and assist in this matter."

"That's Spymaster Sabor," Isla said.

Kaylina grimaced, but she was right. If not for the distance muffling his voice, Kaylina would have identified him sooner. "Was he really supposed to meet you—us—down here?"

"No. I lied. He did call me to the royal castle with a message saying he wanted to discuss Vlerion, but it didn't mention you."

"That sounds right. He barely acknowledged my existence, even when he was offering me as a reward—a *bribe*—if Vlerion did what he wanted."

Before heading up the steps, Kaylina glanced around, hoping to spot another way out, but the only other exit from the corridor was a ladder descending to a lower level.

She crept up the steps, sling in hand, intending to brain anyone who attacked the beast. If she got a chance, she would brain Sabor twice. The bastard.

At the top, the door was secured open, the fog denser than ever. Good. That would make it easier to sneak overboard. Except... Kaylina wanted to stay and help Vlerion if she could.

Maybe she could direct Isla overboard and find a nook from which she could hurl rounds without drawing attention.

Someone jogged past, but she could barely make out the face. A pirate? An assassin? It seemed everyone was preparing to attack the beast.

"It is rare that he who hires an assassin comes to assist with the kill," a cool accented voice came from a railing nearby. That speaker was also familiar. The leader, Venegarth.

"Is it?" Sabor responded. He sounded like he was on the dock near the ship. "I wish to ensure you're successful."

"Do you? You told me little of this aristocrat, of the power that he possesses. Of what he can become."

Kaylina winced, wondering how many witnesses were onboard to hear this. Vlerion's secret was well on its way to becoming common knowledge.

"I assumed you would believe you'd been brought to deal with someone powerful," Sabor said, "else why wouldn't I have drawn from my own troops?"

"I've lost several of my men, several of my well-trained, skilled, and enhanced men. Even veteran assassins who consume the special roots from the desert may not be enough to battle one who can turn into a monster. But I think perhaps you knew that."

"I just hired you to do a job," Sabor said. "From your reputation, I assumed you'd be able to handle it, especially when you showed up with ten men."

"Did you?" Venegarth asked softly. "Or do you have some vendetta against the tribes? Did you lure us here, hoping to see many of our strongest warriors killed?"

"Nothing of the sort." Sabor scoffed. "The tribes are insignificant to the kingdom. Your squabbles with the sandsteaders keep you perennially busy, and your people are no threat to Zaldor. I brought you to do this job, nothing more. And tonight, I've come to see you complete it. Assuming you can."

In the silence that followed, Kaylina shifted, aware of Isla crouching behind her on the steps—and that they would be caught if any of the crew ran belowdecks.

But all movement on the ship had stopped. The pirates seemed to be listening and watching the exchange between Venegarth and Sabor.

"Is it a test?" Isla breathed.

Kaylina looked back.

"Sabor has made it clear he wants to use my son—the beast—to get rid of the Virts and other threats," Isla whispered, "but I don't think he's ever seen the beast fight. Maybe he set this all up with the assassins to see if the beast is as deadly as he's heard."

Kaylina hadn't considered that, but she *had* been confused about Sabor wanting Vlerion dead.

"I don't know," she whispered.

"If that assassin succeeds, I'll kill Sabor myself," Isla said.

"The whales are still circling," someone said from the bow of the ship. "And I saw a shark fin."

"Is he capable of calling wildlife too?" Venegarth asked. "How many other powers does that man possess? How did he gain them?"

"He doesn't have any power except shifting." After a pause, Sabor added, "You said you have the girl?"

"In a cell."

Sabor's voice turned dry. "You might want to check if she's still there."

Kaylina cursed to herself and drew back, bumping Isla. They might have to hide on that lower level and hope for the best.

In case it helped, she tried to reach toward the altered aquatic plant below, willing it to sound that alarm even more loudly, whatever might prompt the whales to bump against the ship again and distract the men. The last few minutes had been quiet and still.

"You didn't mention *her* powers either," Venegarth said. "You didn't mention her at all. We underestimated her."

"Until recently, I wasn't aware that she had any power of significance. Or what she is."

"What is she?"

"Part Daygarii, we believe. Check to see if she's still in your cell."

"You're paying me to kill a man, not take orders about other matters."

Footsteps sounded, someone heading toward Kaylina and Isla.

Help, she whispered in her thoughts, trying to rouse the plant.

The alarm that had been bleeping in her mind earlier grew audible again, and thumps sounded as creatures bumped the ship. It rocked enough for people to curse and grab railings. Kaylina planted a hand on the wall, and Isla gripped her shoulder for balance.

Splashes sounded as the vessel rolled back and forth. Another thump came from the hull directly beneath Kaylina.

Thank you, she thought to the plants. *Keep it up, please.*

"Let's sneak you over the railing," Kaylina whispered to Isla.

But even as she rose, an angry roar echoed across the foggy harbor. This time, it came not from the city but from the dock. The beast had arrived.

28

As the deck rocked, whales thumping against the hull from all sides, a blunderbuss fired. Someone targeting the beast?

With the fog so dense, Kaylina doubted anyone could see him, but the pirates might get off a lucky shot.

"Vlerion?" Isla whispered, angst and fear in her voice.

"He'll be all right." Hoping she wasn't lying, Kaylina gripped Isla's hand. "This way."

"There!" someone shouted as they veered across the deck toward the railing farthest from the action.

Kaylina froze, afraid someone had spotted them.

But something landed on the far railing, claws scraping into wood. No, not someone. The beast.

In the fog, she could just make out his powerfully muscled form under his sleek fur. From the railing, he sprang toward a man on the deck. Toward the assassin.

Crouched with a sword and dagger in his hands, Venegarth waited, ready to meet his furred opponent.

"Look out!" someone barked.

A blunderbuss boomed again, thunderous in Kaylina's ears. The beast blurred as he leaped aside, swift enough to avoid the shot. Rounds slammed into the railing, chipping off chunks of wood.

Isla had been following Kaylina without hesitation, but she halted now, turning into an anchor.

"Vlerion," she whispered, her face contorting with distress.

"He'll be all right." Kaylina tugged, willing her to follow, but Lady Isla wasn't as obedient to druid power as a plant. "I've seen him fight. He can handle this."

She hoped that was true, but movement above caught her eye. Two of the crew ran across the yardarms, cutting something. Not a sail. A net?

"Watch out, Vlerion," Kaylina blurted as it fluttered toward the deck.

The beast either sensed the trap or heard her warning. He sprang back to the railing as the net landed between him and the assassin. He glanced up, snarled at the men who'd dropped it, then bounded over it and toward his waiting foe.

"This way." This time, Kaylina succeeded in leading Isla away, though she didn't take her gaze from the fight as the beast and assassin engaged, claws and blades clashing.

Only when they reached the railing, the harbor water lapping against the hull and a fin gliding past, did Kaylina realize she'd made a mistake. She couldn't hoist Isla over and ask her to swim to shore when there were sharks down there. Usually, nothing more inimical than starfish and sea urchins came into the shallow waters of the harbor, but now... She'd caused this.

Kaylina might swim past the sharks unscathed, but she wasn't positive of that. Especially not when she saw a second fin. The sharks were circling in the water. Waiting for prey to fall overboard?

Since the fur shark she'd encountered in the lake in the catacombs had left ugly scars on her leg, she didn't have faith that these creatures would leave her alone.

"I can swim." Maybe Isla thought she was hesitating because of that concern.

"Yeah, but so can they." Kaylina pointed at a fin, then scooted along the railing.

Maybe they could reach the side of the ship near the dock— assuming it was still *near* the dock. With the fog, she couldn't tell.

Growls, snarls, and scrapes and clanks came from the deck, the beast fighting with Venegarth. A lesser human would have already fallen to his superior speed and strength, but the sage assassin had advantages. Not only greater than normal strength and agility but tricks. He hurled one of his small explosives at the beast's pawed feet.

An irritated roar came from the smoke that billowed away, mingling with the fog. Someone screamed in pain. Not the assassin but one of the pirates. They were ganging up on the beast, trying to help Venegarth, and one had gotten too close.

Kaylina hardened her heart to the scream. These people were getting what they deserved for helping kidnap women.

She and Isla continued along the railing, making their way around the bow of the ship. When they reached the other side, a pirate with a blunderbuss came into view.

He stood with his back to the railing, his focus on the fight, and he didn't see them. With his firearm aimed toward the skirmish, he waited for an opportunity to shoot the beast.

Fury propelled Kaylina to release Isla and sprint at the man. She had her sling and knife but raised neither, wanting to bowl him over the side.

At the last second, the pirate noticed her and turned, swinging the blunderbuss toward her. She reached him first, ramming her shoulder into his torso. The firearm flew out of his hands, hit the deck, and went off, booming into the night.

The pirate grabbed at Kaylina, but she'd knocked him off balance. She tried to shove him over the railing, but he weighed more than she, and even her fury couldn't lend her the strength needed.

He recovered, curling his fingers into a fist. Before he could punch, Isla stepped up beside Kaylina with the discarded blunderbuss. Kaylina was about to say that it would need to be reloaded, but Isla swung it like a club.

The pirate, paying more attention to Kaylina, didn't get an arm up to block in time. The firearm cracked against his temple. Isla struck him again and again, her fear for her son no doubt lending her strength—making the attack more frenzied and savage than one would expect from a fifty-year-old woman.

When the man staggered back, nose bleeding and eyes glassy from the blows, Kaylina and Isla swarmed him. Together, they shoved him over the railing.

He almost landed on one of the whales near the hull below. Several sharks angled toward him.

Drawing back, Kaylina pointed farther down the railing and closer to the dock. "We'll go that way."

Pale-faced, Isla nodded. "I should think so."

Grunts and a cry of pain came from the netting, then the clatter of a sword hitting the deck. The beast slashed toward the assassin's chest. Claws tore into flesh and muscle as the man rolled away, and blood spattered. As Venegarth angled toward his sword, someone threw another explosive to help him escape. Another assassin ran in as well, shouting for his boss to look out as he swung at the beast.

Isla faltered, staring at the battle as fresh smoke billowed.

Kaylina pushed her along, knowing Vlerion would want his mother to reach safety. "There, the gangplank is still down. Get to land."

On the far side of the ship, another pirate aimed a blunderbuss, targeting the beast through the smoke. As Isla continued forward, Kaylina stopped to loose a round with her sling.

She wasn't fast enough to keep the man from firing, but her round struck him in the jaw. He reeled back, dropping his weapon. At least that would delay him from shooting again.

When she turned to check if he'd hit the beast, someone charged out of the smoke at her. She swore, reaching for her knife, but a pirate barreled into her like a taybarri about to flash.

She tumbled backward, striking the rail painfully, then tumbled over it, unable to get a grip to save herself. As she fell, she glimpsed Isla running along the gangplank. Hopefully, she would make it to safety.

Kaylina splashed down into the icy water without landing on any marine life, but that didn't mean she was out of danger. She gasped for air as the cold shocked her system while willing her power to keep the sharks away.

Something glided past, brushing her side. She spotted a triangular gray fin and almost screamed, inundated with memories of the fur shark in the lake chomping into her leg. This time, nothing bit her, though fins were all around, far more ominous from in the water than from above it.

Kicking hard, Kaylina paddled toward shore, or where she believed it to be. The fog made it hard to see far, and within a few strokes, even the hull of the pirate ship grew indistinct.

Another explosion came from the deck. She hoped the beast would survive, that he could handle all the assassins and pirates— and traps—without help.

A piling loomed ahead of her and to the right. Kaylina angled toward it, a gentle wave rolling her in that direction. She caught the barnacle-covered piling, but the dock was too far above for her to reach. She swam under it until she found a rowboat. It was low enough that she could grasp the edge and pull herself into it. From there, she climbed up to the dock.

When she got her feet under her, the fight was still going on the deck of the ship. The fog made the view fuzzy but didn't hide it completely, didn't hide the dead men, eviscerated or beheaded by the beast's powerful claws. Nor did it hide that others were diving overboard, risking the sharks and whales rather than continuing to fight against a more deadly foe.

Kaylina hoped Isla had made it to the waterfront—and that she hadn't noticed all the blood, all the bodies. Even though Kaylina had no delusions about the curse and what Vlerion became, the carnage was something from a nightmare. It would be hard for any mother to know her son had been responsible. Even if these men deserved it.

No, Spymaster Sabor deserved it. He'd orchestrated this.

Sling in hand, Kaylina started to turn, wondering if he'd avoided the beast running out toward the ship and was nearby watching this. But something hard pressed into her back even as she glimpsed a shadowy figure out of the corner of her eye. Sabor.

"Is that—" she started.

"A loaded pistol?" Sabor pressed the muzzle more firmly into her back as he stood close and gripped her elbow. He spoke over her shoulder as he watched the battle on the ship. "It is. I've a dagger and a sword as well. And troops nearby. As you might guess, it would have been foolish for me to come unprepared."

"Why *did* you come? And why did you hire assassins to kill Vlerion?"

As one of the pirates took aim at the beast, Kaylina tightened her grip on her sling, wanting to loose a round at the man. She should have stayed on the ship. Sabor never would have come for her there. He'd been skulking on the docks, avoiding the beast and watching from afar.

Somehow, the beast anticipated the firing of the blunderbuss aimed at him and leaped away before the pellets would have struck. He twisted in the air and came down behind his main opponent. Venegarth whirled, sword ready to deflect a claw slashing toward his head.

"To kill him?" Sabor responded calmly, as if they were in a quiet park instead of witnessing a deadly battle. "I deemed that unlikely, but I wanted to know for certain that this was all worth it."

"Then Isla is right. You *are* testing him."

Sabor turned his head slightly, whispering in her ear. "Not only him."

"Me?" Kaylina longed to ram her free elbow into his abdomen, the creep, but if he fired, that weapon could kill her instantly. And his grip on her was like steel. "You didn't even know I would be here."

"I knew the assassins wanted to use you as bait. Rightfully so. They're not dumb. They figured out what draws the beast."

Kaylina didn't know what to say to that.

Sabor fell silent, watching—or maybe mesmerized by?—the battle. She tried to reach out to the aquatic plants again. Maybe the whales could swim close enough to bump the pilings. The dock wouldn't rock like the ship had, but if a tremor startled Sabor, she could dive back into the water to escape him.

"He's magnificent," Sabor whispered. "Even more incredible than I believed from my research."

"You had to hire assassins to figure that out? You're an ass."

Sabor laughed shortly. "I wanted to make sure. The project I have in mind is long-term and quite the commitment, so it had to be worth it."

"What project?"

"Preparing a suitable location for him and his mate and ensuring his line will continue." Sabor looked at her, his eyes glinting with his schemes.

"What do you mean suitable location?" she asked, though she was getting the gist and doubted he meant the room in the castle tower he'd promised.

"Something far enough from trees—and apparently aquatic life—that you won't be able to escape from me—or him. Drawn by your druid blood, he'll come to you over and over, *mate* with you over and over, and you'll have cursed baby after cursed baby. We'll raise them to be weapons, to serve the kingdom."

Horrified, Kaylina stared at him. "You mean to serve you."

Sabor smiled tightly. "With such an army at my disposal, the kingdom will be mine."

"You're mad. You can't keep him locked up. He's too strong. And I'm—"

"As fascinating as he is." Sabor looked at her again. "I didn't think I was the type to be roused by a pretty girl, but even I can feel your allure, your draw."

His hand shifted from her elbow to her waist, groping presumptuously, and fury surged into Kaylina. Only that pistol against her back kept her from attacking, but she shook with raw anger as the spymaster pressed against her.

Something bumped one of the pilings, and a shudder went through the dock. Unfortunately, it didn't startle Sabor the way she'd hoped. He looked calmly down as a shark swam beneath them.

"Fascinating," he repeated, meaning her, not the shark. "I almost envy the beast his task of taking you, of planting his seed, but you are meant for him. Your cursed babies will be powerful. With them serving me, the world will bow to the power of Zaldor. We'll finally get rid of the Kar'ruk parasites and all those desert dwellers who refuse to come under our rule. None will dare stand against us."

A splash sounded as someone fell or dove into the harbor, and a final scream came from the deck of the ship. The beast gripped the eviscerated body of Venegarth, holding it overhead with both hands—paws. He appeared ready to hurl it after whoever had gone overboard, but he spotted Sabor and Kaylina on the dock.

With the body still above him, the beast jumped onto the railing of the ship. He must have been able to tell that Kaylina was a prisoner because he roared with fury. His blue eyes were savage—almost insane. He hurled the body onto the dock, blood spattering when it landed, then launched himself off the railing toward them.

Sabor shifted the pistol from her back toward the beast. Kaylina stomped on his instep and rammed her elbow into his abdomen. She had the satisfaction of striking him hard enough to make him stumble back. The pistol went off with a fiery flash, but she'd knocked his aim high, and the beast landed on the dock, not wounded, at least not from the firearm. He dripped blood from his other battles, but that didn't make him pause.

A splash sounded behind her. Sabor falling, or more likely *diving*, into the water.

"Vlerion," Kaylina blurted as he sprang not after the spymaster but toward her.

She backed up, fresh fear flowing through her veins. Did he not recognize her as a friend? As his *mate*?

"Vlerion," she repeated as he came closer, meeting those savage eyes and willing him to hear her. She reached for the power to soothe, but did she want to calm the beast now? When Sabor was getting away? "You have to go after him."

The beast engulfed her in his powerful arms, almost knocking her back.

"*Mine*," he snarled in his animalistic voice, and she realized those savage eyes did recognize her. And, after his great battle, he wanted her. "My mate."

"Yes, but you can't stop this time." Kaylina planted her hands against his chest, the muscles hard and taut under that sleek fur. "If you don't take out Sabor, he'll send more assassins after you." No, that wasn't the spymaster's plan, but with paws all over her, she couldn't find the words to voice detailed explanations. He shifted her against a piling, hunger in his eyes, in his touch. The beast wanted her, and he wanted her right there.

The dock shuddered as another shark bumped the piling. Or maybe something larger struck it.

The beast paused, snarling as he glanced toward the water, holding her possessively.

"I command those," Kaylina told him, trying another tactic. "I can take care of myself. And I need you to chase down Sabor." She glanced toward the water but couldn't see if the spymaster was swimming for the shore. He had to be. She couldn't have hurt him badly with her elbow strike. And he'd dived in, not fallen. "He'll continue to be an enemy to us both if you don't get him. Vlerion, do you understand me?"

Her hand tingled with searing warmth, and it glowed green, the light so strong that it bathed the furred and snouted face of the beast. It highlighted his eyes as he looked down at it and then at her. For the first time, a hint of hesitation mingled with the savagery in his gaze.

"Get him, Vlerion," she whispered. "Get Sabor, and then we can be together."

When you're a man, she thought but kept to herself.

The beast snarled, showing his fangs. This close, they were terrifying, but she made herself hold his gaze, summoning whatever power her blood gave her, and repeated her words. "Get Sabor."

The beast leaned in, inhaling her scent deeply, and she

thought she'd failed, that he intended to take her whether she agreed or not, but his lips brushed her cheek, almost a gentle caress, and he sprang away.

With his great muscles rippling under his fur, he ran past lampposts and down the dock, then leaped into the water. For a moment, splashes sounded as he headed in the same direction Sabor had likely gone. And then silence fell.

29

THE ONLY CHOICE IS HONOR.

   ~ Ranger Saruk

Dripping water, Kaylina slumped against the piling while taking deep breaths and second-guessing herself. She worried she'd made a mistake in sending the beast after Sabor.

What if, exhausted from the battle with the assassins and pirates, Vlerion changed back and fell unconscious at the spymaster's feet? He would be vulnerable to a dangerous man who was far from an ally.

In addition to endangering Vlerion, Kaylina realized she'd been presumptuous. She didn't have a right to order him around. Yes, she'd been afraid and grasping for something she could say to get the beast to release her, but she'd made a promise that she didn't plan on following through with. She wanted to lift the curse and make him disappear forever, not mate with him.

"Kaylina?" came a soft call from the fog. Lady Isla. "Are you all right? Where did Vlerion go?"

Kaylina pushed herself away from the piling, willing strength into legs that trembled after the chaotic adventure. Slowly, she walked down the dock toward Vlerion's mother.

"I'm okay. I asked the beast to go after Sabor. I... shouldn't have done it, but he was, uhm. After he fights and protects me, the beast tends to want to... mate."

Isla grew visible in the fog, standing at the foot of the dock. She didn't respond as she digested that.

"I'm sorry," Kaylina said, worried Isla would be upset with her for sending her son into danger again. She would have a right to be. "I was scared and furious with Sabor—you won't *believe* what he's planning—but it might have been a mistake. Vlerion could change back."

"We'll look for him. If we can find the carriage..." Isla peered into the fog along the waterfront, and Kaylina winced as she remembered that two of her men had been killed. "Now that I know Sabor hired those assassins," Isla added, "I hope someone *does* find and kill him, but I worry there will be repercussions if it's Vlerion. Sabor is an important person and at least partially in charge, with the king no longer able to function fully in his role. Sabor has powerful allies."

"He wants to run the kingdom completely. I wouldn't be surprised if he's egging on the Virts to try to get them to assassinate the king and queen and get them out of his way." Kaylina hadn't considered that before, but after listening to Sabor babble about creating beast babies—a future army of beasts—she believed it might be true.

As she reached the foot of the dock and joined Isla, voices came from farther up the waterfront.

Kaylina tensed, wishing her sling weren't wet, that *all* of her weren't wet. She pushed damp hair out of her eyes and debated if they should run. There were bodies everywhere on that ship and floating in the harbor—probably with sharks feasting upon them.

The Kingdom Guard might arrest anyone caught near the scene. Isla might not be held in suspicion, but Kaylina?

"We should go," she whispered, touching Isla's arm and nodding across the street to the buildings—and alleys—facing the harbor.

"Fan out," a gruff male voice said. "Check the ships."

Wait, was that Captain Targon?

"Help has arrived." Isla slumped with relief.

Kaylina did not. Targon, who knew all too well about her fledgling druid powers, might blame her for this. At the least, he would be exasperated that she'd been at the heart of it. She was still tempted to run, but Isla remained rooted.

"The rangers can help us find Vlerion," she said as men riding taybarri came into view through the fog.

Targon led the herd with Jankarr mounted beside him.

"You are quite late, Captain Targon," Isla said firmly—and tartly. She was bedraggled from their adventure but drew herself up regally, her chin in the air. "The bodies of the assassins and pirates who attempted to kidnap us are on that ship." Isla pointed down the dock and didn't mention that she'd been attempting a kidnapping herself.

As long as she was done doing that, Kaylina would keep her secret.

"We would have arrived sooner, my lady," Targon said, more dry than polite and respectful, "if you'd alerted us to your intention to seek trouble at the docks."

He halted his mount in front of her and looked at Kaylina, his lips pressing together. With disapproval, no doubt, as he wondered how she was involved.

Not my fault, Kaylina wanted to say, but she looked toward the city, more concerned about Vlerion.

Isla didn't respond to Targon's dry words, only waving to include the waterfront. "The assassins killed two of my men as well. You'll find their bodies nearby, as well as my carriage. Further, my son was here, and I need help locating him."

Isla looked at the rangers coming to a stop behind Targon, well within earshot. Jankarr's mount came forward and sniffed at seaweed draping Kaylina's shoulder.

"I must speak with you alone," Isla added to the captain.

Targon sighed and dismounted. "I figured."

"Are you all right, Kaylina?" Jankarr asked from atop his mount. He looked at her more with concern than the wariness he'd shown her since she'd successfully commanded the vines in the preserve to release him.

She would have been encouraged by that, but it might have only meant that she appeared extra bedraggled and pathetic. "Yes, thank you."

Crenoch, riderless but with the herd, came forward, joining the other taybarri who was sniffing Kaylina. Its large blue-furred snout had shifted from her shoulder to her pockets.

"Sorry. I don't have any food right now." Kaylina turned to Crenoch as Isla drew Targon aside to explain things to him. Impatient, she whispered, "Can you track Vlerion? He came out of the harbor near here." Thanks to the fog, she hadn't seen where Sabor or the beast got out, but she waved toward the waterfront near the dock. She whispered, "He was not himself," aware of Jankarr nearby.

Crenoch whuffed, as if he'd already known, then trotted toward the dock and started sniffing along the waterfront. Kaylina followed him, looking for puddles on the cobblestones that might indicate Vlerion or Sabor had climbed out.

Targon and Isla spoke tersely and quietly, but she caught Sabor's name often. Kaylina hoped Isla completely and thoroughly ratted out the spymaster. Whatever Isla didn't know, Kaylina would fill Targon in about later. Like his dastardly plan to start a beast army.

She trailed Crenoch along the waterfront as he sniffed and soon spotted a blocky shape in the fog. Isla's carriage. The horses had been unhitched and were nowhere to be seen.

Remembering the invaluable sword left inside, Kaylina jogged for the door. The assassins—or an opportunistic thief—might have taken it, but she hoped she would get lucky.

The lanterns had gone out, so she had to pat around to look for the scabbard. Disappointment swept through her when she didn't find it on either seat. She crawled in to search more thoroughly, and her knee bumped something. Ah! It had fallen to the floor.

Crenoch whuffed softly.

After grabbing the sword, Kaylina returned to his side. He looked at her, whuffed again, then veered toward a street perpendicular to the waterfront. He sniffed the air a few times, then lowered to his belly, pointing his snout at his back.

"You want to give me a ride?" Kaylina glanced at the rest of the herd, the fog shrouding them. Levitke hadn't arrived with them, and Kaylina hoped she was enjoying a well-deserved rest back in headquarters.

Crenoch whuffed again.

With their boss talking, the rangers hadn't dispersed, as Targon had originally ordered. Kaylina thought about calling for some of them to follow her, but if Vlerion was still in his beast form... bringing along men with weapons would be a mistake.

"Let's slip away," Kaylina whispered, gripping Crenoch's fur and swinging up.

The sword made the movement awkward, but she wouldn't leave it. She might yet need it tonight.

Crenoch rose and trotted off. Thanks to the poor visibility, the rangers didn't notice. Either that, or they weren't worried about a trainee riding off with Vlerion's taybarri.

Kaylina wanted to urge Crenoch to go faster, thinking they

might be able to catch up, since Sabor had been on foot, but frequent sniffing sounds promised the taybarri was tracking as he went, following the scent of the beast.

He turned often. Sabor must have been hoping to lose the beast, but Kaylina suspected he could track his prey without trouble.

Crenoch paused to sniff at a dark damp spot on a corner. Blood.

Sabor's? Vlerion's? Crenoch continued, and the situation reminded Kaylina of the hunt that had led them to the bathhouse.

They'd gone more than a half mile before Crenoch paused again. Kaylina recognized the neighborhood. A market square lay ahead, the vendor carts closed or gone for the night, and she spotted the back and one side of Nakeron Inn, lights burning in the windows as people stayed late in the bar and enjoyed their food and drink.

Would Sabor have gone *there* to hide? Or maybe he'd headed toward that nursery across the street. If it had a catacombs entrance, as Vlerion had said, the spymaster might have hoped to escape into the maze of tunnels.

A meow came from a nearby rooftop. Some stray drawn by the approaching *anrokk*. Unfortunately, a cat couldn't help Kaylina the way the sharks and whales had. Even so, Kaylina sent a thought in its direction, silently telling the feline she would have milk for it at Stillguard Castle if it helped her find Vlerion.

The answering meow sounded more saucy than accommodating.

"Cats," she muttered as Crenoch took them around the back of the inn and toward the alley where they'd fought the assassins.

Distant voices came from the street they'd come up. The rangers following them? Someone else?

"Hurry," Kaylina urged.

Crenoch turned down the alley but stopped after a step.

Two lanterns mounted on the outside of the inn provided enough light to see a man in dark clothing standing over another man, a *naked* man with short auburn hair. Vlerion. He'd turned back into his human form. As Kaylina had feared, he lay unconscious and vulnerable.

Enough shadows lingered that she couldn't make out the face of the man standing over him, gripping his ribs as he looked down, but she had no doubt it was Spymaster Sabor.

Fear blasted into Kaylina. He held something in his free hand, and when he turned it slightly, she caught the glint of a dagger reflecting the yellow lamplight.

Sabor hadn't yet noticed Crenoch and nudged Vlerion's side with his boot. Vlerion didn't move. He must have caught up with Sabor and attacked, wounding him, but the beast magic had faded before he'd finished, and he'd collapsed.

"Too much trouble." Sabor lifted the dagger.

Kaylina flung herself from Crenoch's back, drawing the sword before her feet touched the ground. Whether or not Sabor meant to slit Vlerion's throat, she didn't know, but she couldn't take the chance.

Perhaps busy debating Vlerion's fate, Sabor didn't turn until she stepped on shards of ceramic or glass indiscernible in the dark.

He whirled to face her, crouching and raising the dagger. Blood darkened his knuckles as well as the shirt under his cloak, and his clothing was ripped. The beast had landed at least one blow before he collapsed.

"Stay away from him," Kaylina snarled.

With the sword, she swung for the dagger, intending to knock it aside. But, even injured, Sabor glided to the side, easily avoiding her.

She knew he was a skilled fighter but didn't care. She

advanced, launching chains of feints and attacks, as Sergeant Zhani had taught her.

Though he had only the dagger and grunted in pain with his movements, Sabor didn't fall for the feints as he parried the attacks.

"*You're* too much trouble too," he said, knocking her sword out wide so he could lunge for her with his weapon.

She leaped back, whipping the sword back across her body, barely clipping his blade and deflecting it. He was faster than she, and she reluctantly admitted she was outmatched. His injuries didn't slow him enough.

Milk for some help, Kaylina thought toward the rooftop, though she had no idea if the cat remained up there.

"If I didn't need you, I'd find a potion that took *your* power too."

A potion?

His knife swept under her guard, slicing through her wet shirt and finding flesh, and she didn't have time to ponder. A streak of fiery pain lit up her side, and she scrambled away.

"You stay back, or I'll finish off your rider." That was for Crenoch, not Kaylina, and Sabor threw something at the ground in front of the approaching taybarri.

It wasn't an explosive, but it shattered when it struck the cobblestones, and something spattered Crenoch. He drew back, bellowing in pain.

At least that would draw the other rangers. If Kaylina could keep Sabor busy for a moment, they would arrive, and then... then what? Sabor would say she'd attacked him for no reason. And he was their superior officer. If he ordered her killed or arrested, they would obey, even Targon.

Frustrated, Kaylina lunged for Sabor, launching another series of attacks, willing whatever power flowed through her veins to guide her limbs, to make her fast enough to slip past his defenses.

"Stay back, girl. You'll make me forget my plans to keep you around."

She snarled and attacked faster, hardly caring that her fury made her movements frenzied instead of calculated.

Sabor curled a lip as he parried, not giving any ground. "You're every bit as irreverent and disobedient as Targon said."

A feline screech came from right behind Sabor. That startled him into flinching, his grip fumbling.

Though it startled Kaylina too, she didn't hesitate to take advantage. She sprang, giving up on feints and slashing with all her strength for Sabor's neck.

He almost recovered and got his blade up in time to parry. But almost wasn't sufficient. As the cat weaved between Sabor's legs, bumping him and further upsetting his balance, Kaylina slashed the beautiful bejeweled sword of Vlerion's deceased brother into Sabor's throat.

His dagger struck the cobblestones, clattering as he grabbed his neck, trying to stop the bleeding. But she'd struck an artery, and his life flowed out between his fingers.

Kaylina stepped back, relief mingling with horror as she watched a man die before her eyes. She'd never killed anyone before. Despite the ranger training, a part of her hadn't believed she ever would.

Sabor crumpled to the ground, dead.

The ramifications of her choice sank in, the realization that she'd killed an important man in the government, a powerful man with a lot of friends. The king and queen might order her executed when they found out. No, they *would* order her executed. She was common riffraff who wasn't even from this part of the kingdom. There would be no lenience for this crime. She couldn't even honestly say that she'd killed him in self-defense, only that it had been in Vlerion's defense. And to stop Sabor from executing his awful vision.

Crenoch had backed out of the ally, pained grunts almost like sneezes announcing that he remained nearby. Later, she would check on him, and, later, she would worry more about her predicament, but she had to make sure Vlerion was all right.

As she'd noted before, he lay naked on his back, his clothes not ripped, as they usually were during a change, but gone entirely. Maybe he'd lost them in the swim after the battle. Or maybe he'd known he would shift and had prepared ahead of time, stripping before letting his emotions swarm him.

Burn marks and gashes marred his flesh, wounds that had been hidden by fur when he'd been the beast. They were worse than she'd realized, so bad that Kaylina again regretted sending him after Sabor. Her own gash stung but was insignificant in comparison.

When she knelt beside Vlerion, the sword clinking on the cobblestones as she dropped it, he didn't stir. What if he... hadn't survived? What if he'd given everything to battle the assassins and the pirates? What if it had been with the last of his life force that he'd obeyed her order to chase after Sabor? And then the spymaster had thrown some potion at him. Or some *poison*.

She spotted a broken vial near Vlerion's head and gingerly picked it up. A blue liquid lingered in the bottom of the glass tube. She tucked it into a pocket for someone to research later, then touched Vlerion's bare shoulder.

"Are you awake, Vlerion?"

Are you alive?

She didn't voice the question but shifted her touch to his neck to check for a pulse. It thumped strongly beneath her fingers.

"Thank all the moon gods," she whispered. "Vlerion?"

The voices in the street were closer now. The speakers had passed the alley and continued into the market square, but it wouldn't take them long to figure out where Kaylina and Vlerion were. She didn't know if he would stir before they arrived. After turning into the beast, he always fell unconscious, his body drained by the magic and his battles, but the duration was different each time, and she didn't know what Sabor had done to him.

One of the voices in the square grew distinct. "Which way? There's his taybarri."

That was Targon.

Crenoch responded with a whuff-sneeze. Some of that acid, or whatever Sabor had thrown at him, must have landed in his unprotected nostrils.

"If you could wake up now, that would be handy." Kaylina patted Vlerion on the chest. "I think the rest of the rangers are coming. Maybe the Guard and whoever else they've rounded up too. And we..." She glanced at the body, groping for a way that she could explain Sabor's death. "*I* have a problem."

She supposed the Guard wouldn't believe that she'd *found* Sabor with his throat cut? And Vlerion unconscious? At least he was in his human form. Explaining the beast would have been even more difficult.

Vlerion stirred at her words and her touch, his lids opening and his blue eyes focusing on her. Pain made him wince, but he hid it quickly and breathed her name.

"Kaylina." He grasped her arm. "You're well." Relief and even delight entered his eyes as he smiled.

His feelings warmed her, especially when he'd once been so aloof with her, but there wasn't time to bask in them.

"Yeah, but that might not last long." She looked toward Sabor's body as voices drifted to them again. It sounded like everyone was in front of the inn. Any second, Targon and who knew how many rangers—how many *witnesses*—would find them in the alley.

"Spymaster Sabor is dead?" Vlerion pushed himself onto one elbow. "I..." His eyes slid upward as he groped for elusive memories of what had happened. "The beast didn't do that," he said with certainty. "I remember him... He threw some vial, and I lost all my energy."

"I know. I got here and..." Kaylina waved to the sword on the ground beside her. "I don't regret it, Vlerion. I *can't*. You have no idea what his plans for us were. And I wasn't sure if he was going to kill you. I thought maybe he was so pissed that he would. I had to..." She gulped for air that was no longer sufficient for her body's needs. "I'm screwed."

A mounted ranger appeared in the mouth of the alley, gazing in their direction. Captain Targon.

More men on taybarri rode up behind him, and men on horseback as well. The Kingdom Guard.

Vlerion picked up the sword and pushed himself to his feet, turning his face away so Kaylina wouldn't see him wince in pain. But she could see in his body how much he hurt, how badly he'd been battered by all the night's foes.

It wasn't until he stepped in front of Kaylina, as if to shield her from view—from *suspicion*—that she realized what he meant to do. Take the blame for Sabor's death. Accept whatever repercussions came for it.

"Vlerion, don't—"

He stopped her with a raised hand and by stepping closer to Sabor's body. He lifted his chin and held up the sword as he met Targon's eyes.

"Captain, I have a report for you."

Targon was looking at Sabor but shifted his gaze to Vlerion, his face masked. "Does it involve an explanation as to why you're naked?"

"No."

One of the guards snorted. "This looks like a lover's quarrel gone awry."

"Sabor *is* rumored to prefer men."

"Didn't know Vlerion's tastes ran that way."

Ignoring the guards, Targon said, "Meet me back at ranger headquarters, Lord Vlerion." He looked at Kaylina, his eyes narrowed, as if he was positive she'd had something to do with Sabor's death.

With her mouth dry, she couldn't have spoken if she wanted to. She vowed to tell Targon the truth, but it would be better not to admit anything in front of the guards.

"You too, Trainee Korbian." Targon glanced at the sword in Vlerion's hand—did he know Vlerion had given the blade to her? —before looking him in the eye again. "I'll take your report there."

In private, he didn't say, but it was implied.

"Yes, Captain."

Crenoch trotted past the group at the head of the alley. His eyes and snout watered, but he came close so Kaylina and Vlerion could mount.

Vlerion pulled himself up first, then, despite his injuries, offered her a hand up. Ignoring her own stinging wound, she scrambled up on her own, not wanting to burden him. She wrapped her arms around him from behind, half hugging him, half slumping against him with weariness.

She wished they could share a real embrace, that everything would be all right. He patted her hand, perhaps thinking the same.

"My mother was with you," Vlerion murmured as Crenoch passed the rangers and guards, all watching them curiously. "Is she..."

"She's okay." Kaylina didn't want him to worry about Isla and tried to make her tone light as she added, "She didn't even get chewed on by a shark."

He squinted over his shoulder at her. "I'm going to ask you for details on that later."

"I'll tell you everything."

"Go with them, Sergeant Jankarr," Targon said. "The streets are dangerous tonight. Even rangers need an escort."

Bleakness swept through Kaylina as Jankarr said, "Yes, my lord," and nudged his taybarri to follow Crenoch.

She knew Targon wasn't worried about street dangers. He wanted to make sure Kaylina and Vlerion did indeed return to ranger headquarters for that briefing. As much as Targon trusted Vlerion, he probably worried they might both flee from the city and the law, afraid of the ramifications of Sabor's death.

Had Kaylina been alone, she might have, but she knew Vlerion never would. With tears of concern leaking from her eyes, she pressed her cheek against his back.

A part of her wished he wasn't so noble and that they *could* flee together, even if it meant abandoning her business and starting over somewhere far from here—maybe Sergeant Zhani could advise them on opening a meadery in Sandsteader lands. Another part of her loved Vlerion for the man he was, even if his honor and nobility might land him in the gallows.

When she looked back, Targon had dismounted and was checking Sabor's body. Kaylina noticed the second-story inn windows that overlooked the alley, and more dread crept into her. She'd forgotten about those. She hoped all the patrons were on the main floor, eating and drinking rather than in their rooms.

But she glimpsed the curtain pushed back and a woman's face in a window right above a lantern. Was that Jana Bloomlong? The shadows made it hard to tell, but something told Kaylina it was. How long had she been there? What if she'd seen the beast battling Spymaster Sabor and then Kaylina killing him? What if she'd seen everything?

30

THAT WHICH IS DIFFERENT DRAWS CURIOSITY FROM SOME AND SCORN from others.
~ *Lady Professora Nila of Yarrowvast, Port Jirador University*

Having Jankarr riding beside them on the way back to ranger headquarters kept Kaylina from speaking much and certainly not about anything important. She would wait until she and Vlerion were alone together for that. Assuming they got a chance to be alone together.

"At some point, are you going to regale us with the tale of how you became nude?" Jankarr asked as the gate to headquarters came into view.

It had been a short ride—the night's chaotic events had happened near the core of the city—but Kaylina was impressed he'd gone that long without bringing up the matter. The weary slump to Vlerion's shoulders and grim set of his face might have staved off earlier quips.

"I am not," Vlerion said.

Jankarr looked back to Kaylina.

"I actually don't know where his clothes went," she said.

"No?" Jankarr arched his eyebrows.

"*I* didn't take them off."

"Is that true, Vlerion? Your pretty lady friend didn't remove your clothes? From the way she's hugging you, it's hard to believe she had nothing to do with it. Why else would a man remove his clothes?" Though Jankarr smiled easily as he joked, the set of his eyes reminded Kaylina of the way he'd looked when he'd been trying to puzzle things through in the preserve.

"I bathe occasionally."

"Such as before going into battles?" Jankarr eyed the burns, blood, and bruises all over Vlerion's torso.

"Yes. So I'm not too distastefully begrimed when I arrive in Doc Penderbrock's infirmary." Vlerion brushed soot off his arm.

"Maybe you should avoid walking through explosions if you want to arrive there in a tasteful state," Jankarr said.

"I'll consider your advice."

"Doubtful," Jankarr muttered.

"Speaking of your doctor, I hope you'll ride straight to the infirmary." Kaylina squeezed Vlerion gently, glad for his solid and reassuring presence even if she worried about the future.

"I will. Targon can receive his report there as easily as anywhere else. It won't be the first time."

Kaylina almost suggested Vlerion should consider a less dangerous line of work, but the night's events hadn't had anything to do with his career choice. Because he cared about her and his mother, he'd been drawn into Sabor's web.

She felt guilty that he'd been wounded because she'd been used as bait again. At least Sabor was dead. Whatever befell her in the future, she wouldn't regret that. Though if something awful befell Vlerion, she might.

She leaned her face against his back and gently kissed him,

wanting him to know that she understood the sacrifice he'd made for her. His career might be forfeit. His *life* might be. What would his mother think of Kaylina once she learned of the sacrifice Vlerion had made for her?

He patted her hand again.

"Why is Lord Vlerion naked?" the gate guard asked when the two taybarri arrived. Despite his curiosity, he didn't hesitate to open the way for them.

"Apparently, he bathes before going into battle," Jankarr said.

The gate guard looked to Kaylina with the same raised eyebrows that Jankarr had. She shook her head.

"I also thought the clothing removal might have been for her sake," Jankarr said, "but she says not."

"Huh."

Vlerion helped Kaylina dismount, then followed, taking the sword with him. Where his own blade was Kaylina didn't know—with his clothes, perhaps—but he seemed disinclined to let this one go. Maybe he didn't want anyone to associate it—and what it had done—with her.

After he patted Crenoch, promising to feed the taybarri soon, Vlerion walked to the infirmary. Despite the late hour, the door stood open. White-haired Doctor Penderbrock leaned against the frame, as if he'd been expecting them.

"You look like someone lit a fire on you after you were run over by a herd of taybarri." Penderbrock's gaze drifted from Vlerion's damp, sooty hair down to his bruised and burned bare feet. "*Two herds.*"

"That's about right."

Penderbrock looked Kaylina over, his gaze pausing on the bloody rip in her shirt and then lingering longer on the brand he'd once offered to help her remove. But *it* hadn't had anything to do with her troubles, not tonight. Now that the plant had told her that it had only placed the brand to help her access her power, she loathed the mark much less.

Penderbrock's gaze shifted to her shoulder. "Is that seaweed?"

"I think so," Kaylina said. "One of the taybarri sniffed it earlier but must not have considered it tasty."

The doctor grunted. "I wouldn't either."

Vlerion walked past Penderbrock and sat on the closest cot. Kaylina sat next to him and clasped his hand.

"Guess it's a good sign if a woman is willing to touch you when you're that grimy and naked." Penderbrock grabbed water and towels before opening cabinets for whatever ointments and potions could help with the numerous injuries Vlerion had received. He waved at Kaylina's gash to indicate he would treat her as well.

"Jankarr suggested my nudity might appeal to her." Vlerion squeezed her hand.

"It's grimy, blood-spattered nudity, Vlerion." Penderbrock put bandages, sutures, and jars of ointment on the table next to the cot and paused to look him over and squint closer at a couple of the wounds. "It's not appealing to anyone."

"Even a doctor?"

"*Especially* a doctor, but I've the tools to fix them. Once you wash yourself." Penderbrock tossed him one of the towels.

"Some healers might clean a man's wounds for him," Kaylina murmured, taking the towel and dipping it in water.

"That's the work for an *assistant* healer. Or a ranger trainee undeterred by grimy nudity. Have you had your first-aid class yet?"

"No, Sergeant Zhani has only been instructing me on how to use plant patterns in sword fights."

"Maybe you can wrap fern fronds around injured people."

Kaylina patted Vlerion's arm. "Why don't you lie down? Then I can gently and reverently dab your wounds clean."

"Reverently?" he asked.

"Yeah, I'll call you *my lord* a bunch while I'm dabbing."

Vlerion managed a smile, the first since she'd found him in the alley. "It's almost worth being wounded to get such treatment from you."

Voices sounded outside. Some of the rangers returning?

Vlerion held up a finger to Kaylina and rose to close the infirmary door. "Doc, will you give us a few minutes of privacy?"

"You can't wait to talk until I've stitched you up and rubbed ointment on those burns?"

"No." Vlerion pointed to the doctor's office.

"Fine, but if I come back here and find the dabbing and reverence have turned into sex, I'll be irritated with you."

"You don't think I deserve sex after a night of battle?" Vlerion looked wistfully at Kaylina as he returned to the cot, lying on his back as she'd advised.

"It's contraindicated for a man in your condition. Look at all those burns. You're lucky your cock wasn't fried like a rotisserie turkey over flames gone wild."

"Thank you for the garish imagery," Vlerion murmured.

"Think about it the next time you decide to go into battle without clothes." The door thumped shut as Penderbrock sealed himself in his office.

"His bedside manner is lacking," Kaylina noted, taking the damp towel to Vlerion.

"Even in their headquarters, young rangers must be hardened and never coddled, for their travails in following their duty will test their mental and physical ability to endure."

"Quoting the handbook again?"

"As every ranger should be able to do." Vlerion rested his hand on hers, pressing it against his chest to stop the dabbing while he gazed into her eyes. "Tell me what happened tonight from your point of view."

"Still giving orders, are we?"

"Yes, and please obey them quickly." He glanced toward the window. "We might not have much time."

And he needed to figure out what he was going to tell Targon. He didn't say it, but his eyes—and the glances toward the window—did.

Nodding, Kaylina shared what had happened, starting with Isla arriving at Stillguard Castle. She wasn't sure if Vlerion only wanted to know about the showdown in the alley or if he wanted the whole tale, but she had to tell him everything so he would understand why she hadn't hesitated to cut the spymaster's throat. She hoped he understood.

He listened without interrupting. A few more voices sounded in the courtyard—one belonged to Targon—as more men returned.

"I didn't mean for you to take the blame," Kaylina said to finish. "I would never have asked that."

"I know." He patted her hand.

"In the end, it may not matter. There was at least one witness. Jana Bloomlong. I don't know if she saw everything, but..." Kaylina shrugged.

"She probably did. She's a busybody." Vlerion didn't look too worried. Maybe because he'd already come to peace with his choice and accepted whatever fate the future delivered to him?

Emotion knotted in her throat. She didn't *want* him to have to endure anything but the fate he deserved. He was a good man. A hero, not a villain. The kingdom needed to know—

The door opened, and a scowling Captain Targon walked in. After eyeing them both, he glanced toward the closed office door.

"You weren't supposed to be left alone," he grumbled.

If that was true, Kaylina made a note to thank Penderbrock later—or send Frayvar over to help him organize deliveries of new medicines that came in.

Thoughts of her brother made her look wistfully through the

wall in the direction of Stillguard Castle. She hoped the rest of their opening night had gone well.

"Did you think we'd flee the city?" Vlerion asked without humor.

"That thought crossed my mind," Targon said. "Now that I see you're alone in here together, I'm surprised I didn't walk in on you *both* naked on that cot with the legs creaking."

"Due to my wounds, Penderbrock said sex is contraindicated."

"He says that no matter what your problem is. I had a cramp in my calf last month, and he told me not to have nocturnal visitors." Targon glanced toward the courtyard, then closed the door.

"Did you obey his suggestion?" Vlerion asked.

Kaylina shook her head. She didn't want to know.

The wicked smirk Targon gave them promised he didn't listen to his doctor's advice.

The smirk didn't last long. "The word is getting out quickly about Spymaster Sabor's death. You two want to tell me what happened?" He looked steadily at Vlerion as he spoke. Fully intending to blame him for it?

Why, because he didn't think she could have bested Sabor? Indignation lifted Kaylina's chin before she remembered that she nearly *hadn't* bested the experienced veteran. If not for Sabor's wounds and the timely interference from the cat...

Still on his back, Vlerion touched her hip. A reminder that he didn't want anyone to know that she'd landed the killing blow?

"It didn't escape my notice, nor will it escape Milnor's that he had grievous claw wounds as well as a cut throat," Targon added. "And there might have been witnesses in the inn. Why'd you pick *that* alley for your showdown?"

"Sabor was angling for the catacombs entrance through the nursery," Vlerion said. "I managed to catch up with him before he got there."

"You could have followed him *in*. That would have been a

much better place for him to die. Altered orchards, the body might not have been found for months down there. If ever." Judging by Targon's sour expression, Spymaster Sabor going missing would have been a far less consequence-laden event than his death.

"I wasn't myself at the time," Vlerion pointed out. "And I was..." He looked toward Kaylina but didn't continue.

The beast had been doing his best to obey her order. She grimaced.

Targon squinted at her, probably guessing the unspoken thoughts.

"Who's Milnor?" she asked before he could start questioning her.

"Sabor's second," Vlerion said. "Now the head spymaster, I suppose."

"Yes, a former doctor and a detective for the Castle Guard," Targon said. "Not much gets past him. Did Sabor threaten her, or what, Vlerion?" Targon pointed at Kaylina.

"He did," Vlerion said.

"More than that." Kaylina kept herself from explaining how Sabor had died, but she did spit out his plans to Targon, wanting him to know the truth about that, how Sabor had planned to have her birth an army of beasts—and how he'd had ambitions to rule the kingdom.

Targon's only response was to grunt, an utter lack of surprise on his face.

"Did you *know*?" Kaylina asked.

"I knew he wanted to use Vlerion. The rest doesn't surprise me, though that's a long-term plan. He must have imagined he would live well into his old age."

"Maybe he had a longevity potion in his collection." Vlerion touched what might have been an acid burn on his leg.

Kaylina twitched, reminded of the broken vial with the blue liquid she'd recovered. Something that might have forced Vlerion's curse magic to fade, leaving him in his human form. She almost withdrew it, thinking Penderbrock might have ideas about it, but she decided to keep it and enlist her brother to help to research it.

"I suppose." Targon grunted again. "He had a dangerous job though. Potions don't do much against swords." He pointed at the scabbard beside the cot. "That was your brother's sword, wasn't it, Vlerion? Why'd you have it tonight? Especially when you were... You're skirting the subject of Sabor's death, but from what your mother told me, you were furry tonight. The beast doesn't carry a sword, does he?"

"Is my mother all right?" Vlerion asked, even though he'd already questioned Kaylina about that.

He probably wanted to change the subject.

"Fine. Just rattled. And in awe that her cell mate was able to call whales and sharks to the harbor to aid in their escape." For the first time, Targon gave Kaylina more than a glance, as if she might have some slight significance to him.

"Actually, the muskrat was paramount in our escape," she said, inclined, like Vlerion, to change the subject.

"Captain Targon," came a call through the window. "The spy, Lord Milnor, is here to see you."

"That didn't take long." Targon looked at both of them with exasperation. "Vlerion, you're relieved of duty for now, and you're not to leave the city." He looked toward the window. "No, it'll be better if you're out of the city for a while. Go to your family estate, and stay with your mother. I'll come see you to get a more thorough report and let you know... Well, there'll be an inquiry, I'm sure."

"I have no doubt," Vlerion said.

"He's a prisoner?" Kaylina couldn't help but feel affronted on Vlerion's behalf and gripped his hand. As she'd been thinking before, he'd been heroic that night. He'd done the right thing. She swallowed around the lump in her throat. He'd done what she asked.

"On his mother's thousands-of-acres estate with servants to fetch whatever he wishes," Targon said dryly. "I'm sure he'll survive the hardship."

"May I have visitors?" Vlerion said, no objection to the exile.

Targon rolled his eyes. "Yes, yes, your jaunty little *anrokk* can visit you, though I want you to obey Penderbrock's advice."

Vlerion tilted his head.

"About contraindicated activities." Targon headed for the door. "The beast needs to disappear for a while if you're to have any shot of making people forget about him."

"Understood, Captain."

Another call came from the courtyard. Sighing, Targon walked out, closing the door behind him.

"I don't want you to take all the blame for this," Kaylina whispered, facing Vlerion. "I don't want you to take *any* of it. It was because of me—"

"It was not." He raised a finger to her lips to quiet her.

She frowned. Maybe, since he'd been the beast, he didn't remember that she'd ordered him to go after Sabor.

"When the assassin laid his trap for me—for the beast—he delivered a message that he had my mother," Vlerion said. "I assume it was luck that he captured both of you. I didn't know until I arrived at the dock and caught your scent that you were there. Summoning sharks and muskrats." He had to be worried about his future, but he smiled, humor glinting in his eyes. He lifted a hand to brush hair from her eyes. "Once I knew you were there and that Sabor had arranged everything... I would have killed him regardless. Will you come visit me while I'm in exile at the family estate?"

"I would like to, but how many kidnappers will be waiting for me?" After what she and Isla had been through, Kaylina *hoped*

Vlerion's mother no longer wanted to oust her from the province, but she didn't know that.

"No more than four or five, I should think."

"That many? I'll have to bring allies."

"Muskrats?"

"A whole pack of them, yes."

"That should be interesting to see. I'll wait by a window so I can watch your arrival as you lead them up the driveway."

"It'll be magnificent, like I walked out of a fairy tale."

"Of that I have no doubt."

He kissed her, gently and wearily, and she wrapped her arms around him, wishing they could have more time alone together, but the office door soon opened. Penderbrock cleared his throat as he walked back in.

"Targon stopped at my window and said to get you patched up and on your way, Vlerion." He looked at Kaylina. "You too. Then you're supposed to check on your grand opening."

"I will. Thank you." She looked at Vlerion as she said the words, hoping he knew how much she appreciated everything he'd done. How much she appreciated *him*.

He nodded and picked up the scabbard, handing it to her. "Don't forget your sword. I fear the streets will remain dangerous for some time."

"I have no doubt," she murmured. "I have no doubt."

EPILOGUE

"I have a quest for you, Fray," Kaylina said as morning sunlight slanted through the windows of Stillguard Castle, the fog of the previous night gone.

She moved about the kitchen carefully. Every time she twisted slightly, her side twinged where Sabor's dagger had caught her, but Penderbrock had bandaged the wound, saying it didn't need stitches. Fortunately, the spymaster had only grazed her.

Her brother yawned, pushed hair out of his eyes, and drank from a mug containing three parts honey and one part coffee. "Is it to improve upon my salmon dish? It got fewer rave reviews last night than the others, but I have some ideas."

"You can work on that, but I'd also like you to see if you can use your vast research abilities to learn what was in this and what it does." Kaylina showed him the broken vial she'd collected from the alley. The liquid in the bottom had dried, but a faint blue smudge remained.

"Uh, that's not a lot to go on."

"Yes, but you're smart, resourceful, and love puzzles. I'm certain you can figure it out."

Frayvar squinted at her. "Flattery?"

"Naturally. I thought you'd like it."

"More than Silana making marks all over my seating chart and telling me the aisles were too tight. They most certainly were not. I used math—precise computations—to choose where the tables and chairs should go."

"I thought they were perfectly placed."

"So did Sevarli." Frayvar took the vial and lifted his chin. "She complimented the food and the way I ran the kitchen."

"She either likes you or got a lot of tips and was happy."

"She said she'd come back to help again tonight."

"It could be both things."

Pink tinged Frayvar's cheeks, and he muttered, "I'm sure she doesn't *like* me," as he turned away.

Silana walked in so Kaylina didn't point out that a girl his age, who thought his food was good, would be a more realistic person to pursue a relationship with than Lady Ghara.

"Oh, there you are, Kaylina."

"Here I am." On the outside, Kaylina smiled, but she braced herself for censure about how late she'd gotten home. By the time she'd returned the night before, all the patrons had been gone, and the dishes had been washed. Being kidnapped and locked in a cell was a good excuse for being gone, but... Kaylina didn't plan to tell her sister about any of that.

"We missed you last night," Silana said.

"Especially for the cleanup," Frayvar said, though he was studying the vial by the light of a window.

"I'm sorry. I'll handle it all tonight." After her adventures, Kaylina might need a nap before they opened for the evening, but she wanted to make up her absence to her siblings—especially Frayvar, who'd had to endure a horribly maligned seating chart.

"Despite your noticeable absence," Silana said, "the evening was quite successful. I'll report that to Grandma."

Kaylina almost swooned with relief. With so much else going on, she hadn't realized how tense she'd felt over her sister's visit, over the dreaded report she would take back home. She made a mental note to thank Vlerion for putting the word out to the aristocrats and whoever else he'd told about the grand opening.

"We got more bulk orders for your mead," Frayvar added. "I hope it's safe enough for you to venture into the preserve to gather gallons of honey. We'll need it."

"I..." Kaylina imagined showing up in that valley with a cart pulled by taybarri—taybarri who expected a cut of the honey for themselves. She might have to go on an expedition in search of more hives left by the druids. "I'll see what I can do. I need to visit Vlerion later and take his mother some mead."

A bribe to ensure further kidnapping attempts didn't occur.

"We're raising the price," Frayvar said. "With our supply so limited, we'll have to charge more."

"I'm not charging Vlerion's mother."

"Didn't you say she was behind your kidnapping attempts? I'd charge her double."

"Kidnapping?" Silana asked.

"Nothing." Kaylina laughed and waved away the notion while shooting a glare at her brother. "Just a joke."

He made a face but didn't naysay her.

"The people up here are having an influence on you," Silana said. "They're rough. Some of the men and women who visited last night had the demeanor and manner of pirates."

"If you mean the table of guys who kept pinching your butt," Frayvar said, "those were nobles. They're pompous and arrogant. It's why groups of commoners are rebelling."

"Ghastly," Silana said. "At least they tipped well."

Kaylina wondered if she could convince the plant to do some mild defending of any staff who were treated poorly by handsy customers. A vine wrapping around a wrist might startle even a pompous aristocrat into good behavior.

"Anyway," Silana said, "I'll take my leave soon. It looks like you have some decent helpers to run the services, and I miss my husband and children. It's such a long voyage to get up here. I don't know why you had to cross the *entire* kingdom to prove yourself."

"The capital seemed a good place for it," Kaylina said.

"Hm."

"Thank you for coming up to help us." Kaylina lifted her arms for a hug. "Even if you were also spying on us."

Silana snorted but didn't deny it. She returned the embrace.

Frayvar glanced over and, perhaps afraid the hug would be contagious, fled the kitchen.

After they stepped apart, Kaylina said, "When you're back at the Gull, if you see a green-haired man, you might mention that I exist and would like to see him."

"*Any* green-haired man? Or the particular one?"

"The particular one, though I suppose I'd be curious to meet any of them." It was the truth, since Kaylina had more questions than she could wrangle, but she doubted a man who wasn't related to her would sail a thousand miles and more to the north for a chat with her.

"I'll keep my eyes out," Silana said.

"Thank you."

Once her sister departed, Kaylina delved into the cellar to

select a bottle of mead to take to Havartaft Estate. Even though the cooks there were doubtless plying Vlerion with good food, she also boxed up some of Frayvar's bread and leftover lamb for him. She'd tasted them and knew how delicious they were. If the meadery turned out to be a success, she would owe her brother a great deal for it, for drawing so many people with his food.

Kaylina remembered to set out a dish of milk in case the cat who'd helped her came by. It showed up immediately, trailed by ten more, a ragtag bunch with mangy fur and torn ears. They surged to the milk dish like piranhas in the Bloody Basin near the Vamorka Islands.

A stronger-than-usual purple glow from the tower indicated the plant was watching over the premises—or watching over her. It didn't communicate with her, but she sensed an emotion coming from it. Satisfaction? Over how she'd handled the night's events? Maybe it was pleased she was drawing upon her druid power to inveigle help from trees, plants, and seaweed.

A cat licked its lips, meowed, and weaved between her legs.

"Yes, and animals too," Kaylina murmured.

Before leaving, she gave the plant more honey water. It glowed at her with contentment.

If only she could use her burgeoning power to keep Vlerion from getting in trouble over Spymaster Sabor's death.

"Thanks for coming with me," Kaylina said as she rode on Levitke beside Sergeant Zhani and her mount.

They were heading north to Havartaft estate, the afternoon sky a pale blue, the sun warming their faces. Kaylina wore a dress and sandals instead of blacks, and the sword was in a holder instead of belted at her waist, so she didn't feel like a proper ranger on the big taybarri, but Levitke didn't mind. Her hind end sashayed as she walked, her tail swishing back and forth.

"I don't *really* think there will be kidnappers waiting for me, but if Vlerion explained his reason for being exiled here to his mother, she might have changed her mind about me."

"You're welcome, but it wasn't entirely my idea."

"Targon sent you?"

"To make sure Lord Vlerion is where he's supposed to be and that the two of you don't decide to... what did he say? *Hare off somewhere together.*" Zhani slanted a long look at her. "I don't know what happened last night, but the captain was back and forth to the castle three times this morning, scowling every time."

"He scowls *most* of the time."

"I believe that's usually when he's dealing with you. He gives me a nod and a polite *Good morning, Sergeant Zhaniyan* when I see him. Though the nod is occasionally more toward my boobs."

"He's an ass."

"Sometimes." Zhani smiled faintly, like she might not entirely agree.

Kaylina wagered her *boobs* agreed. "We're not going to hare off anywhere." She meant that but felt wistful at the notion. "Unless the king or spymaster's disciple sends an execution squad out here to kill Vlerion."

Zhani blinked. "Is that likely to happen?"

"I hope not."

A worried furrow creased the sergeant's brow.

Since Kaylina couldn't wave dismissively and claim it had been a joke, she forced a smile and said, "If we *did* want to hare off, would your homeland be a good place? It sounds vast and like it would be easy to avoid pursuers."

"It's vast without much water, so it's easy to die if you don't know where the oases and rivers are. The summers are brutal, the winters are cold—though not as cold as here, I'll admit—and the nomadic tribes are cantankerous and dangerous, whether you're behind city walls or not."

"If those sage assassins come out of those tribes, I believe you. Do you ever miss it, or is it better here?" Kaylina waved to indicate the Strait of Torn Towers, the valley, and the mountains, their peaks still snow smothered despite summer's arrival.

"I don't mind it here. I do miss my family, but... it's safer for me here." Zhani bit her lip and, for a moment, looked like she might explain, but instead she patted her sword. "Captain Targon suggested I continue your training while we're out here. He said Lord Vlerion is too injured to entertain you for long."

"Is that so?" Thoughts of her fight with Sabor came to mind, and her gut churned at the memory of delivering a killing blow. Kaylina didn't long to wield the sword anymore and again thought wistfully of escaping. Or at least returning to Stillguard Castle to start planning her next batch of mead. That was far more appealing work than sword fighting.

"Something about contraindications." Zhani shrugged.

Kaylina snorted but dropped the subject. They'd reached the circular driveway that led to the manor, and neither butler nor servant stood in the doorway. Instead, Lady Isla herself awaited them. Kaylina examined the topiaries and trees dotting the manicured front lawn but didn't see any kidnappers poised to spring.

Isla's face was as grave as ever as she lifted a hand to greet them, but she surprised Kaylina with a smile as they approached. After Kaylina dismounted and offered the bottle of mead, Isla stepped forward and hugged her.

"I'm glad you could come this afternoon." Isla accepted the bottle, holding it reverently to her chest, and nodded to include Zhani. They must have met at some point before. "Vlerion is restless."

"Already?" Kaylina asked. "His exile just started last night. Did he even arrive here before dawn?"

"Shortly after. He's relaxing out back—his doctor and I both ordered him to do so until his injuries heal—but he's a man of action. He's flipping his dagger and looking longingly toward the mountains, like he hopes hordes of Kar'ruk will invade the kingdom at any moment."

"That is typical behavior of many rangers," Zhani said. "We are trained to always be prepared for enemy attacks."

"Perhaps so, but I'm sure Vlerion would delight in having female company to distract his ranger mind."

"Some female company more than others." Zhani smirked at Kaylina and pointed toward the stable. "I brought training equipment. I'll set it up for later while you visit with him."

Kaylina glanced at Isla, wondering if she would object to Kaylina being alone with Vlerion. Given their tendency to be drawn to each other and leap into kissing and touching, his mother might prefer a chaperone.

Not remarking on that, Isla said, "I'll have some snacks brought out to go with your mead. Or perhaps some of *our* mead. We'll save this for a special occasion." Isla patted the bottle from Stillguard Castle. "And possibly only for me."

Kaylina didn't object. She was glad Vlerion's mother enjoyed her mead.

After Zhani moved away, Isla pointed around the house. "You'll find him back there. Maybe you can discuss ideas for lifting his curse."

The belief that Kaylina could do that shone in Isla's eyes.

Though glad to have her faith, Kaylina didn't yet know how to do what they both wished.

All she said was, "An excellent topic."

"Yes."

Kaylina left Levitke with Zhani and followed a path around the house. She'd been that way before but hadn't wandered down the flagstone trails that branched off, meandering through gardens of flowering bushes. Bees, butterflies, and birds flitted about, enjoying the area.

At first, she didn't see Vlerion, but one of the trails continued farther behind the house to a small lake, the water almost hidden by reeds growing in the shallows. The flagstones led to a dock that stretched through a gap in the reeds, widening to a square platform at the end with a rowboat tied up next to a diving board. Vlerion and his brother must have played out there as boys.

Now, Vlerion lay on a lounge chair with his shirt off and his feet bare. A book and the dagger he must have been flipping earlier rested beside the chair, but his eyes were closed. Though relaxed, his body always emanated power, reminding Kaylina of a panther that could switch from lounging in the sun to springing upon enemies at any second.

As she approached, she admired his muscled chest. Bandages covered some of the cuts and burns, but she could see plenty of his lean form, and her libido bestirred itself. She imagined walking up and straddling him on the chair, pressing her hands to his shoulders, and leaning down to kiss him. Such positioning probably wasn't properly reverent, but the thought of it was arousing.

Kaylina didn't think she made noise as she stepped from the flagstones to the dock, but Vlerion's head turned, his blue eyes finding hers. She blushed at her thoughts.

He nodded toward her, looking at her dress—or maybe her body—and letting his gaze linger with appreciation. That gaze heated her as much as thoughts of straddling and kissing, and she couldn't help but notice how much privacy the foliage provided back here.

If only...

Vlerion sighed, perhaps thinking the same, and sat up. "Thank you for visiting."

"Of course. Your mom is going to have someone make us snacks but not, she warned me, the mead I brought. She's keeping that for herself."

"So we get something inferior?" His eyes crinkled, and he patted the cushion next to him. He might have winced ever so slightly as the movement made his wounds twinge, but he masked his expression quickly.

Kaylina wanted to tell him that he didn't have to be tough for her, but stoicism was spoken about often in the ranger handbook. He probably didn't know *how* to show his pain.

"Probably mead made on *your* estate." She waved in the direction of hives in the fields between the highway and the manor.

"Ours isn't dreadful, but it's not made from druid honey."

"Few varieties are."

Kaylina sat beside him, their hips touching, his bare torso drawing her gaze again. Using a separate chair would have been safer, but there wasn't one on the dock.

"Do you have a shirt?" she asked.

"Does my nude torso offend you?"

"No, and that's the problem." She lifted a hand, tempted to touch him, to stroke and caress him, but when she spotted the flare of interest in his eyes, she lowered it again.

"Ah." A hint of sadness replaced the interest. "I suppose I shouldn't suggest you remove your dress and swim in the lake then."

"Definitely not. It's not that warm anyway, especially given how cold the waters in this part of the kingdom are."

"And I can't even offer to warm you up afterward. It's a tragic state we find ourselves in."

"I know." Kaylina clasped his hand, hoping that would be safe, that it wouldn't lead to temptation.

Vlerion accepted her grip, and they arranged themselves to sit shoulder to shoulder, gazing out at ducks paddling in the lake.

"Your mom wants us to discuss lifting the curse. She seems to have faith now that I can do it."

"Yes. She shared her version of your adventure last night. I'm thankful that you watched out for her even though she tried to betray you. You may not want to be a ranger, but you've all the honor and courage that we value. That *I* value." Vlerion's eyes flared again, interested and intense, and he brought her hand to his lips to brush them over her knuckles.

A zing of awareness swept up her arm, making her tingle all over, the urge to kiss him returning.

"I just talked a muskrat into helping us," she said to dismiss her role as having been that great.

He didn't look away. "A *muskrat* is not what allowed you to defeat Sabor last night in that alley."

"No, that time it was a cat."

Vlerion snorted softly. Since he'd been unconscious, he wouldn't have seen the cat and didn't know that it had indeed played a role in her surviving that confrontation. Since his eyes were so full of gratitude—and was that even admiration?—for her, she didn't continue to downplay what she'd done.

"I can't regret that the spymaster is dead," Kaylina said, "but I shouldn't have let you take the blame for that."

"Let me?" His eyebrow twitched. "I did not seek your permission before doing so."

"No, and that was rude."

"Or maybe noble."

"Rudely and presumptively noble."

"I am, as you've so often pointed out, a haughty aristocrat. We're trained from birth to be presumptively noble."

"That I believe."

Vlerion lowered their clasped hands to gaze more seriously at her. "I had to protect you, Kaylina. Not only from blades but from less tangible but equally threatening dangers. Besides, my station and service to the kingdom should... if not armor me fully from repercussions, make them less severe than you would have endured."

"Hence why you've been promptly exiled."

"Exiled instead of executed."

"For now," she said softly.

He might have more inkling of how he would be treated than she, but he couldn't know for certain what the future held for him either.

"Yes. I'll deal with whatever blowback comes. After all, it's not like I didn't *try* to kill him myself." Vlerion raised his hand, curling his fingers to indicate claws. "If the magic hadn't faded at that moment, I would have."

"I regret ordering you—the beast—after him. I was just..." Kaylina bit her lip.

"Trying to deter him from celebrating his victory by mating with you," Vlerion said grimly.

"Yes, but I've now twice promised the beast that we *would* mate if he did what I wanted. I feel like I'm betraying him every time I show up."

Vlerion squeezed her hand. "You should do whatever you must to keep him from hurting you or forcing you to do anything. I wouldn't forgive myself if I woke up as a man with you underneath me and..." Eyes bleak, he looked away. "I wouldn't forgive myself if the beast hurt you," he murmured.

Even though he said it was okay for her to make false promises to the beast, her feelings of guilt lingered. It wasn't as if they were entirely different beings. Betraying the beast also felt like betraying Vlerion.

Kaylina leaned her forehead against his shoulder. "While

you're resting and enjoying your exile, I'll find the answer we both long for."

She also felt guilty that she'd been promising that for a while and hadn't had the time to do much research. But now that she'd realized and accepted that she had druid power, she believed she was closer to a solution.

"Then we can be together," she murmured. "Me and *you*, the man."

"I do appreciate that you added that clarification." Vlerion wrapped an arm around her shoulders.

"The beast isn't who I fantasize about when I see him naked."

"Since we can't let ourselves get too worked up, I won't ask you for details of your fantasies." His eyelids drooped as he gazed at her, promising he wanted to.

"You might not like them. They're not reverent."

"Imagine my shock."

"Captain Targon wouldn't approve."

"I won't be consulting *Targon* when we can finally be together."

"Good." Kaylina gazed up at him, tempted by the lips that weren't far from her eyes.

With his lids still drooped, she knew he was tempted too.

Fortunately, one of the servants arrived then, carrying a tray of snacks and drinks. A second man followed him, wordlessly toting a chair up the dock. He set it down and waved that Kaylina could use it, which made her wonder if the reeds didn't offer as much privacy as she believed.

Lady Isla might have faith that Kaylina could one day lift the curse, but she probably intended to keep an eye on her son, especially while he was on the estate, to make sure nothing too arousing happened in the meantime.

Understandable. Kaylina selected a couple of triangle-shaped sandwiches for herself and sat in the chair opposite Vlerion. It was safer that way.

He raised a glass toward her in a rueful salute of acknowledgment. But he watched her over the rim as he drank, his eyes promising that they would one day be together.

THE END

Thank you for reading. I hope you enjoyed the story! If you're ready for more, The Curse and the Crown wraps up in Book 4, *Scions of Change*.